Not My Child

SAMANTHA KING

ONE PLACE. MANY STORIES

HQ
An imprint of HarperCollins*Publishers* Ltd
1 London Bridge Street
London SE1 9GF

www.harpercollins.co.uk

HarperCollins*Publishers*
1st Floor, Watermarque Building, Ringsend Road
Dublin 4, Ireland

This paperback edition 2022

1
First published in Great Britain by
HQ, an imprint of HarperCollins*Publishers* Ltd 2022

ISBN: 9780008471460

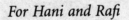

For Hani and Rafi

Denial – is the only fact
Perceived by the Denied
— EMILY DICKINSON

Prologue

The cry seems to come from a distance, singing across the dark water. 'MUMMY!'

Fear pulses through me, but even as I grip the rusty blue railing along the river's edge, my eyes frantically searching the spot where I saw the last flash of Billy's blue duffle coat, my thoughts are wrenched back in time . . .

Mummy. How many times has that single word woken me from the deepest sleep?

'Your turn, hon. Sorry, I've got work in the morning,' Daniel always mumbles, rolling over. I've never minded; I waited years to enjoy night-time cuddles with a small, sleep-warm child snuggled against my shoulder.

Another cry, fainter this time, jolts me out of memory. 'Billy!' Icy mist curls into my mouth as I call his name. I cough, eyes watering, all the while pointlessly scouring the murky green of the River Thames, left and right, up and down, until a slight, sudden movement draws my gaze to the canal boat in front of me.

Rich royal blue with gold scrolling around the windows, the

1

long, low vessel looks out of place among the other houseboats, most of which are more house than boat. With pot plants on their terraces and slatted wooden walkways sloping towards the river bank, they give only the illusion that they might one day sail away.

This boat is different. *New*. It only appeared at the weekend. I know that because every inch of this stretch of the Thames is as familiar to me as Billy's face. Each nook and cranny is our secret hideaway; we've spent hours here, just the two of us, making up stories as we gobble our sandwiches, tossing the crusts to fat, friendly ducks.

'*Billy!*' I try to call out again, but terror has closed my throat, my soundless whisper carried away by the wind. Mutely, I direct my agony towards the tall red-bearded man who has emerged to chop gnarled logs of wood on the boat deck. He pauses, shoving one hand into the bulging pocket of his navy overalls, jerking his head back to frown at the glowering sky.

The clouds hang even lower now; a storm is closing in. The man disappears inside the boat's cabin, leaving me alone with my fear – and fury. 'He's mine! Give him back!' I manage to yell at last, holding my hands up to the moon, appealing to its pale, benign face as it slides out from behind a cloud. I beg it for answers; there are none.

My darling, longed-for child is gone, but my heart refuses to let go; it burns with yearning – and regret at how blind I've been. I've lost the most precious part of me, and it's all my fault. *How did I not see the truth staring me in the face for four years?*

A dizzying kaleidoscope, fragments of the past, begins to crowd my head. Closing my eyes, I give myself up to them, trying to piece everything together – desperate to understand what I ever did to *her* to make her punish me so cruelly: why she took my baby from me.

PART ONE

PART ONE

Chapter 1

The school playground was the last place I would ever have expected her to make her move, and yet, looking back, I can see now that it formed the perfect stage, surrounded as we were by an audience of other parents, each as oblivious as I was to the drama about to unfold.

'Hey, Nish. All ready for your big day?'

That was Bea. Short for Beatrice.

Taupe cashmere coat and an abundance of jewellery deliberately advertised not only the success of her exclusive art gallery, but also her marriage to a wealthy antique dealer.

'Amber's big day, you mean.' Nish stamped her feet to keep them warm. Early-morning frost sparkled on the tarmac playground. 'I can't *believe* my baby's starting school.'

'Actually, no, I meant *yours*,' Bea insisted, stooping to air-kiss her shorter friend. 'The kids are way too excited to be nervous.' On cue, she stepped sideways to avoid being mowed down by stampeding four-year-olds. '*We're* the ones who'll be chewing our nails all day.'

5

'Good job you've booked yourself a manicure, then, Bea.'

Jules. The fourth and final member of our little mum group.

'Very funny.' Bea frowned, fiddling with the end of her sleek, strawberry-blonde ponytail. 'I *need* this spa day, OK? I've got so much shit on my mind.'

'Fuck, it's freezing,' Jules complained. 'Why don't they open the door, already?'

'Teachers love to torture parents. It's the best part of their job,' Bea told her drily. The stiletto heels of her tan suede boots were skewer-sharp; they carved circles of tiny indentations on the icy tarmac as her feet jittered.

Billy let go of my hand and inched closer, staring down in fascination at the bullet-hole-shaped marks. 'Ouch! Aunty Bea! My foot!' Hopping up and down, he screwed up his face in pain, at the same time reaching for the toe of his new, smart black leather school shoes.

'Oh, sweetheart. Is your naughty mummy not paying you any attention?' Bea consoled silkily, squeezing Billy's shoulder while slanting a narrow-eyed glance at me. 'You look miles away, Ruth. What's up? Guilty conscience?'

'Guilty . . . *what*? No, I . . .' Before I could gather my thoughts to explain how anxious I was about leaving Billy, a boy sprinted over to him, holding out a ball.

'Want to play?' he invited with a grin, flicking back a ginger fringe.

Joseph. Jules's son.

He lived with his dad and new stepmum, ever since Jules had lost custody during her divorce. I knew how much she missed him. I understood *exactly* how much it hurt to constantly feel like a part of yourself was missing, and I knew that was why Jules and I had clicked when we'd first got chatting at the school's open day.

Even so, if her ex-husband hadn't turned out to be Daniel's new boss at the bank, I would have run a mile the second I'd discovered that Jules was best friends with Bea.

6

Or *Beatrice*, as I used to know her.

Back when *we* were best friends.

Before the night that changed everything . . .

Appearances can be so misleading. To passing strangers, I was sure I looked just like all the other mums, in my faded jeans, leather ankle boots and comfy green cardigan-coat slung on at the last minute, wavy blonde hair tugged back into a hasty ponytail. Only Bea *wasn't* a stranger – and it seemed she was no longer even pretending to be my friend.

All things considered, she'd been friendly enough during the last six months, and I had played along, almost as though we had an unspoken pact to avoid mentioning our turbulent past. I'd even begun to believe it truly was all forgotten. Only, lately, something seemed to have changed. Bea was definitely acting differently towards me. *Again*.

'God, I miss my boy.' Jules's despairing groan cut across my thoughts.

I smiled sympathetically at her. 'It must be so hard knowing another woman is looking after your son. But you're still his mum, Jules. Nothing and no one can change that.'

'If my husband ever ran off with a younger woman, I'd serve him up a nice cold dish of revenge.' Nish grinned. 'Then rub his nose in it.'

'Far better to have an affair yourself,' Jules countered. 'Poetic justice, isn't it? Making the punishment fit the crime.'

'An eye for an eye. Seems fair,' Bea said blithely. 'Actions have consequences. We're all adults. We have to take responsibility for our mistakes. Don't you think, Ruth?'

'Boys, how about a penalty shoot-out?' I called out, deliberately avoiding Bea's eyes as it dawned on me what she was hinting at.

Feeling myself blush, I lifted my phone, taking a few quick snapshots of Billy to disguise an uncomfortable sense of shock and shame awakening inside me. Images flashed in my head. My throat dried.

7

'My go first!' Joseph yelled, racing Billy towards the goal posts.

I trailed along behind them, my heart pounding as memories came thick and fast now. Glancing back at Bea, I blushed again as I saw her staring intently at me, and in a flash, I realised: *she must have found out what I'd done.*

*

'So, we're all set? Sunday brunch at mine,' Bea said as I re-joined the group, minutes later.

'Sorry. Sunday's out for me.' I grimaced apologetically. 'We're—'

'Oh, I know,' Bea cut in. 'You and Danny are taking Billy to Windsor, aren't you?'

'Windsor?' That was news to me. 'Daniel didn't mention . . .'

'Wives should always check their husbands' phones,' Jules commented bitterly. 'That's how I caught mine out.'

'Now, now, Jules,' Bea chided. 'Danny would never do the dirty on Ruth. He's far too much of a goody two-shoes. No, I think our Ruth here must be the one harbouring a guilty secret.' Her tone was light, *teasing*, but her dark eyes glittered as they fixed on mine.

'Of course not.' I felt myself blush again.

'That's a shame.' Jules sighed. 'I was hoping for a bit of play-ground gossip.'

She and Nish laughed, and in all honesty, I couldn't blame them; they had no idea what Bea had meant about Daniel being a 'goody two-shoes'. But I did, and the barb hit home. It twisted deeper as I pondered how Bea could possibly know his weekend plans before I did. And I *hated* it when she called him 'Danny'.

Back when the four of us were fresh out of university and starting our first jobs, it had been an in-joke that mine was the only name that couldn't be shortened. In camaraderie, we'd all taken to using our full names: Beatrice and Finley; Ruth and Daniel. We'd coupled-up at about the same time and became a tightknit foursome for five years. Then, after that one disastrous night, we'd become strangers. I felt a creeping sense that we were now enemies.

I still vividly remembered our former friendship – the good times and the bad – and often wondered if Bea ever thought of it. Her appearance and lifestyle couldn't be more different, these days: every inch of her home, every item of clothing she wore was refined, expensive, *gleaming*. As though she'd polished her former life, her former *self*, into oblivion.

Yet, increasingly, she'd been dropping hints that she remembered, too. Like the 'goody two-shoes' jibe and snide hint about guilty secrets. She obviously wanted me to know that she *hadn't* forgotten. But how much did she know, and what did she plan to do about it?

'What's the urgency, anyway?' Jules said impatiently. 'We could meet *next* Sunday.'

'Can't. I've, uh, got big news.' Bea linked arms with her. 'I'll tell you later, hon.'

I got the hint: her *big news* wasn't for my ears. Bea was up to something; I could feel it, and I had a growing suspicion that it involved me – and that she'd deliberately waited until now, safe in the circle of friends that were more hers than mine, to throw down a marker.

'Boys! Mind how you go!' a teacher called out, and a sea of heads turned to look.

Diverted from thoughts about what Bea might be plotting, I felt a surge of panic and sprinted across the playground. 'Billy!' My heart was thumping as I watched him chase the ball towards the tall iron gate that stood open. 'Sweetheart, wait. Stop!'

Relieved to see a tall, thin woman standing near the exit, I was about to call out to ask her to grab Billy before he could run through it, when I noticed her shoulders trembling.

'Hey, are you OK?' I asked in concern as I approached. The woman was clearly young, in her early twenties, perhaps, though it was hard to tell exactly, with her face half hidden by a black hoodie. But I immediately felt sorry for her, intuitively understanding

9

how nervous she was probably feeling about leaving her child at school for the first time. I felt exactly the same.

'I'm sure it's not this crazy every day,' I encouraged when she didn't speak. 'They're all a bit hyper, aren't they? First-day excitement. Which is yours?' I added, looking around.

'Yeah, right. Like you don't know.'

'Sorry?' I stepped back, startled by the unexpected rudeness. 'Have we met?'

'Huh. Very funny, Ruth. *Not.*' Edging towards me, the woman mimed a long, slow hand clap. 'Top marks for acting, though.'

I frowned, about to turn away. I didn't need hostility. Not today. I was anxious enough about Billy starting school, and Bea wasn't helping. I knew her spiteful little grenades were a prelude to something infinitely worse. I needed to figure out what.

Yes, handling one toxic friend was enough. Whoever this mum was, I'd be sure to steer clear of her the next time I saw her in the playground. 'Well, anyway. If you'll excuse me, I'd better get back to my—'

'Son?' Her stare was black and unflinching. 'Is that what you were about to say?'

Peeling back her hood, she revealed long dark hair that tumbled around her thin shoulders in wild curls. Her face was pretty, despite a fierce scowl, and as I registered high cheekbones and pale, almost translucent skin, I realised that I *did* recognise her.

'Yes. My son,' I whispered, and a horrible, sick feeling began to coil in the pit of my stomach. Shocking, long-buried images flickered in my mind; I felt myself sway dizzily.

'OK, enough already. It's time to give it up. Give *him* up.' One arm shot out to point at Billy. 'No more lies, Ruth. That boy is mine. I know it. You know it. It's time *he* knows it. I want him back. And if you don't give him to me . . . well, I'll just have to take him.'

Chapter 2

Daniel has always said that Billy gets his speed from him. He runs five miles along the Thames towpath every morning, and occasionally Billy joins him to the halfway point. He's fast; faster even than me. *Except when I'm sprinting away from my own fear.*

I kept thinking this as I pulled Billy through the school gate and along Ferry Lane, past Kew Green and up the hill towards Kew Bridge. As I ran, I glanced alternately over my shoulder then down at Billy, squeezing his hand to reassure him everything was all right. I didn't hear if anyone called after us; I didn't stop to think what the teacher would say when she announced 'Billy Cartwright' for the register and no one answered. I just kept running.

'Keep going, darling. You're doing super well.' My throat felt tinder-dry, but my breath puffed out in incongruously fluffy clouds.

'Slow down, Mummy. My legs hurt!'

'Almost home. Don't stop. Keep going, darling. You're *such* a good boy.' I was panting with the effort to talk, run, hold on to Billy and look behind me, all at the same time.

11

'Did we forget something?' His voice was wobbly, but only from exertion. He was smiling; he wasn't frightened.

If Mummy said he needed to leave school without even saying goodbye to his friends, and run home at full pelt, that's what he'd do. If I told him it was bedtime, he went to sleep. If I said it was morning, he got up. The thought of how much he trusted me made every bone in my body ache with guilt. 'No, love. Everything's fine, OK? I'll explain when we get home.'

'About the lady with the knife?'

'The *what*?' His words sliced through my anxiety, and I stopped dead, grabbing hold of his shoulders and swinging him round to face me.

'Ouch!'

'Sorry, darling. I'm so sorry.' I rubbed my hands comfortingly up and down his arms. 'What do you mean, knife? *What* knife?'

'Like Daddy's army knife. It was in her jeans. Sticking out of her pocket.'

'*Whose* pocket?' For a second, I pictured Bea's glittering eyes and knowing smile.

'The lady with the black curly hair.'

'Oh. Right. I didn't see it, love.' He must have been mistaken. I knew life had been tough for Eve. She'd been just seventeen the last time I saw her, and already she had experienced more horrors than anyone should have to endure in a lifetime.

In fact, that was the very thing that had drawn me to her, I remembered: sympathy for her troubled life. It was also the reason I'd never forgotten her, despite not recognising her at first. But although she'd had a temper, I didn't remember Eve being aggressive. I couldn't believe she'd have been carrying a weapon. Not in a school playground. *Especially* not there.

'I *saw* it,' Billy insisted.

'It must have been a pen or something, sweetheart.'

'Is she my new teacher? Is that why she had a pen?'

'No. No, I don't think so.' I frowned, puzzling over the possibility.

'She's just someone Mummy used to know. A long time ago. She's not important, though. I don't expect we'll ever see her again.' I reached for Billy's hand and urged him quickly onwards.

'Do *I* know her?' he persisted, looking up at me.

'No, Billy.' I couldn't say any more. My lungs were burning now, but we had to keep going. I had to get as far away from *her* as possible. I tucked Billy's new school scarf around his neck, grabbed hold of his hand again and pulled him along with me, fast-walking, half jogging.

'*Look*, Mummy!' Billy jerked to a halt so abruptly, I almost fell over him.

'What? Where?' I turned around in panic, expecting to find her hot on our heels. But all I could see on the pavement behind us was a few harried-looking people in suits hurrying in the opposite direction, clearly late for work.

'A helicopter!' Billy squealed, pointing skywards.

'Ah, well spotted.' His innocent enthusiasm brought tears to my eyes. Plane-spotting, naming cars, waving at trains, making up stories about the passengers: they were all the little games Billy loved. Swallowing my fear, I tried to calm down, act normal and show an interest. 'I wonder where it's going? Who do you think is inside?'

'It's the police! It's over our flat, Mummy. Have we done something wrong?'

'No, sweetheart,' I said hoarsely, almost choking on a mixture of guilt and impatience. *None of this was Billy's fault*, I reminded myself. Gently, I encouraged him to keep moving. 'Whoever they're looking for, it's not us. We've done nothing wrong. Nothing at all.'

*

At last we reached the brow of the bridge, and my eyes fixed on the point where our apartment building pierced the grey sky. I just needed to get there, high up inside our penthouse in the clouds, where she couldn't get to us.

'Nearly home,' I reassured Billy, before mumbling a desperate reassurance to myself: 'We'll be safe there. She can't get to you. *I won't let her.*'

The slip road curled steeply around the corner from Kew Bridge towards the courtyard outside our building, and my leather boots slipped on a patch of ice. I pulled Billy closer. By now, I was carrying his new book bag, PE bag – half carrying *him*.

'What did you say, Mummy?'

'Nothing, darling. Just talking to myself.'

Billy grinned up at me. 'Funny Mummy.'

I smiled into his eyes, loving the sound of his giggle, the warmth of him pressed against my side. Then I tensed as a voice in my head whispered: *Billy might be fast like Daniel, but he doesn't have his straight brown hair and blue eyes, nor his thickset body.*

I thought of how Billy had always been tall for his age, his body slight, all elbows and knees. Such an adorable, gawky child. Daniel was also tall, but in the photos I'd seen of him as a boy, he'd been sturdy – stocky, even.

As we hurried across the marble-tiled foyer into the lift, my legs were trembling; with my back pressed against the mirrored walls, there was nowhere to hide from my conscience. Staring at Billy's reflection, I finally admitted to myself that there wasn't a single resemblance between my son and my husband.

Did Daniel ever notice? He'd never remarked on it, although occasionally he marvelled at Billy's silky black curls, ruffling them approvingly while he played with his Meccano, train sets and Lego. In Daniel's eyes, Billy's dexterity was a sign that he'd inherited his daddy's 'problem-solving mind'.

Loving his pride, I had always agreed, but sometimes, as I'd watched the two of them play, doubt had niggled. For four years, I'd closed my mind to it, blocking it out along with all the shocking details about that night. They were coming back to haunt me now, though.

'Are you crying, Mummy?'

'Just a bit of dust in my eye.' I smiled, fighting tears at the rush of memories.

Our happy family life. I'd craved it for so many years, but now my mind had begun scratching away at the surface, until, like a portrait gradually revealed as a fake, all the imperfections were exposed.

None of the lines quite matched up to those underneath, and I could no longer deny that it was because I had forcibly joined all the dots together to form a different picture: the one I'd *wanted* to see – my perfect world with Daniel and Billy.

'Five, four, three, two, one,' Billy counted down, until the lift pinged, indicating that we'd reached the penthouse level, the door immediately opening onto our private landing.

'Well done, darling.' I smiled, but my hands trembled as I fumbled for the keys to our apartment. Daniel wouldn't be home from work for hours, but a hundred years didn't feel long enough to prepare myself for the confession I was going to have to make now. I could run away from the school, but I couldn't escape my past: it had finally caught up with me.

'Can I watch cartoons, Mummy?'

'OK, love. Just for half an hour.'

Hurrying to the floor-to-ceiling windows that spanned the length of our living room, I glanced down towards the river. There were no signs of unusual activity, but rather than calming my jitters, the everyday ordinariness around me seemed wrong. How could everything carry on as normal, when my entire world was about to fall apart?

'Come on, Ruth. Keep it together.' I reminded myself that it was the start of a new term. The parents and children who usually strolled along the towpath would have headed off to school by now, while the residents of our building would be at work, many, like Daniel, in the City. And despite my paranoia, I hadn't been followed.

There was no sign of Eve.

Then again, it wasn't *her* I'd been running from.

It was Bea.

Eve was a damaged young woman. She'd been through hell four years ago and was no doubt still struggling to come to terms with her tragic loss. It had been an unlucky coincidence, bumping into each other again, and I understood it must have triggered terrible memories for her. *Poor Eve, looking at Billy and imagining she was seeing her own little boy.*

I felt sorry for her; she was most likely suffering from PTSD. I knew all too well that the effects could linger for years. But while unresolved trauma was deluding her mind, prompting her to lash out at me in desperation, her claim was ridiculous. I didn't take it seriously for a second. *Billy was her son?* The poor woman was unhinged. I knew my own boy.

No, I was certain my instincts in the playground had been spot-on: Bea must have found out what I'd done. I couldn't kid myself any longer that our uneasy truce over the last six months had been anything more than a conspiracy of silence. Bea's sense of dramatic timing had always been impeccable – and it was finally payback time.

'An eye for an eye,' I whispered, recalling her sly hint in the playground.

I had to tell Daniel, before Bea made her move. But how much did she know? And what was she going to do about it? I thought of the old saying: *keep your friends close, but your enemies closer*. It was a bitter pill to swallow that, once, Bea and I had been closer even than friends: more like sisters.

16

Chapter 3

'I can't believe we've survived our first month. I've never worked so hard in my *life*,' Bea complained, pouting as she topped up our wine glasses.

'Me, too.' I stifled a yawn. 'And I still have three bar shifts this weekend. I promised my landlady I'd do extra hours. I just hope to God it's not as busy as this place.'

I glanced around the packed Coach & Horses pub in Greenwich Market. Bea's lodgings were in north London, so we usually stuck to Covent Garden for after-work drinks. But that morning she'd texted asking to stay over at my place: 'I need a night off – and I need to pick your brain. About something important,' she'd added mysteriously. We were now on our second bottle, and I was on my last legs.

'What is it they say? No pain, no gain. It'll all be worth it in the end.' Bea raised her glass. 'Cheers, babe. Here's to us and our brilliant careers.' She rolled her eyes. 'Eventually.'

'Cheers.' I clinked glasses with her. 'I hope you're right. I was *so* excited to get an internship, but I'm still broke. And exhausted.'

This time, I couldn't hide my yawn. 'It feels less like a career, more like an endurance test. Last person standing gets the job.'

'Intern is just another word for slave,' Bea scorned. 'At least in Tanya Wade's dictionary. Roll on Christmas, I say.' She frowned, checking her phone as it vibrated.

'Yeah. I'm desperate for a lie-in.'

'And a permanent contract. That's what I meant by *roll on Christmas*. Tanya's making the final decision by then. Which interns stay. Who gets the boot.'

'Really?' I was thrilled but surprised at Bea's inside knowledge. 'How do you *know*?'

'I have my sources.' She tapped her nose, then knocked back her Prosecco.

I slowly savoured mine. We'd pooled the remaining contents of our purses to buy another bottle, and I wanted to make it last. I *had* suggested we drink something cheaper, but Bea insisted we 'deserved the best' and that we should 'live in the style to which we intended to become accustomed'. I knew she'd inherited money from her parents; I also knew she had credit card debts: she wore a different outfit to work every day and socialised most evenings.

I watched her frown at her phone again, taking the opportunity to study her. With her waist-length, dark silky hair, glittering eyes and perfect skin, Bea was beautiful – and she knew it. She also had the self-confidence to match. I wasn't surprised she'd already made an impact at the trendy advertising agency where we'd both started as interns on the same day.

'I'm pretty sure you'll be OK.' I sighed. 'Tanya loved your idea for the Robinson pitch.' I tried not to feel aggrieved that it had actually been *my* idea; Bea often 'leapfrogged' off my suggestions, as she put it. 'And the art director called you a "rising star", remember?'

Bea rolled her eyes. 'He only said that because he fancies me. Sleazebag.'

'You think so? He seems nice to me. Anyway, at least he knows your name. He always calls me Ruby. Or Rachel. Like Ruth is so hard to remember! I daren't say anything, though. I suppose I'll just have to keep plodding on and hope my work speaks for itself.'

'Hope doesn't come into it, babe. If you want something, you have to go for it. Stop being so bloody polite and *make* it happen.' Bea clicked her fingers emphatically.

'Easy to say. Tanya's hard to impress.' Along with the three other interns, I was torn between admiration and fear of our boss.

Bea was the only one who remained unintimidated by her. Although she moaned about the long hours and low pay, she seemed to glide through her work, whereas I was counting the days until I could move on. A job in advertising had seemed the perfect way to save enough money and gain the experience I needed to pursue my real dream: opening my own art gallery. But I was skint and demoralised. Meeting Bea was actually the best thing about my new job.

'Oh, don't let Tanya fool you,' she said with a glint in her eye. 'She's smart, but her *real* genius was marrying a tech billionaire. Then cleaning him out in the divorce settlement.'

I shook my head. 'How do you *know* these things? Oh, right. *You have your sources.*'

'It's not what you know, it's who you sleep with.' Bea chuckled, then scowled when her phone buzzed again. 'Oh, for God's sake. Can't a guy take a hint?'

'Who?' I craned my head to get a glimpse of the screen, but Bea turned it over.

'Oh, just my arsey landlord. As if he doesn't get enough out of me.'

Something in her tone worried me, and I remembered her insistence that she needed *a night off*. 'Er, what exactly *does* he get out of you?'

'As much as he can,' Bea said vaguely. 'Even that doesn't satisfy him. He's always on my case about something. This week, it's his wife's jewellery. I mean, as if I haven't got better taste than to nick her frumpy old pearls!'

'He's accused you of *stealing* them?' I was indignant on my new friend's behalf.

'Not in so many words. He's far too clever for that. But he's dropped enough hints, the creep.' She gave me a doe-eyed look. 'I wish I could tell him to go shove his crappy little box room, but then where would I be? Hampstead rents are daylight robbery.'

'Same goes for Greenwich,' I sympathised.

Bea paused, as though waiting for me to say more, then continued: '*And* he lied in his advert. He made out it was a flat-share. All I get to share is his bloody mortgage repayments.'

And his bed? I wanted to ask, but I'd only known Bea a couple of months – long enough to know she could be volatile; not long enough to trust she wouldn't turn on me if I offended her. 'He sounds awful. Poor you. It must be exhausting living with him.'

'You don't know the half of it.'

She seemed genuinely upset, and I felt bad for her. Racking my brains to think how I might help, I suggested impulsively: 'We should move in together.'

'Really?' Bea sat back, eyes widening until her pupils were glossy black discs.

'Well, I know we haven't known each other that long, but . . . No, you probably wouldn't want to. Sorry, forget I said anything,' I said, feeling myself blush.

Having grown up in a succession of foster homes, I had learned through experience to become fiercely independent, never getting so close to anyone that I'd miss them when it was time to move on. But there was something different about Bea; I'd sensed it as soon as I met her. Despite our differences – she was loud and popular, while I was shy and more reserved – we'd become instant friends, and I loved hanging out with her.

Looking at her shocked expression now, though, I cringed inside, suddenly realising that feeling might be one-sided.

'No, you're right. That's a *fabulous* idea.' A smile spread across her beautiful face.

'Really?'

'*Definitely*. I should have thought of it myself.' Her exuberance drew attention from a group of young guys at the next table, but she ignored them, her eyes locked on mine. 'Flatmates! So exciting. How much notice do you need to give at your place?'

'Oh. I'm not sure.' I hadn't got that far in my thinking. 'I'll have to check my lease. The bedsit over the pub goes with the job, you see. I can't afford to lose my bar work, so . . . But I'll figure it out,' I added quickly, not wanting to put a dampener on Bea's enthusiasm.

'Excellent. Because I have the perfect flat in mind.'

'You do? Wow, that was fast. I mean, that's *great*,' I added as she frowned.

'It so is.' She beamed again. 'It's a two-bed garden flat. Just around the corner from here, actually. One bedroom is huge and the other tiny, but you won't mind that, will you?'

I hesitated, not keen on the idea of being cooped up in a tiny room, when I currently had plenty of space for the artwork I liked to do at weekends. 'Well, I—'

'Fabulous!' Bea clapped her hands together. 'Honestly, you'll love it, Ruth. It's a Victorian conversion, but totally modernised. No creaky floorboards or rising damp.'

'Or live-in landlord,' I chipped in, warming to the idea.

'Exactly. It's a great location, and the flat's gorgeous. Just too far above my budget to rent alone. No point blowing the last of my inheritance to have a spare room sitting empty.'

Bea's excited chatter suddenly dried up, and her face clouded over again. Conscious of another tug of pity, I grabbed her hand. 'I'd rather have parents than an inheritance, too.'

'I wasn't close to them,' she said softly, 'but as soon as they were gone, I wanted them back. Jeez, what a cliché!' She let out a hollow laugh. 'I was such a typical angry teenager. I'm pretty

21

sure the last thing I said to my mum was that I hated her.'

'I never even knew mine. At least your parents left you *something* of themselves. I've got no idea who my dad is. All I know about my mum is how she left me.' I dug my nails into my palms, fighting anxiety. 'She jumped off the hospital roof the day I was born.'

'Fuck.' Bea stared at me, and I felt the tiniest frisson of satisfaction that I'd finally managed to surprise her. I knew she thought she had everyone totally sussed, including me.

'Sorry.' I reached for my drink. 'Too much wine.'

'You and me both.' Bea smiled, her emotional outburst seemingly forgotten. She took out a mirror, unselfconsciously reapplying lipstick. 'That's what I love about you, Ruth. You *get* it. You understand what it's like to feel alone in the world. But we've found each other now, haven't we?'

'Absolutely. We make a great team. Tanya will be *begging* us to stay.'

'We rock!' Bea declared, tucking her lipstick away and giving me a high-five.

'Huh. We do after almost two bottles of Prosecco, anyway.'

'I know, let's go see the flat right now. Come on, knock that back, babe. It's going to be fabulous. Like we're *sisters*!' Bea raised her glass to me, before downing it in one.

'Fabulous,' I echoed, gulping at my own wine, blinking as the room seemed to spin.

I didn't usually drink much, which probably explained why it wasn't until we'd seen the flat and agreed to put down a hefty deposit that I remembered Bea had wanted to pick my brain about something. *Something important*, I was sure she'd said.

Only, when I asked her what it was, she waved the question away with a throaty chuckle, saying she had absolutely no idea what I was talking about.

Chapter 4

Four weeks later, I found myself balancing on a dining chair in front of the ornate Victorian fireplace in the front room of our new flat, stringing Christmas lights around the mirror and smiling at the 'Happy Housewarming!' message Bea had scrawled in red lipstick on the glass.

Once she set her mind to something, Bea wasted no time pursuing her goal. If she wanted something – or someone – she let nothing and no one stand in her way. I knew she was single-minded; I was about to find out that she could also be unscrupulous.

'Oh! Snap!'

'What the . . .?' I glanced in the mirror, watching Bea slink into the room. 'Bea! I *told* you I was wearing this.' Groaning, I stared down in dismay at my favourite red velvet dress.

'Ladies in red. Aren't we hilarious?' She twirled seductively in her dress, identical to mine, only inches shorter, then flicked back her long, dark hair. 'We are so going to rock this party, babe. Oh, come on, Ruth. It was meant to be a joke.'

'Really?' I stared at her uncertainly. 'Right. Well, OK. But you know . . .'

'I know what?' She scowled. 'Fine. Sorry. I'll go and change. I don't want to spoil—'

'No, wait.' I clambered down from the chair. 'It's fine, honestly. I was just surprised, that's all. But you're right. It *is* funny.' I forced a smile. 'And, er, festive. We just need a bit of tinsel, and we're Santa's sexy sidekicks,' I said, trying hard to get into the spirit of things.

'Exactly.' Instantly, Bea was all smiles again. 'Oh, there's the doorbell. Be a love and answer it, would you?'

'Sure.' I strolled to the door, suddenly not looking forward to the evening as much as I had been. 'Coming,' I called out as the doorbell rang again, trying not to sound as flat as I felt.

'Hey, gorgeous.'

'Finley!' I greeted in surprise. I knew Bea had invited him, but I'd warned her that I didn't think he would come. We were lowly interns, and Finley McDermott was the head account director – and Tanya's favourite, if office rumours were to be believed.

'So? Do I get to come in? Or shall we do this here?'

'Do . . .? Oh, thanks.' I accepted the gift-wrapped bottle Finley handed to me, stepping aside to allow him to edge past me into the narrow hallway. 'I'll just put it in the kitchen.'

'Actually, that's not a general offering. It's for you.' Finley nodded at the bottle. 'Early Christmas present slash congratulations gift.' He grinned. 'Go on, then. Open it.'

I tore off the gold paper to discover a bottle of Moët. 'Wow. That's . . . wow.' Bea had told me Finley came from a wealthy family, as well as being a high-flyer in his career, but I was still surprised by his generosity. 'You obviously know Beatrice's tastes well. She loves Champagne. Interns don't usually get to drink it, more's the pity.'

'Good job you're no longer an intern, then.' Finley winked. 'And FYI, when I said it's for *you*, I meant exactly that. It's yours, Ruth. A special gift just for you.' He took hold of my arm, giving it a squeeze. 'You deserve it.'

'Really? Gosh. Well, thank you.' I felt myself blush. 'Wait, is this a consolation gift, then? You said I'm no longer a . . . Is Tanya letting me *go*?'

'Au contraire. She's making you permanent. I merely offered to be the bearer of glad tidings.' Finley gave a small bow. 'The fizz is actually from Tanya,' he admitted.

I chuckled. 'Ah. I see.'

'I *was* intending to steal credit for it, but it's probably best I come clean. You know the boss. She'll lord it over you herself on Monday. Nothing from Tanya comes without strings attached,' he said, a little tersely. 'If she gives you something, she expects double in return.'

'She's a slave driver,' I acknowledged.

'And we lowly creatures, with extortionate London rents to pay, live to serve her.'

'So true.' I laughed. 'Gosh, that's awesome news. Thanks, Finley.'

I set the bottle on the hall table and gave him an impulsive hug, pulling back in surprise when I felt his arms close around me, his lean body pressing slightly too close for comfort.

'Sorry, am I interrupting something?'

'Oh, Beatrice.' I stepped back sharply, turning to her with a self-conscious smile.

She was smiling too, but her jaw was clenched. Bea had never mentioned fancying Finley, and I was sure I'd made it clear that I didn't. Occasionally, she'd teased me about him, and it was true that we shared a love of art, but friendly artistic banter was as far as it went.

'You two had better watch yourselves,' Bea said tartly. 'I'm pretty sure Tanya doesn't allow fraternising between management and interns.'

'That's exactly it.' I couldn't contain my grin. 'Finley's just given me the best news. We're not interns anymore. Tanya's making us *permanent!*' I turned to him as a thought occurred to me. 'You did mean both of us, didn't you? Tanya wants Beatrice too?'

'Of course.' Finley winked. 'Who wouldn't?'

*

25

By midnight, the party was in full swing. I'd given prior warning to our upstairs neighbours, who luckily for us were a young, laidback couple in their twenties. Although they'd declined my invitation for them to join us, they also waved away my advance apologies for loud music.

It was a good job they *had* declined, I thought, as I pushed my way through the crowd to get to my tiny bedroom: the flat was rammed with people I didn't recognise. I knew Bea had spread the word, but it seemed everyone had brought a friend – and a friend of a friend.

'Hey. Caught you.'

'Sorry?' I swivelled around in shock, feeling hands on my waist. 'Oh, Finley.'

'It's OK, no need to look so guilty! I don't blame you for trying to escape. I was hoping for five minutes' peace myself.' He rested a hand on my bedroom door.

'Right.' I looked away, feeling awkward. I'd danced with him a couple of times during the evening, but I'd noticed Bea hovering nearby each time. If she *was* harbouring secret feelings for Finley, I didn't want to upset her. 'Actually, you know what? I think I might call it a night. Um, alone,' I spelled out, determined to nip any flirtation in the bud.

'That's a shame.' Finley's eyes lingered on mine, before moving to my mouth.

'Sorry, but I . . . you . . .' I floundered, taken aback by his closeness. 'We—'

'It's a *shame*, because I was hoping to grill you about that new exhibition at the Tate Modern,' Finley cut in with an innocent expression. 'You've been, haven't you?'

'What? Oh. Yes. Yes, I have. It's awesome. I loved it.' I knew I was babbling, but I was cringing with embarrassment. I'd stupidly assumed Finley was coming on to me, when clearly all he wanted was to chat about art, as we usually did in the office.

'That's settled, then. I'll have to go. Even if I'm doomed to go

26

alone.' His dark eyebrows arched. 'Although, strictly speaking, I could demand you come with me. For research purposes, I mean. New trends and techniques. Now you've been made permanent . . .'

'Right. Well, I do try to keep up with the latest—'

'Or you could call it a thank-you, if you prefer.' Finley cocked his head to one side. 'After all, I did put in a good word for you with Tanya.'

'You did? Oh.' I wanted to believe I'd won my permanent contract on my own merits.

'Of course. You've got genuine talent, Ruth. But to get ahead in life, you know the score.' Finley shrugged. 'It's not what, but *who* you know.'

'That's what Beatrice says,' I muttered, flinching as I recalled her exact words: *it's not who you know, it's who you sleep with.* I recalled, too, that Bea had been the only intern to have advance knowledge about Tanya making her decision by Christmas.

I wondered if Finley was her secret 'source', deciding that if Bea *was* romantically interested in him, the two of them would make a good pair. They were both ridiculously attractive and charming, not to mention fiercely ambitious.

'So, do we have a deal?' Finley prompted.

'Deal?'

'You show me the exhibition highlights. I buy you coffee afterwards. Black, no sugar. That is how you like it, isn't it?' He reached out to smooth a stray curl off my face.

'Yes. Only . . .' I hesitated, grappling with conflicting emotions.

I was keen to see the exhibition again, and Finley was knowledgeable and entertaining about art. His slightly suggestive tone had flustered me, but I was probably misreading it, and although his hint that I owed him my job had annoyed me, I didn't seriously imagine he expected something in return.

'Do you need to ask the audience? Phone a friend?' Finley teased, as I continued to hesitate. 'I'm not proposing a dirty weekend, you know? Just coffee. Maybe a slice of cake if you're really good. You can even keep your clothes on to eat it.'

'Of course.' I blushed harder as, once again, he seemed to have read my mind.

'Who mentioned coffee?' Bea emerged rather unsteadily from the kitchen opposite my bedroom, wine glass in one hand, cigarette in the other, even though she didn't smoke.

'That would be me.' Finley took the cigarette from her and placed it between his lips.

'Hmm, I didn't have you pegged as a lightweight,' Bea taunted.

He grinned, unfazed by her rudeness. 'I'm a man of hidden shallows.'

'You should take *Beatrice* to the exhibition,' I suggested, glancing between the two of them and definitely picking up on a hint of something. 'She loves art, too.'

'I so don't,' she refuted, looking horrified.

Finley chuckled, removing the cigarette from his mouth long enough to say: 'When you're as pretty as a picture, who needs art galleries?'

'Flirt,' Bea responded tartly, but she looked pleased all the same.

Finley winked, raising a hand. 'Guilty as charged.'

'As long as you don't go corrupting my best friend here.' Bea lurched giddily towards me, wrapping an arm around my shoulder. 'Or you'll have me to answer to, Mr McDermott.'

'You're welcome to join us,' I encouraged her, wondering if Finley had in fact only invited me in the first place in the hope that my flatmate would come too.

'Thanks, but I'd rather watch paint dry. Oh, wait, I forgot. That's what we're doing tomorrow.'

'Very funny.' I rolled my eyes, knowing Bea hated it when I got out my watercolours at the kitchen table. As flatmates, our differences were beginning to become more obvious: she was restless and always eager to go out; I enjoyed being home or having friends round.

While Bea had grown up in London, spending her childhood

and teenage years in Greenwich, before moving to 'more upmarket' Hampstead when she started work, I'd only moved to the capital for uni and sometimes found city life overwhelming. Once work was over, I liked my own space; Bea seemed to hate being alone.

In fact, we were chalk and cheese, and I knew she bossed me around. Mostly, I let her – anything for a quiet life – and I did genuinely find her boldness entertaining. Back then, it had also seemed harmless.

'Looks like I've got you all to myself, then.' Finley turned to me with a smile. 'I take it you're free this weekend?'

Bristling at his assumption that I'd have nothing else planned, my reluctance returned. 'Actually, I'm not sure. I'll have to—'

'Excellent! It's a date.' Finley clapped his hands together. 'I can't wait.'

Chapter 5

KEW, SOUTH-WEST LONDON
Thursday, 2 September; 10.30 p.m.

'Where have you *been*?' I couldn't contain or mask my tension as Daniel crept into our bedroom. I felt like I'd been waiting days for him to come home. Looking back on my friendship with Bea had left me anxious and on edge; I'd been sitting in the exact same position since settling Billy to sleep hours ago.

The whole day, I'd tried to keep things as normal as possible – TV, snacks, story time – so that he wouldn't feel unsettled. I'd told him 'silly Mummy' had got his school start date wrong. He hadn't questioned it; he trusted me completely. The thought hurt when it should have comforted, and shame about lying to Billy had made my hands shake as I'd turned the pages of his favourite book, my mind racing in dizzying circles the whole time.

I'd had to come up with a different lie for the school welfare assistant, leaving a message out of Billy's earshot to say he'd had a bad tummy ache and I was keeping him home. Having rehearsed my excuse, I found it flowed more easily when I'd left voicemails for Jules and Nish. I couldn't bring myself to phone Bea, but I knew she'd hear the news: gossip travelled lightning fast around the mum network. By the end of the day, the whole school would probably know.

I'd realised I was weaving a complicated web of lies, but I hadn't been able to think beyond the need to buy myself some time to figure out what to do.

'Ah, you're still up.' Daniel stopped tiptoeing and loudly scuffed off his shoes, shrugging out of his work suit at the same time. 'I thought you'd be asleep by now.'

'I've been waiting for you.' Wishing he would stop buzzing around, I sighed as he pulled off his shirt without unbuttoning it, fully expecting him to let it drop to the floor as he usually did. Instead, he shoved it deep into the linen basket. I stared at him in surprise.

'You have?' He whipped off his belt with a snap, then hooked it over the back of the dressing-table chair. Immediately, it slithered off, coiling into a heavy heap on the carpet.

'Yes. I, uh . . . I need to talk.'

'Was there a problem at school?' Daniel unbuttoned his trousers and kicked them off, seemingly forgetting about the linen basket this time. 'The kids didn't poke fun at Billy about his hand, did they?' He braced his hands on his hips, ready to defend his son. 'I hope you—'

'No. It's nothing like that,' I cut in quickly. Billy had slightly webbed fingers on his right hand, the tendons and skin of his fingers part-conjoined. It had never bothered him, or us, but Daniel had obviously been secretly worrying about Billy being teased.

I wished he'd told me; I wished I'd thought to talk to Billy about it, prepare him. But I so rarely noticed his hand. I didn't see it as a defect, a cause for ridicule; it was just part of him, and every inch of my son was perfect in my eyes.

'Good. Because I won't have my boy picked on. If anything like that happens, tell me and I'll sort it. OK? I'm sorry I couldn't be there today, sweetheart,' Daniel said more gently. 'I really wanted to be. If anyone gives Billy any trouble, I'll—'

'No, honestly, he was fine. But I . . .' My mouth dried. Suddenly, I had no idea where to begin.

I needed Daniel's reassurance, but the energy fizzing off him felt like a barrier between us. It came from the world *out there*, where he was Daniel Cartwright, Senior VP of Global Strategy at an international bank, not *my* Daniel, the man who had made my heart beat faster when he'd turned up at the Tate Modern instead of Finley, the weekend after that party.

I'd been a little hurt but not entirely surprised when Finley had texted: 'Can we take a raincheck on that coffee? Something's come up.' His message was swiftly followed by one from Bea, saying: 'Sorry, sorry, sorry! Please don't hate me!' But after a moment's awkwardness when this strange man had taken his best friend's place, I'd quickly realised that my own treacherous friend had unintentionally done me a favour.

Daniel and I had hit it off immediately; within weeks, he'd become my soul mate, the man I shared everything with: a home, our hopes and fears. *Our guilty secrets.*

'But you . . .?' he prompted when I disappeared into my thoughts, anxiously recalling Bea taunting me in the playground about *mistakes* and *consequences*.

'Oh. I, um, I got a bit rattled this morning, that's all. In the school playground.' I tried to smile, but it wouldn't come. My face, my entire body, felt frozen.

Daniel frowned. 'Right. OK. Well, give me sec, and I'll jump in the shower. Then we can talk, yeah?' Half in and half out of the en-suite bathroom, he paused, one hand resting on the doorframe. He looked like he was about to say more, then he turned abruptly away.

'What's the rush?' I called after him in surprise. 'Did you go to the gym after work? Is that why you're so late? You usually shower there.' *Usually*, too, Daniel crawled into bed whenever he was very late home, saving his shower for the morning.

Preoccupied by my own anxiety, I only now picked up on something different about his mood, too. In fact, he didn't seem his usual laidback self at all, first stuffing his shirt into the laundry basket like he was concealing incriminating evidence from the police, and now dashing into the shower as though to wash away the remnants of a crime scene.

'Nope. No gym this evening. I, uh, bumped into an old client in Richmond. We grabbed a bite to eat. Loads to catch up on. I guess we lost track of time.'

'Sounds fun.' I finally managed to force a smile.

'Yeah. I'm knackered now, though, to be honest. You know what? Maybe it's actually best if we chat in the morning.'

'*No!*' I only recognised the sharpness of my tone as I saw Daniel's eyebrows fly upwards. 'Sorry. I just really need to talk, you know?' I refused to sugar-coat the demand. This situation didn't just affect me; it involved all of us. Me, Daniel . . . and most of all Billy.

'Talk about what?' Daniel huffed, clearly eager to get on with his shower.

Shivering in my silk pyjamas, but from nerves not cold, I wrapped my arms around myself and took a deep breath. 'Well, there was this woman. In the school playground.'

'Ah, right. Now I get it.' Daniel chuckled. 'Playground politics kicked off already?'

'Don't tease, Dan. That's not what I was going to say. I'm not upset because I got left out of a stupid coffee morning. I'm worried that—'

'Well, *don't* worry. Anyone gives you grief, Bea will sort them out.'

'Bea?' Her name in his mouth sent a shiver through me.

'Yeah. That's one thing she *is* good for. Putting people in their place. You've seen her do it often enough,' he said over his shoulder, as he finally disappeared into the en suite.

Exactly, I thought fearfully. 'You're not helping!' I said out loud, glaring after him.

His comments were far too close to the bone. Yes, Bea was more than capable of exacting revenge, and that was precisely the point. But Daniel wasn't paying attention – his mind was clearly elsewhere, just when I needed him to listen very, very carefully to what I had to say. Before I lost the courage to say it.

*

I remained hunched on the bed while Daniel took his shower, reflecting that Bea wasn't the only one who had a talent for *sorting things out*. There had only ever been one problem in our life that Daniel hadn't been able to fix with a snap of his fingers: having a baby . . .

For the first five years of our marriage, we'd tried everything: every fad diet, vitamin supplement, hypnotherapy and reflexology course, eventually taking the plunge and embarking on IVF. Nothing had worked, and the strain had really begun to take its toll on our relationship.

Closing my eyes, I remembered those times, and I knew that if I told Daniel what Eve had said this morning, I would also have to confess what I did five years ago – which would undoubtedly propel us back to the lowest point of our marriage: to the dark days after our latest round of IVF had once again ended in failure, and I seriously began to fear that if Daniel and I never had a child, I might lose him, too.

Chapter 6

Five years ago

'There are tests. The doctors can find out . . . you know. Whether the problem is with my eggs or your . . .' I squeezed my eyes shut, hating the thought of more medical procedures.

Surely having a baby was supposed to be a natural process – something my body simply knew how to do? I felt like a failure; in my darkest moments, I felt like I was cursed.

'I don't *want* to know.' Daniel jerked the curtains open to let in daylight.

'Why on earth not?' I squinted against the brightness – not only because the light hurt my eyes, after I'd spent the afternoon hiding in bed, but also because the reminder that life was going on outside was too much to bear.

It was summer; Greenwich Park opposite was teeming with visitors enjoying a sunny day out. I could hear mums chatting, children laughing . . .

'I don't want it to come between us,' Daniel said, cutting across my thoughts. 'There'd come a point when one of us would be tempted to throw it at the other. I know there would.'

35

'No. Don't say that. Is that really what you think? I'd never do that. We're a *team*.'

I pulled myself upright against the pillows, still watching his face, unsettled by the thought of conflict between us. Daniel had come home early that day, but most days he was staying at the office later and later. He loved his job; I knew that. But he'd always told me he loved me far more. I was worried that might not be the case if our luck didn't change soon.

'I know we are. And that means we win together, and we lose together. OK?'

He came to sit on the bed, giving me the broad smile that had made me fall in love with him on our first official date, two weeks after that unexpected coffee at the Tate Modern that had turned into a long, leisurely lunch at The Ivy, during which he'd spent most of the time apologising for his *fickle best friend*. Bea had thought she'd won first prize by *stealing Finley from under my nose*, but Daniel was all I'd ever wanted from the moment we met.

'How many times, though?' I stared into his eyes, wishing I had the guts to ask the question that was really on my mind: *will you still love* me *if we don't have a baby?* Daniel had never hinted that he was getting fed up of me, but I couldn't think of any other reason for the slight distractedness I'd noticed about him lately.

'As many as it takes.' He shrugged, but his voice didn't carry its usual confidence.

'Really? I'm not so sure.' I saw his look of surprise and added: 'You know how much I want a baby. But not at the expense of our marriage.' I bit my fingernails to hide my awkwardness at having blurted out my worst fear.

'What? Don't be silly. I'm sure it won't come to that.' He stood up and wandered across the bedroom to look out of the window, arms folded behind his head.

It was hardly a ringing endorsement, and my eyes filled with tears as I watched the play of muscles through his white shirt. He was still dressed in his work clothes, having left the office early to come home and see me, saying he was worried when I didn't reply to his texts.

I honestly hadn't been ignoring them; I'd just forgotten to take my phone into the bathroom while I tried to soak away stomach cramps and misery as, once again, my period arrived, heralding yet more failure.

'Won't it?' I said faintly. 'You're completely sure about that?'

'Hey, you're not getting rid of me that easily.' Turning around, Daniel smiled and came to sit next to me again, giving my shoulder a teasing shove. 'So don't go getting *too* comfy hogging my side of the bed, Mrs Cartwright.'

I laughed, but I couldn't completely shake off my anxiety. I had enough self-awareness to realise that my desire to have a child was fast approaching obsession. I'd seen several friends' marriages break apart under similar strain, and I felt panicky at the thought that we might be heading towards the edge of the same cliff.

I was already feeling insecure about Daniel's new assistant: emails and texts after hours; impromptu working dinners alone. Corinne was my friend – I'd even been the one to introduce her to Daniel, to help her get the job with him – and he repeatedly insisted I was imagining any flirtation, or worse, between them. But I couldn't help worrying he might turn away from me if we didn't have a baby soon.

'I was thinking more of the other way around.' I bit my lip, feeling pathetic and clingy but unable to swallow the nagging fear. 'Whether you might decide to trade *me* in for someone less complicated. Someone who doesn't have to pop pills to stop herself going loopy.'

'For better, for worse, Ruth. Remember?' Softly, Daniel repeated our vows, exactly as he always did whenever I had a wobble. 'In sickness, health—'

'And *childlessness*?' I ventured breathlessly. 'Maybe it's time we thought about . . . alternatives,' I suggested carefully. We'd had more than one argument on that subject lately.

'We've discussed that already, haven't we?' He folded his arms. 'It's *our* baby we want, isn't it? Not one that someone else has abandoned.'

'Dan, don't be cruel. You know that's not how it is. There are a million reasons why some parents aren't able to cope with a baby.' I wished for the millionth time that I knew why my own mum hadn't felt able to stick around for hers – for *me*.

'I know. You're right. It's just . . . I know it probably sounds selfish. Egotistical, even. But I want us to have *our* child, sweetheart. A little bit of you; a little bit of me. That's what we planned, isn't it?'

'Your brown hair. My green eyes. Your big feet,' I tried to joke.

'Exactly. I want to look at my son or daughter and see *us*. The child *we* made. Because I love you, Ruth Cartwright. So much. And I know you're going to be an amazing mum.' His voice was husky; I caught a surprising glint of tears.

'You think?' I was beginning to doubt it.

'I *know*. I can't wait to see you hold our baby. You've dreamed of it as long as I've known you.' He took hold of my hand, lifting it to kiss my fingertips one by one.

'Yes. Yes, I have. You're right. Only, sometimes I feel like I was born under an unlucky star, you know?' I sank back against the pillows, sighing.

'Huh. I don't believe in fate. We make our own luck.'

'Luck. This isn't a stock trade, Daniel. Or an annual bonus. Actually, that reminds me. I was thinking . . . What would you say to me stepping back from work for a while?' I watched his face closely. The thought had been on my mind more and more, but I hadn't mentioned it, and usually we shared everything.

'You mean take a sabbatical?'

'Actually, I mean handing in my notice.'

'But you like your job.' He frowned. 'And you've just been promoted.'

'I *do* like it.' Over time, I'd come to enjoy advertising, even discovering a talent for it. 'But maybe my body doesn't. Maybe all the pressure isn't helping it do *its* job. The mind is so powerful, isn't it? Infertility can be partly psychosomatic. At least, Dr Harper said so.'

'She did?' Daniel looked cross. 'Is she sure about that?'

'I think she's concerned about my mental health,' I admitted quietly.

'Why, what's going on? Please tell me you haven't had more blackouts. Or . . .' He hesitated for a moment. 'Have you been having those out-of-body feelings again?'

Automatically, I glared at the pills on the bedside table. 'No,' I lied, not wanting to worry him. 'I'm OK,' I insisted, reluctant to confess the desperate thoughts I'd been having. If I didn't have a baby soon, I was worried I might go out of my mind. 'Just a bit anxious.'

Daniel glanced at the packet of antidepressants too. 'Those aren't helping?'

I shrugged. 'A little. Anyway, I'm thinking of ditching them. Dr Harper said they're only mild. They won't affect my fertility. But I'd like to find alternative ways of coping, other than medication. Painting helps. I'm hoping to do more of it. Not just my volunteer work at the art therapy centre, but my own stuff. The yoga exercises are good for relaxation, too.'

'Mm, yeah. How is your downward dog?' Daniel chuckled as he drew me into the crook of his shoulder. 'I'd join you, but I'm not that bendy.' He paused, his face turning serious again. 'Maybe you should see your old counsellor. Just say the word, and I'll set it up.' He kissed the top of my head. 'I'd do *anything* to make you happy, Ruth. You know that.'

Chapter 7

'OK, then. Shoot. What's the story?' Daniel, wearing his black jersey sleep shorts and still towelling his hair dry, bounced onto the end of the bed. 'You were telling me about a mum glaring at you in the playground. I'm all ears.'

He whipped the towel behind his broad shoulders, and I wondered how long it had been since I'd dried his back for him – how long since Daniel had soaped my shoulders in the bath, his blue eyes sparkling as he slipped his hands beneath the water to caress me.

I'd gone through so much to become a mum that I knew I was guilty of letting family life take precedence over our marriage. *Our happy, messy family.* I couldn't bear it if it was snatched away – if Daniel turned his back on me, once I'd found the courage to confess. But I couldn't just blurt it out. He'd asked for my story; well, it actually began with Eve.

'The woman in the playground, Daniel. It was Eve.' I had no fingernails left to bite, but I chewed them anyway.

'Eve?' He stopped towelling and sat still, frowning.

'Yes, you know – the teenager I met when I had Billy. She was in the bed next to mine on the postnatal ward. You must remember. Tall, dark-haired. Painfully thin.'

'Oh, yeah. I remember.' Daniel stood up and tossed his towel into the bathroom, before climbing into bed, wrapping the duvet around his waist. 'She lost her baby, didn't she?'

'Well, that's just it.' I peeled back my side of the duvet and slid underneath too, but I remained sitting upright against the headboard; my body felt rigid with nerves.

'*It?*' Daniel turned to face me, head propped on one hand.

'Yes.' My mouth dried again as I found myself studying the length of his nose, the breadth of his jaw, straight brown hair so unlike Billy's black curls, blue eyes where Billy's were dark brown. 'The thing is, Eve said . . . Oh, it doesn't matter. She was talking nonsense.'

I understood that Eve was still mourning the loss of her baby; I totally got her distress. I remembered every failed pregnancy attempt, each burst of hope for a new life that had ended in tears. Grief had clearly damaged Eve's mind. Maybe that's why she'd been at the school: she must have a job there. Perhaps it brought her comfort to watch other children.

'No, go on. Eve said *what?*' Daniel encouraged.

'A load of rubbish, actually,' I dismissed, still thinking how best to raise the subject of Bea. 'She was always unstable. The years obviously haven't been kind to her. Poor woman. She's quite deluded. She came at me, pretty aggressively, as a matter of fact.'

'Jesus. Are you OK?' Daniel sat up, looking cross and concerned. 'What did she say?'

'That Billy is her son. Crazy, huh? She's obviously deeply confused.'

'Damn right she is, stupid cow.'

I frowned at his uncharacteristic harshness, feeling bad now. I should have more sympathy for Eve. She was clearly struggling with her mental health; I knew all too well what that was like.

'In fairness, she's had a tough life. She probably—'

'I couldn't care less about her life,' Daniel snapped. 'She just needs to stay the hell out of ours.' His voice was sharp and loud now. 'Billy is her son – what the hell?'

'Shh, you'll wake him.' I rested a hand on Daniel's arm. I needed to talk about *Bea* and regretted mentioning Eve now. She was proving a distraction when, as far as I was concerned, she wasn't an issue. No one could tell me Billy wasn't mine; the idea was ridiculous.

'Billy is *our* son,' Daniel said, unknowingly twisting the shard of guilt deeper inside me. 'I don't need to prove it to her, or anyone. For Christ's sake, what does she expect us to do? Take some sort of test?'

'You mean a blood test? DNA?' Panic surged at the thought of what that might reveal.

'Exactly. Ridiculous.' Daniel glowered. 'So this *Eve* better sort herself out. Billy is ours. End of. Jesus, I watched you give *birth* to him. How dare she?'

The bedroom was dark, apart from a sliver of light from the hallway where Billy insisted I leave a lamp on at night. The glow caught Daniel's profile, highlighting the sensuous curve of his full mouth, now hardened into a thin line. I reached out to rest a calming hand on his bare shoulder; every muscle was tensed. I pulled away, confused by the strength of his reaction.

'Of course you did,' I said to pacify him. 'Honestly, don't worry about Eve. She's just mixed up. Grieving. Desperate, I shouldn't wonder.' I thought back to the first time I'd met her. 'Seriously, I remember her talking about some dreadful stuff in hospital. She even lived rough on the streets for a time, I think.'

'Huh. Doesn't surprise me. There's your answer, then. She was probably making some pathetic attempt at a scam.'

'You mean blackmail?' I was genuinely shocked. I could believe Eve was delusional; I struggled to see her as criminally manipulative. 'No. Really, I don't think . . .'

'Well, I do. She must have googled me. Found out about my job at the bank. No doubt she's hoping for a big fat cheque to stop her shooting her mouth off about us stealing her son.'

I stared at Daniel, astonished that he was taking Eve's idiotic accusation seriously – that we were even still talking about her, rather than my toxic friend . . . and the confession I knew I had to make, before Bea made it for me. 'Stealing her son?'

'Kidnapping, then. Or whatever absurd story she's cooked up. You tell me.'

'I don't care what she . . . Look, she was talking complete rubbish. I'm not scared of Eve.' *But I'm terrified of Bea*, I admitted to myself.

'Nor am I.' Daniel rolled over, punching his pillow to get comfortable. 'She's just another screwball woman. And if she, or anyone else, bothers you again, Ruth, you mark my words. I won't be held responsible for my actions.'

*

The strange thing was, until Daniel reacted so strongly, I hadn't given serious thought to what Eve might want from us, what she could *do* to us. My encounter with her in the school playground had badly shaken me up; it had taken me by surprise at a moment when I was already on edge about leaving Billy for the first time. But mostly it had upset me because it prised open the lid on my own trauma: on long-buried guilt and fear about a night my mind had blocked out for five years. *Until this morning.*

Eve's crazy accusation hadn't made me doubt that Billy was my son, and I strongly suspected she was already regretting her outburst. Now that she'd had time to get over the shock of seeing a little boy who had reminded her painfully of her lost baby, Eve would most likely either disappear or steer clear of me, embarrassed by her deluded accusation.

In a few days' time, no doubt I would forget all about her again, too, as I'd forgotten her for four years. What I *couldn't* blot out of my mind so easily was the fear she'd awakened: not that Billy wasn't mine, but that he might not be Daniel's . . .

Over the years, I'd occasionally wondered about Billy's dark eyes and hair, his tall, slight body shape. There had been times when I'd splashed him in the bath, or cuddled him to sleep, that I had felt a vague, unaccountable, whispery sense of *otherness* about him.

I had wanted so badly for everything to be right this time that I'd ignored it, always making a joke when people commented on how he didn't look much like his daddy. 'Oh, he takes after Daniel's dad,' I would say. Or: 'The stork must have delivered the wrong baby!'

My joy at finally becoming a mum had chased those anxieties to the back of my brain, and gradually I'd forgotten them. Now Eve had shone a stark spotlight on them, and I couldn't stop wondering if the weekend that destroyed my friendship with Bea had also cheated Daniel of being a father . . .

I was terrified of confessing what happened that night, what I had done. I knew Daniel loved me; I hoped he'd be able to forgive a drunken mistake I could barely remember. I doubted he would be so forgiving if he discovered there was a possibility he might be raising the son of his former best friend.

Chapter 8

I heard Billy murmur in his sleep, then cry out – as he did around midnight every night. The wake-and-feed routine I'd established with him as a baby had become firmly etched on his body clock, and I had never been able to help him break it.

Daniel was either asleep, or pretending to be, so I slid my feet to the soft grey carpet, ready to go to my son and comfort him, as I had every night since he was born. *My son.* Not Eve's. But quite possibly Finley's . . .

'Mummy?' Billy wasn't fully awake; I knew that.

'Mummy's here, everything's all right. Go back to sleepies, darling.'

I slotted my thumb into his warm palm and watched his hand curl around it, exactly as he'd done every night since he was a baby. Jules and Nish often lectured me about letting him get into bad sleep habits, and I always smiled and said they were right, not wanting to explain that I wasn't just comforting Billy; these moments also healed *my* pain. I had never known my own mother, but at last I'd become one.

45

Please don't let her take away my son. I wasn't sure how it would be possible for Bea to do so, but I knew that if she had even the slightest suspicion Billy might be her husband's child, she would try anything possible to take back what was rightfully his – and therefore, to Bea's possessive, domineering mind, *hers*.

My own mind was still buzzing as I returned to bed. I felt restless – and thirsty. Deciding to get a drink, I made my way quietly to the kitchen, filling a glass of water at the sink.

The river looked high when I glanced through the kitchen window, and I peered closer at the blue canal boat, squinting to see if I could make out any sign of the occupants. But the curtains were drawn. Whoever was on board must be asleep. In fact, I had an eerie sense of being the only person awake.

Usually, I loved the feeling of being high up – safe, quiet, apart. Despite my initial reluctance to move to the penthouse, I'd never felt isolated there, but now I felt a frisson of loneliness. Daniel had always been my strongest ally, my closest confidant. It felt wrong to let him go to sleep without having made my confession.

Not that there was any chance of sleep for me while I remained on tenterhooks waiting for Bea's next move. 'Maybe I should bite the bullet and go see her. Thrash it out. Let her do her worst,' I murmured, feeling a knot of anxiety tighten inside me at the idea.

About to turn away from the window, a ghostlike form caught my eye. Standing on the wharf at the end of the path leading to our building, shoulders hunched, hands deep in pockets, there was something familiar about the figure's body shape and posture. It was only as floodlights from the canal boat were suddenly turned on that I realised why.

It was Eve.

*

'Are you OK? It's the middle of the night, Eve. What are you doing here?'

46

'I wondered how long it would take you to notice me,' she said, folding her arms.

She was wearing the same torn jeans and oversized black hoodie as she'd had on at the school that morning, and I felt a flash of worry that she must be freezing. Automatically, I tugged at the collar of Daniel's grey wool work coat, the first thing that had come to hand as I'd looked for something to pull over my cream silk pyjamas in a hurry. Thankfully, Billy's bright blue-and-green school scarf and my soft grey suede Ugg boots had also been on the coat stand; a biting wind whipped off the Thames.

'Did you follow me?' I asked, bemused about her reappearance. I'd been convinced I would never see her again. Bumping into her in the playground had been an unlucky coincidence; the same couldn't be said of her turning up outside my home.

'Did you really think I wouldn't? Huh. Typical.'

'Sorry?' I frowned, tiredness and anxiety clouding my brain. I wasn't sure if I was misjudging her mood, but Eve seemed angrier even than at the school earlier.

'Ha. Rich people. Always think the same thing. If something is inconvenient to them, they expect it to just disappear. Problems. *People*. Whatever is in their way.'

'Well, I don't think like that. And I *don't* want you to just go away.'

Eve was troubled, but I was convinced she was harmless. I stared at her pale, gaunt face, debating whether to invite her inside. Maybe she just needed to talk. It had obviously been a big shock, seeing me again, dredging up trauma for her, too . . . convincing her that I was to blame for it.

Only the thought of Daniel stopped me asking her to come back to the apartment with me. He'd called Eve a 'screwball woman'; I doubted he'd welcome her into our home. I didn't want to put him in a bad mood before I talked to him about Bea – and Finley . . .

'Liar,' Eve said softly.

I sighed. 'No, honestly. I don't wish any ill on you. I'm just

47

surprised to see you, that's all. And I don't lie.' *Only to yourself*, I thought bitterly.

'It's OK. We *all* lie sometimes. But some lies are bigger than others.'

'Of course. But a mistake can seem like a lie, when in fact it's an accident,' I said, still thinking of Bea and Finley, trying to reassure myself I hadn't deliberately deceived Daniel.

'The truth is the truth.'

'I'm sure you haven't come here just to tell me that.' Tiredly, I forced a smile. 'It's been a while, hey?'

'Four years and six weeks.'

'Yes. I suppose it is.' Instantly, I remembered Billy's fourth birthday party in July, his excitement when Daniel had un-blind-folded him to reveal the shiny blue bike he'd hidden in the boot of his car. *Poor Daniel*. He adored Billy. I hated the pain I was about to cause him.

'Not a date that's easily forgotten. Even though I'm sure you've tried.'

'Why on earth would I want to forget my son's birthday?' I reeled back, starting to feel uncomfortable. Eve's hostility wasn't softening, and her misguided allegation suddenly hung in the air between us, as oppressive as the heavy dankness drifting off the river.

'So you can pretend it never happened.'

'Pretend *what* never happened?'

'The switch, of course. My baby and yours.'

'*What?* Now, look here, Eve.' I took a step towards her. 'I know you had a terrible time in the hospital. You went through something I wouldn't wish on my worst enemy. But what you said in the playground this morning . . .' I shook my head, too wound up to say more.

I'd spent the whole day in mental torment, forcing myself to confront every blinkered, delusional lie I had ever told myself, any time the lack of resemblance between Billy and Daniel had

48

niggled at me. For four years, I'd basked in the brilliant sunshine of pure joy: *at last, I had the family I'd craved.*

That happiness had blinded me; I could see that now. All my doubts had lain buried in shadows at the back of my mind, along with agonising memories of *that night*. Fragment by tiny, agonising fragment, I had painstakingly unearthed those shameful, guilty memories over the last few hours, trying to piece together what had happened between me and Finley – and it was Bea's loaded hints that had first pricked my conscience.

I'd been half expecting *her* to turn up at any moment. It wouldn't have been a surprise to find *Bea* stalking me – but not Eve. What on earth did *Eve* want with me?

'What I said was true,' she said, hands on her hips. 'You just don't want to hear it.'

'How can it be true?'

'Truth doesn't need an explanation. It just is.'

'No. You need to do better than that. I understand that seeing me again has triggered bad memories. That's unfortunate. It's a terrible coincidence, and I . . .'

I broke off as it occurred to me how much of a coincidence it was. Eve didn't have a child of school age, although it was possible she had some sort of job at the prep school. But she didn't live locally, and unless her circumstances had changed dramatically over the last four years, it seemed unlikely she could afford to rent in this expensive part of west London.

'I'm sure it *was* terrible. For *you.*' She smiled. 'I'm actually happy I've found you.'

'But why were you even *at* the school, if you don't have—'

'A child? Oh, but I do. I told you.' Her head jerked upwards. 'He's up there asleep in your fancy apartment. But in answer to your question, I was there to see you. And my son.'

'*My* son. And . . . my husband's.' Despite my doubts about that, I felt a need to convince Eve that I had Daniel firmly on my side.

She glared at me. 'He knows, you know. Oh, he's very good at

49

putting on a front. *Your husband*. I saw an interview with him in a magazine the other week. A photo, too. Very handsome. Very *smug*. The man who has it all.'

'Hang on, there's no need to be—'

'There was a photo of you as well. And . . . Billy. That's what you call him, isn't it?'

'Yes,' I said absently, trying to remember the name of *her* baby. I'd never forget those tense hours in the hospital, though. Eve's raw screams and anguished pacing around the ward.

She was talking nonsense, but I couldn't simply walk away. It was obvious she'd come here to cause trouble – blackmail being the most likely scenario, as Daniel had suggested. I shivered, remembering Billy saying Eve had been carrying a knife. I glanced at the pockets of her jeans, then at the shadows along the riverside, wondering if she'd really come alone.

'I recognised my little boy immediately,' she goaded. 'As soon as I saw his photo, I knew he was mine. And I knew what you'd done.'

'I've done *nothing*,' I insisted harshly. *At least, not to Eve.*

'It wasn't hard to find you,' she continued, almost chattily. 'Daniel is very meticulous, isn't he? Files his business accounts online bang on time. He's the perfect banker. Perfect husband. Perfect *daddy*,' she said scornfully. 'You told me all about him in the hospital, remember? The perfect life you were going to give your son. Only he died. So you took mine instead.'

'*No*, Eve. That's not true. Look, do you need money? Is that what this is about?' My words echoed inside my own head, sounding as though they were coming from a distance.

'Huh. You see? I was right. Rich people. You think that's the answer to everything. Money. No. I need my *son*. My little boy. Sean.'

'Sean,' I echoed wistfully. 'That's what you were going to call your baby,' I recalled gently. 'But Eve, I know it's so, so hard, but your little boy died.'

'No, Ruth, he didn't. *Yours* did.'

Chapter 9

I stared at Eve for long moments, wondering if stress had finally made me start to lose my mind, or if this was all a bad dream . . . if I'd conjured up her presence out of guilt and fear, my former psychological trauma rearing its ugly head again now I'd stopped taking my pills.

I squeezed my eyes shut for a second, remembering Eve's wild, unexpected appearance in the school playground. Had I simply imagined her? *Was I battling the manifestation of my own conscience?* But Billy had seen her, too, I reminded myself, and when I opened my eyes again, Eve was still there.

She was all too real, and I glared at her, furious that she'd walked back into my life, unannounced, at the worst possible moment. 'What do you really want, Eve? Let's cut to the chase.' I felt sorry for her, but I'd had enough. I wanted to go back inside – back to my family. I hoped I would still *have* a family, after Daniel and I finally got to talk about that night.

'I . . . want . . . my . . . son,' Eve insisted, jabbing a finger to emphasise each word.

51

'OK, so if you're right, and Billy *is* your son,' I said quietly, humouring her even while I felt like my heart was pounding almost out of my chest, 'how can that be?'

'You switched the babies, of course. When you realised yours wasn't going to survive.'

'That's insane.'

'It's criminal, that's what it is.'

'You think there was some kind of mix-up at the hospital. Is *that* what you're suggesting?' If pressure wouldn't work, I needed to try empathy. Her baby had died; she'd clearly been unable to accept that. Perhaps I could help steer her towards that realisation.

'It was no accident. It was theft.'

'Look, you're upset. I get that. But there's no *way* I could have switched our babies. I was in a terrible state after my caesarean. I could hardly stand up. I fainted at least twice.'

'Fine. So maybe it wasn't you that actually did it. I told you. *Your husband knows.*'

'Rubbish.' I rolled my eyes, exasperated as I realised she was about to turn her attack to Daniel. 'And it was *your* son that was poorly, Eve. Remember?' I reached for her arm, picturing her agony after she'd gone to kiss her little boy goodbye.

Admittedly, I'd been woozy with medication for much of my time in hospital, but there was no way I could have dreamed up the midwife's solemn face and Eve's cries of distress. She was obviously rewriting the past in a desperate attempt to change her future. But lying didn't change the facts: Billy had lived; her son had died.

'No. It was *yours.*'

She rejected my sympathy with a stamp of one foot, her black hair flying upwards, reminding me of the wild ponies that wandered the New Forest . . . surrounding the hotel where the four of us had stayed that weekend, *that night.* Bea and Finley; Daniel and me.

Suddenly, I couldn't stop the rush of images. The four of us at the christening, staying in a chintzy hotel afterwards. The evaporation of our friendship over the days and weeks that followed. Bea's aloofness back then, her icy hostility now . . .

Had she found out what happened between me and Finley?

The thought of her telling Daniel before I did, and the multiple, devastating repercussions of that revelation, continued to plague me. Eve's presence was a complication I didn't need. Her accusation was ludicrous – grief had clearly made her delusional – but it was equally obvious she wasn't going to stop making it.

I had to figure out how to pacify her, before she did something rash, like broadcasting her crazy accusation and causing a scandal. She was right about Daniel's success as a banker, and his job required absolute integrity: gossip of this kind would be hugely compromising. I was prepared to help Eve, but I refused to be blackmailed.

'If you won't be reasonable,' I said, as calmly as I could, 'I have nothing more to say to you.' Turning to leave, I began picking my way carefully back up the slippery walkway.

'Are you quite sure you can trust your husband, Ruth?' Eve called after me.

'One hundred per cent,' I said, without turning around.

'And what about Billy? He looks like me, doesn't he? He's *mine*, I tell you!'

'No, he's *mine*.' Deliberately, I kept my eyes fixed straight ahead.

'Don't walk away, Ruth. Do you hear me? I meant what I said this morning!'

'Which bit?' I scoffed, finally spinning around to glare at her.

'If you don't give Billy back to me, I'll have to take him,' she said coldly. 'You have forty-eight hours to hand him over. Don't make me do this the hard way.'

'I'm not *making* you do anything,' I snapped, even as, once again, I pictured Eve wielding a knife. All at once, it dawned on me that she might be psychotic – *dangerous*. 'Look, you need help, Eve. Please, talk to someone,' I appealed to her. 'Before you do something you regret,' I added, trying not to show how that prospect was beginning to frighten me.

'The only thing I regret is trusting you,' she spat. 'He's my son, Ruth!'

'*Prove it.*'

I turned and carried on walking slowly away. My legs were trembling, but I was determined not to appear as flustered as I felt. I didn't want to give Eve the satisfaction of sparing her a second glance, either, but as I reached the gate leading to our building, curiosity finally got the better of me. I turned to take one last look at Eve. She had already vanished.

*

The apartment felt unnaturally quiet when I let myself back in and went to check on Billy. I stood staring at the dark curls falling over his forehead, the long lashes casting shadows on his pale cheeks, and I understood how he might cast a spell over anyone, especially Eve. The need for a child could be overpowering; I'd been driven half-mad by it myself.

I stroked Billy's cheek, my fingertips trailing over his face, tracing the shape of his jaw, his pointy chin, absorbing every feature and comparing it to Daniel's, to Finley's . . .

Did he look like Eve? Yes – and no, I decided. Not enough that I would instantly put them together in a random line-up. The thought made me shudder, reminding me of police enquiries and identity parades. I felt sick at the idea of Daniel being arrested by the police and charged with . . . what? *Abduction?* It was crazy, like something out of a soap opera.

People didn't walk out of hospitals with someone else's baby. I knew Eve was lying. *Bea* was the one who posed the real threat to me, my marriage and my family – and that dreadful night, the weekend of the christening in the New Forest five years ago, held all the answers. I was utterly convinced of it.

Daniel was the innocent victim in all this. I'd betrayed his trust, and I hoped he would give me the chance to make up for what I had done. I hoped Bea would forgive me, too: for stupidly, accidentally betraying our friendship. She was right about actions and consequences, and taking responsibility for our mistakes. That was where I needed to focus my energies: confessing my past misdemeanour, and trying everything within my power to make up for it.

What Eve was suggesting was the stuff of nightmares: *her* nightmares. I remembered her agony, and I felt sorry for her. But it wasn't my responsibility, and it wasn't Daniel's fault. It was one of life's tragedies, and I had experienced enough of those myself to recognise when one happened to someone else. Especially someone as vocal about their grief as Eve had been.

Chapter 10

I wouldn't normally remember a passing stranger so vividly, but Eve had made a lasting impression on me. We had been assigned adjacent beds in the postnatal ward of the Queen Elizabeth Hospital in Greenwich, and our babies were also together in the special care unit. While I felt consumed by worry, locked in my own thoughts much of the time, Eve had never stopped talking – and firing questions at me.

Recognising that she was terrified, too, I tried to distract us both by chatting about Daniel, his job at the bank and our cosy home overlooking Greenwich Park. When I saw Eve doodling sketches in the back of a dog-eared science fiction paperback, I also talked to her about my love of art and how, one day, I hoped to open a gallery.

In return, she told me about her fascination with the supernatural, confiding that she felt like my 'cosmic shadow' – or 'parapsychic echo', as she called it. I'd smiled and told her she read too much fantasy fiction, but she had remained adamant.

'Think about it. I'm tall, you're short.'

'Not *that* short. I'm five foot six.' I was sensitive about my height, having always felt a little stumpy in comparison to Bea's willowy elegance.

'You're all golden blonde, and I'm, like, so *dark*.' Eve chewed her nails, looking me up and down with childlike unselfconsciousness.

'Dark *hair*,' I pointed out. 'Your skin is actually fairer than mine.'

'We had our babies at almost exactly the same time. On the same day. Explain *that*.'

'Coincidence,' I said, laughing.

She glared at me. 'We both had boys.'

'It's just a coincidence, Eve,' I repeated gently. She was young and she'd been through a tough time; if she needed to escape into a fantasy world sometimes, that was understandable.

'They were both born two weeks early. Both poorly. It's like they're twin souls. But maybe there's only so much cosmic energy to share between them. And it's not *enough*.' She was getting worked up now, her pale skin blotchy, pupils dilated.

'You know, I think I should call the doctor, Eve. You look a bit flushed. The midwife said to keep an eye out for any signs of fever, and you do seem—'

'No! I don't want to see anyone. It's too late. No one can change anything now. It's all just . . . meant to be,' she said fiercely, turning away and hiding her face.

'Try to rest, OK?' I rubbed her shoulder. 'The doctors are doing everything they can. I don't know much about destiny, or fate,' I said carefully. 'But I do know that miracles happen in that special care unit. Let's just channel all our, um, positive energy into hoping for one.'

Although I wasn't superstitious, I was scared, too – and more than a little unnerved by Eve's talk of *twin souls*. Rationally, I guessed it was something she'd picked up from one of her fantasy novels, but even so, her paranoia was starting to get to me.

After three anxious days, though, it was her son that was moved to the more urgent high dependency unit, while mine remained in special care, gaining strength by the hour. Still, I shut my eyes in fear when the midwife approached our beds later that day, only opening them again when I heard Eve let out an animal wail.

'Sweetheart,' I said tentatively, slipping through the curtains drawn around her bed, after the midwife had finally left. 'Don't give up. There's still hope.'

'Really? You must have heard what Mary said. She told me to go and say *goodbye*.'

I caught sight of livid red lines crisscrossing Eve's wrists and realised what they signified: at some point, she must have hated her life enough to want it to be over. I resolved to have a quiet word with the midwife, to make sure Eve would get the help she needed.

'Your poor little boy. He must be so unwell.' I held out a hand to her, but she brushed it away. 'I'm so sorry. I know this is agony. I do. Trust me, I know.'

'Sure you do.' Suddenly, she rounded on me. 'You get to take *your* boy home. I bet you've even got a name. There's no point naming mine just to put it on his death certificate.'

'Is there no one who can be with you?' It felt wrong that she had to go through such a trauma alone. For a fleeting moment, I thought about taking her home with *me*.

'No one. Well, I guess there's my old foster dad. He was a right charmer. Only ever got off the sofa to beat me. As for my foster mum . . . yeah, she drank so much, the social worker told me she broke her neck falling downstairs. I was long gone by then, anyway. Oh, then there's the teacher who promised to look after me. Only he decided to rape me instead.'

For a moment, I was too shocked to speak. 'He . . . oh my God, Eve. Is he . . .?'

'The baby's father?' She screwed up her face. 'No idea. I'll sleep with anyone for a spliff. Everyone knows that. They threw me out of college because of it. Actually, the head teacher threw me out

58

because I wouldn't sleep with *him*. There's hypocrisy for you, hey?'

'Eve, you don't have to act tough with me.' Gently, I took hold of her hand, and this time she didn't push me away. 'We're friends, aren't we? I want to *help* you.'

'Then do me a favour.' Her dull eyes glittered for a moment. 'Hold on to your boy. Give him all the love you can. At least one of them has to make it. Maybe mine has to die so yours can live. Like, they're shadows of each other and can't be in the world at the same time.'

'Please don't say that.' The superstitious notion sent a shudder through me. I pulled her closer, hugging her thin body against me and stroking her hair. Finally, she leaned into me.

'I lied about not giving him a name. I was going to call him Sean.'

'Sean. That's a good name.' I blinked back tears.

'It was my dad's. My *real* dad's.'

'Ah. So is your dad . . .' I pulled back, studying Eve's face. 'You said "was".' I hesitated, not wanting to upset her even further. 'Is he . . . is it possible he could help you? I could call him for you, if you like?' I offered, feeling awful about how alone she was.

'No point. My parents were teenage dropouts, too. I was an accident, you see? No one actually *wanted* me. Not my birth parents. Not my foster ones.'

'Oh. I see.' I frowned, running out of options. 'I'm so sorry, Eve.'

'I'm not.' She shrugged carelessly. 'To be honest, I doubt my dad even knew I existed. My foster mum said he was a right playboy at college. Still, that's one less person who's dumped me. You can't be accused of abandoning a kid you never knew you had. *Can* you?'

*

Meeting Eve had been intense, and I'd never forgotten her. But our brief friendship had ended without a trace of guilt on my

59

side. *Babies sometimes died*. I knew that, and while I felt sympathy for Eve, I had a crisis of my own to deal with: a confession I had yet to make to my husband, and a spiteful friend who would take malicious delight in making it for me.

Even so, I couldn't ignore Eve's threat that I had forty-eight hours to hand Billy over. However ludicrous her claims were, she was clearly unbalanced; I couldn't be sure she wouldn't do something stupidly impulsive. After remembering my conversations with her in the hospital, a new worry had also started to grip me.

Eve had dismissed her birth father's importance; I couldn't do the same for Billy's. *A father had a right to know his child*. When I'd demanded that Eve 'prove it', I had been calling her bluff. I *knew* there was nothing she could do to convince me Billy was her son – he was *mine*. Only, I still had no proof or certainty that he was Daniel's . . . or Finley's.

I'd been terrified when Daniel had mentioned a DNA test, but there was no other way to be sure. Finley clearly had no inkling – I hadn't heard a peep from him since that ill-fated weekend, and he was never around when I took Billy for playdates at Bea's house. Lately, there hadn't been many of those, I recalled, pondering again how aloof Bea had become.

'Damn,' I groaned, as it hit me that if she *had* found out about that night, it could only be from one source: *Finley*. And while Bea might be mad at me for betraying her friendship, if Finley had finally put two and two together and started wondering if Billy was his son, he would surely feel I'd betrayed *him* a thousand times over: for keeping him from his child.

Chapter 11

'Daniel. Are you awake?' I whispered, creeping back into our bedroom, after accidentally falling asleep cuddled up next to Billy. I'd only intended to lie down for a moment, to be close to him and draw comfort from his presence, but stress and exhaustion had overwhelmed me.

I envied Daniel's deep sleep: he had his back to me, and the bedroom was dark, but his big body was motionless; he was clearly dead to the world. I knew I wouldn't be able to sleep so soundly until my conscience was cleared – and Eve was gone.

'Dan. Can we talk?' I sat on the edge of the bed, gently nudging his shoulder.

'What time is it?' He frowned, rubbing a hand over his face.

'Early. Billy's still asleep.'

'Ah, good. How are you feeling this morning?'

Guilty. Terrified. 'Worried, I guess.'

Daniel stretched, then yawned. 'Oh? What about?'

'Eve, of course. And—'

'Seriously? I thought we'd dealt with that?' Abruptly, he sat

61

up, grabbing my arm. 'I told you, Ruth. She's a headcase. Forget about her.'

'I wish I could, but . . .' Tiredly, I scrubbed at my eyes, once again picturing Eve's cold glare as she spat her horrible threat at me.

Daniel rubbed my arm now. 'It upset you. I get that. But try not to dwell on it. It was a horrible incident, sure. Maybe chalk it down to experience, hey? In future, stick to your own friends and steer clear of mad women in the playground.' He chuckled, leaning forward to plant a kiss on my cheek. 'The crazies always stand out a mile.'

I couldn't smile. 'I was so excited about Billy starting school. Nervous, but happy for him. He was desperate to go. Seeing Eve . . . it's spoiled *everything*.'

'Then don't let it,' Daniel said philosophically. 'Look, there will always be troublemakers. We can't switch everything up trying to avoid them. We've got to get on with our lives. They have to figure out their own problems. No running away, OK?'

Although that was exactly what we'd done with Bea and Finley. We'd never seen them again after the christening weekend. I also recalled that it was Daniel who had initiated the move from Greenwich all the way to Richmond on the other side of London, saying that our friendship was becoming 'claustrophobic' and that we needed space from it.

Yes, *he* was the one who had pushed for a fresh start – away from the constant presence of our best friends, who were always in the grip of some drama or other. He'd radically changed our lives once to avoid 'troublemakers' – what was different now?

'I don't want to run away, exactly,' I said hesitantly. 'Actually, quite the opposite. I'm finding it hard to . . . to face up to things. What Eve said, it made me think—'

'How many more times, Ruth?' Daniel cut in, clearly losing patience now. '*Forget* about what she said. Listen, why don't you go have a bath? Relax. I'll get Billy up.'

I shook my head. 'No. Let him sleep. I don't want him to go to school today.'

'Seriously? *Why?*'

'Because of *Eve*. I know what you said about her, and I agree. She's deluded. But it's not that simple. I don't think she's just going to walk away.'

'What makes you say that?' Daniel frowned as he swung his legs off the other side of the bed, grabbing black sports shorts and a grey T-shirt from the floor where he always left them, untidily but easily to hand for his regular morning run.

I tutted, watching him, but I was too on edge to tease him about his messiness, as I usually would. 'I . . . well, I saw her last night. Down by the river. You were asleep. I was restless.' I shrugged. 'I noticed Eve outside and thought I could talk some sense into her.'

'You did *what?*' Daniel straightened up and stared at me, open-mouthed. 'You went down to the river alone, in the middle of the night, to see that *nutcase?*'

'I had to do something.'

'Christ.' Daniel groaned, then let out a sigh as I hunched up my knees, feeling tearful and anxious. 'Sorry, sweetheart.' He scooted across the bed to give me a quick hug. 'I didn't mean to shout. OK, so tell me, what happened?'

'She's still saying Billy's her son.' I wiped my eyes on my pyjama sleeve. 'She claims our babies were switched at the hospital.'

I deliberately didn't add that Eve had accused *him*. He was scathing enough about her; I didn't want to fuel any more conflict. Daniel wasn't an aggressive man, but he'd graduated top of his year at Officers' Training Corps after uni; he never let himself be pushed around.

'Look, I told you. She's a screwball. You took a silly risk going down there, but what's done is done. *Forget* about Eve. She'll get bored of her little game soon enough.'

'What if it's *not* a game? Even if it is, shouldn't we call the police? Eve is deluded. She could also be dangerous.' I shivered, remembering the knife Billy was certain he'd seen in her pocket at the school. *Even more reason not to take him there.* 'She told me we have forty-eight hours to hand Billy over. Then she'll take him.'

'No way.' Daniel's body tensed until the veins in his strong arms visibly stood out. 'There's no *way* she can get her hands on Billy. That's a stupid, idle threat.'

'It's still a threat. Shouldn't we report it?'

'Huh. The ramblings of a mad woman? The police would laugh in our faces.'

'So, what, we wait until she actually does something? I can't take that risk, Daniel. I can't take Billy to school, knowing Eve is hanging around.'

'OK.' He thought for a moment. 'If it makes you feel better, *I'll* take him. I'll even bunk off work and pick him up later. I've got a meeting this morning, but I'll cancel. We could spend some time together. Just the two of us. Go for a walk in Kew Gardens. Treat ourselves to brunch. Or, better still, go back to bed. How long has it been since we've done *that*?'

Too long, I thought, and the prospect made my heart leap, only not with romantic excitement, as it once would have. I needed uninterrupted time and space to speak to Daniel alone, to make my confession – and apology – and figure out what was to be done about it.

I was desperately anxious about leaving Billy, but Kew Gardens was only around the corner from his school. We could get to Billy in minutes if Eve *did* show up again – and I had no doubt Daniel would brief the head teacher with the strictest of instructions not to let her, or anyone but us, anywhere near him.

'Actually, a walk and talk sounds like a good idea. Fresh air. A chance to clear my thoughts.' I smiled. 'If you really don't think we should phone the police?' I couldn't put my doubts to bed entirely. 'Eve sounded deadly serious.'

'I bet she did. First sign of paranoia, isn't it?' Daniel said flippantly. 'Believing your own conspiracy theories.' He huffed, then launched himself into a series of stretches, first one leg then the other. 'I'm not giving that woman the time of day. Nor should you. Eve won't get within an arm's length of my son. Not while there's breath in my body.'

'He's everything to me,' I whispered, feeling more tears roll down my face, all my guilt, worry and pent-up emotion starting to feel overwhelming.

'And to me.' Daniel stopped doing his pre-run stretches and pulled me into a hug.

Breathlessly, I clung to him, my confession rising to my lips. 'Dan, I . . .'

'Come on, no more tears. Go run that bath. I'll make a few calls, cancel my meeting, then wake Billy. I'll even get him dressed in his uniform and feed him breakfast.' He pulled back, waggling his eyebrows, clearly trying to lighten the mood and reassure me everything was fine.

It wasn't fine. I wasn't sure it would be ever again. 'OK. Thanks.' Reluctantly, I let go, telling myself there would be time enough to talk once Billy was safely in school.

Strolling to the en suite, I paused in the doorway, turning back to watch Daniel reach for his phone. His handsome face was concerned and thoughtful, and my heart squeezed. He didn't show his softer side to many people; the gentleness underlying his ruthless ambition had always felt like a special secret between us. I opened my mouth to tell him so, when he lifted his phone to his ear.

'Hi. It's me. There's been a change of plan.'

Chapter 12

A leisurely bath, followed by a few stretches of my own – the mindful yoga routine I tried to practise each morning – calmed me a little, and I told myself Daniel was most probably phoning Corinne, his assistant, to say he wasn't coming in today. He'd mentioned needing to cancel a meeting, too; that was all he would have been doing.

No doubt I'd imagined his intimate tone, just as I'd imagined him deliberately hiding his shirt in the laundry basket last night. 'Forget about Eve, *you're* the loopy, paranoid one,' I chastised myself, even as I recalled Bea mentioning a visit to Windsor at the weekend – a plan that was news to me, but I hadn't yet had the chance to quiz Daniel on how Bea knew about it.

'She was just messing with my head. Stirring up trouble,' I groaned. Daniel had always called Bea a *drama queen*, and he was right. That was part of the reason we'd moved away from Greenwich: for a quieter life. 'Daniel isn't having secret dates with Bea. He hasn't seen her in *years*,' I reminded myself.

Just as Finley seemed to avoid my visits to their house, Daniel

66

made sure he was never around when Bea, Nish and Jules came over to our apartment with their kids. We never talked about our former foursome, or the reasons our once close friendship had drifted . . . then died.

Bea's and Finley's names were never even mentioned between us – which was exactly why I was finding it so hard to bring up the past, and confess to Daniel my fears about the consequences of that night. The sooner I came clean to him, the sooner we could organise a DNA test and do as Daniel suggested: move on with our life.

'You wish,' I taunted myself, blow-drying my hair into loose waves.

Deep down, I knew it wouldn't be that simple. If Billy *did* turn out to be Finley's son, it would severely test Daniel's commitment to me. I'd do everything in my power to make it up to him, but, in all honesty, if I were in his shoes, I wasn't sure I could ever forgive such a betrayal of trust.

'Dan? Is that you?' I called out, convinced I'd heard the front door bang.

Turning off the hairdryer, I wandered from the dressing area into our bedroom, not surprised to see our bed still unmade. 'Messy as ever.' I picked up the sleep shorts that now graced the spot where his running shorts had spent the night, before straightening the duvet.

'He'd better not leave the kitchen in the same state,' I grumbled, pulling on fresh black jeans and a soft green jumper, before going to check. 'Where's my best boy, then? Oh!'

Surprised to find the kitchen empty, I made my way back through the apartment, glancing into the living room, before skipping back upstairs to Billy's bedroom.

'Come out, come out, wherever you are!' I sang, as it occurred to me that Daniel was probably playing games with him, having fun on his impromptu day off. The thought made me smile, and I chuckled, peeping into every corner and cupboard.

'OK, I give in!' I yelled at last. 'Daniel? Dan, are you there?'

After jogging downstairs, I checked the kitchen again, then the living room for a second time, before bursting into Daniel's study, guessing he might have taken Billy there to play while he made work calls. The room was empty.

'For God's sake. You could have said goodbye before you left,' I muttered, realising Daniel must have taken Billy to school already. Hunting around for my phone to call him and double-check, I was frustrated that I couldn't find my mobile anywhere.

Come to think of it, I hadn't seen it since yesterday morning; I'd had to leave my messages for the school, Jules and Nish from the landline, after my mad dash home with Billy.

'Ah, that must be it.' I'd probably dropped my phone somewhere between the school gates and our apartment building. 'Oh, well. Might as well go look for it.' It would kill a bit of time while I waited for Daniel to return from dropping Billy at school, and I needed to do something to keep my nerves in check ahead of our *walk and talk*.

Sauntering to the front door, at the last moment I doubled back to Daniel's study, deciding to call him before I set out – maybe even arrange to meet him halfway, so we could head straight off to Kew Gardens. 'Stay calm. No lectures,' I lectured *myself*. I was already anxious about the conversation I needed to have with Daniel; I didn't want to antagonise him with a telling-off about letting me know before he took Billy out of the apartment.

'Come on, come on, pick up.' I wandered through to the kitchen with the handset clutched to my ear, as Daniel's phone went to voicemail for the third time. About to leave a message, I groaned as I spotted Billy's school cap and book bag on the kitchen table.

'Darn it, Daniel.' I disconnected the call, reaching for the blue-and-green hat. 'I should have taken him to school in the first place.' Daniel might be super-efficient at work, but he was infuriatingly scatty on the domestic front.

Glancing at the clock on the range cooker, I was relieved to see it was just before eight. If I jogged to the school, I might catch them before the morning register. Quickly returning the phone handset to Daniel's study, no sooner had I set it back in its cradle than it rang.

'Daniel?' I said automatically, picking it up again.

'Mrs Cartwright? I'm sorry to call you so early. This is Billy's form teacher. How is he this morning? We all missed him yesterday. I got your message. Such a shame to be poorly on his first day. I hope he's feeling better?'

'Yes, much.' I grimaced. I'd hated lying yesterday morning; the staff at the small prep school were all lovely, his form teacher especially. 'It was, uh, probably just something he'd eaten.' Wandering back into the hall, I grabbed my grey jacket off the stand.

'Oh dear. Well, I'm glad he's a bit better. Will he be joining us today?'

'Actually, his dad . . .' It was on the tip of my tongue to say that Daniel was dropping him off and would be there any minute, when I noticed Billy's blazer on the hook beneath where I'd just retrieved my jacket. Glancing down, I spotted his new black school shoes, too. 'Er, do you mind if I call you back?'

'Of course, Mrs Cartwright. And if I *don't* see Billy today, I hope he gets well soon. I know what you said about him having eaten something, but there are some nasty bugs going around. At least it's Saturday tomorrow. He probably needs the weekend to rest, and—'

'Yes. Thank you. You're very kind,' I said absently, abruptly ending the call.

For a moment, I couldn't move, frozen in shock and confusion as I stood staring at the blazer on the coat stand: royal blue with emerald-green piping, it was unmissable. But even if it hadn't been so brightly coloured, there was no way Billy could go to school without his shoes. It was one thing for Daniel to have forgotten Billy's blazer, hat and bag, but his *shoes*?

'What the hell's going on, Daniel?' About to try his number

again, I jumped when the phone vibrated in my hand, its shrill tone jarring my already stretched nerves.

'Ruth? I missed your calls,' Daniel panted. 'Sorry, I was running. Didn't hear the phone. Everything OK?'

'Shit, Daniel. You could have left a note.' Anger surged, even as relief bled through me. 'I thought Billy was *gone*.' I drew in a deep breath. 'I'm surprised you persuaded him to come out for a run with you at all. He hasn't even had breakfast yet. Usually, he won't—'

'Woah, woah. What are you talking about? Billy isn't with me. I went to get him up for school, but he was fast asleep. I didn't want to wake him. Thought I'd squeeze in a quick run first. Are you saying he's not in his bed? Have you looked—'

'I've looked *everywhere*!'

'Fuck. I'm calling the police.'

'Which is exactly what we should have done last night!' I screamed down the phone line, as a dizzying cocktail of adrenaline, panic and terror fizzed through me.

'I know, I know. Calm down, Ruth. Please. Let me think.'

'Calm down? She's taken our *son*, Daniel!' Instantly, I pictured Eve's face, her gaunt features rigid with disdain as she threw down her threat. I had no idea how she'd managed to carry it out, but right now all I could think about was getting Billy back. 'I have to *find* him!'

'Yes. Shit. Look, wait there. I think I know where to look.'

'What? *Where?*'

'Sorry, can't waste time talking. Stay put, Ruth. I'll call you as soon as I've got him. I promise.'

Chapter 13

The lift seemed to take for ever as I stood pressed into a corner, willing the digital numbers indicating the floor levels to go faster. As they counted upwards, the penny dropped: *the lift went direct to our penthouse.* No one else had access to it – which meant that whoever had taken Billy either knew the lift code, or they had broken in to the service staircase.

Even that wouldn't have mattered so much if the front door had been locked, but as I'd left the apartment, I'd discovered that it wasn't. Whoever had managed to gain access to our private penthouse landing would have been able to walk straight into our home.

Bea had been to our apartment dozens of times: she was familiar with the layout of the building; she knew all the codes. Eve didn't, but she was angry and desperate – I'd understood that much last night. Both women had reasons for wanting to get their hands on Billy . . .

'I'll kill her,' I wailed, not entirely sure who I was talking about – which woman I feared more. Eve was wild and deluded, but Bea

71

was clever and manipulative. 'If she's taken my boy, I'll *kill* her.'

In the next second, panic surged again as it occurred to me that I might be jumping to the wrong assumption: maybe *neither* woman had anything to do with Billy's disappearance. A random stranger could have taken him, perhaps someone who had legitimate access to the building – a plumber or electrician – or maybe another resident, or one of their friends over for a visit. News stories about child trafficking flashed horrifically across my mind.

'Oh, Billy. I've told you a million times not to answer the door!'

As soon as I'd had the thought, guilt roiled through me. This wasn't Billy's fault – none of it was. He was a kind, sweet boy, always trying to do helpful, grown-up things. I thought I'd heard the door bang when I was drying my hair. *I should have gone to investigate immediately.*

Daniel had told me to stay home and wait, but there was no way I could do that. I had to get out there and look myself. I'd searched everywhere I could think of: the bench where Billy and I liked to sit each morning and watch the river; the reeds where a family of ducks had recently settled, Billy and I visiting them each afternoon.

I peered into the water, then scanned the decks of every houseboat along our stretch of the river, confident they were the most obvious places the police would want to search.

'Thank God Daniel's finally calling them. The police will find him, even if he doesn't,' I tried to reassure myself, feeling desolate and panicky that I hadn't spotted Billy anywhere.

I had no idea where Daniel was on his run, or where he'd gone to look for Billy. Perhaps the playground, or our favourite café. Or maybe, like me, he'd simply needed to do something while we waited for the police. 'We should have called them *before*!'

Staring up at the lift ceiling in despair, I became fixated on a green light winking in the corner. 'Of course! *CCTV cameras.* They're all over the building.' Renewed hope spurred me on as the doors slid open and I hurried back into our apartment.

It was frustrating that the building's caretaker, Arthur, was off sick – he might have seen something – but at least security footage would give the police a starting point. Even, perhaps, an image of the culprit. *The kidnapper*, I thought in alarm, pacing to the living room.

Immediately, I headed for the window, looking down to the river, hoping to see Daniel – praying Billy would be with him. There was no sign of either of them, and my frantic gaze was drawn to the traffic building up across Kew Bridge, eagerly searching for the flashing blue lights of a police car. Surely, the detectives would be here at any moment?

To keep myself occupied, I rifled through the living-room sideboard to look for a recent photo of Billy. There weren't many: most of my photos were on my phone. Cross that I still couldn't find it, I suddenly realised why I hadn't heard from Nish or Jules since I'd left messages for them yesterday morning, after running away from the school . . . *away from Bea.*

I didn't know for sure that Nish or Jules had passed on the news to her, but I assumed they would have. 'Just call her, Ruth. Talk to Bea. She might even know where Billy is. Maybe he went to her house to see Ophelia before school.'

Unlikely as it was, the possibility made me give up searching for photos and dash to the home phone. But after pressing the button to begin a call, I paused, realising that Bea usually called *me*. I could remember Jules's and Nish's numbers off by heart, but not hers. '*Damn.*'

With the handset still pressed to my ear as I trawled my memory, I recognised the repetitive *beep beep* of the dial tone: there was a new voicemail message. 'Please be Daniel,' I mumbled, tapping in the number to access the messaging service. It wasn't.

'*Ruth, it's me. Call me back as soon as you get this. We need to talk. I know what happened that night . . .*'

I listened to the message over and over, feeling increasingly terrified. Bea hadn't left her name; then again, she didn't need to.

73

I would recognise her throaty voice anywhere, just as I recognised the threat laced through her message. *I know what happened that night.*

Replaying the message one last time, I pressed 'return call', waiting breathlessly to hear Bea's voice, bracing myself for a tirade of fury while also hoping that – somehow, and for whatever reason – she *did* have Billy with her and that we could sort out this whole sorry mess. She hadn't mentioned him, but perhaps she was waiting to speak to me in person.

Frustratingly, voicemail clicked in, which only intensified my anxiety – and paranoid conviction that I was too late: that Bea, always impatient, forever dramatic, had opted to take action rather than waste time on more words.

'Oh, don't be ridiculous. You're letting fear get the better of you. Bea isn't a psycho. She wouldn't break into our apartment. She wouldn't steal your son.' I wiped away tears. 'It's *me* she'll be mad at. She wouldn't take her anger out on a little boy!'

But even as I told myself that Bea wasn't capable of doing anything so rash, so spiteful, my mind filled with a dozen examples of exactly how scary and irrational her behaviour could be. One occasion in particular, when I'd been convinced not only that Bea was devious, but potentially dangerous, too.

Chapter 14

'Oh my God. Have you heard?'

Jason, the IT support manager at the advertising agency where Bea and I were now fully fledged account executives, had accosted me the moment I'd walked into the office kitchen at the end of a long, hard Friday. It was obvious he'd been loitering, waiting for someone to come along so that he could spread whatever news he was burning to share.

'I've been trapped in a focus group for hours,' I told him. 'I haven't heard anything but complaints since I set foot in the building.'

'Eh? I thought Beatrice was facilitating? I set her up with a whole bunch of IT gubbins.' Jason swiped his iPad, frantically checking emails to make sure he hadn't slipped up.

'Don't panic. She won't put you in the naughty corner. Not today, anyway.' I gave him a sympathetic look. 'She asked me to stand in for her.'

Jason pulled a face. 'Ah.'

'Precisely.' Rolling my eyes, I hurried to the coffee machine, in need of caffeine.

'No, I mean, *ah*, as in you really haven't heard, then. About Tanya.'

'Well, whatever it is, it won't be my problem as of three months tomorrow.' I tapped at my phone, not to confirm my leaving date but to triple-check that I'd set a reminder for my next hospital appointment. I was anxious about forgetting.

As if I could. The quest to have a child had come to dominate my life by then; it was the principal reason I'd handed in my resignation. I was convinced my fertility problems were due to stress, and, to be honest, much as I liked Tanya, she caused most of that.

For Bea, too. Only the week before, she'd joked in the pub after work that she wished someone would push Tanya over the edge of the roof terrace café and 'put us all out of our misery'. I'd laughed, saying it was the wine talking, but Bea had insisted she wasn't joking. Our 'cougar boss' was driving her insane, she said, constantly flirting with Finley, inventing after-hour meetings and taking him along to pitches that weren't even for his own campaigns.

'Oh, yeah. You're leaving, aren't you? Lucky you.' Jason gave a dramatic sigh. 'I wish I had a rich husband. Things are only going to get worse around here, after what's happened.'

'Well, I'm going freelance, not becoming a lady of leisure. But anyway. Tell me, please. *What's* happened?' I abandoned my coffee and put away my phone, reassured that I'd set multiple reminders for my hospital appointment.

'There's been an accident,' Jason said in a hushed voice. 'At Tanya's apartment block.'

The look on his face made the back of my neck prickle. 'What kind of accident?'

'You don't have to whisper. It's not a secret.' Bea strolled into the kitchen and opened the glass-fronted refrigerator, taking out a bottle of sparkling water.

'It's pretty tragic. I was just trying to be discreet,' Jason defended himself.

76

'Discreet?' Bea's eyebrows arched. 'That would be a first.'

'Look, can someone *please* tell me what's happened?' I looked anxiously between them, starting to imagine the worst. 'You said something tragic has happened. Oh my God. Tanya's not—'

'Dead. No, more's the pity.' Bea uncapped the bottle, tutting when the water fizzed over her fingers. 'Only kidding, guys.' She gave a throaty chuckle.

Jason looked at me, his eyes widening. He would never dare pass any comment. Bea was senior to him, and more than one IT support person had lost their job after a run-in with her. But I could read his shock.

It mirrored mine, especially as I recalled my conversation with Bea in the pub only the week before. I hadn't taken her seriously then; now I felt a niggle of worry that I should have done. 'I think you'd better tell me the full story, Jason.'

'Tanya fell head first down the stairs last night,' Bea explained before he had a chance to speak. 'There's no great mystery. That concrete staircase in her block is bloody lethal. The building is listed. Loads of character. Horrendous safety record.'

'I didn't realise you'd been to Tanya's apartment?' I queried, frowning.

Bea waved a dismissive hand. 'Senior management thing last year.'

'Really?' It seemed odd that I hadn't known about it. 'How come I wasn't—'

'Anyway, she survived. End of story.' Bea tossed her bottle into the recycling bin, where it landed with a violent crack, the green glass splintering loudly.

Jason winced. 'Well, not for Tanya. Her spine was fractured. She's paralysed. It's so *shocking*. I think the police are—'

'Only paralysed from the waist down,' Bea corrected him. 'I bet you my measly end-of-year bonus she'll be back bossing us about before you can say *personal injury insurance*.'

'What were you going to say about the police?' I asked Jason, trying to process the shock of the news, concern for Tanya and sinking horror at Bea's glib reaction all at once.

'Tanya reckons she was pushed,' he explained, lowering his voice again. 'The trouble is, she didn't actually see anyone. The police have dismissed the case out of hand.'

'CCTV?' I asked hopefully.

Jason shook his head. 'Nope.'

'See, old building.' Bea shrugged. 'Tanya thinks she's posh because she lives in a grand old mansion flat. But you can't fall down a lift, can you? Unless you slip down the shaft, I guess,' she mused, her eyes glinting.

'Well, let's hope it *was* an accident,' I said. 'And not deliberate. That would be—'

'Attempted murder.' Jason folded his arms. 'That's what Tanya's alleging.'

'Really? Oh my God. Who on earth would want to hurt Tanya? I mean, *seriously* hurt her.' I couldn't help flashing a glance at Bea.

'I could give you a list,' she said smartly. 'But in any case, the police think her memory is compromised. She took a blow to the head when she fell. So I heard,' she added lightly. 'Probably slipped in those ridiculous heels. Honestly, the woman dresses like she's still—'

'It must have been *terrifying*,' I cut in, glaring at Bea, thinking that she could at least pretend to feel normal human sympathy.

Her mouth twisted. 'I'm sure a big fat insurance payment will compensate. Money has this funny way of making everything better.'

'Beatrice . . .' I shook my head in despair.

'Oh, come on, guys.' She held up her hands. 'I'm just trying not to be hypocritical. I don't like the woman, so sue me. But you're right, I'm a bad person. Tanya deserves all our sympathy, and I'll send her some flowers, all right? Jeez.'

'We should start a collection,' Jason suggested eagerly.

'Good idea,' I agreed. 'Not because Tanya needs the money, but because she needs to know we *care*,' I told Bea when she raised her eyebrows. 'Will she really never walk again?'

It was hard to imagine the office without our overactive boss striding around it, cracking the whip. Tanya was tough, and I knew she'd adapt to whatever changes the accident wrought; she'd proved her resilience time and again. But if her injury *wasn't* an accident, the mental scars would be as hard to overcome as any physical disability.

'Permanent disability.' Jason mimed horror. 'That's what I heard on the news.'

'It's on the *news*? Wow. I've been trapped in that meeting room all day.' I threw Bea a pointed look, still irritated that she'd ducked out of the tedious session.

'All over the lunchtime bulletins,' she said blithely. 'Finley said there were reporters and TV cameras outside the building within minutes.'

'Are they still here?' I crossed the kitchen to look outside, scanning the crowds thronging Covent Garden for anyone who looked like a journalist or reporter.

'Not here. At *Tanya's* building,' Bea explained, coming to stand next to me at the window. 'Finley had to take some papers over last night for her to sign. Again.' She tutted. 'He said the media vultures were already gathering. Oh, there's Daniel.' Suddenly, Bea straightened up and ran her hands through her hair. 'Um, I just need a word with him.'

'Daniel? What's he doing here?' I felt a flash of panic that I'd forgotten an arrangement. I'd been so preoccupied with doctors' appointments, I tended to forget others. 'Oh, right. It's Friday. His day for squash with Finley.' I watched Daniel pace up and down the pavement, looking repeatedly at his watch. He looked as smart and handsome as ever in his charcoal grey work suit; he wasn't carrying a racquet.

Bea paused in the kitchen doorway. 'OK, I was trying to be discreet, but it can't be helped. *Somebody* has a birthday coming up, don't they? Subterfuge may be required.'

'Ah. Sorry.' I forced a smile, telling myself I was stupid for being suspicious about Bea secretly meeting Daniel, whatever the reason. 'Give Dan my love, then,' I said deliberately.

'Oh, don't you worry,' Bea called over her shoulder, hurrying off. 'I will.'

*

I hadn't thought of that day since, but as I paced the apartment, waiting for Daniel to return from his run – with or without Billy – I was caught in agonising indecision about whether it was Eve or Bea that I feared most.

Eve had been aggressively vocal in her threat, but Bea's sly digs yesterday, and her cryptically intimidating phone message, were equally unnerving. Her callousness towards Tanya had shocked me, and I'd never forgotten it. I realised how easily I could imagine Bea exacting painful revenge on someone – if she believed they had slighted her.

We're all adults. We have to take responsibility for our mistakes. That was what she'd thrown at me yesterday morning, along with snide hints about me having a *guilty secret*.

If Bea was looking for a way to get back at me, she knew my Achilles heel better than anyone. For all her heartlessness, there had once been a time when she'd listened to my woes, month after month, comforting me with wine and platitudes as I sobbed my heart out after repeated failures to get pregnant. She knew that nothing meant more to me than Billy.

Along with mounting fear for his safety, I was conscious of a growing conviction that if Bea *had* found out about me and Finley, she was more than ruthless enough to punish me. *Make the punishment fit the crime*, Jules said yesterday, and Bea had agreed.

What better way to get back at me than by taking my son, the precious, perfect symbol of my betrayal?

Chapter 15

I was so deeply immersed in thoughts of Bea, the sound of the door buzzer made me jump.

'Daniel!'

Racing through the apartment, I prayed with all my might that it *was* Daniel, and that Billy was with him – that he'd wandered off to play by himself somewhere, and, as Daniel had suggested, he'd made a lucky guess where to find him and was bringing him home. I prayed, too, that all my paranoia about Bea was exactly that: irrational suspicion. I prayed that Eve, as Daniel had repeatedly insisted, was merely a harmless, deluded woman making idle threats . . .

Lifting the receiver of the security intercom, I felt breathless and almost dizzy with anxiety as I also activated the video screen. It took me a moment to recognise the face grinning back at me from the grainy image, and when I did, my heart plummeted.

'Hi, babe. Can I come up?' Even through the receiver, the familiar, gravelly voice made the back of my neck prickle. '*Someone* wants to give you an almighty hug.'

81

'What the . . .? Oh. Sure. Hang on, I'll just . . .' Cursing under my breath, I hit the button to open the lift at ground-floor level, wondering again who had either managed to hack or force their way into our private elevator – or trick Billy into pressing the release button.

'Shit,' I cursed again, my boots scuffing the walnut hall floor as I paced in circles, waiting for the *ping* in the corridor outside that would indicate Finley's arrival. Frantically, I rehearsed what to say to him, but every sentence was crowded out by worry about Billy.

'Oh, come on, Ruth. You can handle Finley McDermott,' I counselled myself. Bea had been right about one thing yesterday: *we are all adults*. We also used to be best friends.

Out of fear for Billy, and guilt about the past, I had demonised both Bea and Finley, I realised. Bea's voicemail had terrified me, but in fairness, if she *did* know what had happened that night in the hotel, as she'd claimed in her message, she had a right to talk about it.

I had to calm down. I had to believe that Bea would never physically hurt me, or Billy – and Finley wouldn't hate me, or punish me for keeping quiet about the possibility that Billy might be his son. After all, he had to share at least half the blame for that night . . .

I hadn't deliberately kept the consequences from him. The last twenty-four hours had been as big a shock to *me*. Over the last four years, I'd blotted out that night so completely, it had taken the shock of Eve's ludicrous accusation to trigger memories of it. The possibility that Billy might be Finley's son was something I was still grappling with myself.

Round and round my thoughts went, along with my footsteps, and by the time I heard Finley's jaunty rap on the front door, I had *almost* convinced myself everything would be fine. I felt even more reassured as he strolled into the apartment, dressed in his old favourite outfit of chinos and black sweater, as casually as though he was popping over for coffee: exactly as he'd done several times a week back when we all still lived in Greenwich.

That felt like a different lifetime, yet even though the friendship between us was gone, a strangely poignant familiarity remained. Disappointed as I was that my husband and son hadn't been at the door, at least I had a chance to talk to Finley alone – to make it clear that even if a DNA test proved he was Billy's biological father, Daniel would always be his dad.

'So, about that hug.' Finley came towards me, a broad smile on his face.

'What?' I stepped back, in no mood for teasing flirtation.

'Don't panic. I'm not coming on to you. Water under the bridge, and all that.' He waggled his eyebrows, brown eyes glinting.

'Finley . . .' The blush burning my cheeks was from anger, not embarrassment.

I turned away, wondering if I'd made a mistake letting him in, after all – debating whether it would inflame things disastrously if I simply asked him to leave.

'Sorry. Couldn't resist. You don't have to hug me. But there *is* someone who—'

'*Mummy!*'

I dropped to my knees in shock. 'Oh my God. *Billy.*' Pulling him into my arms, I hugged and squeezed him against me until he squealed, pushing me away.

'I can't breathe!'

'Oh, darling. I'm sorry.' My eyes blurred as tears streamed down my face. I felt sick with relief as I swept back Billy's curls, scanning his face to make sure he was all right, before pulling him hard against me again. 'I thought I'd lost you,' I whispered against his soft cheek.

'Silly Mummy.' He giggled, obviously having no idea why I was so upset. 'I lost my teddy. You can't lose a *boy*.' He rolled his eyes, for a moment looking exactly like Daniel.

'You're right.' Not wanting to scare him, I forced myself to let go of his shoulders, but my legs were trembling as I straightened up.

I clenched my hands together to stop them shaking, too. 'I could never lose you. That would be like losing *myself*,' I joked weakly.

Only, even as I said the words, I realised how true they were: without Billy, I couldn't exist – nor did I want to. But seeing his dark eyes staring solemnly up at me, his soft eyebrows puckering, as they always did when he was trying to work something out, I tried my hardest to smile reassuringly through my tears.

'I guess I just mislaid you for a while,' I said huskily. 'Where did you *go*?'

'To the toy shop.' Billy's eyes lit up now. 'We bought a new train, Mummy!'

'To the . . .' I glanced at Finley, for the first time noticing that he was holding a bag from the twenty-four-hour convenience store next to the apartment complex. Billy loved it because it stocked gifts as well as groceries, and I watched in shock as Finley reached into the brown paper carrier and pulled out a shiny green toy engine, grinning at Billy the whole time. 'You went with . . . Finley took you to . . .'

'He told me to pick anything in the whole shop,' Billy reported happily. 'It's a surprise for Daddy. But I can play with it, too. Look!' He grabbed the chunky toy from Finley's hands. 'It has a little man inside. He drives the train. He looks like Daddy!'

'So he does. Wow. What an amazing train. But huge.' I gave Billy a watery smile. 'Will it even fit on your train track, I wonder?' I added, knowing he would immediately run upstairs to his bedroom to find out, giving me a chance to speak to Finley alone.

'Oh!' Billy's brows puckered again, and without saying another word, he bowled past me towards the stairs, only pausing when he was halfway up. 'Thanks, Uncle Finley!' he called out, before scampering around the corner towards his bedroom.

The second he was out of earshot, I turned to glare at Finley, hissing at him: 'Did you trick Billy into going with you?' I stared up at his handsome face and cheeky grin, feeling acid bile burn my throat, as sickening anger churned in my stomach.

'Trick him? Don't be daft. I'm an old friend of the family, aren't I? I was at a loose end and passing by your place. I figured I'd treat your little boy to a new toy.'

'Billy has enough toys.'

'Sure. OK, so maybe I wanted to hang out with him for a bit. Get to know him.'

'You . . . what? *Why?*' I asked breathlessly, already suspecting the answer.

Finley frowned. 'You're angry with me. Sorry, babe. My bad. But, you know, I did tell Billy to let you know we were going out.'

'He's four years old! You should have told me *yourself*, not sneak him out, and—'

'Woah, I didn't sneak him anywhere. This is *me* you're talking to, Ruth. Hey, come on now. I know it's been a while, but we're still good, aren't we? Ophelia and Billy hang out all the time. Playdates and whatever. I thought it was time I got to know my daughter's pals, that's all.' Finley stepped towards me, eyes and arms both wide in appeal.

I backed away. 'You had no right to take my son.'

'*Your son.*'

With those two words, I could sense the atmosphere in the hall change, as starkly as if someone had switched off the heating. For a moment, Finley's boyish, innocent smile held, then his mouth twisted, one dark eyebrow quirking, reminding me uncomfortably how, throughout our friendship, I had never quite felt certain whether he was teasing or serious.

'Yes. My son.' I folded my arms across my chest, refusing to be intimidated. We were no longer twenty-somethings hanging out in bars after work. I was a wife. A *mother*.

'Sure,' Finley said casually. 'Billy's your boy. But let's be honest, we both know there's a chance he might also be mine.'

Chapter 16

'Daniel's out for his run, then. Still kidding himself he's the fittest and fastest, hey?' Finley winked as I returned to the living room, after dutifully admiring Billy's new train and then settling him for a nap.

There was no way I was taking him to school now, and thankfully his teacher had already sanctioned his absence. Thankfully, too, Billy was still unaware that anything was wrong, but he was clearly exhausted after his early start, not to mention the fun of going toy shopping in his pyjamas, dressing gown and slippers. Barely protesting as I tucked him into bed, he was asleep before I gave him one last, lingering cuddle, burying my face in his curls so that he wouldn't see me having a little cry.

'What's it to you?' I snapped, disliking how Finley had made himself at home. Weak with relief as I was to have Billy back, I was still livid with Finley for taking him. I wanted to know *exactly* how it had happened, and why. If he'd come for a showdown about Billy's paternity, he could have it – and then leave, get the hell out of my life and stay out. 'But, yes. Daniel's out for a run.

86

He's also looking for Billy,' I said pointedly. 'I need to call him.'

'Oh, don't worry about Dan.' Finley crossed his legs, stretching one arm along the back of the black leather sofa. 'I messaged him just now. Like you say, he was running. Didn't pick up my call. Anyway, I texted that I'd found Billy playing outside and brought him home.'

I shook my head. 'Billy never goes out alone. Daniel won't buy that.'

'Au contraire. He was extremely grateful. He texted back effusive thanks.'

'Seriously?' I was certain Finley was lying about Daniel's response, and equally sure Daniel would have picked up that Finley was lying about Billy. He hadn't wandered outside to play; Finley had tricked him into leaving the apartment, no doubt to punish me – and possibly Daniel, too – for having kept Billy from him.

I was only surprised he hadn't shown up before, and I struggled to imagine what could have happened to make Finley suddenly wonder if Billy was his son. Surely, if he'd always suspected so, it wouldn't have taken him four years to decide to 'get to know him'?

'We haven't seen you for years,' I pointed out. 'You're never around whenever I've been to your house to see Bea. With *Billy*, I might add. There's been no contact whatsoever. Then, what, you expect me to believe you happened to be passing by our apartment building?'

'OK, fine. You got me.' Finley held up his hands. 'I wasn't just passing by. I was on my way to see Daniel. I didn't like to say, because . . . well, we had private stuff to discuss.'

'Private . . . uh, what?' *That night. What happened between us. Billy possibly being Finley's son.* I guessed exactly what was on Finley's agenda now, but I refused to acknowledge it until he did. I hated playing games, but Billy's happiness was at stake.

'Unfinished business,' Finley said cagily. 'We were actually supposed to meet at his office. Then I got a call from his assistant,

87

cancelling. I was worried about Dan. Thought I should stop by and check on him. Which is precisely what I texted him an hour ago.'

'And he swallowed that?' I stared sceptically at Finley, still furious with him but also conscious of a tiny bud of relief unfurling inside me: he didn't actually manage to see Daniel, so perhaps he hadn't yet told him about Billy – or indeed that night at the hotel.

I fervently wished I'd made my confession already; Daniel deserved to hear it from me, before either of our former best friends got in there first. At least that was now possible – *I hoped*. Until I got to speak to Bea in person, too, I couldn't be entirely sure.

'Of course he believed me! It's the truth. Apart from the bit about finding Billy wandering around outside.' Finley winked again. 'Admittedly, I made that bit up.'

'No kidding,' I scoffed. 'So how *did* you trick my son into going with you?' I perched on the arm of the sofa, deliberately signalling that I wasn't about to settle into a cosy chat. 'And why the hell would you do something so cruel? I've been out of my mind worrying about him.'

'Point one, like I said, your son, but perhaps also mine.' Finley paused, as though waiting for me to acknowledge that fact. 'Which gives me the right to hang out with him, no?'

My face burned, and I could feel my palms start to sweat. 'Daniel is Billy's dad.'

'Point two, I fully intended to ask your permission,' Finley continued blithely. 'But Billy answered the intercom. I told him I was an old friend of his mummy and daddy. Nothing more, nothing less,' he added with a knowing look. 'Don't worry, I didn't drop any *long-lost daddy* hints. Admittedly, it's been preying on my mind, lately. But my meeting with Dan had nothing to do with Billy.'

I chewed my lip, trying to decide if he was telling the truth. 'You'd swear to that?'

'Absolutely. As if I'd rock up and drop a bomb like that! I *love* you guys. I've *missed* you. Sure, there have been times these last four years when I've wondered about Billy. But you and Dan are solid. I never wanted to come between you. Oh, I can't deny it hasn't been tough sometimes.' Finley let out a long, plaintive sigh. 'Keeping your secret.'

'*Our* secret,' I corrected indignantly, immediately regretting it as Finley smirked.

'Our secret,' he agreed softly. 'But whatever happened between *us*' – he shuffled along the sofa, reaching out to squeeze my knee – 'has stayed between us. I promise. I didn't want to upset Bea, either. I still don't. Which is why I've never told her. She has enough on her plate.'

'Really.' I brushed his hand away, thinking of Bea's voicemail, wondering if it was possible she'd found out what happened that night from someone other than Finley – and hadn't yet confronted him about it. 'She's changed towards me, Finley. She's been so sarcastic. *Frosty*. Are you seriously telling me there's no good reason for that?'

'Oh, there's a reason.' He frowned, then stood up and began pacing the living room, coming to stand in front of the Klimt painting on the far wall. 'I remember her buying that.'

'For Daniel's and my wedding anniversary, yes.' I sighed. 'It's still the most amazing present I've ever been given,' I admitted. 'That she knew exactly what I loved.'

'Huh. Of *course* she knew. Bea made it her business to know every detail about you.'

'I guess. She did have this funny thing about us being sisters.' I winced, remembering. '*Good twin and evil twin*, she used to joke.'

'Yeah. It was more than that, though.' Finley turned to stare thoughtfully at me.

'Sorry?'

'Oh, Ruth, Ruth.' Drifting across the living room to sit on an armchair opposite me, Finley leaned forward, head bowed as though lost in thought. When he finally looked up, his eyes were unexpectedly full of tears. 'Look, you say Bea joked about you being like sisters. Only it wasn't a joke. I honestly thought you must have realised. I genuinely thought that was the reason we didn't hear from you guys again. After that weekend in the New Forest, I mean.'

I frowned, completely baffled now. I was concerned to see Finley's distress, but I couldn't shake my scepticism. 'OK, let's be real. There was one reason and one reason only our friendship drifted apart after that weekend.' I drew in a deep breath, at the same time digging my nails into my palms. 'What happened between you and me.'

'Well, that certainly didn't help.'

'Exactly. And I . . . I guess I ran away. I wasn't sure if Bea knew. I didn't want to tell her. Or Daniel. Fine, I was a coward.' Burying my face in my hands, I let the pain of my guilt rush through me. *I deserved it.* I deserved the mess I was in now, I thought in anguish.

'Don't be too hard on yourself,' Finley consoled. 'It takes two, hey?' He winked.

His flippancy rankled, but I tried not to let it distract me: this conversation had been a long time coming, and I needed to get to the point. 'I feel awful about Bea,' I confessed. 'I know I kept putting off seeing her. Then, uh, I had Billy. Life with kids is so busy, isn't it?'

'Sure is,' Finley agreed affably.

'I did try to get back in touch with her a few times. She never responded. Then Daniel and I moved away from Greenwich, and . . . well, here we are.'

'Yes, here we are. Exactly where I hoped we'd never be,' Finley said cryptically. 'You're right about never seeing me at the house, by the way. I moved out months ago. I couldn't take it anymore, you see? Bea's obsession.' He paused. 'With you.'

'*What?*'

'You've honestly never realised?' Finley sighed. 'Bea is properly fixated on you, Ruth. She has been since the day you met.'

'Fixated? What on earth are you talking about?'

'I know it's hard to get your head around. It took me all of yesterday evening to explain it to Daniel. It blew his mind, too.'

'Understand what? And what do you mean, *yesterday evening*? Dan had dinner with a client last night.' I thought back to his tense manner when he'd returned – when I was trying to explain about Eve . . . and Bea. *Was Finley telling the truth?* But if so, why had Daniel lied?

'Ah. Sorry, I made Daniel swear not to say anything to you. I needed to sound him out first, you know? Before I spoke to you. Like I said, *unfinished business*. We were supposed to talk some more this morning, but . . .' He shrugged. 'Then there was Billy.'

'Exactly. *Billy*. That's what you *really* wanted to tell Daniel about, isn't it?' I sounded braver than I felt; the thought of Daniel finding out about me and Finley petrified me. 'Admit it, that's why you're really here. To lay claim to my son. But, Finley, you can't have him. Even if he *is* yours. Which there is zero proof of, by the way.'

'Easily obtained,' Finley pointed out. 'But, honestly, that's not why I'm here.'

'It has to be! What you said about Bea having a fixation on me . . . that's rubbish!'

'You said yourself she's changed towards you. Why do you think that is?'

'Because of *Billy*, of course. That night,' I said huskily, wondering how many times I was going to be tormented about it – whether the guilt would ever end.

Finley shook his head. 'I told you. Bea has absolutely no idea about that.'

Hope flickered, until I recalled her ominous voicemail. 'But she said—'

'I don't want her *ever* to know,' Finley interrupted fiercely,

91

making me jump as he slammed one fist into the other. 'No, Bea's constant, erratic, increasingly unpredictable mood changes have nothing to do with Billy. Or me. Or anything other than *you*, Ruth.'

I shook my head. 'I don't understand. You're not making any sense.'

'Then let me put this as plainly as possible. The simple truth is . . . God, how do I put it?' He rubbed a hand over his face, groaning, then seemed to rally himself. 'OK, here's the deal. Bea has never just wanted to be your *friend*. Or your sister, or pretend twin, or whatever.'

'So, what *does* she want?' I said, more baffled than ever.

Finley leaned forward in his chair. 'Bea wants . . . has always wanted . . . to *be* you.'

Chapter 17

I counted to at least twenty in my head before I could reply. I was as shocked as if Finley had told me he was in love with Daniel. I'd thought we were skirting around the night we'd had accidental, drunken sex, not that my former best friend was some kind of Single White Female. 'You're kidding me,' I said at last.

'I wish I was.'

I stared at him in astonishment. 'Bea has everything she's ever wanted. She's rich, glamorous, confident. Successful. I'm not putting myself down. It's just, if anything, I've always thought of Bea as, well, *self*-obsessed. What makes you think she's so hung up on *me*?'

Finley sighed. 'First, she manipulates you into moving in with her.'

'No. Hang on. *I* was the one who suggested—'

'Really? She had the lease on that flat drawn up before you even knew it existed.'

'Oh. I didn't know that.' I frowned, wondering if it was really true.

93

'Well, she did. Your landlord told me. Anyway, that's nothing compared to what came next. You must remember how she started dressing like you. Borrowing clothes. Jewellery.'

'Only sometimes. And it was just a bit of fun,' I added uncertainly, as a memory of Bea's red dress at our flat-warming party flashed into my mind. She'd even worn a similar outfit as me for the christening, that ill-fated weekend in the New Forest, I recalled.

'Huh. And was it *fun* when she muscled in when you and I started getting friendly?'

'Friendly. Exactly. We were only ever *friends*, Finley.'

'But we could have been so much more, couldn't we?' He cocked his head, giving me a sad half-smile. 'Only we never had the chance to find out. Bea didn't let us.'

'You were the one who set me up with Daniel. Not that it's a problem. Daniel and I are extremely happy.' *Please don't do anything to spoil that.*

'Sure. But for the record, I didn't mean to. I just didn't want you to be left hanging around at the Tate Modern. Stood up by yours truly.' He pulled an apologetic grimace. 'I had every intention of meeting you. I had tickets booked and everything. Bea railroaded me.'

'Oh.' I frowned, recalling her texts at the time. 'I see.'

'Not that Daniel wasted the opportunity. In fact, he jumped at it.' One dark eyebrow quirked. 'It's not the first time he's tried to get one over on me. Dan's always been competitive with me, ever since uni. He could tell I was keen on you. He couldn't wait to steal you away. He didn't just take you to the café at the gallery, did he? Oh, no. He had to go one better.'

'We had lunch at The Ivy,' I said stiffly. 'And, yes, it was amazing. But, honestly, I wouldn't have cared if we'd eaten in a greasy old café.'

'Hmm, sure. Well, that was never going to happen,' Finley huffed ironically.

'Nothing wrong with working hard and liking nice things,

94

is there?' I glanced around the living room, the heart of our luxurious duplex penthouse. We lived a privileged life now, but it hadn't always been that way, for either of us. 'Anyway, what's this got to do with some fixation, or whatever, that you claim Bea has on me. Sure, she dressed like me sometimes, but—'

'And cut and dyed her hair blonde, exactly like yours. On her *wedding* day.'

'Yes, well.' I cast my mind back, remembering the lavish, glamorous occasion on board the *Cutty Sark* in Greenwich.

Admittedly, I'd been stunned when Bea had turned up with newly blonde hair tumbling in waves around her shoulders, but she'd always liked to make an entrance. I hadn't seen anything particularly odd at the time; if anything, I'd admired her bravery at experimenting with a whole new look, in a way I never felt comfortable doing.

Daniel's and my wedding in the orangery of the Horniman Museum six months later had been a far smaller, more intimate affair, with Bea as my maid of honour, Finley as Daniel's best man, and no more than a dozen other guests. Neither Daniel nor I had any close relatives – our *friends* were our family.

It had broken my heart when that friendship ended; it bewildered me that Finley was now putting it all down to Bea's obsession with me. I was baffled and suspicious that he'd waited until now to tell me. *Something didn't add up.*

'Let's also not forget that Bea loathes art,' Finley said quietly, watching my face. 'You know that better than anyone.' He gave a wry smile, as though he too was remembering Bea's constant complaints about us chatting about our favourite artists, back when we were still a foursome. 'Opening an art gallery has always been *your* dream, Ruth. Not hers.'

'Yes, but hang on. Bea only set up her gallery *after* we stopped being friends. She didn't copy me. We hadn't seen each other for years, by then.'

'Exactly. She saw it as a means of getting close to you again.

She was planning it the whole time she was pregnant. Her idea was that you'd be so thrilled, you would join her. You'd be best friends again. Mums and business partners together.'

'Really? So why did she never *tell* me? I didn't hear from her once after that weekend at the hotel. She didn't even get in touch when I left messages saying I was pregnant. I sent her an invitation to Billy's christening. I heard nothing.'

'Hurt pride. That weekend in the New Forest . . . you and Daniel were so blissfully happy. Bea and I rowed the entire time.' Finley shook his head. 'We fought about *you*, Ruth. Bea's obsession with you. She denied it, of course. Looking back, I think that weekend was the beginning of the end of our marriage.'

'I'm so sorry,' I said, even though I'd had no idea that was how Bea felt. 'I guess that explains why you got so drunk that night. Whereas I . . .' I frowned, remembering how I'd been drowning my sorrows about not being able to get pregnant. *How cruelly ironic.*

'Yeah. I hated seeing Bea like that. It was eating her up. I was also worried about you and Daniel. Because, you know, Daniel was yours. And whatever you had, Bea wanted. She always did, and she still does.'

Chapter 18

'You thought Bea might try to seduce . . .' The idea of anything happening between her and Daniel was so painful, it brought home to me how devastated he would be when I finally had the chance to make my confession about what had happened between me and Finley.

At odd times over the years, I'd been irritated by Bea's flirtatiousness towards Daniel; occasionally, I'd wondered if he secretly enjoyed it. Now I asked myself if I'd been blind to something between them all along.

I had yearned so desperately for my perfect life with Daniel and Billy that I'd deliberately closed my mind to so many things. Ignorance might be bliss, but I was regretting my naïve, stubbornly blinkered contentment now.

'I wish you'd told me all this at the time,' I groaned. 'I could have *talked* to Bea. Helped her work through it all.'

'I'm sorry,' Finley said sheepishly. 'In fairness, it took me a while to realise what was going on. I guess I felt awkward about it, too. It hasn't been easy to come to terms with.'

'Sure. I can understand that,' I said, my anger softening to pity.

'I almost *did* tell you once. At the hotel. At breakfast, the morning after the christening. But I lost my nerve. I'm aware how odd this all sounds. I can hardly believe it myself. But it's true. I thought, if I gave Bea space to find herself again, stop her seeing you guys for a bit . . .'

'She might get over it. Forget all about me,' I finished for him.

'Precisely.'

'So *that's* why we didn't hear from you both after that weekend.'

All these years, I'd believed the four of us had simply drifted apart. Many times, I'd racked my brain to figure out why, forgetting about that night at the hotel. It was hard to take in that Bea's fixation on me was the reason for the rift.

'I'm sorry, Ruth.' Finley stood up from the armchair, crossing the living room to sit next to me again on the sofa. 'I walked away from my two best friends to save my marriage. It nearly broke me. But I did it for Bea.'

'I've always thought she was so confident. So *together*.'

Finley shook his head. 'Granted, she does a good job giving that impression. But I've seen Bea at her lowest.' His voice cracked, as though he was battling his emotions.

'I'm sorry,' I said again. 'I genuinely had no idea.' I felt like the worst friend in the world. For all the years I'd known Bea, I had never realised what was going on in her head. She'd always had an air of mystery, but this was the last thing I would ever have guessed.

'I think it goes back to her parents' car crash.' Finley let out a deep sigh. 'For what it's worth, my theory is that Bea tried too hard to act tough after they died. Hiding her grief. Putting on a front. She lost herself in the process.'

'She did often talk about feeling alone in the world.'

'I think she was. Utterly. Until she met you.'

'She once told me she was so happy we'd met, because I'd been through it, too.'

'Exactly!' Finley threw up his hands. 'Bea *knew* you'd lost your parents at a young age. In fact, I'd go so far as to say that's why she targeted you in the first place.'

'*Targeted* me. That's a bit strong. You make her sound like some kind of stalker.'

'*Isn't* she? Look, if it makes you feel any better, you're not the first person Bea's latched on to. There's a pattern. I've figured it out now. At first, it all seems very innocent. She knows how to be a good friend. She's fun. Lively.'

'I liked her immediately,' I agreed. 'As soon as we started as interns together.'

'Precisely. And Bea made a point of singling you out, didn't she?'

'Maybe.' I cast my mind back. 'No, actually, I spoke to her first. She was more confident than I was, back then. I asked her to show me the ropes. Introduce me to people.'

'Sure. But then what happened? She stole all your ideas, didn't she? Reinvented herself to be more like you. To sound like you. *Dress* like you. She did it with her landlady in Hampstead. Started borrowing her jewellery, acting like *she* was the wife. The poor husband got fed up. He put up with so much, then he gave Bea her marching orders.'

'Her *arsey landlord*,' I said, remembering Bea telling a very different story.

'Quite. Now she's latched on to Jules, and the whole sorry pattern is repeating itself.'

'Jules?' I thought for a moment, picturing Bea's strawberry-blonde hair, her sleek ponytail so similar to her new best friend's hairstyle. 'But don't we all morph into our friends a little? Especially if we're around each other a lot. As we used to be,' I said sadly.

'You're right. Only I'm afraid it goes much deeper with Bea. It's like there's this sort of vacuum where her own thoughts and emotions should be. Take the baby thing . . .'

'Sorry?' I sat back in shock. I'd become so engrossed in what Finley was saying about Bea, I had forgotten the real reason he was most likely here: *to challenge me about Billy being his son*. I bit my lip, feeling my heartbeat start to race.

'Bea never wanted children,' Finley continued. 'But *you* did, Ruth. Really, really badly. Then Bea started going on and on about wanting you to be "mirror mummies".'

'Seriously? Oh my God. That's actually a bit freaky.' I paused, thinking it all through. 'You know, if you're right, if everything you're saying is true, Bea needs help.'

'I know. I've tried my best, but I'm at my wits' end. That's why I'm telling you all this now. I can't keep pretending. Covering up for her. It's the reason I turned to Daniel. He always manages to sort things out. He dug me out of many a hole at uni. Then at Sandhurst.'

'Ah, yes. You were at the military academy together.'

'Yeah, until I got booted out. I always seem to mess up.' Finley's shoulders slumped.

'No. You are not to blame for this,' I told him firmly.

'Thanks, babe. I knew you'd understand.' He looked up with a forlorn smile. 'I wish I *had* been brave enough to talk to you before. I'm only glad I've had the chance to tell you now. Things have really hit a low point. I'm no shrink, but Bea's become almost . . . unbalanced.'

'Unbalanced? In what way?'

'Like, talking to herself all the time. She keeps mumbling about a stolen child.'

My heart leaped. 'A *what*?'

'I know. Crazy, hey?' Finley frowned. 'Although I think I know where it stems from.'

'You do?' My voice was a croak. Now we were getting to the nub of things. *Billy*.

Hard as it was to take in what Finley was saying about Bea having a fixation on me, I could appreciate where he was coming

100

from. But I was convinced he was wrong about Bea having no idea about that night – about the possibility that Billy might be her husband's son.

Her digs in the playground about actions and consequences came back to me, and it seemed impossible that they related to anything other than a friend's betrayal and her husband's infidelity. Bea had to know – *but what was she planning to do about it?*

'Yes. I do,' Finley confirmed. 'I found some letters, you see. That's what I was going to talk to Dan about this morning. Ask his opinion. Check he was OK with me telling you all this. To warn you about Bea's volatile state of mind, but also to ask for your help. You see, the letters were from Social Services. Adoption papers. God knows why she's never told me, but it seems Bea once gave up a baby.'

Chapter 19

Almost a minute passed before I could speak. I stared at Finley's handsome face, more shocked by this revelation than anything else he'd told me. 'When?' I asked quietly.

'The year after her parents died in that car crash. Bea was only fourteen.'

'Jesus. That's so shocking. *Poor Bea.* What did she have? I mean, boy or girl?' I wasn't sure why it mattered, but, somehow, I had a feeling it did.

'Boy.' Finley's mouth pursed. 'I reckon that's the real reason she's like she is. Don't you?'

'It probably explains a lot. Getting pregnant so young. She must have been terrified. Then giving up a child – presumably, being forced to. I imagine that left her with a deep emotional, psychological hole that she keeps trying to fill. But nothing ever does.' I thought of how she always needed to be the centre of attention. *Queen Bea*, Daniel used to call her.

'Exactly. Not me, not our little girl Ophelia.'

'Ophelia was the name I once told her I'd choose if I ever had a daughter.' I glanced towards the Klimt painting of the same name. 'It's why she bought me that.'

'See? That's what I mean. She's obsessed.' Finley huffed and shook his head. 'Anyway, if having a beautiful daughter can't make her feel complete, what chance do I have? I guess there's only one thing that will truly make things better.' He paused. 'Another son.'

'Yes. Of course.' I dry-swallowed, feeling an urge to go and check on Billy, reassure myself he was still safe in his bed. I half stood up.

'Shit, this is all my fault. I'm such an idiot. I should have put my foot down when she insisted we move to Richmond. To be closer to you.' Finley groaned. 'Bea will deny that, too, of course. Half the time I'm not sure she knows the difference between fact and fantasy.'

'She pretended not to recognise me to begin with,' I recalled, slowly sitting down again, thinking back to my first playdate at Bea's house with Jules and Nish, six months ago.

'I guess to make it look like coincidence that your paths *just happened* to cross again.'

'She's become so aloof, though. Maybe it's not actually me she's interested in now.' My heart started thumping as I recalled Finley saying: *whatever you have, she tries to take.* Maybe it wasn't just my son Bea coveted, but my husband, too. 'Uh, what did Daniel say last night?'

'Not a lot. He just called Bea a "screwball woman".'

Immediately, I thought of Daniel saying he wouldn't let Eve or 'any other screwball woman' come near me again. *He must have been talking about Bea.*

I understood now why he'd seemed in an odd mood last night: having spent all evening with Finley, and promising to keep quiet about it, he must have felt awkward. Or was there more to it than that? Once again, I recalled Bea knowing about our weekend plans before I did. Daniel had been derisive about Bea last night, but could that have simply been a smokescreen?

Are you sure you can trust your husband? Eve asked me. I wanted to trust Daniel, but I wished he'd hurry up and come home. I hated these secrets between us: his about last night; mine about that night five years ago. I was going out of my mind with worry and paranoia.

'Daniel will be back from his run soon. I guess I can ask him myself.' I stood up and crossed the living room to look out of the window. The riverside was quiet, the house boats looking shut up and sleepy. Only a plume of smoke twisted above the blue canal boat.

'Let's hope he hasn't gone to see Bea, hey?' Finley stood up from the sofa, too, joining me at the window. 'I'm kidding. But they've always had so much in common, don't you think? Both so driven. Ambitious. Me, I just want to be a family man.'

I looked dubiously at him. 'Really? I seem to recall you saying children ruin your life.'

'I've changed, Ruth. Finding out about Bea giving up a kid. It's made me realise how precious parenthood is. All these years, I've kept my counsel. Kept my *distance*. Not wanting to hurt you. Not wanting to upset *Bea*. But I don't think I can help her anymore. Huh, I don't think it's even me she wants. She's always had a thing about Daniel.'

'Bea's flirtatious, that's all,' I said, swallowing my own doubts.

'Sure. And Dan plays his cards close to his chest. But haven't you ever wondered?'

Hi, it's me, I remembered Daniel saying on the phone earlier, his tone strangely intimate. He'd always been so scathing about Bea; I had to admit this wasn't the first time I'd wondered if his scorn was a decoy for fonder feelings. 'Oh God.'

Finley rested a hand on my arm. 'Look, Dan's always been my best mate. But blood's thicker than water. I guess all this stuff with Bea has made me realise that. If she wants him, so be it. But if there's a chance, even a slim one, that Billy might be mine . . .'

'Please, Finley, you're racing ahead,' I cut in, frowning at him.

'We don't *know* there's anything going on between Bea and Daniel. There's also nothing beyond paranoid worry to suggest Billy isn't his son.' *And Eve's accusation*, I recalled, glancing once again out of the window, peering down towards the wharf, half expecting her to appear out of nowhere again.

Finley drew in a long breath. 'OK, it's cards-on-the-table time. Yes, I came here to see you and Daniel. To talk about Bea. To ask for help. If I'm honest, though, part of me also wanted to see Billy, too. Just to be around him.' His shoulders sagged. 'See if I can spot any signs of similarity between us, I guess.'

I'd been doing the same thing all day. 'Let's deal with one thing at a time, shall we?' I said, panicking. 'I need to talk to Daniel. He should have been back from his run ages ago.'

Finley frowned. 'He can't still be looking for Billy. I already texted him that he's OK.'

'You don't think . . . Dan told me he had an idea where Billy might have gone. You don't think he meant to see *Bea*, do you?' I'd considered that possibility myself when I thought Billy was missing, but only because Billy had been to Bea's house for lots of playdates. It hadn't occurred to me that he might have been there at other times . . . with Daniel.

Finley pulled a face. 'I've never seen him at the house. But, to be fair, it's been a while since I moved out. Shit. I was kidding when I said he might be there. Only . . . I'd best go home and check, yeah?'

'I'll come with you.'

'I'm not sure that's a good idea, Ruth. Like I said, Bea's become unstable. A fight might tip her over the edge. I'll phone you, though. I promise. As soon as I've seen her.'

'I'll call Daniel again.' I turned away, glancing towards the phone on the sideboard.

'Sure.' Finley squeezed my arm, pulling me closer against his side. 'But you know what? If Daniel *is* with her right now – if he's dumb enough to throw away his marriage for Bea – I'll always be here for you, Ruth.'

'Finley . . .' I tried to pull away, but he held me firmly against him.

'I won't let them take Billy and swan off into the sunset.'

'Take Billy?' Horrified, I jerked back, and this time Finley let me go.

'He's a good kid,' he said softly. 'He even looks a bit like me. Don't you think?'

*

As the front door closed behind Finley, I flew into Billy's bedroom, curling up next to him on his bed, pulling him close. The fear that I'd lost him this morning had torn me to pieces; the possibility Finley was suggesting – that Bea's flirtation with Daniel ran deeper than I knew, and that they might get together and try to take Billy from me – was beyond bearing.

It *couldn't* be true; I wouldn't believe it until Daniel said it to my face. Then again, my certainty about everything seemed to have evaporated. I was no longer sure what or who to trust; all I knew was that I would die before letting *anyone* take Billy from me.

'Mummy? I'm hungry!' he complained, waking up.

'I'm not surprised, darling. You haven't even had your breakfast yet.'

After helping him get dressed in jeans and a navy hoodie, I settled him in front of the TV with a bowl of his favourite cereal.

When Daniel still didn't answer his phone, I tried to settle myself next to Billy as I waited: for Daniel to return, for Finley to call with news of Bea . . . and for Bea's next move.

And while I waited, I mulled over everything Finley had told me, trying to figure out the truth, casting my mind back to the day Bea and I had crossed paths again, for the first time since that weekend in the New Forest – accidentally or deliberately, I was no longer sure.

Chapter 20

RICHMOND, SOUTH-WEST LONDON
Six months ago

Meeting Jules at the prep school's open day had, at first, seemed like a stroke of luck. I liked her, and I'd been thrilled when she invited me to join her and her best friends for their regular *coffee and play* get-together. Only excitement had turned to shock when it was Bea who opened the door of the red-brick, wisteria-laced Edwardian semi just off Richmond Green.

To begin with, I'd hardly recognised her. She'd dramatically changed her appearance once before, curling and dyeing her hair blonde for her wedding; now it was closer to Jules's Titian shade of red. But I'd never forget Bea's glittering eyes and haughty cheekbones.

It seemed she hadn't recognised *me*, though, as she ushered me along an exquisitely tiled, wood-panelled hallway to the vast kitchen-diner-conservatory at the back of her house.

'Lovely to meet you, Ruth,' she said coolly. 'Please, grab a seat. Make yourself at home. What can I get you? Skinny latte? Cappuccino?'

Taken aback, I automatically played along, but inside I was

confused about why she was pretending not to know me. Nish and Jules were busy setting out paints at the huge, industrial-chic dining table, and as I watched Billy get stuck in alongside their children, I babbled nervously about how much I was looking forward to getting to know them all.

When Bea put a mug of frothy, milky coffee in front of me – even though she knew full well that I liked it black – I met her dark eyes and we both smiled. Cool, careful, polite.

'Thanks . . . Bea.' I hesitated; it was the first time I hadn't called her Beatrice.

'No problem. *Ruth.*'

I looked quickly away, glancing curiously around her home, wondering when and why she'd moved there from Greenwich, where, apart from a year or so in Hampstead, she'd lived her entire life – feeling sad and guilty that we'd lost touch with each other. I remembered our previous friendship, feeling a spike of hurt that Bea either didn't, or was pretending not to.

There was no doubt that she had achieved the lifestyle she'd always dreamed of: her home was stylish and immaculate, filled with eclectic antiques, a glossy black piano in one corner. All the walls were white, broken up here and there by canvasses of modern art, plus a few framed photos, most of them baby shots or mother-and-child portraits.

One black-and-white photo in particular caught my eye. It was from Bea and Finley's wedding on board the *Cutty Sark*, and I remembered the exact moment it captured. Only the picture had been cleverly cropped into a smiling close-up of the happy couple with, tellingly, no sign of me – the bridesmaid – or Daniel, the best man.

I kept thinking about that photo as the morning passed in chat, more coffee and messy play, and I had goose bumps as I realised there was no longer the slightest hint of the closeness Bea and I had once shared. Nish and Jules were clearly none the wiser, and it would have been far too awkward to suddenly acknowledge our former friendship. But I wondered what was holding us back – why we were both acting.

'I can't wait to get to know you, too, Ruth,' Bea said brightly. 'And your husband. What did you say his name was?'

'Daniel,' I told her, even though I *hadn't* mentioned it. Then again, I didn't need to.

'And what does *Daniel* do?'

'He works in banking. How about yours?' I asked politely.

'Oh, he dabbles in this and that. Finley has a ridiculously short attention span. He adores . . . dabbling.' Bea's eyes met and held mine.

'Bea,' Nish chided. 'You're being way too modest. Your gorgeous hubby has taken the antiques world by storm.' She gestured to the array of pieces perched on every available side table. 'You must have seen him in the glossies, Ruth? He's a bit of heart-throb, is our Fin.'

'I'm just waiting for Bea to dump him,' Jules said. 'I've got first dibs on him to be my second husband.' She grinned at Bea, who raised her eyebrows but said nothing.

'He's very handsome,' I acknowledged, adding quickly: 'I mean, I can see that by his photo.' I glanced towards the gallery of portrait shots. 'I take it that *is*, um, your husband.'

'For now, at least.' Bea smiled at last, and we all laughed. 'But Jules and Nish are right. Fin usually makes quite an impression on people. If you'd ever met him, I'm sure you wouldn't have forgotten. Or perhaps it's just *me* that never forgets a face.'

My heart started racing as my mind grappled for a response, but before I could formulate one, Nish, oblivious of my escalating stress, jumped in with more good-natured chat.

'Have you got plans for more kids?' she asked me with a friendly smile. 'Yash and I are toying with the idea of another. Once my catering business takes off. Here, try one of these.' She pushed a dish of delicate Indian pastries towards me.

'Thanks. They look gorgeous. I bet they're delicious.' I smiled, even though I couldn't stomach the idea of eating anything; I was beginning to feel sick with tension.

'So, your husband's a banker, too?' Jules said. 'Same as Simon. My cheating ex,' she explained when I looked puzzled. She raised her mug. 'Welcome to the club, Ruth.'

'Oh!' The penny dropped. 'He's not called Simon Barker, by any chance?' Daniel had been moaning for weeks about his new boss, Simon, saying he lived far too close for comfort.

'He is. But how . . . Ah. *Dishy Daniel*.' Jules clicked her fingers, grinning as she, too, made the connection. 'Wow. Such a small world, isn't it?'

'Yes. It really is.' I smiled too, but beneath the table I dug my nails into my palms.

'Coincidence, karma . . . I'm a great believer in all that,' Bea said archly.

I tried to hold on to my smile, but inside my head I was cursing. If Jules's ex-husband was Daniel's new boss, it might make things awkward for him at work if I turned down any more coffee invitations from Jules. It wasn't that I didn't like her; she was lovely. But she was also *Bea's* new best friend, and Bea was clearly no longer mine.

I had no idea why she wasn't acknowledging our former connection, but as I looked around her stunning, monochrome, carefully staged house that felt more like a set for a magazine shoot than a home, the huge white walls suddenly felt like they were closing in on me. I wanted to leave – run away – and keep on running.

Bea mopped up an invisible coffee spill. 'Do *you* work, Ruth?'

'No. I . . . I used to do graphic design. For an advertising agency. Billy keeps me busy now, though. You know, being a mum. It's all I ever wanted, really.'

'So sweet.' Bea cocked her head to one side, giving me a fake smile.

'I, uh . . . I keep my hand in with sketching, a bit of painting,'

I babbled nervously. 'I also volunteer at an art therapy centre.' Encouraged by Nish and Jules's friendly smiles, I confessed: 'One day, I hope to open my own art gallery. It's kind of a pipe dream, but—'

'Oh my God.' Jules grabbed my hand. 'This is *too* weird. First our husbands work together. Now you say you want to run an art gallery!'

I frowned, perplexed as to why that was of any significance. 'Yes, well, that's what I've always dreamed of. But . . . weird? Why is that—'

'Because that's *exactly* what *Bea* does!' Jules declared, wide-eyed. 'Gosh. It's like, oh, I don't know . . . like the universe has brought us all together for a reason.'

'And you're doing your level best to drive Ruth away,' Nish interjected drily. 'Look at her face! You're freaking her out, Jules.'

I forced a smile, conscious that everyone was looking at me and knowing my face probably did reflect every ounce of my shock. I opened my mouth to say: *But Bea hates art.* Then I caught the look on her face, and there was no more doubt in my mind that she remembered me. And although I'd been allowed into her home and introduced to her new friends, it was clear to me that it was all strictly on her terms.

The gallery of photos on her vast kitchen wall was Bea's victory parade; she had deliberately whitewashed everything that didn't fit in with the myth she was creating of her life: art connoisseur, doting mum, latte-drinking middle-class wife.

That wasn't the Bea I knew. She'd had a tough start in life, brought up by her aunt after her parents died, dropping out of school before grafting hard to get to uni and build a career. But I'd found myself playing along, unsure why, only sensing that my clever former friend was up to something. I had no idea what, but I had a sick feeling I would soon find out.

Chapter 21

The view over the river was as grey as my thoughts, and I wished the gathering storm clouds would burst and wash away the entire day. Staring down at the wharf, I felt lonelier than I had since I lived in my bedsit over the pub in Greenwich, before meeting Daniel – before meeting Bea. *Were the two of them together right now?*

Finley had promised to call me, but almost as soon as he'd left, it had dawned on me that I still hadn't found my mobile, and I wasn't sure Finley had my landline number. I'd phoned Bea's house repeatedly on redial, trying to stop myself picturing her there with Daniel.

Pacing across the living room, I came to stand once again in front of the painting Bea had given me as an anniversary gift. At least, I'd always *felt* it was intended more for me – and Finley had agreed, even suggesting that it signified Bea's obsession with me . . . that the name of the painting, *Ophelia*, showed how deeply Bea wanted to connect with me, even calling her own little girl after it – the name she knew I'd always imagined for a daughter of my own.

Finley was beating himself up for missing the signals back then, for not realising that Bea was fixated on me. Only, perhaps we had *both* missed – or misread – the signs. Maybe it wasn't me Bea had been interested in at all: maybe it had *always* been Daniel.

Sinking down on the armchair nearest the painting, I stared up at it, letting my thoughts drift back over the years, to the evening Bea had first mentioned the special artwork she'd bought for us – when she and Finley gate-crashed my anniversary dinner with Daniel.

*

'Happy anniversary, sweetheart. Here's to us.' Daniel popped the Champagne cork and poured two glasses, expertly filling the delicate flutes to the brim without spilling a drop.

'For someone who doesn't drink, you're surprisingly good at that. But I shouldn't.'

'One glass won't hurt.'

I sighed. 'You mean it hardly makes any difference. It's not going to stop me getting pregnant, when there's little enough chance of that already.'

'That's not what I meant, but—'

'Sorry. *Sorry*. It's just, every time I see a bottle of Champagne, I can't help thinking of other news we're *not* celebrating.' I took a gulp of my wine, to prove I wasn't being a killjoy.

It was the first time Daniel and I had been out alone for weeks. Mostly, we felt too tired to make an effort; the repeated disappointment each month brought was really beginning to have an impact. I could tell both of us were giving up hope of ever having a child, and I was carrying around more sadness than I could hold without my face giving away the strain.

'It's fine. I understand,' Daniel reassured me. 'But maybe we need to give ourselves a night off from worrying about the future. Let's just enjoy the present, hey? We don't often get the chance to be alone. Just the two of us.'

'You're right. I guess neither of us realised that our wedding vows included *till our best friends leave us alone*.' I laughed. 'Love them as I do, I love having time with you more.'

'Ditto. And I fully intend to make the most of having you all to myself. It's time *we* had a bit of fun, don't you think?' Reaching for my hand, he wove his fingers through mine.

'Oh.' I put down my glass.

'Hey, I'm only teasing,' Daniel said quickly. 'We have *plenty* of fun. I only meant—'

'No, it's not that. It's . . . well, *look*.'

Daniel followed the direction of my gaze towards the door, where Finley was laughing and patting the head waiter's back, while Bea scanned the restaurant.

'Christ. What are *they* doing here?' Daniel withdrew his hand. 'I mean . . .'

'It's OK. I get it. Tonight was supposed to be for us. I don't think I mentioned us coming here. Did *you*?' I bit my lip, trying to remember if I'd let it slip to Bea.

She'd insisted on coming shopping with me at the weekend, to help me buy a new dress especially for my anniversary. I couldn't swear I hadn't told her Daniel was taking me to our favourite local Italian restaurant to celebrate.

'Of course not,' Daniel said quickly. 'But I guess this is their regular place, too. Just an unlucky coincidence.' He stowed the Champagne back in the ice bucket, looking thoughtful.

'Hey! Great minds think alike,' Finley called out, catching sight of us. 'Look who it is, babe,' he said, turning to Bea.

'Love the earrings, Ruth. And those shoes are to die for.' Bea's eyes were all over my outfit, after she and Finley made their way through the other diners to our table. 'I take full credit for the dress, of course,' she added, before bending to kiss Daniel on both cheeks. 'Gorgeous, isn't it? In fact, I loved it so much I bought one for myself.'

'Ha. Well, you picked a good one,' I told her. 'At least, my handsome husband seems suitably impressed.' I beamed at Daniel, but my smile dipped as I watched Bea pick up a white linen napkin and wipe her lipstick off his cheeks. 'Are you guys here to collect a takeaway, or—'

'Just waiting for Gino to find us a table,' Finley chipped in. 'Busy here tonight. Go ask him if he's found something yet, babe? Your charm's far more persuasive than mine.'

'You *used* to think so,' Bea threw at him over her shoulder as she headed to the bar.

Daniel's fingers squeezed the stem of his Champagne flute. 'We booked ahead.'

'Bea did, too,' Finley said, oblivious to the tension. 'I guess there's been a mix-up. Never mind. If they can't fit us in . . .' He leaned casually on the spare chair at our table.

'Please, join us,' Daniel invited politely, flicking an apologetic glance at me.

'Yes, do,' I added, mouthing *sorry* at Daniel. I was sure I must have let our plans slip to Bea. How else could she have found out where we would be? It seemed too much of a coincidence for her and Finley to turn up at the same restaurant, at almost the exact same time. I was frustrated, but it was fairly typical of Bea. She hated to miss out on a party.

'Nice suit, Mr C,' she complimented, returning to the table and seating herself next to Daniel. She leaned against him. 'Nice tie, too. Finley never wears one. He says it makes him feel like he's on a leash.'

Daniel quirked an eyebrow. 'Indeed. Well, one aims to please.'

'Oh, you are very . . . pleasing.' Bea winked at him, then knocked back the two vodka shots she'd bought at the bar.

'Hey, slow down.' Daniel rested a hand on her bare arm as she lifted it to summon the hovering waiter. 'For your own good,' he added, as Bea pouted at him.

'Who wants to be *good*?' She wound a silky, blonde curl around her fingers.

Daniel sighed. 'You don't always need alcohol to have fun.'

Bea poked her tongue out playfully. 'I think you've forgotten how to enjoy yourself, Mr Goody Two-Shoes.'

'On the contrary. Ruth and I were having a terrific evening.'

Bea looked hurt. 'Fine. Well, I know what will make it even better. You must come back to our place afterwards.' She grabbed his hand. 'I've got you the *best* anniversary gift. Gino's is all very well, but we need to celebrate *properly*.' Reaching for the ice bucket, she looked around for a spare glass, but there were only two Champagne flutes and both were taken.

'Hey, save some of that for Ruth,' Finley said, as Bea generously filled a water tumbler instead.

'Don't worry. My beautiful wife can have mine.' Daniel caught my eye and smiled as he slid his untouched glass across the table towards me. 'Like I said, I don't need alcohol to have fun.'

'Just unbridled sex, hey?' Bea teased, bumping shoulders with him.

'Party's over, Beatrice.' Finley stood up, shoving back his chair. 'But don't let that stop you guys. We'll head off. Leave you to it.' He grabbed Bea's arm, at the same time nodding at Daniel. 'See you at squash tomorrow, as per?'

'Sure. If you can make it,' Daniel said lightly.

Bea sighed. 'Well, like I said, you're welcome at our place for dessert and a celebratory nightcap.'

'Actually, I've made my own tiramisu,' I told her, waiting for her to roll her eyes. Bea always used caterers for dinner parties.

Instead, she clapped her hands. 'Fabulous! I've got a gorgeous Marsala wine that will go *perfectly* with that.' Finally, she stood up, her eyes still fixed on Daniel, looking curiously bright and almost . . . desperate. 'Meet you guys back at yours in an hour, then. OK? I'll bring the wine. Oh, and the painting, too. I promise, you're going to *adore* it.'

Chapter 22

'Oh, pull yourself together. Bea's a flirt. She's also jealous, over-dramatic and possessive. But Finley's wrong. She's not a stalker. Or a psychopath. Nor does she steal husbands. Or children,' I added breathlessly, still conscious that I hadn't managed to get hold of Bea and had no idea what she was thinking, let alone planning to do.

Irritated that Daniel still wasn't home, I decided that it was pointless waiting for him. Some fresh air would clear my head, and a stroll along the riverside might help me to prepare my confession. Even if Daniel was with Bea right now – *especially* if he was, and she was maliciously feeding him her side of the story – he would return, and I needed to be ready.

Hurrying into the hall, I pulled on my grey jacket and grabbed Billy's blue duffle coat, along with his yellow wellington boots, before making my way to the bottom of the stairs.

'Billy? Come on, sweetie, we're going on an adventure!'

'Can I take *this*?' he asked, appearing almost immediately.

I sighed, not keen on him keeping the gift from Finley. 'Well,

117

it might get spoiled,' I cautioned, as he shuffled downstairs on his bottom. 'Boats like the water. Trains, not so much.'

'OK.' He abandoned it on the stair, pleasingly unfazed. 'Is Daddy coming?'

'Is Daddy coming where?'

'Daniel!' I swivelled around at the sound of his voice. 'I didn't hear you come in.' Instantly, I felt my heart start to thump. 'Where have you *been*?' I demanded, torn between irritation, relief and a weird sense of déjà vu. Was it really only twelve hours since I'd asked him the same question, after he'd returned from his secret dinner with Finley last night?

'For a run,' he said, even though his grey T-shirt looked bone dry and his short, spiky hair was as neat as ever. 'How's my best boy?' Crossing the hall, he crouched in front of Billy.

'It took you long enough to come home and find out,' I muttered.

Daniel didn't respond. 'What's that you've got there, kiddo?' He nodded at the train.

'A new engine! It's s'posed to be a present for you, Daddy.' Picking up the chunky green train, Billy chewed his lip, staring hopefully at Daniel.

'Well, you know what? *You* can have it.' Daniel winked. 'So, where are we going?'

Billy hugged the train against his chest, then sprinted back up the stairs towards his bedroom, as though fearing Daniel might change his mind.

'Hey, we were about to go out!' I called after him.

'He's fine,' Daniel said. 'Let him play. We need to talk.'

'Sure.' I shrugged out of my jacket. 'I mean, yes, we do.' I put Billy's boots and both our coats away, conscious that I was dragging my heels a little. My nerves were raging.

Following Daniel into the living room, I perched on the sofa, still finding it hard to believe that our former friend had been sitting there less than an hour ago. Everything he'd told me whirled around my head. 'Finley was here,' I blurted out. 'He said he saw you last night.'

'Ah.'

'Yes, *ah*. Why didn't you *tell* me, Dan?'

He settled himself on the black leather armchair where Finley had so recently sat, his long, bare legs astride, arms folded. 'Because I promised him I wouldn't.'

'And your first loyalty is to Finley, is it?' I snipped, feeling hurt.

Daniel gave me a sharp look. 'Uh, that's a bit rich, coming from you.'

'Sorry?' My heart felt as though it skipped a beat.

'He told me everything last night, Ruth. About that weekend in the New Forest. After John and Maxine's christening.' His fists clenched. 'How you got drunk with him in the bar. Told him all our problems. How I couldn't give you a baby.'

'Oh.' Relief surged through me, followed by stabbing guilt – and panic. *Had Finley been working up to tell Daniel what else had happened? What he suspected about Billy?* He'd insisted he hadn't, and Daniel clearly had no idea, but I was convinced Finley still planned to tell him. I had been on borrowed time for the last twenty-four hours – it was fast running out.

'That stuff's private, isn't it?' Daniel leaned forward in the armchair now, frowning at me. He looked baffled and wounded. 'I don't like Finley knowing my business.'

I winced in sudden understanding. 'Is that why you were so tense last night?'

'Well, yeah, I guess. That and other stuff.' He paused, frowning. 'Finley was rabbiting on about Bea, too. He did my head in. I could hardly keep up with what he was saying.'

'He thinks Bea is obsessed with me,' I said simply.

'Huh, does he indeed?' Daniel shook his head. 'Look, I've known Finley a long time. He's a player. If he's laying shit on Bea, he must be trying to cover his own tracks. He's done something. You can bet your life on that.'

119

I couldn't stand it any longer. 'Dan, there's something I need to tell you. I've been wanting to tell you since last night. After I saw Eve.'

Daniel threw up his hands. 'Jesus, haven't we already dealt with that situation?'

I thought of Eve's threat, and my terror when Billy had gone missing. But it had been *Finley* who had taken him, not Eve. I still didn't entirely trust why Finley had done that; it had been a cruel, extreme way to make the point that he had a potential right to see Billy. But Daniel had clearly been spot-on about Eve: she'd been talking nonsense, making idle threats.

There was no physical danger to Billy; the only threat was to my *marriage*, and a betrayal I needed to confess. Right now. 'Have we dealt with it? I hope so. Eve certainly seems to have gone quiet. But . . . there's more. Something I haven't thought about in years.'

'You didn't like my speech at our wedding. I knew it,' Daniel joked, but I could tell I had his full attention now.

'Our wedding was perfect,' I said huskily, suddenly tearful. 'No. It's about something I only started thinking about yesterday. Seeing Eve – what she said about Billy being her son.' I brushed away my tears. 'It brought it all back, you see? It made me question . . . everything.'

Daniel's eyes narrowed. 'Question what? You need to be a bit more specific than that.'

I couldn't meet his eyes. He had always been my staunchest ally, my biggest comforter; it terrified me that I was about to change everything.

'Not that Billy might be Eve's child,' I said slowly. 'I have no doubt he's my son. I gave birth to him. How could he *not* be mine?'

'Which is precisely what I said yesterday. Eve is deluded. She—'

'But what she said . . . it made me look at Billy and wonder. His dark hair, dark eyes. I started to worry that Billy might not be—'

'*Mine?* Is that what you were going to say?' Daniel's sharp intake of breath was audible in the quiet of the living room. 'Why the hell would you doubt that Billy is *mine*?'

'I'm so sorry. I didn't mean for anything to happen. Honestly. It was just one time,' I said breathlessly, my words tumbling over each other. 'After John and Maxine's christening.'

'That bloody weekend.' Daniel jerked out of the armchair and stood staring out of the window. 'You were feeling so low. I was, too. The IVF process was a nightmare.'

'Yes, I remember that much.' I pulled up my knees, hugging them against my chest.

'You went back to the hotel to rest.' Daniel turned back to face me now. 'So, what, after baring your soul to Finley in the bar, you chatted up some other guy?'

His face was bleak rather than angry, and I felt my heart break. Fleetingly, I wished I'd kept quiet, but it was too late to turn back now. Even if Finley or Bea had no intention of telling Daniel, which I found hard to believe, I loved him so much and owed it to him to confess everything myself, whatever the cost. 'It wasn't like that. I promise. I just—'

'I'm surprised you had the energy, after your little heart-to-heart,' Daniel interrupted, hurt thickening his voice. 'As I recall, Finley was absolutely wired that night. Firing on all cylinders. He'd had a blazing row with Bea, and boy, did we all know about it.'

I sighed. 'Yes. They were arguing about me, apparently. About Bea's fixation on me, or whatever it is. Like you said, I'm not sure that makes any sense, but . . . Anyway, that was the reason he got so drunk. Why he kept plying me with vodka, and—'

'Wait a second.' Daniel launched himself towards me, his blue eyes blazing. 'You're saying that you . . . and *Finley*?'

Chapter 23

My jaw ached, I was grinding my teeth together so hard. This was the most painful thing I had ever done – harder, even, than buying hundreds of pregnancy tests, only for them all to go in the bin, one by one: an endless plastic trail of failure. Daniel had been with me every step of that agonising journey; now I felt him moving further away from me with each word I spoke.

'I found the christening so hard, remember?' I wanted to beg for his understanding. 'Holding the baby, not being pregnant. Like you said, I had to get out. Go back to the hotel to sleep. Only I didn't. I mean, I did – go back. But Finley was there. We got talking, drinking.'

'You were completely out of it when I got back to the room.' Daniel began pacing slowly up and down the living room. 'Fast asleep, reeking of alcohol and dead to the world.'

'I'm so sorry. Please don't hate me. I don't even remember it.'

He turned to glare at me. 'You don't remember sleeping with my best friend? While I was stuck at a damned christening – in a church, of all places. With *your* best friend. His wife.'

Shame flooded through me. 'It's all a complete blur,' was all I managed to croak.

'Sure. Well, alcohol tends to have that effect.' Daniel rubbed his hands over his face, before returning to the armchair. Arms folded and legs crossed again, he suddenly looked calm and contained, his expression impassive, hiding his thoughts. 'OK, so what *do* you remember?'

I hugged my knees tighter. 'Nothing, really. Not of that evening, at least. Only vague flashes.' They had been returning to me in brief, tormenting glimpses ever since Bea first dropped her hint yesterday morning in the school playground about my *guilty secret*.

'Convenient,' Daniel commented drily.

'But I do remember the next morning. You'd left something in our hotel room. You went back to get it after breakfast. I followed you – to use the bathroom.'

Daniel looked puzzled. 'And?'

'I found something. In the bin. A, uh, a used condom.'

'Right. I see.' Daniel's voice was flat, emotionless.

'I felt sick. I wanted to ask you about the night before – whether you and I had . . .'

'No, Ruth. We didn't. Like I said, you were asleep. Or passed out, is perhaps more accurate. Does that make things clearer for you?'

'I'm so sorry. I've been feeling so guilty. It meant absolutely nothing, I swear.'

'Are you sure?' Daniel jerked out of the armchair, crossing the room to crouch in front of me, taking hold of both my arms.

'No, I'm *not* sure.' I sat back, feeling intimidated, even though his touch was gentle. 'Like I said, I barely have any memory of it. That's why I've never said anything, Dan. I never even thought of it again. Until yesterday morning.'

Daniel remained absolutely still, saying nothing.

'I haven't lied to you, I promise! I don't remember having sex that night. Things only started coming back to me when I saw

Eve, and she said that Billy . . . I started thinking about dates, timing. How the IVF had never worked. How Billy has dark hair and eyes, just like—'

'I meant, are you sure it meant nothing.' Daniel's fingers were squeezing harder now.

'*What?*'

'There's always been something between you and Finley.'

'No. You're wrong, Daniel. There hasn't. *Honestly.*'

'Sometimes, I've even wondered what might have happened if Bea hadn't muscled in on him. If I'd just let Finley stand you up that day at the Tate Modern. As usual, I was trying to get him off the hook. More fool me.'

'Well, that's typical Bea, too, isn't it?' I bristled at the reminder that Daniel and I had met on an accidental blind date – under duress, as far as he seemed to be concerned. It also felt like the pot calling the kettle black, with my doubts still simmering about Daniel and Bea. 'She always wants what I have. Finley said so himself. But he was never serious about me.'

'Yeah, right.'

'He *wasn't.* That coffee date wasn't even supposed to be a date. We were just going to see an exhibition. It was purely a spur-of-the-moment thing.' I thought back to the flat-warming party, how Finley had plucked the suggestion out of the air almost to tease me – perhaps, even, as a ruse to get Bea to join us.

Daniel shook his head. 'Fin only went to your flat-warming party to see you. He told me so. Only Bea railroaded him. As she does everyone,' he acknowledged lightly.

'I don't believe it. Finley's a flirt, but he's only ever had eyes for Bea. He's been so worried about her. He's devastated that things have gone wrong between them. He must have told you *that* last night? He said he wanted to sound you out about it, how to help her.'

'Oh, he said a lot of things last night. Most of it rubbish. Bea's the flirt. But Finley is a complete flake. Why do you think

I wanted us to move away from them?'

'Sure.' I had my doubts about that, but it didn't feel like the right moment to raise them. 'Anyway, I'm sure he can sort his own problems out. I'm not interested in *Finley*. I only care about *you*. You, me and Billy. That's all that matters to me.'

Daniel stood up, striding towards the window again. 'You claim it was an accident. Honestly, though, I can't help but wonder. We tried everything to have a baby, Ruth. I couldn't give you what you wanted. Perhaps you thought Finley could. Perhaps that's why you slept with him. Unconsciously, maybe, but even so.'

Somehow, his quiet, controlled agony was more wounding than an angry attack would have been. 'No, Daniel. *No!*' That he could think such a terrible thing of me tore me apart, but in fairness I couldn't blame him.

I was the guilty one. Finley, too. Only, as Bea had pointed out: I was an adult, accountable for my own actions. I would leave Finley to his own conscience about that night; he clearly had a complex situation to untangle with Bea.

One thing was certain, our friendship was over for good. I just had to hope that a paternity test would soon put an end to this whole nightmare, too . . . that while I may have lost Daniel's trust, he wouldn't lose his son.

'I need to think,' he said, still staring out of the window.

A sudden shaft of autumn sunshine caught his face, and the blue eyes I'd fallen in love with ten years ago had never looked more beautiful. At some point, I had stopped really seeing Daniel, I realised, maybe even coming to take him for granted. But he was completely wrong about Finley. Daniel truly was all I'd ever wanted. I prayed we could prove that Billy was his son, and that *I* could prove I still deserved to be his wife.

'I still love you,' I said, panicking. 'I'm so, so sorry.'

'Me too,' he replied, but he didn't look at me as he walked slowly across the living room, pausing for a moment before quietly shutting the door behind him.

Pressing myself into a corner of the sofa, I pulled a cushion against my chest, hugging it tightly. Then I buried my face in it, allowing my tears to flow.

I let them all out, along with a torrent of memories I hadn't realised I'd been bottling up for five years – which Bea had first started to unleash with her toxic insinuations in the playground, followed by her ominous voicemail.

Eve's ludicrous accusation and furious, futile threat hadn't helped, but once again I pushed it to the back of my mind, knowing that the horrible predicament I found myself in now was entirely due to the events of *that night*. I closed my eyes, and finally let myself relive it.

Chapter 24

Five years ago

'Get a move on, Ruth. We're going to be late.'

For a weekend that was to change my life so dramatically, it had all started rather banally, with Daniel standing in our bedroom, dressed only in his black boxer shorts after a shower, glowering as he tried to choose between two pretty much identical-looking shirts.

By the time Bea's strategic move on Finley had turned into genuine romance, followed by a whirlwind marriage, I'd known beyond any doubt that I was in love with Daniel. I'd been thrilled when he asked me to move in with him, and although we'd only intended to stay in our rented Georgian townhouse opposite Greenwich Park for a few months, with our best friends Beatrice and Finley close by, we'd ended up buying it and staying for five years.

'This isn't some kind of early Halloween trick, then?' I said, not moving from the bed.

I could hear the recycling lorry lumbering up Maze Hill and pictured the park already busy with joggers . . . and parents with prams. The thought of them – their buggies and baby carriers and bottle warmers – was making me want to cry. Lately, I had even started to avoid the Pavilion Café at the top of the hill, anxious about encountering the groups of mums that congregated there, and it had always been one of my favourite places.

'Nope. It isn't. I'm serious.' Daniel tutted. 'We *have* to go. Everyone will be there.' He pulled on his trousers, buttoned up his carefully chosen shirt and straightened his tie. He was wearing his best black suit; his thick brown hair was cut short, his strong jaw freshly shaven.

'Everyone?' I shifted around to look at him, my fingers anxiously pleating my new navy shift dress and jacket, laid out next to me on the bed. I had already showered and dried my hair in soft curls, but I was still wearing my dressing gown, reluctant to accept that in less than an hour we were supposed to be setting off to the New Forest.

'Everyone that matters to us, I mean.'

'Oh. Right. Sure.'

'Our best friends, Ruth.' Daniel frowned. 'At least, that's what I *thought* they were.'

'Yes. No, of course they are.' I told myself I was being selfish to want Daniel all to myself, for once. Even though we lived together now, we were rarely home alone. Either Finley would pop round, or Bea would text to invite us over.

'Huh. Well, they can't wait to see *us*. Finley hasn't stopped going on about it. He's booked us rooms in some chintzy hotel. And *Beatrice* has been messaging me non-stop.'

'Oh? She has?' I frowned, wondering why she would be texting Daniel.

'Apparently, she's worried you'll back out.' He gave me a knowing look.

I felt myself blush. I hadn't told Bea that I was getting cold feet about the christening, but she'd obviously picked up on something. 'Beatrice just likes bossing people around.'

'Ha! Ain't that the truth.' Daniel chuckled. 'Anyway, whatever *Queen Bea* thinks, it would be bad form if we're the only no-shows.' He reached up to the top cupboard built into the alcove, pulling out his leather holdall.

'Sure,' I said, without enthusiasm, still wondering why he was so keen to go.

'Besides, I reckon it'll be fun,' he continued, as though reading my mind. 'The vicar's wife is an old friend of John's. She's opening up the vicarage for the reception. Aren't you curious to go to a vicar's tea party? There might even be a few tarts,' Daniel teased.

I sighed, not in the mood to joke around. 'Be serious, Dan. This isn't about getting drunk and fooling around.' I chewed my lip as I realised how prudish I sounded.

'I never said it was. Not for me, anyway.' His eyebrows rose, and I knew he was thinking of Bea. She and Finley were always the ones who ordered 'just one more bottle' whenever we went out as a foursome, which was most weekends and several times in between.

'Sorry.' I pulled an apologetic face. 'I know you don't drink. It's just, this is supposed to be a *meaningful* occasion, not a house party. We're making a spiritual commitment to a baby, aren't we?' I stood up and shuffled towards the window, opening the heavy crimson drapes just as the streetlight directly outside went out. It felt like a bad omen.

'Maybe.' Daniel huffed. 'But neither of us really believes in all that stuff, do we?'

'Then why are we going?' I turned to look at him, feeling my eyes fill with tears. 'Why did we even agree to be godparents?' I added desperately.

'*Because*,' Daniel replied, his voice lilting playfully, 'for some strange reason, our friends seem to think we'll make good role models for their daughter. Buy her lots of presents on her birthdays, or whatever.' He waggled his eyebrows.

'Wow. And God be with you, too.' I'd been so frightened of

falling apart once I held someone else's baby, that I couldn't help taking the moral high ground once again. But Daniel clearly didn't buy it, and he refused to let me off the hook.

'Oh, come on, sweetheart. You know I'm joking. Anyway, this isn't about God. It's about people. *Friends*. Celebrating the birth of their first child. You of all people should know what that will mean to John and Maxine.' He gave me a pointed look as he reached for the gift-wrapped box propped on the dressing table.

It was a silver photo frame. I'd chosen and ordered it online, unable to face going to the shops and browsing for baby clothes and toys, picking through gifts I longed to buy for a baby of our own. I watched Daniel tuck the present inside his holdall, trying not to imagine the christening photo of her baby girl I knew Maxine would spend hours choosing to put in it.

'You're right. I *do* know,' I said, feeling a tear roll down my cheek. 'But I just can't do it. I can't stand in that church and hold a baby. Wishing she were mine. Feeling like a horrible person for being jealous instead of just *happy* for them.'

'Then pretend,' Daniel instructed bluntly, laying black jeans and a grey sweatshirt inside the bag. 'That's what I'm doing.' He shoved a bottle of aftershave into his washbag, then zipped it up, but not before I'd caught a glimpse of shiny, square foil packets inside.

'Not much call for *those* these days,' I said wryly, nodding at them. 'We need the opposite, don't we? Something to aid pregnancy, not prevent it.'

'What? Oh, yeah. I'd forgotten about those. They've been in there ages. Hmm, let me think. Since the days when sex was for fun, not just baby making.'

'Right. Sure.' I turned away, feeling hurt.

'Hey, I'm kidding!'

'Very funny.'

Daniel was smiling, but I wondered if that was really what

he thought. There was no doubt that trying to get pregnant had come to dominate our lives.

To begin with, we'd been philosophical about it. Setting up home together had been fun, and we'd stretched the honeymoon feeling as long as we could. As time had gone on, though, worry had started to creep in, followed by despair . . . and then desperation.

Over the last few weeks, we'd settled into a kind of frozen acceptance that we might never become parents; we stopped talking about it as much, but I knew it was constantly on both our minds.

Happy as I was for John and Maxine, work colleagues of Daniel's, I'd known their baby's christening would rub salt into the wound left by every false start and dashed hope, every failed IVF treatment. I was terrified of breaking down in front of everyone.

'Look, just grit your teeth and smile for the cameras. I'll be right there with you,' Daniel added more gently. 'You're far tougher than you know, Ruth. You've come through a hell of a lot worse.' He flipped the lid of his bag shut and came to stand in front of me.

'Exactly. That's *exactly* why this is so painful for me. Don't you see?'

'Of course I do.' He opened his arms, and I went willingly into them. 'It's hard for me, too. I want us to have a child more than anything. But we can't put our life on hold indefinitely. Finley was only saying at squash yesterday that—'

'You talked to Finley about it? About us? *Me?*' I felt bad as I heard the shrillness in my voice, but I was upset at the thought of Daniel complaining about me to his best friend.

'Absolutely not. You know I don't discuss our personal business. Finley was just saying he's had an epiphany himself. Apparently, he's glad Beatrice never wants kids. To quote his exact words: "Being a parent swallows everything else." But, you know, that's what's happening to us, and we're not even parents, just trying to be, and everything else is—'

'What? Swallowed up? And what do you mean by *everything else*. There *is* nothing—'

'Nothing else. I know. That's my whole point, Ruth. There *is* nothing else for you but having a child.' Daniel sighed. 'I get it. I do. But where does that leave me? *Us?*'

We had a good marriage, but I knew the strain of childlessness was beginning to show. I also knew I was being crotchety and unreasonable. I hated myself for it, but I loved Daniel and didn't want to hurt him. 'I'm sorry. You're right.'

'It's not a case of who's right or wrong.' He shrugged. 'It is what it is.'

'I guess. Only it's so hard – to stand there in front of everyone, holding that baby. Knowing it will never be me. Mine. *Ours*. A little bit of you. A little bit of me.' I crumpled against Daniel, and he held me tightly against him, trying to absorb my pain.

'You don't know that for sure. *None* of us knows what's around the corner. But it sucks, and I'd give anything to be able to make it happen. Dammit, I've spent every bonus I've ever earned to pay for all the treatment, and still we—'

'I'm sorry,' I said again, feeling even guiltier.

I tried to pull away, but he refused to let me go. I could hear the steady thump of his heartbeat; I tried not to think of silent ultrasound scans, the heavy hush in hospital consulting rooms as yet another nameless doctor gently tried to persuade me there really was no sign of a baby – that the symptoms I'd been convinced I was experiencing were simply the latest in a long, sad line of phantom pregnancies.

Ghost babies, I thought in distress.

'And before you even think it, Ruth. I couldn't care less about the money. I'd pay whatever it costs to make it happen for us. It's *you* I care about. I'm so proud of you, sweetheart. You're a good person. Kind. Caring. Selfless. I know you can do this. For our *friends.*'

Chapter 25

Daniel was right, and I did as he asked: I pulled myself together, hugged the proud parents and kissed their daughter as she was passed between her new godparents. Finley seemed as reluctant as I was to hold the baby, while Bea, astonishingly, hardly let go of her.

I did my best to smile for the cameras, but by the end of the service, I was desperate to get out. At first, Daniel begged me not to leave him alone with 'the Queen Bea'. But eventually he agreed it would be best if I skipped the reception and had a nap at the hotel.

'I'm sure you can handle Beatrice,' I reassured him, as he walked me to the church lobby. 'You know she's only like she is because of her family. Losing her mum and dad like she did. She craves love and attention, that's all. To fill the void they left, I guess.'

'Sure. It's a bottomless pit, though. No amount of attention ever fills it. It wouldn't surprise me if she bumped her parents off for the sympathy. Huh, and the inheritance.'

'Don't be cruel. Beatrice isn't a psychopath. She's just a little . . . high-maintenance.'

Daniel rolled his eyes. 'So you don't think it's weird she's done her hair all curly like yours? *And* she's wearing almost the same dress. I thought you two went shopping together?'

'We did. I bought this navy outfit. She bought a red one.' I pondered for a moment. 'I guess, well, you know she has this funny little thing about us being like sisters.' I screwed up my nose. 'It's just one of her pet foibles. Don't say anything, though. Not today.'

'As if!' Daniel huffed. 'She's like an unexploded bomb right now. I'm terrified to make any sudden moves around her. She and Finley have had a fight, apparently. A big one.'

'Oh? She didn't say. Well, Beatrice loves a drama, doesn't she? Ooh, you smell nice.' I couldn't resist stroking Daniel's cheek as he bent to kiss mine. 'New aftershave?'

'Yeah. Thought I'd make an effort for the vicar.'

'Very funny.' I rolled my eyes, then gave Daniel an impulsive hug.

'Mm, what have I done to deserve that?'

'Nothing in particular. Just, you know, I love you.'

He hugged me back. 'Me too you.'

'Anyway, see you later.' Suddenly, I felt exhausted, the effort of maintaining a happy pretence all day finally catching up with me.

I walked slowly out of the church, then strode more quickly as I spotted a waiting taxi. It had no doubt been ordered by another christening guest, but right now my need for escape was greater than anyone else's, I excused myself.

'Be good!' I called over my shoulder to Daniel.

'Aren't I always?' he quipped, closing the heavy oak door of the church behind me.

*

As the taxi trundled through narrow country lanes, I didn't bother to look out of the window to admire the wild ponies roaming free. At one time, I would have been entranced; now, even the sight of gambolling foals winding around their mothers' legs reminded me how fickle nature could be. I seemed to be surrounded by motherhood, a constant taunt to my own barrenness.

On impulse, I made the driver stop so that I could pick up a bottle of vodka from a little village shop near the hotel. Normally, I didn't touch alcohol in between courses of IVF, only in that moment my need for oblivion was overpowering. I'd planned to have a consoling drink alone in my room, but as I crossed the hotel reception area, I was surprised to spot Finley.

'Hey, Finley!' I called out, but he didn't hear me. Sitting in front of a roaring open fire in the rustic, oak-beamed lounge bar, he was knocking back his own bottle of vodka like it was iced water on a hot summer's day, instead of a cold, foggy autumn evening.

Remembering what Daniel had said about his fight with Bea, I was debating whether I should leave him in peace to calm down, when he finally looked up and beckoned me over.

'Hey, yourself,' he greeted, standing up to kiss me on both cheeks.

Finley's initial spark of flirtation towards me had long since died, and we'd settled into a comfortable friendship in and out of work. While Bea loved the thrill of winning accounts, her husband was more interested in the creative design side of advertising, as was I.

Maybe one of our arty chats would help lift *both* our moods, I decided, eyeing the comfy fireside sofa. 'Mind if I join you?'

'Please do. You did a runner too, hey?' He gave me a knowing look.

'Just feeling a bit tired. It's been a long day.'

'God, hasn't it just. So much baby talk. I couldn't stand any more. Who needs it? Little fuckers ruin your marriage, your career, your whole damned life.'

'Woah, steady on,' I said, surprised by his vitriol. 'You've changed your tune, haven't you? I thought you liked kids?' I added, before recalling what Daniel had said about Finley having had some kind of epiphany. I frowned. 'Even Beatrice seems to have had a change of heart. She's usually the one who's anti-babies. Not today, though.'

'My wife is many things,' Finley said drily. 'Often contradictory.'

'I thought she was going to smuggle that baby out of the church in her handbag. Not that I blame her. Gorgeous girl.' I bit my lip, hating the jealousy raging through me.

'Ah, yeah. Sorry. I was forgetting about you and the, uh, baby thing. Still no luck?'

The baby thing. Such a banal way to describe the years of dashed hopes and depressing pep talks from well-meaning doctors. I forgave Finley's lapse of tact, though; he was usually far kinder. It was Bea who insisted she'd *rather die than have kids*. 'Not yet,' I said, remembering Daniel's insistence that we 'make our own luck'. So much for *that* theory.

'Hey, have you been crying, babe?' Finley rested a hand on my arm.

'Everyone cries at christenings, don't they?'

'I thought that was weddings. Or funerals. Ha! Same difference.'

'Well, I remember crying at *your* wedding.' I didn't add that it had actually been Daniel's unexpected marriage proposal during the reception that had brought me to happy tears. 'And I'm sure I'll cry when you have a baby, too. Whatever you say, I bet you'll be a lovely daddy.'

'Huh. Sure. Well, don't hold your breath. It'll take a bloody miracle.' Finley grabbed a glass and filled it with vodka. 'Anyway, go on. Drink up. It'll make everything better. Or you'll forget all about it. So, you know, win-win.'

I swallowed obediently, wincing at the taste of the pungent liquid. 'Miracles do happen, you know? Just not to me,' I said self-pityingly. 'Anyway, I know what Beatrice says, but she'll change her mind. You saw her with Maxine's baby. If other people have something, she wants the same. Only bigger and better.'

'Yep. My darling wife always has to be the prima donna. It's her raison d'être.'

'Motherhood might even force her to slow down a bit at work,'

I mused, thinking how Bea seemed to live life at breakneck speed. 'Tanya's given her, what, four promotions now?'

'About half as many as Daniel, then. The guy's unstoppable. I can't keep up with him.'

'Do you have to?' Finley had a trust fund and didn't need to worry about supporting himself and Bea in the style to which she'd always intended to become accustomed.

'Nope. But I'd *like* to. I can't believe he's a VP already.'

'You know Daniel thrives on his job.' I sighed. 'Although, to be honest, I think it's probably as much a distraction. Until we . . . you know. Have a family.'

'Maybe he's firing blanks,' Finley said bluntly, topping up his drink again.

'Sorry?' His second tactless comment took me by surprise. 'Er, exactly how many of those have you had?' I took a mental count of the collection on the table in front of us.

'Not enough. Here. Have another.' One eyebrow quirked as Finley sloshed more vodka into my glass. 'We're here to *celebrate*. In fact, we should raise a toast.'

'To Maxine and John. Sure,' I said, trying hard to summon up enthusiasm.

'Actually, I was thinking more of your husband's meteoric rise to the top.'

'Beatrice's, too. They're both high-flyers.'

'True. God gave them the brains. You and I got the artistic flair. Hey, here's an idea. Maybe Daniel and I should wife swap.'

'Oi!' I punched his arm. 'Don't joke.'

'Who says I'm joking? They both live for work, don't they? While you and I . . .' Finley stared into my eyes, and I felt his hand come to rest on mine, fingers lightly entwining.

'I couldn't hack it anymore,' I said, pulling away and inching sideways on the sofa. Finley had always been touchy-feely, but he was clearly in a strange mood after rowing with Bea. I wanted to avoid giving off any accidental signals that we were sharing

137

anything other than a friendly drink.

'Hack what? Daniel's overbearing ambition? So there's trouble in paradise, hmm?'

'No, I meant working for Tanya. Living up to her expectations while trying to get pregnant. The strain almost killed me.'

'And your marriage?'

'What? Well, I—'

'Marriage isn't only about having kids, sweetheart. Sex can be just for fun, you know?' Finley winked, draining the last of the vodka into my glass. 'Fun being *my* raison d'être.'

I decided to ignore his comment, but I felt a pang as I remembered Daniel saying something similar. 'And that, in a nutshell, is why you're not a VP yet.' I winced. 'God, I've drunk too much. You too. One more, then that's it.'

'Spoilsport.'

'You were going to propose a toast,' I reminded him.

'Oh, yeah. Except I seem to have run out of vodka.' He looked around plaintively.

'Here. Allow me.' I reached into my handbag and pulled out my own bottle.

Finley gave me an approving smile. 'See? I always knew we were kindred spirits.'

He reached out to sweep a stray curl behind my ear, and instantly I was reminded of him doing the same thing at our flat-warming party . . . and how I'd met Daniel soon after.

'Maybe. But not soul mates,' I said, suddenly missing Daniel, wishing I'd stayed with him at the church and simply enjoyed time with him at the reception afterwards. 'Sorry, Finley. I have to go. Here. Take this.' I handed over the bottle of vodka. 'You have it. I don't want it.'

Finley took the bottle, but instead of setting it on the table, he uncapped it and filled my glass. 'One toast, then I'll let you go.'

'No, really, I—'

'Oh, come on. I'll keep it brief. No speeches, I promise.'

I hesitated a moment longer, then gave in. If I was going to leave Finley to drown his sorrows alone, I supposed the least I could do was raise a toast with him before I left. 'Cheers,' I whispered hoarsely, as the vodka burned my throat.

'Here's to happy couples,' Finley said against my ear.

'Sorry?' I pulled back. 'I thought we were toasting Beatrice and Daniel?'

'Ah, yes.' Finley's brows arched as he filled my glass again. 'Silly me. So we were.'

Chapter 26

As Halloween revellers began filling up the bar, we sat by the fire for the next couple of hours, finishing the bottle. I kept trying to leave; Finley kept insisting on 'just one more toast'. And when I woke up the next morning, I found myself upstairs in the four-poster bed, in the chintzy bedroom, with Daniel fast asleep and snoring beside me. I felt like I'd been hit by a truck.

All I could remember about the night before was Finley hauling me up the stairs, then hoisting me over his shoulder to carry me into my room, when I seemed to have lost the ability to walk. I could recall giggling as he'd let me slide down onto the bed, before belly-flopping next to me, while I lay staring at the ceiling, willing myself not to throw up.

Having not touched any alcohol for weeks, I had a low tolerance to it: the vodka had obliterated all my powers of speech, thought and movement. *And memory*, it seemed. Everything from that point onwards was a complete blank, no matter how hard I tried to work out whether I'd managed to change into my pyjamas by myself, or whether – embarrassingly – Finley had helped me.

Leaving Daniel to sleep, I dragged myself into the bathroom, puzzling over my aching limbs, wondering if it was all due to alcohol or if I was coming down with some kind of bug. As I stood beneath the shower over the old-fashioned, claw-foot tub, even the gentle stream of water dispensed by the ancient appliance stung my skin. I felt sore all over, and as my hands moved slowly over my ribs and abdomen, carefully soaping, tentatively exploring, I was conscious of a dull, throbbing ache deep inside.

'Huh, it's not your period, and you're definitely not pregnant,' I mumbled, before wondering if my body felt so battered because of the lingering after-effects of invasive IVF treatment. 'Damn. It shouldn't hurt like this. I'll have to call the doctor.'

Turning off the shower, I clambered awkwardly out of the tub. A sudden sharp pain around my pelvic region made me double over. 'Wow, you're seriously out of shape, girl. You need to get to the gym. The doctors *told* you physical fitness can help fertility.'

Deciding to call the clinic immediately and book a check-up, I leaned across the hand basin to reach a stack of fresh linen piled high in a wicker basket. After wrapping a pleasingly soft white towel around me, I stared wearily at my reflection in the bathroom mirror.

Deep shadows under my eyes reminded me why I'd more or less given up late nights and alcohol – and why Daniel never drank at all – but an odd cluster of dark marks on the right side of my neck caught my eye. 'What the heck?'

My first thought was that I must have drunkenly sleepwalked into the unfamiliar four-poster bed, but as I leaned closer to the mirror, examining my reflection, it told a different tale: the bruises – five of them – were small, round . . . and distinctly fingertip-shaped.

Tentatively, I pressed shaking fingers against them, wincing at their tenderness as I tried my hardest to match the shape of my hand to the purple pressure points, still determined to believe I'd inflicted them on myself but baffled as to how.

'What on earth did you *do*, try to strangle yourself?' I genuinely wondered if, drunk and overheated, I had grappled with the heavy covers on a strange bed, clawing at the thick damask bedspread in my sleep and in the process marking my own sensitive skin. Yet even as I considered that possibility, another one made the ache inside me cramp more violently.

'God, no. *Please* tell me you didn't do something so stupid.' I tried to convince myself there was no way Finley and I would have slept together – that those fingertip bruises weren't the legacy of drunken sex, his long fingers entwining my neck in clumsy, heated, illicit passion.

But I couldn't get the thought out of my head as I scrutinised the rest of my body, puzzling over what might or might not be similar marks on my thighs, before crawling back into bed and lying rigid with fear next to Daniel.

Sleepily, he wrapped an arm around me; twice, I opened my mouth to ask him if we'd made love. Then I squeezed my eyes shut and prayed for the world to disappear – anything other than admit that I couldn't remember; that I'd drunk myself into unconsciousness.

Daniel was vehemently teetotal. Confessing that I'd found oblivion at the bottom of a vodka bottle would do nothing to lighten the recent tension in our marriage. And if he said we *hadn't* had sex, that was even worse. Not only would it mean that I might have drunkenly, accidentally slept with his best friend, it would present me with a terrible dilemma: whether to tell Daniel what I'd done, or bury my guilt and try to live with it.

Daniel and I had a good marriage. We never kept *anything* from each other; we talked about all our worries, big and small. But infidelity was massive. I wasn't sure our marriage would survive the shadow of such a betrayal, especially given the strain already created by the endless, seemingly futile quest to have a baby.

Chapter 27

Later that morning, everyone seemed unusually quiet around the breakfast table, but I tried not to read too much into that; no doubt we were all tired and thoughtful about going home.

I stared pensively into my coffee, feeling self-conscious about the bruises on my neck that I'd thankfully managed to conceal with make-up.

'Damn,' Daniel said suddenly, making me jump.

'Everything OK?' I tried to smile, but guilt made butterflies whirl in my stomach.

'Yeah. I just remembered what I forgot.' He chuckled, and I let out a slow sigh of relief. He didn't look cross, just preoccupied.

'What did you forget?' I wished I could remember what my own mind had blotted out.

'Nothing major. Just my washbag. I think I left it upstairs when I put our bags in the car. I should probably fetch it.'

'No rush, is there? We can pick it up after—'

'Be back in a minute.' Abruptly, Daniel pushed back his chair, and stood up.

'Damn. That reminds me.' Bea set her cup back in its saucer. 'You didn't happen to notice if I left my necklace on the bedside table, did you?' she asked Finley.

'Sorry?' Turning to her with shadowed eyes and a deep frown, Finley gave off the impression that he wouldn't have noticed if Bea had waltzed downstairs stark naked.

'My locket. Oh, don't worry yourself. I'll go and check *myself*, shall I?'

I looked between them, astonished to realise they still hadn't made up. I wondered why, and whether it had anything to do with what might or might not have happened between Finley and me last night. So far, he hadn't looked at me once. Not in an obvious look-anywhere-but-at-me kind of way. He simply ate his breakfast and drank his coffee.

Perhaps he'd forgotten what happened, too, I reflected. Or maybe nothing had. I was going out of my mind trying to decide if I was letting my imagination run away with me.

As Bea stalked across the dining room, following in Daniel's footsteps, I thought of his surprising revelation that she'd been texting him; I wondered if she'd told *him* what her row with Finley had been about. He clearly knew something. I was hurt that Bea hadn't confided in me and thought about following her, but it would look ridiculous if I left the table, too.

I wished I could, though; my heart was thumping so loudly, I was sure Finley must be able to hear it. I kept my eyes down, praying yet fearing he would say something – *anything* – about the night before, but he seemed glued to his phone.

'Oh, for God's sake.' Suddenly, he thumped the table so hard, the cutlery rattled.

'Don't tell me you've forgotten something too,' I joked awkwardly.

He turned to look blankly at me. 'What?'

I nodded towards the stairs, in the direction Bea and Daniel had just disappeared.

'Oh, right. No, I haven't. But Tanya has. I *told* her I was taking today off. She's only gone and booked an emergency board meeting.'

'Sounds typical.' I knew how demanding my former boss could be, and according to Bea, who still worked for her, she'd become even more so after her accident six months ago.

'Sorry, Ruth. I'll have to call her.'

'Of course. No problem.' Inwardly, I sighed in relief that he was leaving.

'Don't rush off, though,' he added, frowning as he stood up. 'I, um . . . I did want to chat to you about something, actually. Something important.'

'Really?' I shifted in my seat, feeling myself blush, but before I could formulate my panicky thoughts into a coherent question – *Did we have sex last night?* – Finley's phone rang.

'Tanya!' he said brightly, faking enthusiasm as he answered the call. Giving me one last frown, he strode out of the dining room, iPhone pressed to his ear.

'Dammit, Ruth, you should have just asked him.'

Anxiously, I worked my way through a second pot of coffee, and when the waiter offered to bring me another, I realised that if I drank any more, I'd burst. Assuring him that we'd return to settle the bill before we left, I headed for the stairs, a glance out of the window on the way up confirming that Finley was still engrossed in his phone call – a heated one, judging by the way he was pacing in circles around the hotel car park.

I wondered if Tanya was giving him a telling-off. At least he didn't appear to be struggling with any morning-after guilt, which reassured me a little. Surely, if something had happened between us, he would be showing more remorse, or at least awkwardness? But, if anything, he seemed unusually aloof and distant.

'Oh! Have I gone the wrong way?' I jumped, startled to bump into Bea as I rounded the corner where I was expecting to find Daniel's and my room. Then again, the last time I'd come this direction, I'd been drunk and Finley had been carrying me, I thought wryly.

'No, it's me.' Bea stepped quickly around me. 'Zero sense of

145

direction. My room is *this* way. See you downstairs in a bit.'

'Yes, sure. I won't be long. Actually, I was hoping we could have a quick chat.'

Guiltily, I wondered if Finley had mentioned anything to her. My memory of last night was hazy, but I would still rather talk it over with Bea – even if *she* hadn't confided in me about her fight with Finley. Whatever, she was my best friend. Although right now she seemed even more icily distant than Finley had at breakfast . . .

'Not now, babe. Got to rush.' Checking her appearance in a mirror on the wall, Bea patted her blonde curls, so like mine, before sashaying away from me, glancing back once, eyes glittering.

I stared after her thoughtfully for a moment, before carrying on to find my room at the end of the corridor and pushing open the heavy oak door. 'Got everything?' I asked Daniel.

'What? Oh, yeah. Washbag was in the bathroom. Uh, did you forget something too?'

The old floorboards creaked beneath the worn floral carpet as he paced agitatedly up and down the room, one hand rubbing backwards and forwards across his short hair.

'No. Just need the bathroom.'

'Sure,' Daniel said distractedly, fussing with the heavy pink damask bedspread now.

'They do have people to make the bed and clean the room, you know?' I teased.

'What? Oh. Huh. Yeah, I know. Force of habit, I guess.'

'Really?' I chuckled. Tidiness wasn't one of his strengths. 'Feel free to bring that habit home and introduce it to our kitchen,' I joked, perking up at the thought of being back in our cosy Greenwich home, just the two of us.

I couldn't wait for life to get back to normal – to leave this horrible weekend behind. I'd known it was a mistake coming, but I had wanted so badly to prove to Daniel that I cared about him as much as having a baby. Needing a hug, I took a step towards him.

'Anyway, see you downstairs,' he said, quickly sidestepping me, just as Bea had moments before.

'Oh. OK. Is everything all—' But he was gone before I could finish my sentence. Frowning now, I hurried into the bathroom, where I blundered tiredly around, knocking over the bin. 'Damn.' I squatted down to gather up the spilled contents, and my heart started racing. 'What the . . .?'

Tucked inside an empty packet of the hotel's complimentary, individually wrapped cookies, I found a used condom. Horrified, I quickly buried it beneath a mountain of scrunched-up tissue. Burying my guilt proved a lot harder.

Either the condom belonged to Finley and I *had* been unfaithful, or it was Daniel's – one of the stash I'd spotted in his washbag before we came – and he'd had sex with me while I'd been practically unconscious, bafflingly using contraception. Neither was a scenario I wanted to shout about. *So I didn't.*

Perching on the side of the tub, I weighed up the damage a confession would do to my friendship with Bea, not to mention my marriage to Daniel. After much soul searching, I decided with a heavy heart that the whole thing was best put down to a bad night. I couldn't actually remember a thing, and Finley wasn't saying anything, which probably meant there was nothing to tell. No doubt it was all in my imagination.

The four of us split the bill for a breakfast none of us had eaten, said our goodbyes and headed off to our respective cars. And that was the last time we saw each other, until Bea and Finley unexpectedly moved to Richmond. But from that weekend onwards, nothing was ever the same between the four of us: our friendship had died.

Chapter 28

'OK. Let's go have that adventure.'

'Sorry? What?' I looked up, astonished to see Daniel, now changed into jeans and a pale blue hoodie, his old khaki army jacket slung over one shoulder, standing in front of me. Billy was at his side, wearing his blue duffle coat and yellow wellingtons, a grin on his face.

'We've both had a shock,' Daniel said quietly. 'Let's go down to the river. Blow out the cobwebs. Maybe when the dust settles, we can talk again.'

'Really?' I stared hopefully at his handsome face, hardly daring to believe it was possible we might come through this together. 'Thank you,' I said tearfully. 'I'd like that.'

'Good. Just don't get too close to the water,' Daniel joked, as Billy skipped happily out of the living room, heading for the front door. 'Or I might be tempted to push you in.'

*

An hour later, after grabbing sandwiches from the café, strolling along the riverside with them and watching Billy throw his crusts to the little family of ducks he adored, we returned to sit on our favourite bench. Daniel and I had barely exchanged a word, but I could tell he was turning everything over in his mind. Thankfully, Billy's chatter had filled the void between us.

'Mummy!'

'Yes, darling?' Immersed in my own troubled thoughts, I looked up to see him waving at me. 'The lady said I can go on her boat. Is that OK?'

'Good boy for checking,' I called back, hurrying to his side, leaving Daniel on the bench. Perhaps a little time and space between us would be a good thing.

'It's Captain Jack's boat. He's a pirate. The lady said so. She said he'll show me the engine.' Billy's eyes couldn't get any wider.

'Captain Jack, hey? Ah. Is *this* his boat?'

I stared at the blue canal boat, torn between worry about letting Billy go on board and curiosity to see inside it myself. Having been thrown overboard by bullies on a school trip down the Thames when I was a child, I'd remained scared of the water ever since. I had come to love living next to the river, but I still preferred to keep my feet on dry land – Billy's, too, wherever possible.

'*Please*, Mummy? Can I see it?'

'Yes, *can* he?' a familiar voice echoed. 'Go on. Let the poor boy go.'

I looked up in horror at the dark-haired woman standing on the boat deck. 'Eve . . .'

'Yep. I'm still here. I told you, I'm not going till I get what I came for.'

It was a huge shock to discover she lived on the canal boat. *No wonder she'd vanished so quickly last night.* The realisation that she was staying within sight of our apartment gave me goose bumps, underlining that nothing about this situation was a coincidence. Our paths hadn't randomly crossed: as Eve had told me herself, she'd deliberately tracked me down.

'Daniel!' I called out urgently, when Billy took Eve's request as permission and climbed onto the gangplank. Hurrying after him, I glanced over my shoulder to check that Daniel had heard. 'It's Eve,' I said breathlessly, as he sprinted towards me.

'I'm calling the police.' He was already reaching into his jacket pocket.

'No, don't.' I pulled up short, frowning as I caught sight of Eve's malicious smile. Thinking quickly, I realised that the worst thing we could do now was antagonise her further. 'Why don't the three of us sit down and talk?'

'You're kidding.' Daniel was already aboard the deck, having effortlessly bypassed me on the gangplank. The water held no fears for him; he'd always wanted a boat himself.

'I reckon we can have a sensible conversation. Don't you, Eve?' After all, Daniel knew the truth now about what had happened between me and Finley. I had no more secrets to hide – together, perhaps we could put Eve's nonsense to bed, once and for all.

'Absolutely. I'm pleased you're finally seeing sense.' She rolled her eyes.

'Fine. But we're not staying long.' Daniel grabbed Billy's arm. 'Stay with me, son.'

'Ah, sweet,' Eve mocked, then recoiled as Daniel turned to glare at her.

'Where's Captain Jack?' Billy looked eagerly around. 'Is he really a pirate?'

'Well, he's a builder,' Eve admitted. 'But it's fun to pretend. Just for a little while, anyway. You can't live a lie for ever.' She turned to stare pointedly at me, eyebrows arching.

'What do *you* do?' Billy asked her, oblivious to the mounting tension I could feel around him. 'Do you count the treasure?'

'I wish.' Eve grinned. 'No, I'm an artist. I carve little animals. Birds and things. We travel all around the country, along canals

150

and rivers. It's like one big adventure. We stop off wherever we like. So I can sell my art at markets. People love it. Wanna see some?'

'Yes, please!' Immediately, Billy launched himself across the deck.

'Don't run off, sweetheart,' Daniel warned, grabbing his hand and pulling him back.

His voice was mild, but his eyes blazed at Eve, and I remembered him saying that she would never get her hands on our son while there was breath in his body. I felt a surge of emotion that, even in spite of my confession, he still felt that way: Billy was his little boy and he was determined to protect him.

We had to get that paternity test. Eve was muddying the water at a time when we most needed clarity. Perhaps, if we spent a bit of time with her, it would snap her out of her delusion that Billy was her son. It would finally sink in that she was suffering from PTSD and should get help.

I would even be prepared to help arrange that – *pay* for it – anything to get her out of our lives, so we could focus on what was important: repairing the broken trust in our marriage, and proving that Billy was Daniel's son, after all, and not Finley's. I prayed that was the truth.

'Please, Daddy!' Billy begged.

'What's five minutes?' Eve said, crouching down to ruffle his black curls, before looking coldly up at me. 'Especially when you compare it to almost five years.'

Chapter 29

The canal boat was bigger inside than it appeared from the outside; it was also surprisingly clean, cosy and brightly lit, with a couple of lamps perched on top of bookshelves – stuffed with fantasy novels, I noticed, remembering the one on Eve's bedside cabinet in hospital.

A long wooden table seemed to be made out of an old door, while the benches either side appeared to be upcycled church pews. Further down, I spotted a small kitchen area, and beyond that what looked like bunks behind a heavy, half-drawn blue curtain. At the very far end of the boat, I glimpsed a sliding door, presumably leading to a shower or washroom.

'So where's Jack?' I said, looking curiously around the cabin.

'Gone to get more wood. For my carvings.'

'Ah, right.' I wondered if that explained the mystery knife in her pocket at the school.

'It's how we heat the boat, too.' She nodded at a wood burner in one corner.

'Sure.' I thought of the plume of smoke I'd seen drifting out of its chimney in the middle of the night. I had never, for a second, imagined Eve was inside, stoking the flames.

'You can feed it, if you like, Billy?' she invited with a grin. 'Like this.' Striding towards the wood burner, Eve opened the door and poked in a shard of wood, pulling Billy back as the flames licked around it, leaping higher. 'Don't get too close. Fire burns, remember? Even on the water. We don't want the whole place going up in smoke.'

'Come here, son,' Daniel said. 'Stay with me, OK?'

For a moment, Eve looked as though she was about to contradict him. Then she shrugged and wandered back to the table. 'Suit yourself.'

'Oh, I will.' Daniel sat down on an ancient-looking armchair, hauling Billy onto his lap.

Hunching on the bench by the table, Eve gestured for me to sit opposite her. I did so, continuing to look around, taking in that while everything on the boat was mismatched and repurposed, it was arranged snugly and stylishly. There was a bowl of fruit on a sideboard, with carved wooden wildlife figures perched on every shelf lining the white walls of the boat, interspersed with framed sketches.

The charcoal drawings were unexpectedly good, and I wasn't surprised Eve managed to survive by selling her art. I thought of my dream to open a gallery for undiscovered artists: she would have been exactly the kind of talent I'd have loved to showcase. It was a bitter irony.

'Seen enough?' Eve said brusquely.

'You've made a comfortable home here.' I refused to be intimidated.

'We even have coffee.' One eyebrow arched. 'Can I get you one?'

'No. Thank you. This isn't a social visit. Or a playdate.' I glanced at Billy, pleased to see he was preoccupied now playing rock-paper-scissors with Daniel.

153

'Whatever.' Propping her elbows on the table, Eve studied me. 'You haven't changed.'

'Haven't I? *You* have. I don't mean physically,' I qualified.

'Oh?'

'I mean, it feels like we're enemies. I remember thinking in hospital that we'd become friends.' I deliberately tried to sound amiable, to re-establish a sense of connection – before I used friendly persuasion to convince Eve to walk away.

'Huh. Friends don't leave without saying goodbye.'

'Don't they?'

That was exactly what Bea and I had both done four years ago, I reflected: silently disappeared from each other's lives. *Until Bea forced herself back into mine*, I thought, frowning as I recalled Finley's account of her obsession with me.

He still hadn't phoned, as he'd promised he would this morning, and I wondered what was happening . . . if he'd seen Bea, and whether she'd admitted that Daniel had been at her house when he was supposed to be out running and looking for Billy. If Finley had managed to persuade Bea that what happened 'that night' was history and their marriage could be repaired.

Gazing at Daniel, I hoped ours could be, too. He was here, and that was a start. He was prepared to fight for his son – and it felt good that he trusted me to do that my way.

'Look, you've had your fun, Eve.' Abruptly, Daniel stood up, propping Billy on his hip and heading towards the cabin doors.

'Oh.' *Obviously, I'd been wrong about him doing things my way.* 'Perhaps if we—'

'Fun?' Eve cut across me, glaring at Daniel. 'I'm just getting started.'

'Well, tough. I'm ending it. Right here, right now.' He flicked the briefest glance in my direction, and I wondered if he was talking about our marriage, too. 'I know Ruth feels we can talk this out. I don't. Enough is enough.'

'Enough for who?' Eve scoffed. 'Not for me.'

'Then *deal* with it,' Daniel said bluntly. 'We're going. And if you leave us alone, I'm prepared to pretend this never happened. I'll say no more about it. To *anyone*,' he emphasised, obviously trying to make his threat clear, without scaring Billy by mentioning the police.

'Oh, feel free to tell who you like,' Eve said glibly. 'I have nothing to hide. Do you?'

'Is that a threat?' Daniel hooked his hands on his hips. Tall and broad, he cut an intimidating presence in the confines of the cabin, and I could see Eve recoil slightly.

'Of course not. I just meant . . .' For the first time, she looked unsure.

'Look, Eve. You need to *move on*,' Daniel said calmly.

'I've been moving on for four years. But something pulled me back.'

'Sure. Money.' Daniel glanced briefly at Billy, who was now happily engrossed examining Eve's carved figures on a shelf. 'I'm right, aren't I?'

'No. You're not. But I'll go. When I get what I came for.'

'Please, stop this,' I begged, stepping forward. 'It's not fair to . . .' I stared at Billy, my heart thudding as he reached out to take the hand Eve offered to him, after crossing the cabin to crouch down next to him.

'Captain Jack will be back soon,' she said brightly. 'I promised you he'll show you the engine. I always keep my promises. You can trust me, OK?'

'OK!'

'I bet you'd *love* to live on a boat, hey?'

'Oh, yes!' Billy bounced up and down. 'So would Daddy. Mummy wouldn't. She doesn't like the water. She's scared of it. I can beat her at swimming,' he declared proudly.

'Wow. That's awesome. I can't even swim at all. And I *do* live on a boat. How funny is that?' Eve mimed breaststroke, pretending to sink under water.

155

Billy pointed at her hands. 'What are those marks?'

'Sweetheart, we don't make personal remarks,' I said automatically, remembering the jagged red lines I'd noticed on Eve's wrists in hospital. I didn't want her frightening Billy by mentioning what had caused them. 'And your daddy's right. We need to go.'

We weren't getting anywhere, and I had to concede that Daniel had indeed been right: Eve was a disturbed woman, and it was clearly pointless trying to appeal to her better nature.

Eve ignored me. 'You can ask me anything, Billy. It's not good to keep secrets. Far better to tell the truth. Lies *hurt* people.'

'I never lie. Pinky promise!' Billy held up a hand, crooking his little finger.

'Aw, you've got magic fingers, too, haven't you?'

'That's what Mummy calls them.' Billy grinned at me, his dark eyes shining in recognition of our pet phrase for the slightly webbed fingers on his right hand.

'Well, she's right. They *are* magic.' Eve gave him an extra gentle high-five.

'It's OK. It doesn't hurt. My hand was born like that.'

'I know it was, sweetheart. Mine, too. See?' Eve held out her hand, pointing out scars I'd never noticed between her long fingers. 'Only *my* mummy – well, my foster mum. She didn't call my fingers magic.' Her mouth twisted. 'She didn't like them at all.'

Billy frowned. 'She sounds mean.'

'Well, she wasn't that nice, I'm sorry to say. But I suppose she did try to help me. In her own way. Sometimes grown-ups think they know what's best for children.' Eve's cool gaze flicked between me and Daniel. 'They don't always get it right.'

'We all make mistakes. We have to live with them,' Daniel said lightly. 'I'm sure you've made plenty, Eve. Don't make others pay the price for them.'

'You don't believe in second chances, then?' She cocked her head, staring at him.

'Nope.'

I watched Daniel's expression harden and wondered again if he was talking about me, our marriage. 'Eve, we really do need to go.' I couldn't wait to get out of there now.

'Well, I believe in them,' she said, as if I hadn't spoken. 'If you want something enough, you have to *make* it happen. I believe that, too. Someone said it to me once. I think they were right. There's nothing that can't be fixed if you try.'

'Daddy fixes my trains for me.' Billy's eyebrows puckered, as they always did when he was trying to figure something out. 'I bet he could fix my hand. But I don't mind it.'

'That's the spirit.' Eve grinned at him. 'My foster mum made the doctor fix mine. That's what those marks are. From where he separated my fingers. See?' She held up her hand.

'Snap!' Billy said, giving her another high-five, harder this time.

'Is that true?' Goose bumps started to prickle all over my body.

'I told you, Ruth. I don't lie. About *anything*.'

'You're special too!' Billy hopped up and down again. 'We're *magic*!'

'We certainly are,' Eve agreed, winking at him.

'Abracadabra.' Billy waved his magic hand around, as if casting a spell with it.

'All right, son. Let's calm down a bit, hey?' Daniel scooped him up in his arms, and I wondered if he had the same sick, panicky feeling inside as I did.

'I know a better magic spell than that,' Eve told Billy, with an even bigger grin now.

'What is it? *Tell* me!' he demanded, eyes shining.

Leaning towards him, she whispered: 'It's . . . *hereditary syndactyly*.'

She spoke slowly, and I knew it wasn't for Billy's benefit, but mine and Daniel's. I also saw the exact moment the connection formed in Daniel's brain: *Hereditary syndactyly – webbed fingers – a genetic defect passed down from parent to child.*

It could only have one explanation – and one implication?

Chapter 30

Kew, South-West London
Friday, 3 September; 12.25 p.m.

'Do you like photos, Billy?' Yanking open the door of the brightly painted, shabby chic sideboard, Eve rifled inside.

Instantly, I was reminded of doing exactly the same thing that morning – after Finley had taken Billy, and I'd been desperate to find a picture of my son to give to the police.

The police. Daniel was right about that, too. We should have called them, I thought desperately.

'Mummy takes lots,' Billy said happily, oblivious to the anxiety rippling through me. 'We take pictures of the duck. We call her Lucky Ducky. She has six babies!' Concentrating hard, he counted them on his *magic fingers*.

'That's so lovely. Lucky Ducky.' Eve looked over her shoulder at him. 'I like photos, too, sweetheart. I've got one here somewhere that I wanted to show your mummy.'

'Leave it, Eve.' Daniel stepped forward, grabbing her arm.

She brushed him off. 'You must be curious to see it too, *Daniel*?'

'There's nothing you could possibly show me that holds any interest whatsoever. In fact, this whole situation is getting very boring indeed. Come on, Ruth. We're leaving.'

'Oh, here it is!' Triumphantly, Eve held up a small, square photo. 'Your mummy asked me to prove something to her, Billy, you see? Here. Take it,' she snapped, thrusting it at me.

Our hands brushed as I took it from her, but it wasn't the fleeting contact that made my fingers tremble. I looked down at the smiling face of a teenage girl with long black hair and dark, fierce eyes. Then I glanced up to see the same smile on the pale, oval face in front of me. Back down again at the image of her younger self . . .

It was unmistakably Eve. She had her back to a window, and bright sunshine streamed into the room. Her eyes glinted at the camera, boldly challenging, and it felt like I was falling into their darkness. Black eyes, a perfect match to those of the baby she held in her arms.

A tiny, crumpled face peeped out above a soft white fleece, tufty dark hair, a rosy mouth. One hand had escaped the swaddling blanket, stretching upwards in search of a mother's kiss. *They count the fingers; they count the toes.*

Every inch of him was perfect in my eyes; the syndactyly on his right hand had never worried me. I'd noticed it the day he was born – the day this photo had been taken, I realised, staring at the webbed fingers of his splayed, starfish hands, starkly captured by the camera.

I blinked away tears, clearing my eyes so that I could be sure I wasn't misreading the childish blue scrawl on the bottom of the photo. I read it again silently in my head, each word like a knife to my heart: 'Eve loves Sean for ever.'

The date was July the fifteenth. Billy's birthday.

*

I refused to stay on the boat a moment longer, but Eve insisted on coming with us. Surprisingly, Daniel agreed, saying we needed to talk. I thought about protesting but didn't. My head was spinning.

All I wanted was to feel safe in my own home, exactly as I had yesterday morning after running away from the school.

Eve had followed me then, too, but I had been so busy worrying about Bea, even more so after her unsettling voicemail message this morning. *Had I missed what was staring me in the face?*

The similarity between Eve's webbed fingers and Billy's had shocked me; the photo knocked me sideways. I was struggling to dismiss the combined evidence of the two things. If nothing else, it meant we could no longer simply ignore her: the *police* certainly wouldn't.

'Everything's fine. Stop panicking, Ruth,' Daniel told me firmly, as we made our way back down the hall in our apartment, after settling Billy in the living room with his new train. 'We'll get blood tests. Proper, official DNA testing. In the hospital. You'll have to be there,' he warned Eve, as we reached the kitchen, where we had left her – keeping as much distance between her and Billy as possible.

'Oh, I insist on it,' she said, sipping the coffee I'd made for her on autopilot.

'We'll need a lawyer present. Maybe even a police officer,' Daniel added, arms folded across his chest as he stood watching Eve. 'I'm sure they'll have lots of questions.'

'Whatever you want,' she replied, acting meek now.

Daniel took a step towards her. 'What I *want* is for this to all go away.'

'You mean, you want *me* to go away,' she sneered, as she had to me last night, and I had to admire her fearlessness. Daniel's gaze was so intense, I thought it might scorch her skin.

'Look, we need to discuss this properly. *Calmly*,' I said, step-ping into the tension between them. But I was lecturing myself more than anyone else. I didn't feel calm; far from it. 'This is all incredibly distressing. And confusing. I just don't understand . . .'

'What's not to understand?' Eve helped herself to more coffee. 'You saw the photo.'

'Yes, but it's just a *photo*. Of you holding a baby. Who admittedly looks like Billy as a baby. Or perhaps it even *was* Billy. Our boys were in the special care unit together. They were born on the same day. Which explains the date, of course. But that doesn't prove—'

'The babies were next to each other, weren't they?' Daniel cut in. 'Midwives are extremely busy. It wouldn't surprise me if Mary handed you the wrong baby by mistake.'

'Mary, that's right,' I echoed, surprised he'd remembered the midwife's name. 'She took you to see the babies, didn't she? Poor woman. She was looking after an entire ward of new mums practically by herself. No wonder she picked up Billy instead of Sean.'

'Seriously?' Eve rolled her eyes. 'I thought a picture would make things easier for you.' She glanced around the kitchen, her eyes lingering on a few framed sketches, before she wandered over to look at a watercolour of the Thames – a view of the river from our apartment that I'd painted as a 'new home' gift for Daniel. 'You're an artist, aren't you?'

'Graphic designer,' I said tightly.

'Same difference. You like pictures. You told me that when we were in hospital, remember? About how you can *see so much* in them. How they *reveal the truth* in people.'

She reached up to the canvas, tracing a finger over the colourful houseboats I had spent hours working on. There was a space between them – a gap that Jack and Eve's canal boat now filled. Turning towards the window, I thought back to the first time I'd noticed the distinctive vessel.

It had been a typical Saturday morning, with Billy and I sharing our toast while Daniel went for his run. Afterwards, we'd wandered down to feed our leftover crusts to the ducks and make up stories about the mysterious strangers who lived on the houseboats. Nothing I could have imagined about Eve's would *ever* have come close to the truth.

The truth. I still wasn't sure what that was.

161

'I was talking about art,' I snapped. 'Not a quick Polaroid taken by an overworked, over-busy midwife. Presumably it *was* Mary who took the photo? You had no other visitors.'

Nor did I, I thought, remembering my disappointment when Bea hadn't responded to my text that I'd had a baby. I only found out that she'd had *hers* by reading an announcement in *The Times*, shortly after we'd moved into our new apartment.

Billy was born two weeks early, which meant that Bea and I must have fallen pregnant around the same time, I realised, frowning as I grappled with dates, thinking again about that weekend . . . when either the IVF had finally worked, or Finley's condom hadn't – and he'd made me pregnant.

'You're right. I had no visitors.' Eve strode back to the breakfast bar, setting down her mug and drumming her fingers on the granite surface, and it seemed to me she was deliberately drawing attention to her hands, painting another picture for me of the physical connection between her and Billy. 'But you're wrong about Mary. She handed me the right baby.'

'I'm sure we'll be able to find her and verify that,' Daniel said tersely.

'She retired years ago. But if you're up for a wild-goose chase . . .'

'There's no need to be facetious, young lady.'

'Hey, I'm not the one who's done something wrong here.' Eve glared at Daniel. 'I'm trying to put it *right*. But we can do it the hard way, if you like. Involve the authorities. I'm sure Billy would love a ride in a cop car.'

'No!' My heart started to race as I pictured my little boy being driven away by the police. 'Please, let's slow down. I need to think this through. You can't just turn up out of the blue making demands. We're a *family*. Billy's our boy.'

'No, he's *my* boy. And like I said, I want him back.'

Despite my good intentions, I felt rage boil up inside me. 'Over my dead body!'

Chapter 31

I ran from the kitchen to the living room, desperate to hold Billy. Daniel reached out to stop me, but I brushed his hand away.

I badly needed his comfort, only I was reluctant to accept it while I still had questions to ask *him*. For one thing, he still hadn't explained why it had taken him so long to return from his run this morning. I was still half-convinced he'd been with *Bea* all that time.

I had been so completely on the back foot since making my confession this morning, preoccupied by fear for Billy, and then Eve, as well as battling my own guilt, but after recalling the events of the christening weekend, I was beginning to worry that Finley might have been right to hint at something going on between Daniel and Bea.

If Daniel is foolish enough to throw away his marriage for Bea . . . That's what Finley had said, and I'd convinced myself he was talking nonsense.

Throughout our former friendship, I'd noticed flirtatiousness between Daniel and Bea – mostly on her side – but I had never seriously suspected an affair. When Bea had claimed to be meeting him in secret to plot my birthday surprise, that Friday at work, I'd believed her; when Daniel had insisted he wanted to move house to get away from her, I hadn't doubted him.

Only, the timing of Bea's pregnancy was beginning to niggle: Ophelia must surely have been conceived very close to that weekend . . . when I'd seen Bea hurrying away from our hotel room. She'd claimed to have got her directions muddled up. *Had she been lying?* Was that what she and Finley had *really* argued about that weekend?

I wondered again if Daniel's impatience with Bea was simply a smokescreen – that they were both playing a game for which only they knew the rules. Perhaps Bea's 'urgent' voicemail was yet another strategic move in that secret game. After all, she still hadn't answered any of my calls, or phoned me back.

Was that because she'd already achieved her goal? Maybe her message had been intended purely to scare me into making my confession to Daniel about having slept with Finley, to give him the concrete reason he needed to leave me – and get together with Bea.

Finley had fanned the flames of suspicion about them, but at some level I must have always had my doubts, and they were pressing to the forefront of my mind now. *Daniel* had been the one to insist we move to Kew. But Bea had followed, moving to nearby Richmond, barely ten minutes' drive away.

Had the move been a secret plan between them to throw me and Finley off the scent of their affair? What other possible reason could Daniel have had to be so adamant about us leaving Greenwich? In such a hurry, too, only a few days after Billy had been born.

One thing Finley said earlier was definitely true: Daniel *did* always hold his cards close to his chest. Looking back to the day we'd moved into our new apartment, I wondered what secrets lay hidden in those cards . . . and the more I wondered, the louder alarm bells began to ring in my head.

Chapter 32

'So *this* is how the other half live,' I joked, adjusting the baby carrier strapped to my chest, shifting Billy so that he could look at the grand entrance hall of the enormous apartment – even though, at only a few days old, he was mostly either asleep or gazing at my face.

'Stunning, isn't it?' Daniel strode ahead of me along the polished walnut hallway. 'We've both worked hard. I reckon we deserve a bit of luxury. Don't you?'

I peeped into a kitchen gleaming with granite and stainless steel, before following Daniel back down the hall into a huge living room, staring in awe at the tall white walls and sweeping expanse of windows that overlooked the River Thames, gliding beneath Kew Bridge.

'It's certainly beautiful,' I agreed. 'Bit cold, though.'

'Maybe because it's unoccupied. The previous owners worked in the City, too. They left a few weeks ago, to take up jobs abroad.'

'No, I meant impersonal. Beautiful but sterile. Don't you think?'

'I believe the correct estate agent speak is *blank canvas*.' Daniel stood in the middle of the high-ceilinged room, hands on his hips, grinning like a Cheshire cat. 'All ready and waiting for someone to transform it into whatever they want it to be.'

'Reinvent their life, you mean,' I teased. I couldn't disagree that the penthouse was luxurious, but I felt no immediate connection to it – not in the way I'd loved our Georgian townhouse the second I walked into the cosy kitchen, instantly imagining Christmas dinners cooked on the Aga, happy family meals around the stripped oak table. 'What's wrong with the one we have? Besides, I love our house.'

Admittedly, it was impractical – and a money pit. We had damp in the cellar, a tiny courtyard for a garden and no parking. All of the sash windows needed replacing, too. But it was the first real home I'd ever had, and I adored the quirky character of its imperfections far more than the pristine flawlessness of this vast white box at the top of a shimmering glass tower.

Daniel shrugged. 'So do I. But then there's the rising damp, leaky boiler, not to mention three rickety flights of stairs to carry all his lordship's stuff up.'

I kissed Billy's soft head. 'I don't mind. I'm happy there. I thought you were, too?' I said quietly, picturing the gorgeous nursery Daniel had only just furnished, secretly and lovingly.

We were already making memories there; little pieces of our soul had been absorbed into the bumpy walls and rickety floorboards of the tiny but homely room where I spent hours nursing Billy, daydreaming while he slept, reading him stories when he woke up.

'*Were*. Exactly. That's precisely the point. I *was* happy there. It was perfect when it was just us. But we're a family now. We're going to need somewhere with more space. A bit more modern and practical. And we can afford it, now I've had my first vice-presidential pay rise.' Daniel chuckled.

'Hmm. Someone's very proud of themselves.'

'I've sweated blood for that bank. I want us to enjoy reaping the rewards. Is there anything wrong with that?'

'Nothing at all. If you *really* want us to look for somewhere bigger . . .' I swallowed my own disappointment as I saw the eager pride on his face. 'I've passed a few lovely houses on the other side of Greenwich Park. There's no rush, is there?'

'None at all. Except, well, I thought . . . I hoped . . . what with Billy being born . . .'

Surprised to see Daniel falter – he was never lost for words – I crossed the living room to give him an awkward hug, with Billy wedged between us.

'What is it, Dan?' Anxiously, I took hold of his hand.

'We've waited so long to have our little boy, Ruth. I want us to have a fresh start.'

I frowned. 'But we can have that in *our* house, can't we?'

'A *completely* fresh start,' he emphasised. 'Well away from . . . OK, I'll spell it out, if I must. Away from Beatrice and Finley. They're always breathing down our necks.'

'They used to be,' I pointed out. 'We actually haven't seen them for ages. *Months*. Not since . . .' I chewed my lip, trying to remember. 'I'm pretty sure the last time we saw them was that weekend in the New Forest. You know, the christening for John and Maxine's baby?'

'Right. Yes. Sure. I remember.' Abruptly, Daniel turned away and began busying himself examining the fixtures and fittings around the vast room.

'I've tried to call Beatrice. I've texted her loads of times. I even sent an invitation to *Billy's* christening.' I rolled my eyes. 'Not that we got one to Ophelia's.'

'Ophelia?'

'That's what they've called their baby. I read the birth announcement in *The Times*.'

Daniel stared at me. 'They announced it in *The Times*? Who the hell *does* that?'

'Beatrice, apparently. Odd considering she wanted to keep the pregnancy quiet. Then again, she's always loved bragging about her achievements.' I pulled a face. 'Ophelia. Pretty name, hey?' I tried to smile, but I'd been deeply shocked at the time.

'Isn't that the name *you* always wanted?' Daniel said crossly. 'If we had a girl, I mean. And Beatrice knew that, didn't she? It's why she bought us . . . I mean, it's why she gave you that Klimt painting. Honestly, that woman.' He tutted. 'What a bloody cheek.'

'Well, what's done is done. And we've got our gorgeous boy, anyway.' I nuzzled Billy's head again, inhaling his newborn scent. 'I wouldn't swap him for a dozen girls.'

'But Beatrice didn't *know* we were having a boy, *did* she? I certainly never said so.'

I frowned. 'Oh. Have *you* seen her, then?'

'No. Not for ages. Not since, er . . . probably that christening weekend, as you say.' Daniel strolled towards me again, a grin on his face now. 'Which suits me fine. Like I say, things were getting claustrophobic. We all needed a change.'

'This would certainly be a big one.'

'Yes. But it'll be good for us. Look at this place! It's incredible.'

I stared at the huge windows. 'The view is definitely spectacular. I'd love to paint it.'

'And so you can. Every day, if you like.'

'But the upheaval,' I worried. 'This little chap takes all my attention. Don't you, sweetie pie?' I crooned, as Billy opened his eyes and stared up at me. 'What big, brown eyes you have,' I sang, lulling him back to sleep when he started to whimper.

'No need to worry about packing. A removal firm does the lot. In fact, it's all sorted.'

'*Sorry?*'

'All you need to carry is this little fella.' Daniel patted Billy's back. 'And your new front door keys, of course.' He dug into his suit pocket, then held up a shiny bunch of them.

'Wait. Are you telling me . . .?' My heart was thumping; I

couldn't believe he would have made such an enormous decision without consulting me first.

'The apartment's ours, Ruth,' he confirmed. 'I signed the paperwork yesterday.' He leaned forward to give me a kiss. 'Happy new home, darling.'

'But our house . . .' I stared up at him in bewilderment. Then I saw the excited, proud expression on his handsome face, and I bit back my protest. I could see how much this move meant to him. I felt surprised and hurt, but I knew Daniel's heart was in the right place.

He worked so hard – he wanted to give me and Billy everything. It was old-fashioned, but sweet, and I loved him for his generosity. I cuddled Billy tighter, reflecting that in becoming a mum, my own biggest dream had already come true. If living in a penthouse overlooking the Thames was *Daniel's* dream, I felt churlish saying it wasn't mine.

'Buyer is ready to move in as soon as we move out,' Daniel said. 'Good surprise?' He smiled hopefully. 'Bad surprise?' he added, looking crestfallen as he watched my face.

'Yes. No. Just a very big one.' I forced a smile.

'Well, size matters,' Daniel quipped, buoyed up again now. 'Plus, there's a private lift. Not to mention an underground car park. Twenty-four-hour caretaker by the name of Arthur.' He grinned. 'State-of-the-art security systems. Oh, did I mention the view?' He wrapped an arm around me, urging me towards the window.

'It feels like we're in the clouds,' I murmured, watching a flock of birds fly past.

'Precisely. Our very own palace in the sky. Nothing and no one can get to us here, Ruth. We're untouchable.'

Chapter 33

As I gave Billy one last cuddle, it was on the tip of my tongue to ask him if Daddy had ever taken him to see *Aunty Bea*, as he called her, alone, without me. I couldn't shake the thought that her house in Richmond, ten minutes up the road from our apartment, was where Daniel had guessed Billy might be, after he'd gone missing . . .

But I didn't want to worry Billy; all I'd ever wanted was to give him a happy life. If Daniel was having doubts about sharing that life with me, he needed to say so. *No more secrets.* I wanted the truth, and as soon as things were resolved with Billy, I would demand it.

'If this is all so straightforward, why didn't *you* bring the police? Or a lawyer?' I heard Daniel say as I returned to the kitchen, leaving Billy to play with his new favourite train.

I saw Daniel step quickly away from Eve, and I groaned as I realised they'd been arguing the whole time I was out of the room. I hated this conflict in our home; it wasn't doing *any* of us any good, least of all Eve, by her pained expression.

170

'I didn't have time to arrange one,' she said, her pale face flushed and blotchy now. 'I only saw your photo last week. It didn't take me long to find you, but Jack had to sort out mooring rights for the boat.' She huffed. 'People always think boats can go anywhere, but there's so much paperwork. Records to fill in. A whole history of names, dates, times—'

'Presumably you looked up the bank where I work.' Daniel frowned as he held up a hand, cutting her off. 'You must have found a phone number. Why didn't you just *call* me?'

'I wanted to see Billy first. To be sure. But if you'd like to give me your number now.' She took a phone out of her pocket, dangling it between her fingers.

'Oh. That's *mine*.' Immediately, I recognised the sunflower case with a cracked corner: Billy had broken it last week, and I hadn't got around to replacing it. 'I thought I'd lost it,' I said, wondering how on earth Eve had got hold of it.

'You did. When you ran away from me at the school. And I found it.'

'It wasn't actually you I was running away from,' I muttered, still thinking about Bea.

'When you ran away from your guilty conscience, then.'

I held out my hand. 'Please. Just give it back.'

'I haven't finished with it yet. I've been enjoying the pictures of Billy.' She started swiping through them. 'You really should set a passcode on your phone, you know?'

'Give it *back*,' I said, more sharply now. I couldn't bear the thought of Eve looking through my private everyday snaps – little moments with Billy that I'd wanted to capture for myself. It felt like she was invading my life – my *family*.

'Sure.' Eve tucked the phone into her pocket. 'Once you've given back my son.'

*

'Billy's hand condition is pure coincidence,' Daniel said five minutes later, as we sat awkwardly together on the leather ottoman in the hall, watching through the open door as Billy played with Eve in the living room. 'Tests will prove he's ours.' He frowned. 'Well, yours.'

'Yours, too, hopefully.' I bit my nails. 'I know what happened with Finley—'

'I'd rather not talk about it,' Daniel cut in. 'Let's focus on Billy first. Our marriage later.' He gave me a sideways glance, but it wasn't unfriendly.

'Sure.' *I had a long list of questions already lined up for him.*

'By the way, you were right to try the gentle approach with Eve. Talking to her on the boat – on her home ground. That was a smart move. She isn't responding to, uh, tough talk.'

'Well, letting her play with Billy – giving her a chance to get it out of her system. That's a good idea, too,' I acknowledged politely.

'I guess we'll find out.' Daniel folded his arms across his chest, glaring at Eve.

'You really think it's a coincidence?' I whispered. 'Eve claimed the syndactyly is genetic. *Hereditary*. But she could have noticed it in that magazine photo, couldn't she?'

'Exactly my thought. Then conveniently incorporated it into her story. For a bit of extra colour and authenticity,' Daniel sneered.

He was still insisting Eve was a blackmailing con artist; I knew in my heart it wasn't money she wanted. I stared at her, sitting cross-legged on our living-room floor. She was smiling, but I remembered her raw grief after she'd been told her baby wasn't going to survive.

The idea that it had been *my* baby who had died was so unbelievably painful, not to mention far-fetched, that I had so far refused even to dwell on the possibility. Now, with Billy safe in our home, and Eve under our watchful eye, I allowed myself to unpick Eve's claims.

'I wish I could remember what he looked like.' I sighed, leaning back against the wall.

Daniel stared straight ahead. 'Who?'

'The other baby boy. Our *son*?'

'*Billy* is our son.'

'I must have seen him,' I continued, tormenting myself for a moment with the possibility that Eve was right. 'Like you said, he was right next to Billy in special care. I didn't really notice him. Did *you*?'

'Newborn babies all look pretty much the same.'

'They had identity bracelets, though.' I shook my head. 'I just don't get how, or when, a switch would even have taken place.'

'Mistakes happen.'

'What?' I turned to stare at Daniel in shock. 'You think it *was* a mistake, then?'

'It's . . . possible,' he admitted for the first time.

'Oh my God. But *how*?' I clasped my hands together to stop them shaking.

'Busy hospitals, overworked staff. You've seen the headlines. Patients dying on beds in corridors, left unnoticed for hours.' His eyes were still fixed on Billy.

'That's exactly it. You read about things like this in the tabloids. Babies switched at birth. Reunited with their birth parents years later. Only there *is* no other child. We can't just swap back.' I felt like there was a rock pressing on my chest.

'No,' Daniel agreed, a muscle in his cheek twitching.

'You really think there's a chance our son might be *dead*?' I croaked.

'All I know is that we're not giving Billy up. We've come this far, Ruth.' Daniel's fists clenched. 'I'm not turning back now.'

'Turning back? From *what*?'

'I meant turning my back on Billy. Giving up on him.'

'What if we're not given a choice? I know what Social Services are like. They act first and ask questions later.'

173

'No judge is going to hand over a child to a complete stranger.'

'But what if Eve *is* his mother?' I said faintly, hardly able to believe the words coming out of my own mouth. 'How did she get that photo with him, for instance? Why would the midwife have let her take a picture with *our son*?'

'No idea. I was at your bedside on the postnatal ward the whole time, remember? In any case, biology isn't the be-all and end-all. It doesn't remotely qualify anyone to be a good parent.' Daniel's mouth twisted. 'In every way that counts, Billy's better off with us.'

'So our defence is that we're rich and Eve's poor?' I frowned, watching her tease Billy, biting my lip as I saw him laughing in response. 'Billy doesn't love us because we give him toys and live in a penthouse, Daniel. Material stuff is the *least* important consideration here.'

'I don't disagree. But you're a good mum, Ruth.' At last, he turned to look at me.

The compliment brought more tears. In normal circumstances, I wouldn't have needed his affirmation that I was a good parent; now I found myself clinging on to it. I had always done my best for Billy. I wanted what was best for *him*, even more than for myself.

'And you're a good dad,' I admitted, wondering how we'd got from worrying that Finley might be Billy's father, to fearing that I wasn't his mum, either.

'You dreamed of having a child for years. You *wanted* this.'

'I did. I *do*. But what about Billy?' I watched him build a bridge out of train track, loving his imaginative play, hating the thought of not seeing it every single day, missing seeing him grow up and all the thousands of mundane but infinitely special moments of our everyday life together – the deeply layered bond that was already rock solid between us.

'He loves us. We love him. What more is there to say?'

'Eve has *plenty* to say,' I pointed out.

'I'm not giving up on our son, Ruth,' Daniel hissed. 'Even if you are.'

I gasped, then forced a fake smile as Eve looked up, not wanting her to see the tension between me and Daniel. Our marriage was rapidly falling apart – exactly as Bea had intended when she left that voicemail, I suspected – but I didn't want Eve to know that.

'Of course I'm not,' I said through gritted teeth. 'Eve is wrong. But it's obvious she's not just going to drop this. If she reports us to the police, you could lose your reputation. Maybe even your job. She might sue *us* as well as the hospital.'

'She can only sue if there's a basis in fact. Which there isn't. And I don't give *that*' – Daniel clicked his fingers – 'for my job. Nothing is as important to me as Billy.'

At one time, he would have added: *and you*. This whole situation had torn us apart, I realised, and I had a bad feeling the worst was yet to come.

'Shh. I don't want Billy to see us fighting. I don't want him unsettled. Or confused. Even though I am. Totally,' I admitted tearfully.

'Then let me make things crystal clear,' Daniel said in a low, hard voice. 'We may or may not have lost one son, but I refuse to give up another. I don't care what it costs me. Or what I have to do. Whatever it takes, I want Eve gone. By the end of the day.'

Chapter 34

My entire body tensed as I turned to see Daniel's stony expression: a rich, successful man accustomed to getting whatever he wanted. Jobs. Promotions. Penthouse apartments. *A son?*

Having a child hadn't just been my dream, I reflected; it had been Daniel's, too. And after all the failed IVF attempts we'd endured, he had promised me that, this time, we would bring home a child. He'd sworn on his own *life* that it would happen.

Telling him I needed a glass of water, I hurried to the kitchen. I wasn't thirsty; I just needed space away from him to think. Pulling up a bar stool, I laid my pounding head down on the cool granite breakfast bar, casting my thoughts back to the day Billy was born, trying to remember everything that had happened.

I wanted to denounce Eve as a liar and an imposter, but something nagged at the back of my mind. She'd pointed the finger of blame squarely at Daniel, but he had barely flinched, which reminded me how easily he'd lied about seeing Finley last night. I was also beginning to suspect he'd lied about his feelings towards Bea, too.

Daniel was an expert at putting on a front. Perhaps because of his military training, I pondered, once again remembering Finley say how he always kept his cards close to his chest. Feeling increasingly anxious, I found myself questioning what else Daniel might be hiding.

*

I'd been re-organising my hospital bag for the hundredth time, on the afternoon I went into labour. Sitting at the kitchen table in our old house in Greenwich, I could barely move for the stacks of cardboard boxes around me. Daniel had ordered every gadget on the market: baby monitors and swing chairs, play mats and sterilisers.

But while his mind was on practicalities, mine was on choosing the perfect first outfit for our baby. My bag was so full of clothes for him, there was hardly any room for mine.

'You still have two weeks to go, you know?' Daniel strolled into the kitchen, grinning.

'Yes, I know. But I can't relax unless everything's absolutely ready. I've been feeling a bit crampy today. It's giving me the jitters. What? Why are you laughing?'

'I thought Beatrice was the control freak, but you sound just like her. I, um, I take it you haven't heard from her?'

'No, not for ages. I even knocked on their door the other day. No one there. Or at least no one answered.'

I tried not to sound as hurt as I felt. Daniel had actually seemed much happier now we weren't 'living in our friends' pockets', as he'd described it. I didn't want to admit that I missed them sometimes. Especially Bea.

'Ah, well. They won't be able to complain when we're not available for babysitting.'

'Sorry?' I almost fell off my chair in shock. 'Beatrice is *pregnant*? But she never wanted . . . How do you . . .? Have you heard from *Finley*, then?'

Daniel sat down at the table, picking up a sleepsuit. 'Nope. Max, one of the guys at the squash club, mentioned it. Sorry, I forgot to say.' He tucked the sleepsuit in my bag.

'Oh my God. I can't believe she hasn't *told* me. I texted her as soon as I knew the IVF had worked. She never replied.' I shook my head, feeling sad. 'So, uh, when is the baby due?'

'No idea. Max didn't say.' Daniel screwed up his face. 'Come to think of it, I seem to recall him saying it was all a bit hush-hush. I think I was supposed to keep it under my hat.'

'Really? That doesn't sound like Beatrice, either.' I frowned, worried about her.

'Maybe they haven't made up their mind yet. If they want to keep the baby, I mean.'

'*No*. I can't believe Beatrice would . . .' I took out my phone, deciding to call her. *Again*. I couldn't even remember why we'd stopped talking, but I had been so preoccupied with my pregnancy that I'd lost track of time passing. Once again, though, the call rang out, as it always did, without even going to voicemail.

'Shit. I feel bad now.' Daniel ran a hand across his hair as he watched me.

'Why? You're not the one keeping baby secrets.'

'No, just blowing them.' He winced. 'Anyway, while I'm on a roll, I guess I might as well blow another one.'

'Sorry?'

'Ah, patience, Ruth. Close your eyes and come with me.' Reaching for my hand, he hauled me to my feet, guiding me through the stacks of cardboard boxes cluttering the kitchen.

'What's going on?' I laughed nervously as he helped me up the steep, narrow stairs.

'Ta-dah. Open your eyes and see.'

I almost dropped to the floor when I saw where we were standing: in the middle of what had always been Daniel's study but was now filled with dozens of soft toys, plus a bookstand stocked with brightly coloured storybooks. A pile of blankets was heaped at the end of the white-painted cot, with a small mountain of baby clothes stacked on a nursing chair.

I looked around in astonishment. 'Oh, Daniel. It's really happening, isn't it? We're actually having a baby. *Our little boy.*'

'Hey, don't rush him. We don't want him coming out until he's fully cooked.' Daniel wrapped his arms around me, his big hands cradling my belly.

'Ouch.' A sharp pain in my side made me jump.

'What is it?' Daniel snatched his hands away as though he'd hurt me. 'Are you OK?'

'It's just these cramps. I think they might be getting worse.'

'Hey, little man. You stay in there a while longer. Daddy says so. And what I say, goes, OK?' Daniel added, bending over and pretending to address his instructions to my baby bump.

I laughed. 'Oh, *really*?'

'Absolutely. We're bringing our boy home, Ruth. I swear to you on my life. Forget about Beatrice and Finley. The past is over and done with. Onwards and upwards. Nothing and no one can stop us now.'

Chapter 35

The next few hours were a blur of activity, as the first sharp cramps intensified into contractions which had me doubled over in pain. Daniel never left my side, and I kept my eyes on him throughout the caesarean operation, taking strength from his steady blue gaze.

The midwife briefly passed my new son in front of me, but even as I tried to imprint the image of his tiny, screwed-up face on my brain, I was gripped by panic at the sight of his blue-grey skin, the spindly arms that hung limply at his side. Any sound he made was swallowed by the oxygen mask quickly clamped to his face.

I begged for one last look, just one touch, but the midwife whisked him away. After giving me a hasty kiss, Daniel followed closely behind her, but it was to be hours before I saw either him or my baby again. Each second felt like an eternity, and I was thankful that I had Eve for company as we both waited nervously for news of our baby boys.

*

The corridor was packed when I finally got the all-clear to visit the special care unit, Daniel pushing my wheelchair frustratingly slowly.

'So many people,' I said, feeling claustrophobic.

Daniel huffed. 'I know. Like having a baby is so easy, anyone can do it.'

'Look, they're taking their baby out into the world for the first time.' Wistfully, I watched a couple smile at each other, eyes shining as they held a car seat between them.

'Our turn next.' Daniel reached down to squeeze my shoulder. 'In fact, here we are.' He spun my wheelchair around with a grand flourish as we finally arrived at the small, crowded reception area for special care. 'Are you ready to meet your son, Mrs Cartwright?'

'Let's have a quick word with the doctor first, shall we? Check everything's OK.'

I closed my eyes, remembering how delicate, how poorly my little boy had looked after he was born. Suddenly doubting myself, I realised how little I knew about looking after a premature baby, albeit that he'd only been born two weeks early. My antenatal classes had concentrated on caring for a full-term newborn, and I was terrified at the thought of doing something wrong. Daniel had no such doubts, though; he'd refused even to attend the classes, saying it was *our baby* and we would look after him *our way*.

'You talk to her, if you like,' he said gruffly. 'I can't wait a second longer.'

'What?' I opened my eyes to see him striding off. 'Dan, wait!'

But he was already gone, quickly following two doctors through the security-activated entrance to the special care unit, leaving me to stare after him as the doors closed.

'I've got one of those at home,' a woman sitting nearby said with a chuckle.

'Sorry?' I frowned at her. Dressed like me in a flowery blue hospital gown, she shifted uncomfortably in her wheelchair, looking like she was smiling through pain. After a few awkward moments, I recognised her as another mum from the postnatal ward.

'Controlling husband.' She rolled her eyes.

181

'Oh, right.' I laughed, too. 'Maybe a little. But I think he's anxious to make sure our baby's OK. It's our first, you see?'

'Fourth for us,' the other mum said. 'Never gets any less scary, though.'

I knew she was trying to be kind, but all I could think about now was seeing my baby for myself. Staring at the nurse behind the reception desk, I tried to catch her eye, but she was deep in conversation on the phone. I waited for a few minutes, but there was no sign of the call ending, so I looked around for someone else who might wheel me in to special care.

'Can *I* help?' a soft Irish voice said behind me.

I swivelled around to see a motherly face I also couldn't place for a moment. Medication still blurred my thoughts; my head felt muzzy. 'Oh! Mary. Sorry.'

'That's OK. You're used to seeing me on the postnatal ward. You too, Mrs Hall,' the midwife added, turning to the other mum. 'I'll take Mrs Cartwright in first, if that's OK? You saw your little girl yesterday. Ruth here hasn't even met her son. Does he have a name yet?'

'Yes. No. We, uh . . . we haven't made a final decision.' *I'd been too worried about something going wrong*, I thought, recalling Daniel constantly insisting we needed to pick a name, while I said I wanted to wait until I'd held my baby for the first time. Secretly, I wanted to call him Billy, after Daniel's late father, but I didn't want to share that with the midwife – not until I'd told Daniel.

'Well, no rush,' Mary said kindly. 'The doctor wrote "Baby Cartwright" on the notes for now. He's in good company. Plenty of little lambs in there still waiting for their parents to make up their minds. Anyway, how are you feeling, Ruth? Bit nervous?'

'A little. I wish Daniel . . . Oh, there he is. Daniel!' I called out, watching him re-emerge through the double doors. But he didn't seem to hear me, striding towards the waiting area further along the corridor, before slumping into a chair and resting his face in his hands.

'It's not uncommon for dads to have a delayed reaction to the stress,' Mary said kindly, following the direction of my gaze. 'I expect you've had a tense few days waiting to go into labour, haven't you? Then there's all the drama of being rushed into hospital.'

'Daniel was amazing.' I felt a surge of love for him, and tears pricked my eyes.

'Of course he was. It's the father instinct kicking in. Plus, don't forget, men are pretty much helpless bystanders for most of the pregnancy. Mums going into labour gives them something they can actually *do*. He's probably having an adrenaline crash, love.'

'You think?' I was still staring at Daniel, willing him to look my way.

'Absolutely. I see it every day. An emergency gives dads a focus. Dashing here and there, making sure everything is all right. Afterwards, they often feel a bit overwhelmed.'

'But everything's definitely OK with our baby?' I asked anxiously, panicking that Daniel's agitation was due to bad news he didn't want to tell me.

'Absolutely,' Mary assured me. 'I've been looking after him myself.'

'You have?' I perked up hearing that. 'And the doctor's happy with his progress?'

I turned as the two women in white coats Daniel had followed into special care also re-emerged through the doors. Strolling along the corridor, they seemed absorbed in intense conversation, although one of them paused to rest a hand on Daniel's shoulder.

'See?' Mary pointed out. 'That's the doctor. Everything's *fine*. She's already checked your boy over. Filled out her forms and whatnot.' She leaned over, rubbing my arm reassuringly. 'He's grand, love. Honestly. Your husband, too. He could probably do with a breather, that's all. Which is just as well, as it's your turn to have a mummy cuddle. Yes?'

'A mummy cuddle,' I echoed in wonder, as Mary began pushing

my wheelchair. I took one last look over my shoulder, but Daniel was still sitting in the waiting area, head in hands.

'It's been quite a day for you, hasn't it?' Mary said chattily.

'The best and the worst. The happiest and the hardest.' Conflicting emotions rampaged through me. I was excited, but also exhausted, mentally and emotionally, having waited not just for hours in the hospital but also for so many years, dreaming of this one, single moment.

'I hear you. That's the funny thing about this place. So many contrasts. Life, death. Joy, despair. Rush, rush, then hang around for hours.' Mary laughed. 'But you're doing brilliantly. So is your little man.'

'Are you sure?' I squeaked, my mouth drying as we entered the surprisingly bright, open ward. I'd been expecting something terrifying: babies hooked up to machines and wires. But while there was plenty of equipment, the calm, almost serenely peaceful atmosphere took me by surprise. 'Can I take him home *today*?'

'Not today. But soon. He's a tough cookie. A proper sweetheart. See for yourself.'

Mary gave another soft laugh, but my heart was pounding as she positioned my wheelchair in front of two cribs in the furthest corner of the ward. Gripped by momentary panic, I swivelled round to ask her which was my son, but she was already on her way out – no doubt heading off to speak to Mrs Hall, waiting impatiently outside to visit her own baby.

Turning back to the cribs, I braced my hands against the arms of the wheelchair, levering myself to my feet, trying to ignore how badly my legs were trembling.

'Hello, darling. Happy birthday,' I said softly, staring down at the first infant. 'You too, gorgeous,' I added, frowning as I looked into the next crib.

Side by side in their adjacent cots, both babies were dressed in white sleepsuits. Their bodies were tiny, their little pink faces crumpled, eyes closed and mouths pouting like rosebuds. I looked uncertainly from one to the other, blinking to clear my suddenly blurry eyes, trying to peer closer at the name tag around the tiny wrist of the baby closest to me.

'Don't be frightened, darling. Mummy's here,' I slurred thickly, grabbing hold of the side of the plastic crib. 'Precious boy. I've waited so long to meet you,' I murmured, seeing his eyes flicker open. 'Or you,' I said, muzzy with confusion as I glanced again at the other baby.

Reaching inside the crib, desperate for a cuddle, I gasped as a jolt of pain exploded deep inside me. My body felt like it was being sucked into the ground by a powerful magnet, while at the same time I felt weightless, as though I were about to float away.

'I just want to hold my boy,' I sobbed, but my hands were shaking uncontrollably as I reached for him, and in the next moment my knees buckled. 'Oh!' Slumping over the crib, it took all my strength to hold myself upright, not to crush the baby beneath me.

Darkness began to seep around the edges of my vision; I fought it, concentrating on a fleeting glimpse of black eyes peeping at me. 'Billy,' I crooned, desperately trying to focus on his tiny nose, his cherub mouth. But my head felt like it was spinning into space.

Finally, my legs gave way completely, and I sank back into the wheelchair. Nausea rushed up as the room went dark, and the next thing I knew, I was waking up in my bed on the postnatal ward with Mary saying my name, over and over, while Daniel sat on the end of my bed with a face like thunder.

Chapter 36

Three days later, Billy was thankfully given the all-clear to go home, but I barely slept during that whole time, worrying incessantly about what might still go wrong. Fear never left me, especially as Eve's baby continued to struggle in the high dependency unit.

She was a wreck – understandably so – and I did my best to comfort her, keeping her company as she filled the long hours of waiting for news with a constant stream of nervous chatter. 'I wished on a shooting star, once,' she told me. 'When I was a little girl.'

'What did you wish?' I asked, happy to indulge any distraction from her anxiety.

'I wished that, one day, I'd be able to give a child a better life than I've had.'

'That's a lovely wish. Sad, though. Although, I suppose I feel kind of the same.'

'Really?' She stared at me with wide, shadowed eyes.

'Yes. I've wanted to be a mum for ever. So has Daniel. Wanted to be a dad, I mean.'

'He seems nice,' Eve said quietly. 'Confident.' She chewed her fingernails, thinking for a moment before continuing. 'You guys won't mess up like I would have.'

'What? *No*, Eve. Don't lose hope.'

'Huh. Hope is for mugs. Me? I made a deal with the universe.'

'A deal?' I queried softly, sensing she needed the comfort of her little superstitions, now more than ever.

'Yeah.' She gripped her hands together, as though in prayer. 'I promised I'd forget about all the bad stuff that's happened in my life, if I could give my boy a better one. Good stuff cancels out the bad, you know? Like connecting a cosmic circle.'

'Wouldn't it be lovely if that could be true?'

'It *is* true,' Eve insisted, scowling. 'I'll prove it.'

'Of course,' I said quickly. 'I hope you do. I mean, I'm sure you will. Your little boy *will* get better, Eve. You'll give him a wonderful life. Don't lose faith. I only meant—'

'*You* don't need to worry, though. Your boy's a fighter. I could tell that as soon as he was born. He has his mum's fighting spirit.'

'Is that how you see me?' I was genuinely surprised.

'Totally. Look what you went through to have your baby!' Eve shook her head. 'I know what IVF is like. A teacher at my school had it. She was a fruitcake by the end.'

'Yes, well, I had a lot of support.' I sighed, thinking of Daniel, feeling bad that Eve was all alone. Not one single person had come to visit her in hospital.

'But you're his mum, Ruth. You made him. You shape what he becomes. You're strong, he'll be strong. You're kind, he'll be . . .' She tailed off, tears getting the better of her.

'I hope you're right.' I rubbed at my eyes, too, her tears having set off my own.

'I am. I know that for sure because I was in the same delivery suite as you.'

'Oh?' I looked at her in surprise; I hadn't known that.

'You went in as I came out. That's when it happened. Our souls touched, Ruth. Our boys', too. We're bonded, I tell you.'

'That's a nice thought,' I said, smiling through my tears.

'I just wish . . .'

I shuffled over to her bed, sitting down next to her. 'Tell me. What do you wish, Eve?'

'Doesn't matter. Huh, guess I'll have to wait for another shooting star.'

*

Later that day, after Eve had returned from visiting her son for the last time, her mood had darkened and she started lashing out. I'd understood that her rage wasn't really directed at me, and I did my best to comfort her again, letting her cry in my arms before settling her to sleep.

The curtains were still drawn around her bed when Daniel and I were finally able to take Billy home, and I'd felt bad leaving without saying goodbye. Then I remembered the young couple carrying their baby in his new car seat, and I knew Daniel was right: it would be kinder to let Eve sleep, rather than her having to watch the happy moment when we took our son out into the world . . . took him *home*.

Eve didn't even have a proper home, and tragically it seemed increasingly unlikely she would have a son. I'd wished I could have done more to help her; I even had the mad impulse again to take her home with me. The thought never entered my head that I'd taken home her little boy instead.

Chapter 37

I still wasn't sure what had happened. In one way, those intense days in the hospital remained vivid in my mind; in another, they were a blur of such mixed emotions that I couldn't work out what was real – and what I'd imagined. All I knew was that the babies had worn identity bracelets, and the neonatal unit was rarely quiet: people had been constantly milling around.

Plus, Billy had his 'magic fingers'. Although I had seen him only fleetingly after my caesarean, before fainting when Mary took me to visit him in special care, I'd seen him again soon after that and distinctly remembered noticing his webbed hand. An *accidental* mix-up seemed so unlikely, given Billy's unique physical characteristics.

As far as I was concerned, that left only two possibilities. First, and least likely in my mind, was that Eve was right and a crime had been committed. But I struggled to think how: only the doctors and midwives had direct access to the wards.

Admittedly, visiting times were chaotic, but only Daniel had visited me, no one had come to see Eve, and I doubted *anyone*

189

could swap two babies without the medical staff noticing.

Moreover, I was still far from convinced that such a swap had even taken place. Billy's syndactyly condition *could* have been a coincidence, I reminded myself. After struggling with grief for so long, it was possible that when Eve had seen Billy's photo in that magazine, she'd remembered their shared characteristic and had seized on it as false proof of something more.

The thought also reminded me of the deluded, possibly dangerous state of her mind. 'Are you sure it's safe to leave them alone?' I said, as Daniel joined me in the kitchen.

'I've double-locked the front door. Billy's going nowhere. Nor is Eve.'

His harsh tone made the hairs on the back of my neck prickle. 'How is he?'

'Fine. Actually, he's having fun. He wants Eve to stay for tea. I've told him she can spend the afternoon. Maybe that will help her get this . . . insanity out of her system.'

'If only it were that simple.' I sighed, swallowing hurt at the idea of Billy having fun with Eve; afternoons had always been *our* time for games and play.

'She can't replace you, Ruth,' Daniel said quietly. 'Billy has loved you his whole life.'

I shouldn't have been surprised that he'd picked up on my deepest anxiety, but with the continued tension between us, and all manner of suspicions festering in my mind, somehow it hadn't felt like he was still on my side.

It was a relief to feel some of our old affinity returning; it prompted me to confess the worry weighing most heavily on me. 'Shouldn't I have known?' I whispered.

Daniel flicked on the kettle, before turning back to look at me. 'Known what?'

'You said I've been a good mum. What's wrong with me that I never realised?'

'There's nothing wrong with *you*.' His voice was flat and hard. 'Eve is the crazy one.'

'Are you saying you still don't believe her, either?' My heart leaped with hope. 'It's still most likely that this is all a scam, isn't it?'

'Yes, Ruth.' Daniel let out a heavy sigh. 'I've said so all along, haven't I?'

'Billy's hand condition could be *coincidence*. Grief does terrible things to your mind. I should know,' I said huskily. 'That magazine article probably pushed Eve over the edge. Seeing the photo of Billy. It must have reminded her of him. Me. *Us*. Everything we have that she doesn't. She had to do *something*. Try anything.'

'Exactly. We can't let her get inside our heads.'

'It's not even that convincing,' I said, talking myself out of any lingering doubts. 'If Eve truly believed our babies were switched, why wait so long to do something? What kind of mother walks away from her own child?' *Bea had*, I remembered. She'd been young at the time, but I had never heard her mention her lost baby, and for a time we'd shared everything.

'Look.' Daniel spun my bar stool around, so that I was facing him. 'There's still a way out of this. Once Eve has spent time with Billy, she'll realise how being a parent would cramp her style. She lives on a boat. That's what *she's* always wanted. Or so she said. She likes her freedom. I'm sure we can find a way to . . . uh, convince her to disappear.'

A chill ran through me; I deliberately shrugged it off. Daniel had left the army years ago. He was a senior executive at an international bank; he wasn't a backstreet thug. He wouldn't harm Eve simply to make her go away.

'You mean a court battle?' I said, to be absolutely clear.

Daniel shrugged. 'Of course. What else?'

'Wouldn't blood tests be easier? Like you said, a DNA test would give us categorical proof.' I felt a flutter of panic at the thought that it might not give us the result *Daniel* wanted. 'Eve can't argue with science.'

'No. She can't. But things might still go to court. We'd have to prepare ourselves for that. The good news is that Eve is hardly a reliable witness. A young girl growing up on the streets.' He shook his head. 'No judge is going to hand over a child to someone like that.'

'Maybe.'

'Definitely. Ultimately, the courts would have Billy's best interests at heart.'

'I hope so.' It suddenly hit me why Eve had been so keen to get Billy on her boat. He had followed her on board easily, happily. Children were adaptable, and they were adopted all the time. Billy would survive. *I wasn't sure I would.*

I couldn't bear the thought of him living in a different home, with another mummy. I'd moved from foster family to foster family as a child, always feeling that something wasn't right. The sense of being an outsider had become embedded within me; I refused to let Billy grow up with that same feeling of *unbelonging*.

It tore me up to think of telling him I wasn't his real mummy; I ached at the thought of him wondering, even for a second, if I'd lied to him. *If I had stolen him.*

Once I'd admitted the worry to myself, I couldn't shake it off. 'Maybe I did know.'

'What?'

'What if Billy really *isn't* ours, but I've shut my mind to it? Buried it. What do they call it? Repressed memories. The mind blocking out something it doesn't want to recognise. They've done studies on that kind of thing, haven't they?'

'You're talking about major trauma.' Daniel turned to look at me. 'Damaged people who've endured something horrendous, their brains dissociating from triggering incidents. Or even shutting down memories entirely, to protect their sanity.'

'Isn't what I've been through traumatic enough? IVF is brutal. All those months, *years* of trying to have a baby, only to result in . . . you know.' *Ghost babies*, I thought, tormenting myself.

I knew I didn't have to spell it out more clearly – remind Daniel of how many times I'd convinced myself I was pregnant . . . the frantic, hopeful trips to hospital, always ending the same way: with grave-faced doctors proposing a psychiatric referral.

Daniel had been right there, every step of the way, patiently carrying me through my agony, forever masking his own.

'I would have done *anything* to have a child,' I said at last, when he continued to gaze silently, impassively at me. I drew in a breath. 'And so would you.'

Chapter 38

'Let me get this straight. You actually think I'm guilty. That's what you're saying? That Eve is right. I saw our baby wasn't going to make it in hospital, and I switched him with hers?'

I forced myself not to take a step back, either from Daniel's tall body towering over me, or from the confrontation I knew had been brewing for hours – from the moment I'd made my confession. Daniel had withdrawn into his thoughts ever since, but I'd known he was silently working everything through, his clever mind weighing up options before deciding what action to take. He was a planner. A *fixer*.

'You weren't shocked, were you? When I told you what Eve said in the playground.'

'Wasn't I?'

I shook my head. 'You just called her "another screwball woman".'

'Which she is.'

'But the thing is, Daniel, I know you lied to me. About who you spent yesterday evening with. It makes me wonder what else

194

you might not have been strictly honest about.'

'Strictly honest.' He frowned. 'Honesty has no half measures, Ruth. You either tell the truth, or you lie. And I've *never* lied to you.'

'One of us has to be guilty.'

'And you've decided it's me. Have I understood that correctly?'

'Finley told me—'

'Finley.' Daniel rolled his eyes. 'Am I *never* to be free of that leech? Look, I told you, he *asked* me not to say anything. I'd even go so far as to say that he *begged* me not to. God knows why. He didn't want to worry you, I guess. Nor did I. Huh. More fool me.'

'I guess I deserve that. But I'm not a child. You should have told me about seeing Finley. And *he* should have told me before about Bea's fixation. Still, at least I know now.'

'Likewise,' Daniel snipped, folding his arms.

'Sure,' I said guiltily. 'Although, I, uh . . . I have a feeling I don't know the full story when it comes to Bea.' *Like, have you been having a secret affair with her for years?*

'How much more do you need to know? She's always been a nightmare. It's a miracle Finley's put up with her this long. He's divorcing her. Did he tell you *that*?'

'He mentioned that he'd moved out.'

'About time. He's put up with enough shit from her.'

I frowned, wondering if this was yet another part of Daniel's smokescreen. Only this morning, he'd talked about Finley playing games – using Bea to cover up his own mistakes. Now he seemed to be blaming Bea. 'Well, there are always two sides to every story.' *Or, in our case, several*, I thought bitterly, despairing that I didn't know *who* to trust.

'I'm sure Bea has conjured up a good one,' Daniel scorned.

'If she has, I haven't heard it yet. Have *you*?' I probed, hoping to catch him out.

'I've told you before, Ruth. I'm not interested in anything that nutcase has to say. I'm surprised you are, given this weird fixation she has on you.'

195

Perversely, the more Daniel criticised Bea, the more sceptical I became: about his true feelings for her, and about the obsession I only had Finley's word was even a thing.

I know what happened that night, Bea had said in her message. Earlier, I'd feared what she might do in revenge; now, I was desperate to know why, so far, she had done precisely nothing. I knew she'd had a spa day yesterday – but surely she was home by now?

'You really think the same as Finley, then?' I said slowly. 'That Bea wants to be me?'

'I'm a banker, Ruth, not a psychologist. All I know is that she's always been too much in our faces. It's why I wanted us to move away from Greenwich in the first place. To get you as far away from her as possible.'

Or as far away from the hospital – the scene of the crime? I thought fleetingly, casting my mind back again to that time, trying to unravel the truth. But every thread I unpicked seemed to lead to Bea. 'Maybe it wasn't *me* that Bea wanted to be around.'

There. I'd said it. Feeling my heart start to pound, I slid off the bar stool, crossing the kitchen to sit down at the kitchen table, needing to put distance between me and Daniel.

'Bea doesn't fancy me,' he dismissed instantly. 'Never has.'

'And you don't fancy her?'

'What? *No.*'

I took a deep breath. 'So why was she in our hotel room, that weekend in the New Forest? I *saw* her, Daniel,' I said, when he looked startled. 'I saw Bea coming out, just as I was going in. Two minutes later, I found that blasted condom in the bathroom bin.'

'She . . .' He ran a hand across his hair. 'Ruth, nothing happened. Honestly.'

'Bea followed you back to our room after breakfast. You were pacing up and down looking like you'd been handed a terminal diagnosis.' I wasn't going to let him off the hook. I'd made my confession; it was high time he made his.

'OK!' He held up his hands. 'Bea made a half-hearted pass at me. But that's as far as it went. I knocked her back, I swear. She was mad at Finley, that's all it was. It was just a way of trying to get back at him. Make herself feel better. Oh, who knows how her mind works.'

'You've never had an affair with her,' I persisted.

'Of course not.'

'Or any secret conversations.'

Daniel frowned. 'About what?'

'Bea mentioned a trip to Windsor at the weekend. How could she know about that?'

He shrugged. 'News to me. Look, I've never slept with Bea. I didn't steal Eve's baby. They're two screwball women, both cut from the same cloth. *Troublemakers.*'

'Sure,' I said doubtfully.

'I *told* you, we can't let them dictate our lives, Ruth. I refuse to be pushed around by either of them. It ends today.' He glanced over his shoulder, towards the kitchen door. The sound of Billy's laughter floated along the hallway outside. Daniel frowned. 'Right now.'

Chapter 39

I stared into Daniel's clear blue eyes, wishing and hoping I could believe him. He held my gaze and, for a few seconds, it almost felt like we'd turned back time on our relationship – to the days when everything was far less complicated. Before that stupid christening weekend. Before my confession. Before Eve decided to show up and make trouble . . .

Then his mobile rang, breaking the moment, making us both jump.

'Aren't you going to answer it?'

'It's not important.' He took it out of his pocket, glanced at it then turned it over, screen-side down on the breakfast bar.

It rang again. This time, Daniel didn't bother to check the number. He let it ring out, the phone vibrating against the granite. When it rang a third time, I stood up and reached for it. Daniel's hand got there first, but not before I'd seen the name flash up.

It was Bea.

Uncertainty rushed through me again. Daniel talked a good talk, but I had no way of corroborating his version of events.

Now here was Bea phoning him, when he'd spent the last six months – the last four *years* – saying he wanted nothing more to do with her.

'She wants to see *you*,' Daniel said, after I'd insisted he listen to her message, and there was the tiniest hint of vindication in his expression.

'Oh.' *Of course.* I'd been waiting for her to get in touch again. I didn't know why she hadn't answered my calls, but I knew full well what she wanted: *it was payback time.*

I took the phone, reminded that I still needed to get mine back from Eve. It had all gone very quiet in the living room. 'Check on Billy, would you?' I asked Daniel, waiting until he'd left the kitchen before tapping the screen to call up Bea's message.

The hairs at the back of my neck stood up as I heard her throaty voice.

'Danny, hi. I've been trying to get hold of Ruth. Can you ask her to meet me at Climbers and Creepers. Three o'clock? Loads of love. Oh, and it's urgent.'

Her message sounded breathless, and considerably less antagonistic than the one she'd left for me on our home phone. The 'loads of love' was galling but hardly indicative of a full-blown affair. Bea was always theatrically exuberant in her affection – except to me, these days.

I leaned my elbows on the kitchen table, feeling trapped in mistrust and indecision. Fleetingly, I wished I could speak to Finley and ask what he thought, but I didn't have his number, and I still had no idea where he was, or why he hadn't phoned *me* as promised.

He'd left the apartment saying he was going back to the house he'd shared with Bea before he moved out, to check if she and Daniel were together – which Bea's latest voicemail neither confirmed or disproved. After all, she could have seen Daniel earlier and forgot to tell him that she was trying to get hold of me: *to talk about that night.*

Daniel had insisted he'd been for a run this morning – and he was sticking to that story, despite his sports shorts and T-shirt being bone dry when he'd returned. Wanting to scream in frustration, I slammed the table with both hands, wishing I knew who to trust – and what to do.

The situation with Eve remained painfully unresolved, and I wanted to stay and work out what had happened in the hospital four years ago. But Bea's arch comments and unsettling message had tormented me for hours. She was clever. Unpredictable. *She still scared me.*

'You should go see her, Ruth. I'll sort things out here.'

I looked up to see Daniel watching me from the doorway; I hadn't heard him return, and I wondered how long he'd been standing there. 'If only that were possible.'

He leaned on the doorframe, his eyes piercing blue and harder than I had ever seen them. '*Anything* is possible, if you want it enough.'

Chapter 40

Twenty minutes later, I strode away from the Elizabeth Gate entrance to Kew Gardens, past Kew Palace, then cut across the grass towards the Climbers and Creepers play centre. I walked quickly, still worrying about Eve, and now about Daniel, the intensity I'd sensed in him.

Please don't let him do anything stupid, I prayed, and I was on the verge of turning back when I spotted a familiar taupe cashmere coat and strawberry-blonde ponytail.

'Bea!' I called out, making my way slowly, reluctantly, towards the bench in front of the playground where she was sitting.

'Oh. Ruth.' She looked up, sounding surprised, even though she'd been the one who had messaged asking to see me. Twice. 'How's Billy? Jules texted me he was sick.'

'He's better, thanks. Uh, Daniel's looking after him, so I can't be long.'

I didn't want to fill her in on the situation with Eve; it would take far longer than I intended to stay. I wondered if the mention of Daniel's name would provoke any reaction in her, but Bea seemed flat, almost uninterested, when I'd been expecting thunderbolts of fury.

'Sure,' she said wearily. 'You look cold. Fancy a coffee?'

'You said in your messages it was urgent, so . . .' I refused to play more games.

'Suit yourself.'

I checked my watch. 'Who's picking up Ophelia? And covering you at the gallery?'

'The nanny. And I've closed it. Only for a few days. Just while I sort a few things out.'

'Right.' I bit my lip, grimly suspecting *annihilate Ruth* was top of her list.

'I'm thinking of giving it up, actually. You should take it over.'

'Sorry?' I tensed, recalling Finley describing Bea's plan for us to become business partners and 'mirror mummies'. I wondered if this meeting was all part of her weird strategy.

'Well, you're far more knowledgeable about art than I am. You always were.'

'Oh. Right. Thanks.' It was the first time in six months that Bea had acknowledged our former friendship, and, unexpectedly, the reminder of how close we'd once been brought tears to my eyes. It also confused me. Ever since that first playdate, we'd both stuck to our scripts as supposedly *new friends*; now, once again, Bea had changed the rules without warning. 'That's kind of you, but what with school hours . . . and I've had a few art commissions.'

'Ah, that's great. Good on you.'

'Plus, I'm looking forward to hanging out with Billy after school.'

'I don't blame you. He's a cutie. Ophelia's *far* too pushy. Just like her father was.'

I stared at Bea, my confusion deepening. 'Sorry? *Was?*'

'Oh, Finley isn't Ophelia's dad.'

'He . . . *what*?' I stared at her. 'Then who *is*?'

Suspicion about her and Daniel returned in a rush, along with another flashback to Bea emerging from our hotel room that weekend. I also recalled Daniel's indignation about Bea choosing the name Ophelia for her daughter.

At the time, I'd thought he was upset on my behalf. Now I couldn't help wondering if it was because he was the father of Bea's child, and she'd named their baby without asking him.

'Some guy I met at a trade fair.' She shrugged. 'I can't even remember his name.'

'No way.' Bea was incredibly picky; a one-night stand didn't sound like her.

'Sorry if that shocks you.' She didn't *look* sorry; she looked like she was enjoying my reaction. Suddenly, the spark had returned to her eyes. 'Oh. I see,' she added slowly. 'Daniel isn't Ophelia's father, if that's what you're worrying about.'

'Well, I . . .' I felt myself blush, anger mingling with embarrassment. I may have jumped to the wrong conclusion, but that was due in no small measure to Bea's behaviour.

And Finley's, I thought, recalling his hints about Bea and Daniel earlier. An image also drifted across my mind of him pointedly toasting 'happy couples' that night in the hotel bar.

'No doubt it's my fault you're even thinking that,' Bea said intuitively. 'And I probably owe you an apology.'

That surprised me. 'Huh, really. For what, exactly?' *Sleeping with my husband?*

'For that wretched christening weekend. You know, at that hotel in the New Forest.'

I gritted my teeth, certain she was about to come to the point now: about me sleeping with Finley, her affair with Daniel. 'Sure,' was all I could manage to say.

'OK, confession time. I deliberately let you think I'd slept with Daniel that morning.'

'You . . . *what*?' I almost fell off the bench in shock. 'You deliberately . . . Hang on, I saw you coming out of our room. Are you telling me you *staged* that?'

'I planted a condom in your bin, too.'

'Shit.' I stared at her in disbelief. 'Why?'

'Because Daniel rejected me. Told me to get the hell out of your room. So I did. But not before I'd used the bathroom. My bladder was bursting. I was already pregnant, you see?'

Little fuckers ruin your whole life, I suddenly recalled Finley saying in the bar. All the time we were drinking together, talking about Bea never wanting children, Finley insisting he felt the same, he must have known she was already pregnant.

'And you knew for sure that Finley wasn't the father?'

'We'd stopped having sex by then.' Bea's lips pursed, as if the thought was distasteful.

'Oh. I see.' So that was why Finley had ducked out of the christening – why he'd got so drunk, I realised: Bea had been pregnant, and he knew the baby wasn't his.

I guessed that must also have been what their massive row was about that weekend, and although I felt pity for Finley, I also felt intense relief that Daniel wasn't the father of Bea's child, nor had they been having an affair. Clearly, Bea wanted to get back at me; I had no doubt she would take great delight in gloating about it if she and Daniel had slept together.

'Anyway, the morning sickness was horrendous. I puked my guts up in the toilet, looked around for breath freshener. Daniel's washbag was open, I spotted the condoms. Bit of soap, it looked like the real thing. It was just a silly, spiteful trick to stir up trouble.'

She had no idea how much trouble she'd caused. That condom was the sole reason I'd believed I slept with Finley – the root of all my agonising over the last two days.

I stared at Bea, struggling to take in what she'd done – and what the implications of it might be. If I *hadn't* had sex with Finley, there was zero chance that Billy could be his son.

'Why would you *do* that?' I croaked, feeling as though the world had just shifted on its axis once more, tipping all my theories upside down, leaving me more confused than ever.

Bea let out a long sigh. 'Because you fucked my husband, of course.'

Chapter 41

'Finley told me you didn't know.' I didn't bother to deny it; the look on Bea's face confirmed it would be pointless. In any case, my mind was too jangled to formulate a lie.

'Huh. Of course he did.'

'For what it's worth, I totally didn't mean to. I was so drunk that night, I wasn't even sure I *had*. Slept with Finley, I mean.'

Had I slept with him or not?

I still wasn't a hundred per cent sure, but the fact that Bea had planted that condom only increased rather than lessened my anxiety: if Finley and I *did* have sex that night, no condom meant Billy's paternity remained worryingly uncertain in my mind.

Bea smirked. 'I bet he was thrilled to know his performance was so forgettable.'

I ignored her jibe – Finley deserved it – but I registered that Bea seemed more her usual self now: spiky and acerbic. 'I haven't given that night a second thought for years,' I emphasised. 'Not until yesterday, in fact. Your, uh, comments in the playground set me thinking. About me having a guilty conscience. Adults taking responsibility for their mistakes.'

'Yeah. Sorry about that. I was pissed off at Finley. I guess I took it out on you.'

I thought of her message: *I know what happened that night.* 'What made him finally confess? I mean, *something* must have prompted him to tell you now?'

I'd wondered the same thing earlier: why had Finley suddenly wanted to get to know Billy? His confession to Bea and urge to hang out with my son had to be related. I was desperate to know the connection; I couldn't shake the feeling Daniel was the common factor.

'Oh, I've always known. Ever since that night. Finley couldn't *wait* to tell me. Actually, show me. Photos,' she clarified, when I stared blankly at her. 'On his phone.'

I felt sick. 'Oh my God. He took pictures.' *So it really happened. I slept with Finley.*

'I made him delete them, of course. But looking at them . . . I suppose I felt rage. I wanted to hurt you, too. Hence my clumsy attempt to seduce Daniel the next morning.'

I covered my face in my hands. 'I'm so sorry, Bea.'

'Oh, I'm over it now. But I admit I find it hard to let go of a grudge. When you turned up at my house for that first playdate six months ago . . .'

'You pretended not to know me.'

'I was still mad at you. For a while, anyway. Eventually, I softened.' She shrugged. 'I'd had a one-night stand myself. I could hardly take the moral high ground. Whatever, by then, Nish and Jules believed we'd never met. I'd have looked idiotic if I admitted I'd been acting.'

'You could have told *me*. I wish you had. And I wish I'd told *you* . . . well, about what happened that night. I wanted to. Actually, I tried to the next morning. When I saw you coming out of our hotel room. I guess I lost my nerve. I'm sorry.'

207

'Probably best you didn't, anyway. I might have chewed your head off,' Bea admitted.

'I did text you later. Loads of times, in fact. I sent you an invitation to Billy's christening. I heard nothing.'

'Finley intercepted all my mail. He blocked your number, too. I didn't realise at the time, of course. Yeah, he's a controlling bastard,' she said, when I looked at her in horror.

'He didn't want me to find out that you knew,' I surmised. 'That we'd slept together.'

'Always likes to keep a trump card up his sleeve, does Finley. Then whips it out when he needs it. To get him out of whatever his latest fuck-up might be.'

'Daniel said the same thing about him. They had dinner together last night.'

'Huh. Smart guy, your husband. I always thought he had Finley sussed. Don't tell me, Daniel was the one who suggested you move to Kew. To get away from his flaky best mate.'

'Sort of.' I didn't add that he'd wanted to escape Bea, too. She and I were finally talking; I didn't want to spoil it. Not until I knew everything, even if that did include her having a secret affair with my husband.

Bea cocked her head to one side. 'What else did Daniel tell you about last night?'

'Not a lot. Only that Finley must have done something wrong himself to be, uh, laying shit on you. Sorry, Bea. I shouldn't have listened to him. I wasn't sure who or what to believe.' I sighed, staring across the playground, thinking of Billy as I watched a little boy throwing a ball to his sister, the lively siblings giggling as they played. 'I've had so much on my mind.'

Suddenly, I remembered Bea saying the same thing to Jules yesterday morning: that she had *so much shit* on her mind.

I realised now that she must have been referring to Finley, her marriage breakdown, but that still didn't explain how she'd known about Windsor, or why things seemed to have come to a head both for Bea and Finley yesterday – prompting Bea to turn on me, and Finley to all but kidnap Billy. Something else must have happened. *Was it to do with Daniel, after all?*

'Bea, sorry, I have to ask you,' I said carefully. 'Yesterday, in the playground . . . you mentioned Daniel and I going to Windsor at the weekend. How did you—'

'Finley told me. He appears to have been having secret meetings with Daniel.'

'Oh?' As far as I was aware, there had only been one. *Last night.*

'Finley suggested *you* were the one seeing Daniel. He dropped hints about it earlier, when he came to our apartment. In fact, he rushed home to check if you and Daniel were together at your house.'

Bea shook her head. 'I haven't seen Finley at all today. I haven't seen *Daniel* for years.' She paused, watching my face. 'This has really got between you guys, hasn't it? You believed Finley's crap. You thought Danny was cheating on you.'

'I haven't known who to trust,' I admitted bleakly.

'Not Finley, that's for sure. He's a shit-stirrer,' Bea said bluntly. 'He's always been jealous of Daniel. Ever since they were at uni. Both of them are competitive, but Finley . . . Jealousy is like a disease with him. He wants everything Dan has.'

'Finley said it was the other way around. That you wanted Daniel because I had him.'

'See? The guy's screwed up. He projects all his own needs and neuroses onto other people. I know everyone thinks Fin's the golden boy. Nish and Jules adore him. I did, too, when I first met him. That's why I married him. He's charming. Good looking. Filthy rich.' Her eyebrows arched. 'I can't deny that was a big part of the attraction. But our marriage has been a sham for years.'

'God, Bea. I had no idea.'

'Let's just say we're both exceptionally good at acting.' Her mouth slanted in a wry smile. 'But Fin's never been faithful. Remember Tanya Wade?'

'Seriously?' I knew Finley was our old boss's favourite; I'd thought it was professional admiration. I winced, thinking how little I'd really known about my former friends.

'Believe you me, I would never joke about that woman. Finley got fed up of her eventually, of course. Her constant demands. She was far too high-maintenance.'

I stared at Bea, unable to believe she perceived no irony: I had never met *anyone* more demanding than her. 'How long were they seeing each other?'

'The whole time he worked for her. Why do you think I insisted he resign?'

'Ah. So starting his own antiques business—'

'Was my idea. Not that it stopped him seeing her. In fairness, they were already at it before you and I started as interns. I just didn't know it. I thought he only had eyes for *you.*'

I felt myself blush. 'That didn't stop you making a move on him,' I pointed out.

'I never claimed to be a saint.' Bea smiled faintly. 'I see something I want, I have to have it. It's like there's this horrible, needy monster inside of me that needs constant feeding.'

I was about to mention the child Finley told me Bea had given up, wondering if that explained how she felt – why her craving for attention seemed to be a *bottomless pit*, as Daniel called it. But I bit back the words. I was beginning to doubt the truth of that story, too.

Finley had sworn blind that Bea had no idea we'd slept together; he'd obviously lied. He seemed to have fabricated his account of *everything*, not to mention deliberately sabotaging Bea's and my friendship, intercepting – and blocking – all contact between us. But why would he do that? What could he possibly have to gain?

'That weekend at the hotel,' I said thoughtfully. 'You and Finley had a row before the christening. Finley said it was about me. I assumed that was why he got so drunk.'

'Oh, Finley wasn't drunk that night. We didn't argue about

210

you, either. Not till the next day, anyway. No, he was mad at me for sleeping with someone else, the hypocrite. It was also a blow to his ego that another guy had got me pregnant. But Finley isn't interested in kids.'

I frowned. 'He told me he just wants to be a *family guy*.'

'Finley says whatever he needs to, to get whatever he wants.'

Thank God he doesn't want Billy, I thought in relief. Despite Finley's insistence earlier that he wanted to get to know him, it was clearly all talk. More game playing. I only wished I knew what his real agenda was, or perhaps he didn't have one beyond winding Daniel up. 'Which is what? *Tanya?*' I asked curiously. 'Does he still see her?'

'Yeah. The stupid thing is, he doesn't even like her. I thought their affair might have petered out when we moved to Richmond. Stupidly, I thought Finley genuinely wanted us to have a fresh start – to finally be a couple. The move was his idea, you see?'

'He told me it was yours.' I shook my head at the extent of his duplicity.

'Huh. That doesn't surprise me. Not now, anyway. Back then, I guess I was still blaming you. But none of this is your fault, Ruth. I forgive you. I want you to know that.'

'Oh, Bea.' I swivelled around on the bench, taking hold of her slim hand.

'Sisters, remember?' Her fingers laced through mine. 'I forgot that for a while. Stupid me. I should never have doubted you. The moment you turned up for that playdate, I should have known. That moving so close to you guys was another step towards Finley's endgame.'

'Which is what? What *is* it he actually wants?'

'You really have no idea?' Bea said, uncannily echoing what Finley had said to me at the apartment only hours before. 'Oh, Ruth. I honestly thought you must have realised. I genuinely thought it was the reason I didn't hear from you again after that weekend.'

Her eyes filled with tears, reminding me even more of Finley's emotional confession – his insistence that Bea was obsessed with me; that, chameleon-like, she'd tried to *become* me. Suspicion rose up again. Someone was playing me; I knew that. But was it Finley – or Bea?

Chapter 42

'Tell me more. *Everything*. About you and Finley.' I'd already realised I didn't know either of them as well as I thought, and I wasn't sure which of them to trust, or what they wanted, but I had to start with bare facts to have any chance of understanding what I was up against.

'We've been living separate lives for years.' Bea's voice cracked. 'But last week, I hit a wall.' Tears spilled over now. 'I told Finley I want a divorce.'

He told Daniel he was divorcing Bea. 'Well, from what you've said, divorcing Finley sounds like the right thing. I wouldn't waste your tears on—'

'Oh, I'm not upset about *that*.' She dashed away her tears with her coat sleeve. 'I should have got shot of him years ago. No, it's . . . I had some news the other day.'

I've got big news, I recalled her telling Jules in the playground. 'Oh?'

'I wanted to tell you, Ruth. Honestly. Only, Finley has been winding me up so much. Telling me he married the wrong woman.

213

Taunting me that he should have married *you*.'

'I had noticed you'd turned frosty towards me.' That much rang true.

'Sorry.' She winced. 'Anyway, things came to a proper head the night before last. I suppose that's why Finley had dinner with Daniel yesterday. To rehearse his version of events.'

'Which was?'

'We had a fight. The worst ever. Finley was incandescent with rage. About something personal I shared with him. Something I'd never told him – told *anyone*.'

Her face turned deathly pale, and instinctively I was convinced she was telling the truth. Either that, or she really was an incredible actress. 'Look, you don't have to tell me if—'

'But I want to, Ruth. I'm sick of secrets. I finally want to live the life *I* want. It's always been about Finley. What *he* wants to do. Which, nine times out of ten, was whatever you were doing. No disrespect, but when the four of us were friends . . .'

'We spent more time as a foursome than two couples.'

'Finley couldn't leave you alone. Even on your bloody wedding anniversary. Remember your special dinner at Gino's? Finley was determined to gate-crash it.'

'Ah.' I winced, recalling that I'd blamed Bea for that at the time.

'Oh, I know I tried to turn it into a party. It helps, you know? If I keep moving, keep *having fun*. Then I don't have to stop and think. About what happened to me when I was a kid.' Her eyes filled with tears once more; this time, she let them roll down her face.

'Giving up a baby,' I said softly.

'Two, actually. Only one died. The girl. I never even saw her. The midwife at Greenwich Hospital took her. They were twins, you see? As if I could look after even one child! I was fourteen. My parents were dead. I guess I went off the rails. Slept around. Lost myself for a while. Teenagers think they're invincible, don't they? I certainly did. I never thought I'd end up living with my

214

spinster aunt and a baby I hadn't a clue how to look after.'

'You'd have figured it out. I know you would. You always do. But that must have been incredibly hard for you. Not having a mum. Becoming one yourself at such a young age.'

'See? I'm an idiot. I should have told you before. I knew you'd get it, Ruth. I wish I *had* told you. I was petrified when I got pregnant with Ophelia. I . . . I wasn't sure I could keep her. I was scarred by what happened before. I didn't tell anyone about the pregnancy for ages.'

I remembered Daniel saying a friend at squash had told him Bea was pregnant, insisting it was all *hush-hush*. 'But you *did* keep her, Bea. And you're a brilliant mum,' I said sincerely. 'What happened to your little boy?' I asked curiously.

'Adopted by some family up north. I never saw him again.' Her tears came faster now. 'I know I gave him up, Ruth, but it really feels like he was *stolen* from me.'

'I know,' I soothed, realising where Finley had got the idea of Bea muttering about a *stolen child*. Only, he'd let me think she was talking about Billy, I thought furiously.

'Anyway, I got a letter from Social Services. That's what I was going to tell Jules. My son's turned twenty-one. He wants to meet me. It's *karma*, Ruth. I'm getting my boy back!'

'Oh my God. Bea, that's *awesome*.'

I stared at her face, ten years older than when I'd first met her, yet physically hardly changed. She was still glamorous; still beautiful. But there was a vulnerability about her that I'd never seen before. I wanted to weep for our lost friendship – and her lost baby girl. I wanted to dance with joy that she had a chance to get her son back.

'Isn't it?' She beamed. 'I thought so. But Finley didn't.' Instantly, her smile faded. 'He told me he wants nothing to do with any child that isn't biologically his.'

'Wow. Nice.' I shook my head in disbelief, and I couldn't help thinking about Daniel – how even though he couldn't be certain

215

Billy was his son, not Finley's, he still adored him.

'I shouldn't have been surprised, but I was. Devastated, in fact. So I decided to hit him where it hurts. I told him about Ophelia.'

'That she's not his daughter. Hmm, I think I can guess how he took that.' *So that's why everything had come to a head – why Finley had rushed to take Billy this morning.* He didn't really want him; he only wanted to get in his side of the story first.

'Exactly.' Bea frowned. 'He said, if I brought *another bastard child* into his house, he would kill me – and them.' She sucked in a ragged breath. 'Just like he tried to kill Tanya.'

I froze, certain I must have misheard her. 'Say that again?'

'Ironic, hey?' Bea let out a humourless laugh. 'Oh, I know everyone at the agency thought I was the one who shoved Tanya down those stairs. Maybe I did fantasise about her coming to a nasty end.' She shrugged. 'But Finley actually tried to pull it off. He was sick of her. The worst thing is, the poor cow was so besotted with him, she never told the police.'

'Jesus. Have *you*?'

'That's what we fought about. I was going to call them. Finley snatched my phone off me. Smashed it to pieces. He told me I could kiss goodbye to Ophelia, if I told anyone.'

'You were on edge at school yesterday, too.' I pictured her jittery, restless manner in the playground, shaken to realise that while I'd been trapped in my worst nightmare, Bea had been dealing with a crisis of her own. Neither of us had known what the other was going through: Finley had made sure of that. 'I guess you were worried about leaving Ophelia. In case Finley came for her?'

'I was terrified. I told the head teacher, strictly no one but my nanny was to collect her.' Bea paused, watching a little girl slowly climb to the top of the slide, before launching herself down it, arms flung high, joy lighting up her sweet face. 'Ophelia will be safe at school, won't she? I mean, it's not like just *anyone* can walk into a school playground, is it?'

Eve did. She strolled back into my life, propelling me into a tailspin, at the worst possible moment. Immediately, I remembered Bea's voicemail. 'Your message, Bea. You said you knew what happened *that night*. You meant me and Finley at the hotel, right?'

Bea shook her head. 'No. I meant the night Finley pushed Tanya down the stairs. If he could do that . . . I'm scared, Ruth. I'm really worried he's lost the plot.'

'It certainly sounds like it. Can't you call the police without him knowing? From a public payphone?' I suggested, remembering Bea saying that Finley had blocked my number; he obviously had easy access to Bea's phone, or at least her network provider.

'You're right.' She sat up straighter, flicked back her ponytail and grinned, suddenly looking even more like her old self. 'Thanks, Ruth. I'm so glad we're friends again.'

'Please, you don't have to thank me.' I'd slept with her husband – drunkenly, accidentally, but I would never feel OK about that. I should have been there for Bea; I felt awful that she was dealing with all this alone.

'I *do* need to thank you. It's really helped to talk it through. I thought I was going *mad*.'

'Textbook gaslighting,' I told her. 'I can hardly believe Finley would do it, but—'

'He said he's going to find my boy. He said he'll do whatever it takes to keep him from me. To teach me how it feels to lose the one person I truly love. Exactly as he has.'

'Tanya, you mean?' I squinted at Bea in confusion.

'No, Ruth. I mean *you*. That's Finley's endgame. It always has been. He wants you. Not me, not Tanya, and certainly not Ophelia. I'm just terrified how far he'll go to get you.'

Chapter 43

I left Bea sitting on the bench, promising to call her later. Then, for the second time in two days, I found myself running across Kew Bridge, desperate to get home.

I wasn't sure I believed that Finley wanted me; I wished I could be more certain that I could completely trust everything Bea had told me. I'd been so moved by her longing for her lost son, but some of the things she'd said had weirdly echoed Finley's accusations about her. *Which of them was the player – and which was telling the truth?*

It felt overwhelming, just as their friendship used to be. I genuinely wanted to help Bea, but I needed to concentrate on my own family first. It had been hard enough leaving Billy; now I couldn't rest until I held him safe in my arms again.

I burst into the apartment and dashed through to the living room, with love, longing and fear coursing through me. 'Where is he?'

Daniel looked up calmly from the sofa. 'Everything all right?'

'I think we've had enough of trains now.' Eve, sitting on the

218

floor next to Billy, got slowly to her feet. 'Up you get, sweetheart.' She reached out a hand to him. 'Billy's just going to put some toys into a backpack. Something to play with while we're on the boat.'

'Sorry?' I looked between Eve and Daniel. 'On the *boat*?'

'Eve and I have come to an agreement,' Daniel said lightly, but his cheeks were flushed. 'We'll spend an hour with Billy on the boat. She'll leave us in peace. Right, Eve?'

'What, just like that?' I stared doubtfully at her face that was equally flushed and wondered exactly what had gone on while I'd been at Kew Gardens talking to Bea.

Running home, I'd replayed over and over what she'd said about Finley, trying to decide if he really was a threat to her safety – or mine. Noticing that Daniel was still displaying the edge of controlled aggression I'd sensed in him earlier, I felt even more unnerved.

'I *told* you I'd sort things out.' His placid smile somehow made me more nervous.

'Sure, but . . .' I looked dubiously towards the windows. 'It'll be getting dark soon.'

Eve threw me a mocking glance. 'Yes, but you see, we have this strange, mystical power on the boat. It's called e-lec-tri-city,' she said, elongating the word sarcastically.

I glared at her. 'Yes, of course. I meant, it's not that long till Billy's bath time.'

'Please, Mummy,' Billy begged. 'I want to go on the boat!'

I glanced at Daniel. 'It won't take long,' he said quietly. 'Then it will all be over.'

*

Five minutes later, as we followed Eve down to the wharf, I was gripped by an ominous sense that Daniel's idea of how to ensure everything would soon be 'over' might mirror Finley's.

Still processing everything Bea had told me, I felt increasingly certain that more had gone on between the two men than I was aware of – during secret meetings I'd known nothing about – and that the competitiveness between them ran far deeper than I'd ever realised.

We didn't speak as we approached the canal boat, its shadowy deck lit only by lamps inside the cabin, which cast a deceptively cosy glow. I could feel Daniel's tension at my side, and suddenly I recalled him joke earlier about me staying away from the river, in case he was tempted to push me in. I glanced anxiously at Eve, remembering her say she couldn't swim.

Stop it, Ruth! I lectured myself silently. *Daniel isn't Finley. He's a kind man.*

'That's not a knife, is it?' I quipped nervously, as he fretted with his jacket pocket.

He kept his eyes straight ahead. 'Brains not brawn, Ruth. That's what it takes to win.'

His comment made me think of Jack, and as we climbed aboard, I glanced around warily. But the deck was empty, eerily so, and all of the surrounding houseboats seemed to be in darkness. I shivered, again ordering myself to stop being ridiculous. As Daniel had implied, violence wasn't the answer; there was no need to be checking out potential witnesses.

I stumbled as the wind picked up, and as I looked upwards to the dusky sky, I saw the clouds turn thundery. A flock of birds squawked and took flight from the riverbank opposite. I wished I could join them: grab hold of Billy and launch us both into the air. Setting foot on a boat was unsettling enough; being trapped on board in a storm was a terrifying prospect.

'Make yourself at home,' Eve trilled as we entered the cabin.

'Come on, son. Let's stoke the fire.' Daniel ushered Billy towards the wood burner.

'He's a good daddy,' Eve said, watching them. 'I told you he would be.'

'The best,' I choked out. 'He loves Billy to distraction.' *Even if he doesn't love me anymore*, I thought sadly.

Daniel and I still hadn't had the chance to talk about our marriage, or what was left of it. My every thought was for Billy – although concern for Bea now hovered at the periphery of my mind. I still hadn't heard from Finley; his absence was making me increasingly nervous.

Black eyes stared into mine. 'Is love enough, do you think?'

'Sorry?' I frowned at Eve, until it dawned on me what she was suggesting – what she was manipulatively trying to demonstrate by bringing Billy back onto her boat: that he would be as happy living with her, even though she was poor. *Because she loved him.*

'You heard me. Daniel might love Billy to distraction. But so do I,' she said hoarsely, confirming that I'd guessed correctly.

'Having lots of toys and a nice home isn't what makes Billy love us, Eve. No more than being well-off is what makes Daniel and I good parents. It's about *unconditional* love.'

'Absolutely. If we love someone, we'd sacrifice *anything* to make them happy. No matter how badly it hurts us.'

'I only want what's best for Billy,' I said wearily, tired of mind games: Eve's, Finley's, possibly even Bea's. It felt like I was surrounded by lies – and liars.

'I know you do. And I want to show you something. Come with me.'

'Show me what?' Reluctantly, I followed her towards the thick blue velvet curtain at the end of the boat, feeling a slight frisson of fear as it swished closed behind me.

'These.' She gave me a light shove towards a narrow bunk covered by a jumble of clothes. *Baby* clothes.

'Who do they belong to?' I asked curiously. Picking up a couple of sleepsuits, I held them to my face. They smelled new, and I was reminded again of the day I'd gone into labour – the excitement on Daniel's face as he'd showed me the nursery he'd secretly filled with toys.

'Sean.' Eve sat down at the head of the bunk, watching me.

221

'Your son,' I said gently, sitting down at the other end.

'What's going on?' Daniel's eyes were narrowed, his mouth a taut line, as he poked his head around the curtain.

'Eve's just showing me her little boy's things,' I told him. 'I'll be out in a minute.'

'You'd better be.' Daniel glared at Eve. 'Or I'll be back before you can say *life sentence for bribery and blackmail.*'

Chapter 44

'Was there a funeral?' I asked, once Daniel had retreated.

Eve and I were finally alone, on her territory, just as she'd wanted. Whatever more aggressive plan Daniel had in mind, I was still convinced that talking things through empathically was the best way to help release Eve from her deluded obsession with Billy.

'No,' she said shortly.

'Oh.' I paused, thinking. Eve looked so closed-off; this was going to be harder than I'd imagined. 'A little life slips away, and that's *it*?' Suddenly, my chest felt tight with sadness.

'Mary told me the hospital would sort everything out.'

'Mary? Oh, yes. The midwife.'

'She said they take care of babies all together, at the same time. They scatter their ashes in a remembrance garden. At Mortlake Cemetery, or somewhere. I didn't go.' Eve's mouth twisted. 'You weren't the only one who ran away.'

'What do you mean? I didn't *run away*. I went *home*.'

'Your husband rushed you out of hospital like you had thirty seconds to catch a plane.'

223

'We thought you were *asleep*. We thought it best not to disturb you. How long *did* you stay in hospital?' I was determined to steer the conversation back to her.

'About a week. Mary helped me find a place in a hostel. That's where I met Jack.'

'Who we *still* haven't met.'

I frowned, wondering what he was like – if he even existed or was yet another figment of Eve's overactive imagination. Then, in the next moment, it occurred to me that if she *did* have a boyfriend, he might be the one who had put Eve up to this scam.

I wondered how they planned to get away with it. *By force?* Daniel might rely on brain power, but he'd been a soldier once. He wasn't scared of a fight. I had been half joking when I'd asked him about a knife in his pocket, but it still niggled that Billy had mentioned seeing one in Eve's. If this 'Jack' was a builder, he would surely have plenty of tools, too. Sharp ones, I thought with a shudder, glancing around the bedroom, which suddenly felt claustrophobic.

Had Daniel and I just walked into a trap?

'Jack's cool,' Eve said dismissively, seemingly oblivious to my burst of anxiety. 'He was building the extension at the hostel. You'd be surprised how many homeless teenagers there are in London.'

'Actually, I wouldn't. There's never enough funding for social care.' All my years in foster care had taught me that. 'Hospitals are always overstretched and understaffed. Doctors and midwives have more patients to cope with than they can manage. Sometimes—'

'Sometimes mistakes happen – is that what you were about to say?' Eve's dark eyes glinted in the riverside lights filtering through the small porthole window.

'No! Of course not. Look, there hasn't *been* any mistake, Eve.'

'You're damned right there hasn't. No mistake. No misunderstanding. Deep down, you must know that.'

'OK, I've had enough of this.' I stood up. 'I've tried to be kind to you, but—'

'Our babies were swapped at birth, Ruth. Snap out of this ridiculous denial.'

'*Me* in denial? That's rich coming from you.' Instantly, I recalled Daniel saying the same thing to me about my betrayal with Finley. He'd been right that I had something to hide, but Eve was wrong, and I was tired of humouring her. 'Enough, OK? I'm leaving.'

'I know for a fact our babies were swapped,' Eve said quietly, and her eyes were huge, black and curiously dead.

I remained standing but didn't move, deciding to make one last attempt. 'That neonatal unit was like Fort Knox. Security cameras everywhere. The hospital has a first-rate reputation.'

'Does it? It was just the nearest one when I went into labour. One of the guys in the squat took me. Which was kind of him, except he just dumped me outside and left.'

'I'm sorry to hear that,' I said politely, but my sympathy was wearing thin now.

'I don't want your pity. You can keep it.'

'OK, fine. Have it your way.' I strode towards the curtain, but Eve grabbed my arm.

'Wait. We're not done yet,' she hissed.

'Eve . . .' I thought about calling for Daniel, but I didn't want to scare Billy.

'Sorry.' Instantly, she let go of me and sat back on the bunk, raising her hands innocently. 'I don't want to hurt you, honest. I just want you to *understand*.'

'Fine. Then let's cut to the chase.' I stepped away from the curtain but stood with my back to it, where I could call for help if Eve decided to get physical again. 'You think someone swapped our babies, switched their identity bracelets and medical notes,' I summarised briskly. 'This mythical *someone* deliberately did all this, in the full knowledge that one of the babies was dying. And, miraculously, no one noticed.'

'Correct.'

'That would be gross hospital negligence,' I said sternly. 'Not

225

to mention that whoever would do such a thing would have to be a seriously disturbed person.'

'Or someone who never wanted to be a mother in the first place.'

Chapter 45

'Someone who . . .' I echoed in shock. 'What did you say?'

'You heard me. Don't make me say it again.'

I stared at Eve, even as my mind was pulled dizzyingly back over the years to the day Billy was born. 'You're saying that you . . . that *you* switched our babies?'

'Yes. That's exactly what I'm saying, Ruth. Because *that's what happened.*' She folded her arms, looking like a sulky teenager.

In truth, she was little more than that, and part of me wanted to shake her, tell her to grow up – to stop play-acting and start being an adult. 'You're lying.'

'You know I'm not.' Eve's eyes gleamed, but suddenly the anger seemed to have left her. She looked defeated . . . broken. 'I was raped by my teacher. I told you that.'

'You said you didn't know who got you pregnant!'

'Who wants that stigma hanging over them? Anyway, I never told anyone about that. Apart from Mary. She wanted me to report it. Huh. Who's anyone going to believe? A respected teacher or . . . me. Whatever, I didn't want a baby, anyway. But *you* did.'

227

'I wanted *my* baby. I wanted to be a mum. I still do,' I whispered.

My head was spinning, and I was struggling to take in what she was saying. Despite all her claims, despite the baby photo she'd showed me, and the webbing she and Billy obviously had in common, somehow, I'd still been holding on to hope.

Or denial, as Eve had accused.

Perhaps, in the end, they were the same thing.

'I know how much you wanted a baby,' Eve continued quietly, hunching up her knees. 'I saw how you were in the hospital. It made me realise I just didn't feel that way.'

'That's not true. You were distraught when Mary said your baby was poorly.'

Once again, I cast my mind back, remembering Eve's anguished cries as she pummelled her pillow, throwing her books across the ward, screaming at anyone who came close to her. She'd sobbed herself to sleep every night.

'Sure. But, you see, I was pretending. I had to make it *look* like I was devastated when "my baby"' – she mimed speech marks – 'took a turn for the worse. But I wasn't. Huh. I guess I'm a good actress. I didn't feel a thing. Hardly surprising, when you think about it.'

'You mean, because of your teacher?'

'That and the fact that I've got bad genes.' She hugged her knees even tighter, rocking herself. 'My mum obviously never wanted me. Why else did she give me up? I guess I take after her more than I realised. I looked at my baby, and I felt *nothing*.'

'Eve, didn't Mary talk to you about postnatal depression?' I said gently, feeling a renewed flash of hope. Eve was struggling with PTSD. I'd guessed it the moment she'd accosted me in the playground, and I was growing more certain by the minute.

Everything she was saying, her memories of that day, the birth of our babies . . . it had all got jumbled up in her mind. I'd been worried about my *own* memories being repressed and distorted by trauma; it seemed to me that was definitely what had happened to Eve.

'Oh, Mary did better than that. She helped me.'

'Really.' I rolled my eyes. 'A respected midwife with a forty-year career to lose.'

'She *cared* about me.'

'I guess she must have done, to break the law so horrendously.'

'We made a connection,' Eve insisted. 'I was in hospital for days before my contractions turned into the real thing. I got to know Mary. She grew up in Greenwich, too. And she had a tough childhood. She knew exactly what it felt like to have nothing and no one.'

Out of nowhere, I thought of Bea, remembering her saying the same thing, ten years ago. It was what had first drawn us together, back when we weren't that much older than Eve was now. Bea had given up her baby son, but that didn't mean Eve had. I hardened my heart. 'Plenty of people know that feeling. My mum left me, too.'

'Mary's the only person who ever asked me what *I* wanted.' Eve was crying now.

'Which was what? To abandon your baby?' I was trembling with fury at her continued pretence, even as pity for her circumstances surged through me. Once again, I thought of Bea – pregnant and alone at fourteen. 'What about adoption?' I felt a knot of pain inside as I pictured Bea, young and traumatised, handing over her son. 'Did you never consider that?'

'What, hand over my baby to Social Services?' Eve wailed, as though she'd read my mind. 'Fat lot of help they ever were to me. No, *I* wanted to choose my little boy's future. I saw you going into the delivery suite just as I came out. You looked like the kind of mum I'd always wanted. Gentle, pretty. Kind.'

'You mean, our souls touched.' That's what she'd told me at the time, I recalled.

'*Exactly*. So when Mary told me your little boy wasn't going to make it, it felt like it was just . . . meant to be.'

'Hmm. Like we were *parapsychic echoes* of each other,' I said drily, more of her words coming back to me.

'Don't mock me. I meant it, Ruth. I felt a *bond* with you. I knew you wouldn't let me down. I knew you'd take care of my boy.'

'But I saw the webbing between his fingers. Hours after he was born.'

'Mary was looking after both babies. Things didn't look hopeful for yours, right from the start. She knew that he . . .' Eve broke off and started chewing frantically at her nails.

'She knew *what*?' I scoffed. 'She knew my baby was going to die, so she swapped him with yours straightaway? To make it look like it was *your* baby that became so ill? Is *that* what you're telling me? Is that seriously what you expect me to believe?'

'It's the truth.'

'You mean, the first time I properly saw my son, it wasn't my son at all. It was yours.'

'Yes. Mary wasn't a monster. She knew it was wrong. But she was a kind woman. And I told her straight. Either she helped me, or I'd carry my baby up to the roof, and—'

'Jump,' I finished for her.

Instantly, my mind flooded with the image I'd had nightmares about throughout my entire childhood. All I knew of my own mother was that she'd thrown herself off the hospital roof the day I was born. She must have been desperate; I'd always understood that. I stared at Eve, watching her pull her hoodie sleeves down over her wrists to hide the scars, reminded that there was a time when *she* must have felt that same desperation.

Mary would have seen those scars, too – and, like me, I'm pretty sure she would have known what they signified. She'd worked in that hospital for more than forty years: her entire career. She must have seen hundreds, if not thousands, of troubled young mums like Eve.

Like Bea, too, I thought, struck by a similarity between the two women, both physically and in terms of their tough starts in life. Both were convincing actresses, too; I'd struggled to know whether to believe each of them. But I wasn't surprised Mary had taken Eve's threat seriously – if indeed she'd made such a threat. For the first time, doubt began to creep in.

'I would have done it, too,' Eve confirmed defiantly. 'I would have jumped. If Mary hadn't told me about your baby being so sick, I wouldn't be here today. Or Billy.'

'No. Please don't say that.' I shut my mind against horrific images. 'Mary should have told someone. A counsellor, doctor, *anyone*. Wait, what about Billy's medical notes?'

Eve leaned over and opened the top drawer in a small wicker chest next to the bunk. Reaching inside, she pulled out a handful of papers, then thrust them at me.

'Here. Look for yourself. If you need proof, this is it. But you don't, do you, Ruth? Because in your heart of hearts, you know I'm telling the truth. Come on, admit it. You've *always* known.'

Chapter 46

'These forms.' At first, I skimmed through them, barely looking at the lines of closely typed details. 'They name you as the mother. And Sean . . . webbed fingers . . .' I read random snippets aloud, and the more I read, the closer I stared at the hospital notes. Feeling my fingers start to tremble, I pressed the papers tightly against my chest. 'Where did you get them?'

'Mary. They're the doctor's original notes. Obviously, Mary sorted new ones for you.'

'She forged them, you mean.'

Eve shrugged. 'She knew she was saving my life. And Billy's. She called it her "final act of kindness". She was retiring the following week.'

'She *was* kind to me,' I said, remembering. 'And you . . . all those questions you asked me about my life, my husband . . .'

'I had to check you both out, didn't I? I couldn't leave my son with just anyone.'

'So where's Mary now? If the hospital found out – or the police . . .'

'I've no idea where she is. She helped me get my place at the hostel, but that was it. We didn't stay in touch. She said it was better that way.'

'Better for *her*. She could go to prison.'

'She retired because of ill health. I don't even know if she's still alive.'

'We'll find her,' I said confidently. 'Daniel will find her.'

'Oh, *really*? And what will he do, exactly?'

'I don't know, but—'

'Look.' Eve sighed. 'All that really matters now is that Billy is alive and well. Isn't it? My little boy is happy and healthy. I'm in a good place, too. Much better than I was four years ago.' Slowly, she reached out and took the papers from me.

Her so-called proof. Evidence. Her ticket to claim my son.

'But you said it yourself, Eve . . .' Panic like I had never known began to take hold of me, filling my lungs with fear. 'Billy is happy. He's happy with *me*.'

I was running out of excuses. Little by little, denial had given way to doubt – and then despair. But thinking about Billy fired every ounce of determination inside me. I might have brought home the wrong child, but he was with the right mother. I had never been more certain of anything in my life, and I refused to let him go.

'Sure. I don't deny that,' Eve said quietly. 'I've seen your home. I guess I wanted you to see mine. It's nowhere near as fancy as yours, of course. I also know that's not the most important thing. What really matters is that Billy—'

'No!' I didn't wait to hear any more. I leaped off the bunk, baby clothes scattering as I barged into the velvet curtain, bundling it out of my way.

'Ruth, wait! Please, just hear me out!'

I didn't turn around. I ran through the cabin, dashing towards Billy with my arms outstretched. Frightened by the sudden disturbance, he threw himself against Daniel's side, cowering under his arm.

'Billy, darling,' I said, hating myself for causing the fear on his face.

'You look funny, Mummy.'

'Ruth. Stop! We need to talk!' Eve shouted, stumbling towards me.

But I couldn't; there was no way I could stand there and listen to her tell me that she may have given up her son, but now she wanted him back.

The walls of the cabin seemed to close in on me. I had to get off the boat.

I turned around, and I ran.

PART TWO

PART TWO

Chapter 47

Billy's cry sings across the dark water. 'MUMMY!'

I've been his mummy for four years; *I've never been his mother.*

Closing my eyes, I remember a thousand nights, smoothing soft curls back from his hot forehead, stroking away the bad dreams, Billy's hand curled trustingly inside mine like a small, hibernating mouse.

Feeling nausea rush up, I grip the rusty iron railing along the riverside, shivering as the clouds press lower; the dampness of an impending storm chills my skin.

My eyes are glued to the spot where Billy last stood, his blue duffle coat a bright smudge in the icy mist as he called out to me. I watched him searching, running back and forth across the deck trying to find me, before disappearing back down the short flight of stairs and through the double doors into the cabin.

To Eve.

Jack – the bearded man – has finally appeared. He's on the

237

deck now, chopping wood; the cracks ring out like gunshots, splinters spraying up like shrapnel. I watch him lift his eyes to the sky, before disappearing inside the cabin.

To Billy.

'He's mine! Give him back!' I yell, but the wind steals my voice. *He's not mine . . .*

The moon looks on, benign and impassive. Silently, I beg it for answers; there are none. No one can tell me why my baby died; no one can give him back to me.

My poor, precious boy. How I longed for him, but he didn't even live long enough to know how many years I'd waited to hold him in my arms, how much I loved, needed and cherished him.

In despair, I turn away from the river I have loved so much but which will now for ever be the place where I am finally forced to accept the truth: my child was stolen from me.

Twice.

The first time, I didn't know. Eve *took* my baby – without asking, without giving me a chance to hold him, to kiss him goodbye, to hold his tiny hand as he gasped his final breath. Now she wants to take back the child she willingly gave up; the little boy I have loved to distraction for four years, who has become a part of me, inseparable from myself.

If I lose him, too, I am nothing.

How did I not know that the darling son I've been raising is not my child?

The truth has been staring me in the face for four years, but the intensity of my love for Billy has crystallised into denial, and guilt about my own actions has blinded me to other people's. Finley's. Bea's. Even, perhaps, Daniel's. And now Eve's . . .

I'm floored by her pitiless deception, and tormented by her continued, stubborn, heartless torture of me. *What have I done to her that she wants to punish me for so cruelly?*

Closing my eyes, I think back over everything that's happened, trying to make sense of the past – dreading a future without my sons.

Both of them.

The one I lost, and the one I may yet still lose.

Chapter 48

'You shouldn't have run, Ruth. I had everything under control. I know what I'm doing. You have to *trust* me. I meant what I said. I'm not giving Billy up.'

Daniel's low voice only penetrates the swirling depths of my thoughts as he places a hand on my arm. Dragged slowly and painfully out of the shadows of memory, I open my eyes to see him standing next to me on the towpath. Turning in sudden panic, I see Billy sitting on our usual bench, throwing a pile of stones into the water, one by one, his legs swinging.

I stand and watch him until he looks around, giving me a toothy grin. I smile back, blinking away the tears filling my eyes. They blur as I follow the direction of his arm, pointing excitedly at the sky. It's a deep, dark grey, cut with jagged purple swathes; clouds billow and roll dramatically. The storm is holding back, but not for much longer.

'I'm not giving up, either. It would kill me,' I tell Daniel, my smile dropping as Billy turns back to the river. 'If I lose him, I can't live anymore.'

'Don't say that.' Daniel's chest is heaving; his breath puffs out in clouds on the icy air.

He must have run straight after me as I fled from the boat, I realise. I have no idea how long I've been standing on the wharf, thinking, remembering. Trying to piece together how we got to this dark place – where we go from here. 'Why not? It's true.'

'I'm not going to let that happen.' Daniel reaches out to take my arm again.

'You said that before.' I brush his hand away. 'You swore on your *life* we would bring home our son. But we didn't. We brought home *hers*.'

'This whole situation is a mess. I know that.' He takes a step back, turning away from me to pace up and down the wharf. 'But we can figure it out,' he insists, finally returning to stand in front of me, holding out both hands in appeal. 'Ruth? Don't give up. Please.'

'You called her a screwball woman. You didn't even take her *seriously*!'

'Did *you*?' he says drily, a glint of challenge in his blue eyes now.

'I . . . no. Yes. Eventually, yes,' I insist.

'And now we know. Everything,' he says flatly. 'So we can deal with it. *All* of it.'

'But why is she *doing* this? Why has she come back?' I search his face for answers I know he can't possibly give me. I want to throw myself into his arms, seek comfort from him. But my body feels frozen with cold; my heart is numb with grief, pain and terror.

'I don't know. But something still doesn't add up. What Eve said about the magazine article, our photos. Tracing us.' He shakes his head.

'It was all a lie,' I say bitterly. 'She knew where Billy was the whole time.'

'Exactly. She pretended to you – to *us* – that she'd believed Billy was dead. That it was only the magazine interview that convinced her otherwise. Clearly, that was nonsense. No, she's lying about something. I just need to figure out which bit.'

Daniel glances over his shoulder to check on Billy; I haven't taken my eyes off him. 'She did lie about the magazine article,' I say bleakly. 'But not the rest.'

'I mean, Jesus. Where are the police?' Daniel huffs, as though I haven't spoken. 'Why didn't she bring them with her, if she's so convinced a crime has been committed?'

'Because *she* committed it.' I refuse to kid myself any longer.

'What? What do you mean?' Daniel frowns, looking confused.

'Didn't you hear what she told me?' I was sure he must have been listening to every word Eve said. 'She swapped our babies, Dan. Because she didn't want hers, and the midwife told her ours was dying.' I cover my face with my hands, desperate to blot out painful images.

'What the hell? Are you *serious*?'

I nod, unable to speak or even look at him.

'And we're a hundred per cent sure about that?'

I open my eyes to see his handsome face twisted with unbearable pain. 'As sure as I can be about anything.' I can tell he's still hoping; I've gone beyond that point. 'I saw the papers with my own eyes. The medical notes. Details the doctor would have filled out when the babies were born. Measurements, medical history, physical attributes.'

'She could have forged them.' The hope on Daniel's face tears my heart to pieces.

'Billy isn't ours, Daniel,' I whisper. 'He isn't Finley's. He isn't yours. *He isn't mine.* This is really happening. I can't believe it, but it is. What Eve said, it's true. There was a switch. Our babies were swapped.' Finally, I force my legs to move, lurching towards him.

Daniel's shoulders start to shake as I press myself against his tall, strong body. He stands silently weeping, arms hanging limp at his sides. I press my cheek against his chest, listening to his heartbeat, as I've done a million times before.

Finally, he rests his chin on the top of my head. 'I think my heart just died.'

It's so rare for him to show his feelings that the shock of his emotion unleashes mine. My tears leave a dark, wet patch on the pale blue hoodie beneath his army jacket. I squeeze him harder, wanting to be absorbed by his strength, needing it to carry me through the pain.

'I'm so sorry I doubted you. Even for a moment,' I say, needing to clear the air of any lingering misunderstandings between us. 'About what happened at the hospital. About you having an affair with Bea.' I have to give him the benefit of the doubt; I can't survive the heartache I know is yet to come without having *someone* to trust.

'It's what she does best. Plant doubt in people's minds.'

'Finley too. You were right. He's no better. Probably a hell of a lot worse.'

I want to say more, tell him everything Bea told me in Kew Gardens, but I can't deal with our friends right now. Bea might be searching for her lost son, but at least he's alive. The thought of mine dying alone, without me by his side, will haunt me for the rest of my life.

'I think our double-dating days are over.' Daniel pulls back to look down at me.

'I'm so sorry about what happened that night.'

'Shh. It's all forgiven. Oh, I was angry at first. Hurt. But I know what Finley's like. He's a devious little shit. I'm convinced he was having an affair the whole time he was married to Bea. Every squash game I booked for us, more often than not, he cancelled.'

'You think he used playing squash as a cover to see Tanya?'

'Tanya?' Daniel frowns. 'Ah, is that who it was? He tried to convince me it was *you*.'

'What? When did he say *that*?'

'Last night. He spent the whole evening yacking on about it.

I dismissed him out of hand, of course. I knew he was talking rubbish.'

'So that's the real reason you were on edge when you came home last night.'

'Sorry, sweetheart. I didn't want to bore you by relaying all of Finley's crap.'

'You know, he called Bea unbalanced. I reckon he's the crazy one. Actually, she thinks he might be trying to hurt her.'

'Pah. Finley is all bark and no bite. Anyway, let's not worry about them. They're as bad as each other, in my book. Always playing games with people's lives. They dug the hole they're in. They can dig themselves out of it. I'm done rescuing Finley from disasters of his own making.'

'Sure, but Bea . . .' I'm still worrying about her, and it's only when Billy skips up to me, slipping his hand into mine, that my thoughts return to my own family – and how to hold on to it.

'Hey, Billy Boy.' Daniel crouches down to pull Billy into his arms. 'I think I saw some hot chocolate on the boat earlier. Want some?'

'Ooh, yes, please!'

Looking up at me, Daniel says quietly: 'I tried it your way, Ruth. It's time to play hardball. Are you up for one last conversation with Eve?'

'Yes. Whatever it takes,' I whisper. 'I won't lose my little boy.'

Silently, I turn my face to the sky, pleading for a sign that all the fantastical nonsense Eve spouted four years ago in hospital is true: that there really *is* such a thing as a spirit world, and my poor little lost boy, the most precious part of me, is sleeping safely there – that, one day, I will feel his presence again.

'Silly Mummy,' Billy says, jolting me out of my thoughts. 'I'm right here! I told you. You can't lose a boy. I'm going nowhere. Daddy *promised* me.'

Chapter 49

'Hello?' Ominously, the boat is shrouded in darkness as I step cautiously back onto the deck. The tall red-bearded man – Jack – is chopping wood at the far end, his bulky form silhouetted by the lights along the riverside. But there is no sign of Eve.

'Keep going, Ruth.' Taking my elbow, Daniel urges me on.

The sound of his deep voice draws Jack's attention. He pauses, turning to frown at us, and for a moment I have second thoughts. I glance around, again looking for tools – anything that might be used as a weapon. Straightening up, Jack lifts his axe, watching me. I shiver.

'Oh, you're back,' a low, raw-edged voice greets me.

'Eve!' I jump as she opens the cabin doors, nodding for me and Daniel to walk past her. Still I hesitate, getting a bad feeling about the situation. I can't bring myself to take a step further, until Billy rushes eagerly ahead, with Daniel close on his heels.

Eve turns on the lamps; I wonder why she was sitting in the dark. The flame in the wood burner is dwindling; wind whistles down the chimney. The cabin no longer feels welcoming; it's a hostile place, and I know that when I leave it, life will have changed for ever.

'We have unfinished business.' Daniel positions himself in the middle of the cabin, feet planted wide. 'We made a deal. You appear to have reneged on your part.'

'Ruth, are you OK?' Eve ignores Daniel, bypassing Daniel and coming to stand next to me. Her face is even paler than usual; her eyes are red-rimmed. There's a bruise on her neck.

'Are *you* OK?' I counter, pondering whether Jack gave her that bruise.

'Where's the hot chocolate, Mummy?'

Billy jumps up, bowling towards us, and my heart almost stops as, for a moment, I think he's going to run to Eve. Then he beams up at me and bundles in for a hug. I meet Eve's eyes and read the same thought in hers: *She gave birth to Billy, but I'm the one he turns to.*

'I'll make some in a second,' she tells him. 'How about some juice for now?' Grabbing a carton from a compact fridge in the neat kitchen area, she pours a glass. 'Here you go, buster. Why don't you build me a tower out of those wood bricks by the door? I'll make that hot chocolate. Maybe a coffee for your mummy, hey?' She sets a kettle to boil on a small hob.

'I'm not thirsty.' I sit down at the table, staring at Daniel, waiting to follow his lead. As he said, we tried it my way, now it's his turn to sort things out. *Once and for all.*

'Nor am I,' Eve says, opening a jar of instant coffee. 'But it gives me something to do.'

I glance back towards Billy, then lower my voice. 'Should we talk in the bedroom?' I suggest, even though it's the last place I want to be.

Eve shakes her head, as though she, too, can't bear to return to the scene of our traumatic conversation. 'Here's fine. I just want to get this over with.' She abandons the coffee and comes to sit on the bench opposite me, elbows propped on the table.

246

'As do we.' Daniel continues to loom over her, arms folded stoically across his chest.

Eve's eyebrows arch. 'Then we agree on *something*, at least.'

'Um, I noticed Jack is back,' I say to defuse the tension. 'Doesn't say a lot, does he?'

'He can't. Speak, I mean,' Eve clarifies. 'That's why he works as a labourer. He's never had much luck with office jobs. Anyway, he likes to build things. Work with his hands.'

I look at her in surprise. 'Wow. So how do the two of you—'

'Sign language.' Automatically, she shapes the words with her hands. 'Anyway, Jack isn't a big one for words. He's happy enough to let other people do the talking. Mostly me.'

'Oh. I see.' I'm not sure I believe her: the image of a quiet, compliant man that she's painting doesn't fit with the intimidating stance of the one who seemed to follow our every step across the deck with hostile eyes, axe held threateningly aloft. 'Well, I'm glad you've found happiness,' I say pointedly, thinking: *I won't let you destroy mine.*

'Thanks. I have. I know Jack looks tough.' Eve raises her eyebrows, clearly reading my scepticism. 'But he's always been there for me. Every man I've ever known has let me down. Except Jack. He's, um, he's actually the reason I'm here.'

'Sure.' I remember thinking that Jack might have been behind the blackmail plan. Despite her insistence about Billy, the continued tension on the boat tells me there's more at play here: I know Eve wants her son, but I sense she's after something more.

'Go on, then. Tell us. What does *Jack* want?' Daniel says derisively.

Eve doesn't turn around. 'Billy, of course. No more, no less.'

My heart sinks. *Bang goes that theory.* 'Right. So we're back to square one.'

'Hang on, Ruth. Let me speak,' Eve urges. 'You ran out just now before I could finish what I was saying. I was just getting to the hard bit.' She laughs nervously. 'If you don't let me say it

247

now, I might not be able to. You see, what Jack really wants is to be a dad.'

'Tell him to get in line,' Daniel sneers.

Eve ignores him. 'I told him I didn't want kids. Actually, I can't have any more.'

'So you thought you'd take back the one you made earlier!' Daniel huffs. 'Nice.'

Eve turns to glare at him. 'If you'll *please* let me finish.'

'Why can't you have more children?' I ask, beginning to grasp Eve's predicament. Jack is all she has. If he pressured her about having a child, the compulsion to do something rash to please him, to give him what he's always wanted, must have been enormous.

'Rape is brutal.' She wraps her arms around herself. 'It didn't just screw up my head.'

I stare at her pale face and dark, haunted eyes and feel another surge of pity. Digging my nails into my palms, I fight it. I can't let it get into my head that, in taking Billy, I'll be condemning Eve to childlessness. In giving him up, I would be ripping out my own heart.

'Did you tell Jack about your teacher assaulting you?' When Eve hangs her head, I encourage: 'If he's as kind as you say, he'll understand the damage that did to you. Not just physically, but emotionally. He'll appreciate why it made you want to give up your—'

'Actually, no,' Eve cuts in. 'I haven't told him. Not about the rape, or that I gave up my baby. I, um, I told Jack you stole him.'

'What?' I leap up, trembling in fury and sudden, gut-clenching fear. 'You did *what*?'

Chapter 50

'I didn't mean to,' Eve protests, looking more like a child caught stealing cookies than a grown woman who has told the most heinous lie. 'It just sort of came out that way.'

'*No*, Eve. You can't accidentally lie about something like that. It's obvious you told him that to get yourself off the hook. To cover up the fact that you didn't want a child. That's bad enough, but didn't you think of the consequences for *me*?'

'I never thought I'd see you again. I didn't think it mattered.'

I glare at her. 'You told Jack I stole your baby, and you didn't think that *mattered*?'

'I didn't just come out with it! Jack started talking more and more about us being a family. I kept stalling, making up excuses about our life on the boat, not having enough money. But I was scared he'd leave me. Then I really would have nothing.' She fiddles with the collar of her hoodie, and I glimpse another bruise, on her collar bone this time.

'Eve, does he hurt you?' I lower my voice now, forcing myself to calm down.

249

'No,' she snaps, too quickly. 'He's got a temper, sure. But he'd be a great dad, if that's what you're thinking.'

'Oh, really,' Daniel says scathingly, pacing up and down now. 'The man you can't even bring yourself to be honest with, would make a good father. I don't think so.'

'Don't you dare judge me,' Eve spits. 'I'm not calling you on *your* mistakes, am I?'

'What precisely are you referring to?' Daniel's tone could freeze water.

'Are you telling me *you* never looked at Billy and suspected he wasn't yours?'

'Not every child is the spitting image of their parents. They can take after grandparents. Aunts. Uncles. We don't analyse every little feature. We love Billy for who he is. The whole of him.' Daniel moves to stand closer to Eve, towering over her, glaring down at her. 'If you know you're not guilty, you don't look for a crime.'

Immediately, I guess that his use of the word 'crime' is intentional. We *haven't* done anything wrong, but Eve has. The balance of power, of *morality*, surely lies in our favour. I know it, but I feel uncomfortable pressurising her, as Jack clearly has. Eve has made mistakes, mostly at my expense, but I haven't completely given up on finding a solution without threats.

'I don't feel guilty about what I did,' Eve says defiantly, looking from Daniel to me. 'I honestly thought leaving my son was for the best. Then I saw that magazine article. It actually started as a joke. I said to Jack: "That looks like the little boy someone stole from me."'

'Very funny,' Daniel scoffs. 'And Jack didn't suggest you go to the police, *because* . . .? Ah, I see. He has a criminal record. Steers clear of the law. Or – wait. He's on the run.'

'It was *self-defence*. He was being bullied about his speech impediment. He snapped.'

'Wow. Like I say, perfect father material.' Daniel rolls his eyes.

'He's changed. Honestly. He wants to settle down. Have a

family. I wanted to give him that. The article – it spurred me into action, I guess. I tracked you down. In my head, it made sense. I gave Billy away, but he was mine. I could take him back.'

'Children aren't toys, Eve,' I cut in hotly. 'You can't put them to one side when you lose interest, then pick them up again when you feel like it.'

I turn to watch Billy piling little bricks into a tower, laughing as they keep falling into a heap. He's getting nowhere, but he keeps on trying. He won't give up. *And neither will I.*

'I know that now,' Eve acknowledges, so faintly I can barely hear her.

I sit back down on the bench, reaching across the table to take her hand, surprised when she doesn't shake it off. 'I'm not going to just hand him over to you. You must realise that.'

'You've given my boy everything I wished *I* could have given him,' she admits, looking back at me with dark-shadowed, tear-filled eyes.

'But you want to take it away,' Daniel snaps, and I can tell the 'my boy' has got to him.

'I wished on a star once.' Once again, Eve ignores Daniel and keeps her eyes fixed on me. 'I told you that, didn't I? And my wish came true. Everything is exactly as I imagined it would be. You've been a good mum, Ruth. The best.'

Gently, I press her hand, encouraging her to keep talking, heartened that she finally seems to be softening. 'You said if your son could have a good life, it would cancel out the bad stuff in yours,' I remind her.

'Yeah. Karma. I've always believed in it.'

The word 'karma' once again makes me think of Bea, and as I continue to hold Eve's fiery yet fragile gaze, it strikes me how very much she *does* remind me of my troubled friend. It occurs to me that if Bea's baby girl hadn't, in fact, died at birth, but had somehow miraculously survived, she would have grown up to look and be a lot like Eve.

251

'I know you do,' I acknowledge, still thinking of Bea and her conviction that finding her lost son was karma – wishing she could get her daughter back, too. 'But, Eve, two wrongs *never* make a right. You gave Billy away. Please don't make it worse by taking him back.'

'He's brilliant at drawing, isn't he?' Suddenly sitting up straighter, Eve wipes her eyes.

'Sorry?'

'When I was in your flat, I asked him to draw a picture of what makes him happy. He was so sweet, sitting next to me. I thought, *this is what a mummy does with her little boy.*'

'It's what *I* do with him.' I can barely say the words; my throat feels raw.

'He drew three stick people. He wanted me to write their names. Mummy, Daddy and Billy. It made me cry. I thought to myself – he doesn't need a new daddy. He already has one.'

'He . . . what?'

'And he has the sort of mum I wish *I'd* had.'

'Eve . . .' I dash away tears that suddenly won't stop.

'I know I dropped a bomb on you,' she continues, and her black eyes look enormous in her gaunt face. 'I came here hell bent on forcing you to give Billy up. I was wrong. I know that now. Not because you live in a penthouse and I live on a boat. But because he's with *you*, Ruth. You've given him a family. A proper, real, happy family. I can't take that away from him. Not now. Not ever. My little Sean. Please, just promise me you'll look after him?'

Chapter 51

'You made me doubt *everything*. Suspect *everyone*. Why did you *do* that?'

Even as a torrent of relief floods through me, I feel an unstoppable surge of anger at what Eve has put us through – how she's turned my life upside down and now wrong-footed me at the eleventh hour. I came on her boat determined to take Billy; now she's telling me she's decided to simply let him go.

'It was safer than telling you the truth.' She shrugs. 'Like you said, Mary committed a crime. *I* did. I knew if I just rocked up and came clean, you'd call the police.'

'As *you* threatened to do,' Daniel points out. 'You took a risk. I could have phoned them at any point.' He glances at me, reminding me that I was the one who'd stopped him.

'Daniel's right. We could have called the police immediately. We only *didn't* call them because . . .' *Because Eve is right*: deep down, I was worried that either Daniel or I was guilty. 'We wanted to help you,' I insist. 'I thought you had PTSD. That you were

253

deluding yourself. Living in a fantasy world. Looking at Billy and seeing your little boy.'

'Sorry. I never claimed to be a saint.' Her mouth twists and she looks and sounds more like Bea than ever. 'Here. Take this.' She digs into her pocket, then places my phone on the table. Somehow, it feels symbolic: like a truce has been acknowledged between us.

I reach out to pick up the phone; instead, I take hold of Eve's hand again. 'But you are a good person.' Despite everything, I believe that. 'You'd have been a good mum, too.'

Her eyes fill with tears. 'We were meant to meet, that day in the hospital. I made a deal with the universe, and I won. I needed to find Sean a mother. I found *you*.'

'You made a beautiful, perfect little boy.' I rub her small, almost childlike hand, watching a tear splash onto it. I blink, realising it's mine.

'Thank you for saying that.' She brushes away her own eyes with the sleeve of her hoodie.

'You don't have to thank me. It's true.'

'So why bring us here?' Daniel says through gritted teeth. 'You spent all afternoon in our apartment. You could have told us at any point.' He slams his hand down on the table. 'Bam. All sorted. Ruth was right. You've fabricated this whole charade. Pulling our strings every which way.'

'No. Honestly, that's not what I was trying to do! It wasn't like that. I promise.' Eve shakes her head until her hair flies about her face.

'Look, we're all upset. Let's not make things worse,' I say calmly, even though my pulse is racing. With her frightened eyes and tumbling hair, Eve reminds me again of a wild pony. I don't want to startle her into running away: changing her mind and forcing us to leave.

Without Billy.

'I'd gone so far, that's all,' Eve protests. 'I was scared of owning up.'

'To *us*? Or to Jack?' I say intuitively. Everything she's said about him tells me their relationship is based on a power dynamic that is neither equal, nor safe.

'I didn't bring you here to mess you about,' she insists, ignoring my question and, in doing so, answering it.

'Huh,' Daniel interjects.

'You have to believe that, Ruth,' Eve continues, keeping her eyes on me. 'I didn't make up my mind until we were all here. On the boat. I was confused. I showed you the birth papers to give you proof. But it was as much to convince myself that I really *did* have a baby. I look at Billy and . . . he doesn't actually feel like mine.'

'That's because he isn't,' Daniel states coldly. 'He's *ours*. We've raised him. We're the only parents he knows.'

'What about the photo, Eve?' I say gently. I share Daniel's frustration, but I know it won't help the situation. 'Surely that reminded you that you had a baby?'

'I didn't even want Mary to take it. But she said that, one day, I'd want to remember. I was sure I wouldn't. I wanted to *forget*. And I did. I blocked everything out of my mind. When I showed you that photo, it was the first time I'd looked at it in years.'

'I'm glad you *did* show it to me. And told me your story. It's helped me to understand.'

'Yes. That's it!' Eve's eyes widen even further, and for a fleeting moment, she looks exactly like Billy. 'I wanted you to know I'm not a bad person. I needed you to understand what I'd been through. Why I did what I did. I couldn't just blurt it out in your living room, could I? I needed you to come here. To *my* home.'

I sigh. 'I guess I can see that.'

'I thought, maybe, one day, you might tell Billy a bit about me?'

'The good bits, you mean,' Daniel mutters scathingly.

I raise my eyebrows at him, then turn back to Eve. 'I'm sure he will remember you.'

'Really?' She straightens up, looking brighter. 'Jack got this book from a library. It said a child's memories don't, you know, *stick* until they're about four. He convinced me that was good. That if Billy came with us, he wouldn't . . .'

'That he'd forget about us.' The thought of being pushed out of Billy's life, and then wiped out of his memory, is so appalling, I'm too rattled to say more.

'But I thought of all the *good* memories he'd lose, too.' Eve's shoulders slump again. 'To be honest, I wasn't sure I can make better new ones for him.'

I look into her eyes. 'I promise you I'll do my utmost to fill Billy's life with happy memories.' I turn to watch him, his tongue poking out in concentration as he piles up wooden blocks. 'And you know what? I think his time with you on this boat will be one of them.'

'See? I knew you were the one.' Eve grins, and I realise it's the first genuine smile I've ever seen on her face. 'Billy is adorable. But I know in my heart I don't feel the way you do. I can't, can I? Or I wouldn't have given him up. No matter what.'

'Well, it's not quite that simple, Eve, but I understand that—'

'You don't hate me, do you?' she says, suddenly serious again. 'I was doing this for Jack, and . . . He kept going on and on about us having a child. To do the stuff neither of us did when *we* were kids. Oh God!' she groans. 'He's not going to be happy with me.'

My own anxiety starts to spiral again as I realise that even though Eve's had a change of heart, her boyfriend might yet throw a spanner in the works. 'Are you *frightened* of him?'

'Of course she is,' Daniel chips in impatiently.

Eve glances towards the cabin doors, as though expecting Jack to barge in at any moment. 'He's got a temper, sure. But he hasn't really done anything wrong. Not like—'

'Did you hear that?' Daniel cuts her off, then crosses swiftly to the window, peering out into the darkness.

'What?' Eve leaps to her feet, too, and dashes to the window, just as a loud thump draws all our eyes to the boat's ceiling.

'*That.*' Daniel clenches his fists.

'It's probably Jack tidying up before the storm hits,' Eve says breathlessly, but she runs to the window on the other side of the boat to check.

I jump as the forgotten kettle finally reaches boiling point with a piercing scream; a second later, the strident noise is drowned out by the sound of loud cries.

A sudden volley of shouts seems to be coming from up on deck. All three of us stare at each other, before turning almost as one towards the cabin doors.

Chapter 52

It's so dark, I can only just make out the shape of Daniel ahead of me. I reach out to him, and he grabs hold of my hand. 'Stay back, Ruth.'

I crouch low on the steps leading up to the deck, my back pressed against the cabin doors. I can hear Billy on the other side, asking Eve what's going on. An hour ago, she felt like my worst enemy; now I have a feeling she might have become my truest friend.

She was right about one thing: Billy's happiness – his safety – is all that matters now, and I need her to look after him as though her own life depends on it. Whatever Jack is, or wants, or has done in the past, Eve needs to be strong now and stand up to him.

'There's no point hiding, Jack,' Daniel calls out, making his way across the deck.

Faint sounds drift across the water: voices from evening dog walkers wandering along the towpath, mingling with laughter from the terrace of a houseboat further along the river. I take comfort from the noise of people around us. *Witnesses*, I think with a shiver. But there is silence on Eve's boat, and the black water that surrounds us is a circle of my childhood fear.

'Come out, man. I just want to talk to you.' Daniel's voice echoes louder now.

As my eyes adjust to the darkness, I see his tall body silhou-etted against the indigo sky. The height and breadth of him is surprisingly intimidating, and I make a mental comparison with my brief glimpse of Jack, also recalling Eve saying her boyfriend can't speak.

That obviously explains why he's not replying, but his silence unnerves me more. I know he's been in prison; I wonder about the violence of his crimes. I wonder, too, if he was listening to Eve confess everything she's done, growing more furious by the second as he heard her give up on the devious plan he forced her into – give up on the little boy he wants.

'Daniel, come back,' I whisper, frightened for his safety.

'Go back into the cabin, Ruth. And stay there.'

'No. I'm not leaving you,' I say firmly, making my way up the steps to the deck.

By the time I reach the top, my legs are trembling, and as I straighten up I'm buffeted by a gust of wind. I hear a loud snap, followed by an electrical fizzing sound. Automatically, I duck, raising a hand to shield my eyes from the dazzling floodlights that are now on full beam.

'Over there!' I call out to Daniel, pointing urgently towards the wharf as I spot a figure half-illuminated by the floodlights. But Daniel is too far away. He doesn't hear me and carries on searching the far end of the canal boat. I fix my eyes on the man picking his way across the gangplank. 'Oh my God. *Finley.*'

'It's OK. Everything's going to be OK. I'm here,' he slurs, holding out his arms.

I back away. 'Have you been drinking?' It occurs to me that the shouts we heard moments ago might have come from him. It seems unlike him to cause a scene. Then again, nothing I've discovered about Finley today fits with the person I thought he was.

'Champagne, darling. And why not? I'm celebrating my freedom!' He raises his hands triumphantly, before stumbling sideways.

'Steady.' Instinctively, I reach out to him.

'Thanks, babe. Can't keep your hands off me, hey?' He winks suggestively.

'Finley, don't.' I glare at him, then look frantically around for Daniel.

'If you're looking for the ginger thug with the axe, he's chopping wood. Over there.'

I try to follow the direction of Finley's vague wave. 'Where?'

'Scared the living daylights out of me,' he says theatrically. 'I gave him a piece of my mind, though. The idiot tried to stop me coming aboard. I told him: "Stand aside, man! My best friends are on there!"'

'Friends. Sure.' I'm under no illusion about that anymore. 'Where have you been, anyway? You said you were going home to find Bea. You said you'd *call* me.'

'Sorry, babe. I couldn't find her. My beautiful wife appears to have vanished off the face of the earth. Huh. Good riddance to bad rubbish, I say. I expect she's done a runner in shame. I told you what she's like. Fickle. Feckless. Frigid.' His mouth curls in a sneer.

'I saw her, Finley. This afternoon.' I glare at him. 'She told me everything.'

'Well, bully for her. Bea's a liar and a fantasist. So whatever she said, I—'

'How did you know we were here, anyway?' I ask curiously, cutting him off.

'I spotted you from the towpath. I went to your apartment first, of course. See? I told you I'd come back for you. Beautiful you.'

He lurches towards me, and I have to brace my hands against

260

his chest to shove him back. 'No! Don't! Stop it!'

'Oh, come on, Ruth. No need to act coy. It's *me*, remember?'

'Yes, and you shouldn't have come here. You need to go home and sober up.'

'You're right, babe. As always.' He sighs. 'Although, it's so lonely in my little bachelor pad. Maybe I could have a lie down in there.' He nods at the cabin and starts heading towards it. 'It looks pretty cosy. Care to join me?' he throws over his shoulder.

'What? No, Finley, wait!' Billy is inside that cabin, and he's had enough to deal with already. I grab hold of Finley's arm as he passes me.

'Hey, no need to grab the goods, sweetheart. They're all yours.' He reaches for my hand. 'If you come with me, I might even let you unwrap them.'

'Oh, for God's sake.' I snatch my hand away. 'You're drunk. You don't know what you're saying. And this boat is *private*. You can't go inside that cabin. You need to *leave*.'

'OK, calm down!' Finley rolls his eyes. 'What the heck are you doing on a boat anyway?' He looks around curiously. 'Don't tell me Daniel's got himself a new boy toy.'

'It's not his. It actually belongs to Jack. The guy with the axe,' I say pointedly. 'Which means that technically . . .'

'I'm trespassing,' Finley finishes for me, holding up his hands. '*Mea culpa*. So how come you two got an invite? No, let me guess. This *Jack* is one of Mr Big Shot's clients,' he says scathingly, pointing at Daniel, who is now striding towards us across the deck.

'What the hell are *you* doing here?' Daniel barks.

'Finley's had too much to drink.' I'm stating the obvious; he can barely stand up.

'I told you, babe. I'm *celebrating*!' Finley declares. 'Thanks again for our chat last night, man.' He gives Daniel a double thumbs-up. 'I'm so much clearer about *everything* now.'

'Go home, Fin.' Daniel shoves his hands in his jacket pockets.

'We're in the middle of something here. You need to sort out your own—'

'Shh!' Finley lurches towards Daniel and pulls him into a bear hug. 'Seems crazy you guys have lived so close all this time. I can't believe the four of us have never hooked up.'

Daniel pushes him off. 'Yeah, well. There's been a lot of water under the bridge.'

'Huh. You see what you did there? Water. Bridge. Boats. And I thought Ruth was the clever one.' He winks. 'You are, aren't you, babe? You've figured it all out, haven't you?'

'Which bit?' I think back to my conversation with Bea. There are so many crimes and indiscretions Finley has to account for, I don't know where to start.

Daniel comes to stand between us. 'Leave Ruth out of it, mate.'

'Mate,' Finley spits. 'You're not my *mate*. You don't know the meaning of the word.'

'Look, just go home,' Daniel repeats calmly.

'Home? I don't have one anymore. My bitch of a wife has stolen it from me.'

'Where *is* Bea?' I ask anxiously, realising I haven't heard from her since I saw her at Kew. I wasn't expecting her to call or text, but suddenly I feel the need to check she's OK.

'At home. In *my house*. Bought with *my money*.'

'With Ophelia?' I ask breathlessly. 'Did you actually go back there?' A minute ago, he said Bea was gone. 'Did you speak to them? Are they all right?' *Did you hurt them?*

'Oh, Bea's fine. Getting dressed up. Painting her nails. Waiting for her lover. My so-called *mate*. You figured it out, didn't you?' he repeats, casting me a plaintive look. 'Your husband and my whore of a wife have been making fools of us both.'

'That's *enough*,' Daniel shouts, and in the blinding, artificial light flooding the canal boat, his eyes are like blue steel.

'Still keeping up the act, hey? Bea refused to admit it, too. What a pair you are. See, Ruth? I told you once, we should have

262

swapped partners. But no one ever listens to me!'

'Bea refuses to admit what?' Daniel takes a step closer to Finley, his fists clenched.

'I checked our home phone, dude. You called her this morning, didn't you? Who the hell phones his best friend's wife at six in the morning?'

I have a sudden flashback to Daniel in our bedroom, whispering into his phone. *Hi, it's me. There's been a change of plan.* Doubt takes root again. I swallowed everything Bea said to me at Kew; I felt desperately sorry for her, even fearful for her safety. *Had she played me?*

'I was trying to get hold of *you*, you idiot,' Daniel mocks. 'To cancel our meeting. I phoned my assistant first, told her to call you. Then I thought I'd best call you myself. But you didn't pick up your mobile. I forgot you'd moved out and tried your home phone instead.'

He'd phoned Corinne first. His familiar tone had been for his long-time assistant. Rushing off for my so-called relaxing bath, I hadn't heard his subsequent calls to Finley.

Almost dizzy with relief, I grab hold of the boat's guardrail. I grip it tighter as my thoughts return to Bea and Ophelia. 'But, Finley, how did you even get into the house, if you've moved out? Did Bea let you in?' *Somehow, I doubt it.*

'Of course not, darling. I have a key. I can come and go as I please,' he says arrogantly. 'She might earn a fortune from her pathetic gallery, but it's still my name on the title deeds.'

Daniel shakes his head. 'That's not how it works, man. Show a bit of respect for Bea. Whatever's gone on between you guys, she doesn't deserve—'

'Fuck you, Daniel Cartwright,' Finley spits. 'You don't fool me. I know your game. Oh, you can act all decent and honourable, but I know the truth. You're a nasty piece of work. You always have been. And I'm not going to sit by and let you muscle in on my family.'

Daniel rolls his eyes. 'Jesus, give it up, already.'

'Never,' Finley vows dramatically. 'You might have taken Ruth off me, but you'll never get your hands on Bea. *Or* Ophelia.' He steps closer to Daniel, leaning close to his face. 'Even if you *are* her father.'

Chapter 53

'You're being ridiculous.' Daniel braces his hands against Finley's chest. 'I have absolutely no idea what you're talking about.'

'Course you don't. Butter wouldn't melt, eh?'

Daniel shoves him away. 'It's not *me* who's been playing away from home. I have one word for you. Tanya.'

Finley's eyes narrow menacingly. 'What the fuck do you know about her?'

'Please, you need to calm down. *Both* of you,' I add, appealing to Daniel, too.

I haven't told him yet what Bea alleged about Finley – that he pushed Tanya down the stairs, desperate to get her out of his life – but I can tell her name is a red flag to him. If what Bea said was true, and Finley is capable of violence, I don't want him anywhere near Billy.

'Anyway, what the hell do you mean, I took Ruth off you?' Anger is still coming off Daniel in waves, but his voice is lower, his manner more controlled now.

Finley folds his arms. 'I liked her first.'

265

'So you told me. On your *wedding* day,' Daniel says pointedly. 'But we're not ten-year-olds in a playground. Ruth's a grown woman. She can make her own decisions.'

'She's also standing right here,' I point out, irritated even as I'm shocked to hear confirmation of what Bea said about Finley wanting me. I had no idea he had any feelings for me beyond our friendship – and even *that* evaporated after the christening weekend.

As for Ophelia being Daniel's daughter, I know the truth about that: the one-night stand Bea had in retaliation for Finley's infidelity. I trust she told me the truth about that, at least. She'd never admit something that painted her in a bad light, unless it was true. I can't swear that she wouldn't lie about Finley, to get back at him, but looking at his behaviour now, I strongly suspect everything Bea said about him was true – and fear for her returns in a rush.

'I need to speak to Bea.' I dig into my jeans pocket for my phone.

'I wouldn't bother,' Finley says, making a grab for it. 'I told you. She's a liar.'

'Hey. Go easy.' Daniel steps forward, brushing Finley's hand away from me.

'You've always got to be in charge, haven't you?' Finley huffs. 'The great Daniel Cartwright speaks, and everyone has to listen. You think you're so smart. So special. But you're *nothing*. Just an ordinary bloke who got lucky!'

'I am lucky,' Daniel says mildly. 'And the trick is, I know it. Whereas *you*—'

'Me? Lucky?' Finley stares at Daniel as though he's gone mad.

'Absolutely. You have a wife who's loved and stood by you when most women would have told you to take a hike years ago. You have a beautiful daughter, who—'

'Yeah, right.'

'Ophelia is *not my daughter*,' Daniel insists through gritted teeth.

'Please,' I cut in, appealing to him. 'I need to speak to Bea. I'm worried about them.'

Finley sidles up to me, so close, I can smell his aftershave. A sickening memory stirs. I back away, but he follows, lifting his hands and placing them gently around my neck, his fingertips slowly caressing my skin.

'I told you, Ruth. Forget about Bea. She's history. It's all about *us* now, babe.'

'Let her *go!*' Roughly, Daniel grabs hold of Finley's arm.

'Not until I've finished with her,' Finley spits, shoving him off. Returning his hands to my neck, his fingers squeeze tighter. 'I know you want me. You proved it to me that weekend in the New Forest.' His breath is hot on my face. 'When you begged me to fuck you.'

'When I . . . *what?*' My legs almost give way and I stumble.

Daniel reaches for me, but I'm already lurching away from him – from Finley – towards the side of the boat. I cling on to the guardrail, leaning over it to drag in a cold lungful of air, my mind plunging back once again to that night, almost five years ago: to the turning point in our friendship . . . in the rest of our lives.

Chapter 54

Five years ago

'Whoops! Easy does it.'

'Sorry. You go ahead.' My slurred words echoed inside my pounding head; I shook it to try to clear my muzzy thoughts. 'I seem to have lost the ability to walk.' I leaned against the wall, trying not to giggle as other hotel guests looked curiously at me on their way past.

I'd thought I was fine when we were sitting in the bar; it was only as I tried to get up to leave that I realised I could barely stand. I couldn't remember the last time I had felt so drunk, and I glanced at Finley, surprised to notice that he looked as cool and together as usual.

'I'm going nowhere. I'll *never* leave you, babe,' he vowed passionately.

'Well, *I'm* never drinking alcohol again.' I groaned. 'Daniel's going to give me such a lecture in the morning.'

Finley leaned closer, whispering in my ear: 'I won't tell him if you don't.'

'He'll know.' I prodded Finley's chest for emphasis. 'Daniel knows *everything*.'

'Well, he's perfect. Didn't you get his memo?'

I looked up at him. 'Are you saying my husband is . . .' The word slid away from me.

'A goody two-shoes?' Finley rolled his eyes.

'That's what Beatrice calls him. I hope *she's* behaving herself.' I felt a bolt of guilt that I'd left Daniel alone with her at the church. *Or were they at the reception already?*

I pictured the vicarage, where we'd gathered before the christening, then imagined the guests all dressed up as tarts and vicars. I was sure Daniel had said something about fancy dress. *He would hate it.* And Bea would tease him about his refusal to drink, as she always did. Finley, too. Only I knew the real reason for it: the alcoholism that had killed his father.

'My wife behave herself?' Finley huffed. 'Never.'

'We should join them.' I turned around, retracing my steps towards the bar.

'Bit late for that.' Grabbing me around the waist, Finley steered me the other way.

'Why, what time is it?' I lifted my wrist to my face, but my watch looked all blurry.

'Bedtime. Come along, Sleeping Beauty. Up we go.'

'I wish I *could* sleep for a hundred years. My head's thumping.' I slumped back against the wall, sighing as I looked down the corridor leading to the staircase at the end: I couldn't even walk in a straight line, let alone climb stairs.

'Here. Take one of these.' Finley reached into his suit jacket pocket and pulled out a foil packet, popping a little green tablet. 'Painkiller. That'll sort you out.'

'Thanks.' I swallowed it dry. 'Yuck. That tastes weird.'

'I'd offer you some vodka to wash it down, but . . .'

'Oh, you're hilarious,' I slurred, then slid down the wall into a crumpled heap. 'I *so* can't remember how to walk.' I rested my head on my arms, feeling sick. Then, in the next moment, I felt like I was floating upside down as strong hands lifted me off the floor.

'Then I guess I'm going to have to carry you.'

*

Finley was tall, but he was also lean, and I was surprised at how strong he was as he carried me along the corridor and up the stairs, then along another corridor to my room. I couldn't remember the number, and he had to call out 'Sorry!' three times after pushing the key – that I'd eventually found in the bottom of my handbag – into the wrong doors.

'Here we are. Hand delivered to your four-poster, princess.'

'Thank you,' I slurred. 'If you could just point me in the direction of . . .' As he set me down, I stumbled into the room, wincing as I cracked my shin against a chest of drawers.

'Oh, I think I can do better than that.' Finley hoisted me up over his shoulder, then strode towards the bed and let me slide down onto it.

'Ouch,' I complained, falling face first. Pressing my face into the pillow, I still felt like I was moving. 'Is the bed rocking? I feel like I'm on a boat. Daniel has always wanted a boat. I hate them,' I added, yawning. 'I'm so tired.'

'Don't fall asleep in your clothes, darling. You'll be uncomfortable. Here. Pyjamas.'

'Pyjamas . . .'

'And a goodnight kiss for your Uncle Finley.'

The bristles on his jaw rasped against my cheek. His aftershave was so strong, it caught at the back of my throat. 'Kiss?' I echoed faintly in confusion, as the room started to spin.

'If you say so. Don't mind if I do.'

I wondered when the painkiller he'd given me would kick in, because my skull hurt like it was being compressed by a vice.

Then I realised it *was* being squashed: beneath Finley's chest. I opened my mouth to protest, but a pillow pressed against my face absorbed my cry for help. I tried to gasp for air, but my lungs burned as fingers squeezed tightly around my neck.

I had a sudden thought that I was going to die without ever having become a mum, and then I felt a sharp, stabbing pain low down between my legs, and I was convinced it was all over. 'Stop! That *hurts*!' I managed to cry out, fighting back.

I tried to kick my legs, but every part of me below the waist felt rubbery, while above the waist I felt crushed beneath a tonne weight. All I could see was black, with tiny pinpricks of light, like stars, swimming in front of my eyes. I knew I was either going to faint or die.

'It hurts a lot less if you don't resist,' a low, gravelly voice said in my ear. 'Come on, babe. You know you want it. You've been begging for it all night.'

'No, no, no . . .' I thrashed my head from side to side, but it only made the choking nausea surging up inside me worse.

'It's OK, sweetheart. It's all going to be OK,' the voice cajoled. 'I'll take care of you. You know I can. Give me a chance.' His fingers dug into my thighs again.

'No. *Please*.'

'Ah, sweet of you to ask so nicely. I knew you wanted me. Now, let me show you *exactly* what you've been missing with that loser husband of yours.'

Chapter 55

'You bastard. *You assaulted my wife.*' Daniel throws the first punch, but Finley was clearly expecting it. He ducks, then circles around me, using my body as a shield.

'Rubbish. She begged me to fuck her,' he sneers.

His fingers dig into my waist, reminding me so horrifically of that night that I almost black out. 'Let me go,' I plead.

'I told you, *never*,' Finley rasps, and I can feel his spittle on my cheek.

'Did he rape you?' Daniel asks me directly, and his blue eyes are fixed and furious.

'Yes,' I croak, wondering why it isn't obvious, before realising that the sickening pictures were only in my head – Daniel couldn't see them.

And Bea made Finley destroy the photos on his phone, I recall, so I don't even have proof. Reliving that night in my imagination doesn't prove it, either. But I'm no longer in any doubt: I didn't have drunken sex with Finley. *First, he drugged me. Then he raped me.*

272

No wonder that night completely evaporated from my memory, until Bea's barbed reference in the playground to *guilty secrets* pricked my conscience, with Eve's accusation then forcing me to put two and two together . . . and make five.

Finley's date-rape tablet wrought evil witchcraft on my mind and body that night. I've been prescribed enough medication in my life – pills to cheer me up; others to calm me down – and I've become an expert on the subject. I know all about Rohypnol and the like.

I know it renders the body powerless and compliant, causing dizziness, confusion and sleepiness – and nausea. All of which I felt that night . . . and the following morning. Worst of all, it numbs the mind, blocking memory, not just in the moment, but in the minutes and even hours before and after it's taken. Add to that the shock of trauma – Finley's brutal assault – and I'm no longer surprised I blotted that entire weekend out of my mind all these years.

It took another trauma to unfreeze my memories: *the threat to my son.*

'Billy!' I call out, sobbing now.

'Leave him,' Finley instructs. 'We don't need a kid around cramping our style, do we? Even if he *is* my son. Like I said earlier, Billy even *looks* like—'

'Don't you dare mention his name ever again!' I scream. 'And he is *not* your son.'

Forcibly, Daniel wrenches Finley away from me. 'Ruth, are you OK? I'm so sorry. I should never have left you alone that night. It's my job to *protect* you. What this piece of shit did to you . . . I'll never forgive him. I can't forgive *myself*.'

'It's not your fault. None of it. It's *his*.' I glare at Finley.

'I'm so sorry,' Daniel repeats, sounding as broken as he did when he first realised Billy was Eve's son. Then, in the next moment, his chest puffs out in rage as Finley grabs at me. 'I said, let her *go*!' Daniel yells, so loudly that I feel the vibration of his anger all through me.

273

'I let her go once,' Finley hisses. 'I'm not making that mistake again.'

'I'm giving you once last chance,' Daniel warns. 'Back off, or I'll make you.'

'Huh. That old threat.' Finley throws back his head and laughs. 'I've used it a dozen times. It doesn't work, mate. Not on women. And definitely not on me.'

'Tanya,' I whisper, wondering painfully how badly she suffered at Finley's hands.

I think of her outspoken, demanding demeanour at work – even before Finley attacked her – and it dawns on me that she must have been overcompensating: for the powerlessness she clearly felt inside, trapped in a destructive, manipulatively seductive relationship, unable to break away from Finley's gaslighting veneer of charm that masked coercive control.

I was fooled by him too, I think. His flippancy has often unnerved me; I've never been entirely sure if he's joking or serious. He knows how to play on my insecurities; he's deliberately made me doubt myself. He let me think I betrayed my husband – shamefully, drunkenly – irresistibly drawn to his own fake, brittle charm.

But Finley doesn't want me; I'm certain of that. He only wants to prove he can have me, to get one over on Daniel. He's in love with no one but himself, and I despise him. He's a coward and a liar – and a rapist. The thought makes me shudder in horror at what he did to me, and I thank God that there is no longer any question in my mind that he is Billy's father.

'Huh. Tanya was a prick tease, too.' Finley scowls. 'Always picking me up and putting me down, whenever it suited her. Promoting Bea every few months, just to make herself feel better about screwing her husband. Playing me off against my own damned wife. Telling me she'd only promote *me* if I kept sleeping with her.'

'Tanya pressured you into sleeping with her?' Daniel scorns. 'Don't be ridiculous.'

'You don't have to overpower someone physically to take advantage of them,' Finley asserts slyly. 'When I put up a fight, Tanya played dirty.'

'You had a row with her on the phone. At breakfast, the morning after the christening,' I say, realising that if I get him talking, divert his attention, I can slip out of his arms.

He'd also said there was something he wanted to talk to me about, I recall. He never got around to it, and I'm convinced now that it wasn't about Bea's fixation on me, as he improvised earlier. I'm certain it was about what happened between us the night before.

He'd wanted to check if I remembered the rape.

Finley takes the bait, launching into a verbal attack on Tanya. 'Ha! I had a hundred rows with her. She never stopped calling me. Texting me at all hours. She wouldn't shut *up*. No matter what I said, or did. Nothing would stop her until she was literally at death's door.'

'I know you pushed her,' I tell him, hoping the threat of that knowledge will finally convince him to back off. But Finley merely laughs.

'The crazy thing is, she *knew*. And she's never told the police! How twisted is *that*? She told them it was attempted murder. She didn't have the bottle to give them my name.'

'Maybe she genuinely cares about you.' I'm horrified by his callousness as I remember what Bea told me at Kew Gardens about Tanya being *besotted*.

'Maybe she knew it gave her the ultimate hold over me, more like. I put her in a wheelchair. I could hardly abandon her, could I?'

'You're sick, man.' Daniel's face is wreathed in disgust. 'You belong behind bars.'

As if on cue, flashing blue lights fly across Kew Bridge, a siren blaring as two police cars speed towards the high street . . . in the direction of our apartment building.

Within moments, a small crowd gathers on the towpath, and I

see yellow high-vis jackets and hear the crackle of a police radio.

'Shit,' Finley curses. 'The bitch. She must have called them, after all.'

'I think Bea has more than earned that right, don't you?' I say coldly.

'Bea? What?' Briefly, Finley turns to look at me, his dark brows drawing together in a puzzled frown. 'I told you, she's . . . she *can't* have called . . . That's impossible. No, I meant . . . Fuck.'

Seeing officers striding towards the canal boat, Finley throws me roughly away from him, before making a dash towards the gangplank. Picking myself up from the deck and rubbing my bruised arms, I'm filled with relief that he's finally gone.

Until I look up and see a tall, broad figure blocking Finley's exit. It's Jack.

Chapter 56

'I told you already. Are you deaf, man? Get out of my way,' Finley yells.

I watch Jack inching across the gangplank towards him, and my legs seem to turn to jelly. I know it's Billy he wants, not Finley. 'Billy!' I jerk into action, bolting to the cabin.

'Let's get him and go,' Daniel instructs, catching up with me.

'I think we should take Eve with us.' Despite her attachment to Jack, I'm worried about leaving her alone with him. 'We can talk some more about Billy's future.'

Daniel hesitates. 'I'm not sure. What if she tries to run off with him?' He puts a hand on my arm to stop me opening the cabin doors.

'I don't get the feeling she will. She said it herself – he's where he's meant to be.'

'She's changed her mind once. What's to say she won't again?'

'It was Jack who changed it for her.'

'Huh, well, don't worry about Jack. I can handle him. He has no claim on Billy. It's *Eve* we need to worry about. But I know

277

how to handle her, too. I'm pretty sure I can persuade her to sign something relinquishing her rights. I'll hire a lawyer. I'll hire *ten* lawyers.'

'That would scare her off,' I whisper, conscious that Eve is on the other side of the cabin doors. 'She's terrified of anyone in authority. Understandably, given what she did.'

'Then we'll handle the whole thing on the quiet. Adopt Billy without telling anyone.'

I sigh, wishing it were that easy. 'I went through the foster system, Daniel. Nothing happens simply. And what about Jack? He could put something in writing, painting *us* as the bad guys.'

'But we're not!'

'And by the time the courts figure that out, what state is Billy going to be in? Would they even let him stay with us while they investigate what's happened?'

'They can't take him. On what grounds?'

'Jack only has to repeat what Eve told him – that we stole her baby.'

'He wouldn't dare,' Daniel says grimly. 'Besides, I have the feeling he's going to have his own crimes to answer for, before he has a chance to bleat about ours. Jack doesn't have a licence for this boat, Ruth. I checked this afternoon. He's in breach of his parole terms.'

'What?' I turn to look back towards the wharf, watching police officers escort both Finley and Jack away. 'Thank God the police are here,' I say, clutching Daniel's arm.

'I don't know about God, but we've got *someone* to thank for calling them.'

'Bea?' I'm still hoping it was her – that she finally found the courage to report Finley and tip the police off about the most likely place they would find him. *At my home.* 'I hope she's OK. Ophelia, too. I'm worried Finley went round there. I hope he didn't hurt them. Damn, I need to call Bea.' I take out my phone, frustrated when I can't get a signal.

'Well, whoever it was who made the call, I'd like to shake their hand. Both of those losers will get what they deserve now.' Daniel nodded towards the wharf. 'End of story.'

'Not quite. *Poor Eve.*' I'm reassured to hear her chatting calmly to Billy behind the cabin doors, but I feel bad for the shock that's about to hit her. 'She's going to be devastated that Jack's been arrested. He's all she has. We need to help her, Daniel.'

'Don't worry. I'll make sure Eve is taken care of.'

His tone gives me goose bumps, but the cabin doors fly open before I can reply. Billy charges into my arms, and I sit down on the steps to cuddle him, sending up a prayer that we can get back to normal now.

Life as we knew it, only better, with all the secrets and misunderstandings finally washed away. Jack will be safely in custody, Finley too. Hopefully, neither will ever be able to come near us again.

'I kept him inside as long as I could,' Eve says, emerging from the cabin. Her eyes are huge and luminous with fear as she watches Jack being led away by the police officers.

'I'm sorry, Eve.' I rest a hand on her arm. 'I know you love Jack.'

'What's he done?' she wails. 'He's not the bad guy here. He doesn't deserve—'

'Wait here. I'll find out what's going on,' Daniel cuts in. He ruffles Billy's hair, then pulls up the collar of his jacket before striding off.

'Will they arrest me, too?' Eve says anxiously. 'I know I shouldn't have come here. But I didn't hurt you, did I? Nor did Jack.'

'I don't think it has anything to do with our situation,' I tell her, recalling what Daniel said about the boat licence. 'No one even knows about it. I haven't told anyone. Have *you*?'

Eve shakes her head until her hair flies upwards, trailing on the wind. 'Me and Jack keep to ourselves. We won't cause any more trouble. I promise.'

279

'Don't worry. Daniel will fix it,' I tell her confidently. 'He always does.'

'Yeah,' Eve says bitterly, rubbing at her eyes. 'It's easy for men like him, isn't it?'

'Sorry?'

'Look at him! Doors open for guys like your husband. Now look at Jack.' She points to her boyfriend, who despite his height and bulk, looks cowed and broken as the police lead him away. 'They always slam in his face. Oh, God, he's going to be so mad at me.'

I frown at her. 'Who? Jack? But if he's broken his parole conditions, Eve, then—'

'No, I mean Mr Cartwright.'

'Daniel? Why would *he* be mad at you?'

'For the police being here.' Eve starts biting her fingernails, her eyes wild and darting. 'He'll think I called them. You will tell him I didn't, won't you?'

'Of course. But, honestly, he won't think that for a moment. He knows it wasn't Jack.' I still think it was most likely Bea who phoned the police, but I frown as I recall that when I suggested as much, Finley looked puzzled at the idea, insisting she couldn't have done that.

Fear for Bea and Ophelia's safety rushes up once more. Finley raped me, and he tried to kill Tanya. *What the hell has he done to Bea and her daughter?*

Yet again, I try to call Bea, groaning in exasperation when I'm forced to concede that I can't get any reception on the boat. It must be in a black spot.

'Are you sure?' Eve persists, looking doubtful.

'Sorry?' For a moment, I've forgotten what she's talking about. 'Oh. You mean Daniel. Yes. Absolutely. Look, I know you two haven't got off on the right foot, but my husband is a good, kind man. He'll take care of everything. I promise.'

'If you say so,' Eve whispers. But, if anything, she looks even more worried.

Chapter 57

'Take Billy back inside the cabin,' Daniel instructs Eve, as he returns a few moments later. 'Just until the police have wrapped things up.'

'I'm not tired,' Billy protests, yawning.

'I can see that.' Daniel smiles. 'How about you do some colouring, then? I hear you drew a nice picture this afternoon. Do you think you could do another? For me?'

'OK, Daddy.'

'That's my boy.' Daniel bends to give him a quick kiss. 'Be good for Eve, son. Ten more minutes, then it will be time to say goodbye to her.'

'What happened?' Eve asks anxiously. 'What did the police say?'

'Maybe we should talk later?' I suggest, watching Billy's eyes widen at the mention of the police. I'm about to give him a hug when I feel a sudden, hard shove against my back.

Instinctively, I reach out for Billy's hand, but as I hit the deck, I sense rather than see a tall, dark figure rush past me – and sweep Billy up into his arms.

'Finley!' Daniel yells, striding after him, muttering: 'Fucking hopeless police. They had him in the palms of their hands. Why can't people just do their *job*?'

'Mummy!'

Momentarily stunned, I blink rapidly as I look up to see Billy hanging over Finley's shoulders, his head bobbing low against his back, arms flailing helplessly. 'Billy!'

The deck seems to grow ever longer as I dash across it, my legs pumping, heart pounding. The blackness of the water stretches all around us, but I don't look at it: I keep my eyes fixed straight ahead, on Billy's face.

Seconds later, a shadow looms into my peripheral vision. Jerking my head to one side for a better look, I see long hair flying out behind a pale face.

'Eve! He's got Billy!' I scream pointlessly: she's younger and faster than me, and this boat is her home. She knows every obstacle, leaping effortlessly over heavy coils of rope and trailing piles of old nets.

At least ten strides ahead of me, Eve reaches the edge of the boat in one final, desperate dash, throwing out her arms to make a grab for Billy's hands. She almost makes it.

'Put him *down*!' she screeches.

'With pleasure.'

I lurch forwards, diving towards Billy just as Finley lifts him above his head, swinging him out over the edge of the boat. He holds him there, smirking while Billy's legs kick frantically. Then he bends his knees, garnering momentum, before jerking his arms and releasing Billy into the air.

'BILLY!'

As black as the night sky and wide with shock, Billy's eyes meet mine. He flies upwards, seeming almost to hang in mid-air for a moment, his arms waving above his head, as though trying to catch hold of the stars. Then he plummets out of sight.

My mind goes dark. I can hear the wind and smell the acrid

saltiness of the water; I can feel the guardrail, the cold iron rough against my hands. I brace one foot against the lower rung, hauling myself up to look down at the murky river rushing below.

A dark shape bobs on the water before spinning around, cast upwards by a wave from a passing boat. It's Billy, his curls flattened against his head, his little face rigid with cold and terror, before the water sucks him under.

'No!'

The scream seems to be all around me, and I realise that Eve's cry echoes mine. I throw myself forwards but an elbow, sharp against my chest, knocks me back, winding me. I fall backwards, and the last thing I see is Eve flying through the air. I hear a splash, and then my head cracks against the deck – and I'm swallowed by blackness.

Chapter 58

The stars remind me of Billy's bedroom. I covered his ceiling with them, painting each one with luminous paint so he could lie in bed and imagine he's floating through space. But Billy's walls are grey; the sky above me is endless black. I feel like I'm plummeting head first into it.

'Mummy's eyes are closed. Is she asleep?'

Billy's alive!

'She's had a bit of a bump on the head, son. They're taking her to the hospital, OK?'

'Will they fix her?'

'Of course. They have very clever doctors there. Just like when you were a baby.'

'I want to go with her.'

'I think that's a good idea. They'll want to have a look at you as well, son.'

'Is that why they wrapped me up in foil? To save me for later? That's what Mummy does with my sandwiches.'

'Something like that, sweetheart.'

'Will you come too?'

'I'll never leave you, Billy. I'm your dad. It's my *job* to make sure you and Mummy are OK. The doctors will look after you. I'll take care of everything else. Just like I always do.'

'Has Uncle Finley gone? Why did he drop me, Daddy? Was it a game? He scared me.'

'Yes. He's a very silly, very bad man. He thought he was stronger and cleverer than Daddy. But don't worry. You'll never see him again. The police have taken him away. I won't ever let him come near you again.'

'You're the best daddy in the world. You *saved* me.'

'You're a super brave boy, Billy. You kicked your legs. You didn't give up. That's the spirit you need. If you want something, you have to *fight* for it, son. And you did.'

'Eve is brave. She dived in. I saw her. She tried to hold me up. But her magic fingers didn't work. I thought they'd make her swim. But her face kept going under the water.'

'I'm sorry, darling. Sometimes we have to make our *own* magic.'

'She told me she wished on a star when she was little. And her wish came true! Look! The stars have come down to see her.'

'It's just the reflection on the water, son. But you're right. It does look like stars.'

'It looks like heaven. Is that where Eve has gone, Daddy? I hope so. I think she'll like it. She told me she knows a little boy who lives there.'

*

I'm so cold; the stars have gone out.

'There's Captain Jack, Daddy. Can we go on his boat again tomorrow?'

'Jack might not stay on the boat, son. It doesn't belong to him.'

'But he's the pirate captain. He needs a boat.'

'Well, let's see. Maybe Daddy will sort that out for him. As a favour. If he does one for me too, we'll be quits, won't we? Like when you trade your football cards with Joseph.'

'He might give you one of Eve's wooden animals. *That* would be a good swap.'

'Oh, he doesn't need to give me anything.'

'Really?'

'Nuh uh. Maybe he could *keep* something for me, though. A little secret, perhaps.'

'Jack doesn't speak. I bet he's good at keeping secrets.'

'Excellent. But first we have to get Mummy better, hey? She'll be so worried about you. You'll help me look after her, won't you? She didn't have a mummy of her own. All she's ever wanted was to be *yours*.'

'She's the best mummy ever. Do you think she'll make me pancakes for breakfast?'

Chapter 59

The blue canal boat is gone. It's the first thing I notice when I look out of the kitchen window, staring at the lights twinkling along the towpath. They make the river look like it's dressed for a party; my mood couldn't be less festive.

I can't sleep; I've had headaches ever since I was finally discharged from hospital yesterday evening. The doctor said there is nothing wrong with me – physically. Nothing that rest and being at home with my family won't cure.

It feels strange to see the gap between the houseboats. Daniel said he spoke to Jack while I was in hospital, and that they had parted on 'reasonable terms'. Given the complex and tragic circumstances, I imagine it wasn't an easy meeting, but I know Daniel would have handled it brilliantly. He's coping remarkably well, given the trauma of the last few days. I envy his strength to deal so calmly with change – and loss.

So much loss. Finley. Bea. Eve. *My little boy* . . . They're all gone.

Finley is still in custody, being interrogated about what he did, not just to Billy but also Tanya, who I'm guessing finally did make that call – not Bea.

She's in Scotland now with Ophelia. I know that because she sent a jubilant text saying she'd 'found her boy'. I replied wishing her well, hoping to see her on her return. I half suspect she won't come back. Finally, she's found her lost, stolen child: the missing part of herself.

And Eve . . . I can't stop dreaming about her – about Bea, too, actually: the two women who each changed my life, in different ways.

Bea was the first real friend I ever had; then I thought she became my enemy. Eve started out as my enemy, then I realised she was my truest friend. She came here to take my boy from me; instead, she gave me something I didn't know I was missing: the truth.

'Come back to bed, darling.'

'Oh, I didn't hear you.' Sighing, I turn to smile at Daniel.

'You were lost in thought. Good ones, I hope?'

'Some. But you should get some sleep, too. Billy wants to play football with you in the morning. The doctor said fresh air and exercise is the best thing for him, while he's off school. To help him get back to normal, and forget about . . .'

'Ruth? Are you OK?'

'Sure. Just, you know, flashbacks.'

'Yeah. Billy's still having bad dreams. He just called out.'

'Oh, no. I'll go and—'

'It's fine. I've settled him,' Daniel tells me, pulling me against him in a hug.

'Wow. That's new. I'm usually the one who drags myself out of bed in the middle of the night.' I smile to show I'm not serious.

I couldn't have coped, these last few days, without Daniel's support. After everything we've been through, we've *both* been changed, but I'm sure – I hope – our marriage is now stronger and more honest than ever.

'What can I say?' he teases. 'I'm turning over a new leaf.'

'Well, it is autumn. Out with the old . . .' My words dry in my throat as I realise that what I was about to say feels wrong. Our old friendships are well and truly gone, but they're not easily forgotten; they've left scars I'm not sure will ever heal.

'We need to keep looking forwards, sweetheart,' Daniel says, pulling me closer.

'I'm not sure I can yet. At least, not until the inquest is done. But they haven't even called us in to be interviewed. Is that *normal*?'

I'm still anxiously rehearsing how to present Billy's complicated situation to the authorities, as well as wondering whether to mention Finley's assault on me. It would be my word against his, and I already know how persuasive and plausible he can be.

'I reckon so. There were several witnesses to Eve's drowning. I'm sure the police will speak to everyone who was on the riverside on Friday night. As for Finley, they've got him bang to rights,' Daniel says unsympathetically. 'I made a few calls. Sounds like Tanya finally told the police everything. If you feel up to making a statement about what he did to you . . .' Daniel tenses. 'Let's just say Finley won't be walking the streets for a very long time.'

'I'll be glad when I never have to hear or say his name again.'

'Hey.' Daniel tilts up my chin to look at him. 'I'm right here, and I'm going nowhere. And if you *don't* feel up to making a statement, no pressure.'

I make up my mind. 'I'll do whatever it takes to make sure he gets what he deserves.'

'Good. So we can forget about Finley McDermott. We need to concentrate on *us* now. You, me, Billy. Our family. Onwards and upwards. Nothing and no one can stop us now.'

I have a sudden feeling of déjà vu, my mind spinning back to the day I went into labour. 'You said that when Billy was born.'

'Well, it only took us four years to make it so.' Daniel chuckles.

'You really think this whole nightmare is over? What about Jack?' I ask fearfully.

'Oh, he won't be back to bother us. Let's just say we had an exchange of paperwork. He gave me Billy's hospital notes. I had the canal boat officially transferred into his name. Sorted out his registration and insurance. He'll leave us alone now. I'm sure of it.'

'Eve would have been happy about that. She loved that boat.' I turn to look out of the kitchen window again, even though there's just an empty space where the canal boat used to be. 'Transferred from who, though?' I ask curiously. 'Who owned it?'

'No one you know. It was just a rental.'

'Ah. That figures. Boats aren't cheap. You know that better than anyone. You've always wanted one. Sorry,' I add. 'I know my stupid fear of the water must be annoying. I just hope Billy gets over his.'

I close my eyes to try and stop the images spooling through my head: Billy in the river, his terrified eyes staring up at me, the riptide dragging him under.

'He'll forget. Kids do. The doctor referred him for counselling, too. When the time is right. The most important thing is that he's safe. Here, with us.'

I feel a sob form in my chest. 'I always wanted to give him the perfect life. I feel like I've failed. I didn't even dive in and save him. *You* had to do it.'

'You were going to,' Daniel reminds me. 'Eve barged you out of the way.'

'She knew I was terrified of the water. But I reckon it was more than that.' I think for a moment, remembering the young woman who, I'm convinced, gave her life to save Billy's. 'My hunch is, she felt she had to do something to make up for the trouble she'd caused.'

'Or she was making a statement that she was Billy's mother. That only *she* had the right to save him.'

'*Die* for him, you mean. She couldn't swim.'

'So she wanted to be a hero!'

'I don't think so.' I glance up at him in surprise. Eve put us

290

through a tough time, but she was a troubled woman who has just lost her life. It isn't like Daniel to be unfeeling. 'She made mistakes, but she'd been through so much. It *damaged* her. She wasn't a bad person.' I'm glad, at least, that I got to tell her that. I pray she also died knowing her son was safe.

'Huh. I can't believe I'm hearing this. After everything she did? You're too kind, Ruth. And Eve Parker was a manipulative little madam. She had you well and truly fooled.'

'For a time. But in the end, I think I understood her. She said she felt a connection with me when we first met. I felt it, too. I must have, or I wouldn't have remembered her. And after what she did . . .' I pause, remembering the baby clothes she had kept, the pain on her face when she recounted her story. 'There will always be a connection between us.'

'What?' Daniel looks cross. 'No, Ruth. She's gone. Let it go. Let *her* go.'

'She called her little boy a shadow of mine,' I say sadly, fighting tears. 'But it was the other way around. *Our* baby was the shadow. He died, and hers lived.'

'I guess I just think of Billy as ours. I always have, since day one.'

'Well, yes. But we did have a son. I'll never forget that. Or him.'

'You think I will?' Daniel jerks back. 'That was the worst day of my life.'

'You mean the day he was born?' I frown. 'Or when Eve told us he'd died?'

'Both. The whole damned mess. Jesus, it feels like a nightmare that will never end.'

'But it is over, isn't it? Like you said. We need to let go of the past and concentrate on the future now. Starting with trying to get some more sleep.' I wind my arms around his waist.

'Sure. We've lost enough of it over all this.' He loops his arms around me, too. 'Ha. The only comfort is that Finley will be spending the night in a *very* uncomfortable place.'

'Good. Thank God Tanya finally called the police. Or Bea.

Anyway, whoever it was, I owe them a big thank you. If the police hadn't showed up when they did . . .'

'OK, confession time.' Daniel steps back, holding up his hands.

'Sorry?'

'It wasn't Bea. Or Tanya. *I* made that call,' he admits sheepishly.

'What?' I stare at him in astonishment. '*When*?'

'While you were talking to Eve on the boat. We heard shouting, remember? I went up on deck to investigate. I didn't find Jack, so I nipped over to the towpath. Had a scout along there. Then I phoned the police. Anonymously, of course.'

'*Why*? I mean, I'm glad you did. But I am surprised. I thought the last thing we wanted was the police hanging around us, poking into our business. Asking questions about Billy.'

'Well, like I told you, Jack didn't have a boat licence. He was in breach of his parole terms. I may also have thrown in that he was acting threateningly.' Daniel's eyebrows arch.

'Huh. That's true enough.'

'Yeah. Anyway, I figured the police would keep him talking for a while. Long enough for us to get Billy off that boat.'

'So it was just luck that Finley happened to turn up at the same time?'

'I don't believe in luck. I'm a banker, Ruth. I believe in attention to detail. I told you before we even went on that bloody boat that I had it all figured out. Brains not brawn is the way to win. I never leave *anything* to chance. Not when it comes to my family.'

Chapter 60

I still can't sleep. After my conversation with Daniel in the kitchen, my thoughts are churning.

Sitting upright in bed, I stare down at his bare, powerful shoulders. He's lying with his back to me, but his breathing has been steady for the last twenty minutes. He's sound asleep, and for the second time in what has been the worst four days of my life, I envy him.

Maybe he's sleeping so soundly because his conscience is clean, I reflect, whereas I can't stop beating myself up for things I didn't do: be a better friend to Bea; see through Finley's devious charm; stop Eve plunging over the edge of that boat . . .

For a moment, I consider digging out my old sleeping pills or antidepressants. But I want to be calm, not numb. I spent too long cocooned in a state of denial: I never saw the truth; I saw only what I wanted to believe. I won't go back there; I need to find other ways to deal with the dark thoughts I suspect will nag at me for a long time to come.

Deciding a hot drink might help, I slip out from under the

duvet and tiptoe downstairs towards the kitchen, pausing only to peep into Billy's bedroom to check he's OK. Thankfully, he's sleeping soundly, too. I hope a mug of mint tea will help me to do the same.

'Poor Eve,' I whisper, staring out of the window towards the wharf as I fill the kettle.

Feeling restless as I wait for it to boil, I pace through the apartment, pausing outside Daniel's study when I hear the sound of rustling paper. Opening the door to investigate, I see the window over his desk has been accidentally left open; papers are blowing everywhere.

'Oh, *no*.' I think of Daniel calling himself a meticulous banker. 'This won't do at all,' I mumble, hurrying into the study and shutting the window, before flicking on the desk lamp.

Kneeling down, I scoop up handfuls of paper, bundling together notes and invoices, letters and official-looking documents. Then I make myself comfortable on the leather captain's chair in front of Daniel's desk. 'If I can't sleep, I might as well make myself useful.'

Yawning widely, I begin sorting the jumble of paperwork into piles, scanning the contents to organise everything into *work* and *home*. 'Not very scientific, but it's a start.'

The repetitive process becomes hypnotic, and I'm about to give up and go back to bed when my attention is caught by an unfamiliar logo. Peering closer, I realise it's some kind of government emblem. 'Hmm, maybe I'm married to a spy. Nothing would surprise me now.'

I look closer at the document. At first glance, it looks like a simple log of financial transactions and registration numbers. 'Boring old bank stuff,' I dismiss, until the words 'blue paintwork, gold scrolling' leap out at me. 'Ah. The boat registration stuff for Jack.'

Curious to see who *did* own it, I skim the paragraph, picturing Jack's red hair and beard, his hard eyes and rugged face, feeling cross at how quickly he agreed to disappear.

His grief for Eve was short-lived, I think bitterly. He was more interested in the money Daniel offered him – not so much a bribe as 'compensation', as Daniel put it, to help Jack move on. The man had no moral or legal claim on Billy, and Daniel had already set in motion our own legal representation for the official adoption process.

'I wonder how much your silence cost, Jack,' I mutter, scanning the blur of figures underneath his name. 'Oh. That's odd.' I frown, noticing Eve's name under the section headed 'owner'. Looking closer, I'm astonished to notice the hefty price originally paid for the canal boat; it cost far more even than I imagined.

'How on earth did you get your hands on that kind of money, Eve?' I whisper, running a finger down the list of transactions, trying to figure out if I've misunderstood something. I rub my eyes in disbelief when I notice a set of familiar initials.

'DC,' I read aloud, holding the paper up to the lamp. It almost slips through my fingers when I read the earliest entry on the log: ownership transferred to Ms Eve Parker . . . from Mr Daniel Cartwright. The date of the transaction is the eighteenth of July. Four years ago.

*

'MUMMY!'

Billy's voice is loud but sleepy. I force myself not to move – not to leap up, revealing that I'm already wide awake. Instead I try to relax, control my breathing, not give away that I've been in Daniel's study for the last half an hour and have only now returned to our bed.

'Your turn, I think.' Daniel rolls over, his blue eyes glinting in the half-light.

'Already on my way,' I tell him, yawning as though I've just woken up.

'Thanks, sweetheart. What time is it, anyway?'

'Um. Not sure. Late. Or early. Depending on which way you look at it.'

'Always two sides to everything, hey? Even time.' He folds his arms behind his head.

'Totally. Anyway, I'll just go and see to . . .' I climb slowly out of bed, resisting the urge to rush out of the room, not wanting to flag up to Daniel that anything is different.

Everything is different.

I still believe Eve swapped our babies of her own accord; I'm also certain that she only came back for Billy because Jack persuaded her to. I know how mixed up she was, unwittingly allowing herself to be manipulated by stronger personalities. But, essentially, she was a good person who found herself in a terrible situation. Suddenly, I'm not sure Daniel is as innocent.

He pretended to be as shocked, as devastated by Eve's revelations of the baby switch as I was, yet how can that have been the case?

He bought her a boat. Three days after Billy was born.

'OK, darling? Time to get up.' I smooth the curls back from Billy's forehead, trying not to picture his wet hair plastered to his head as he bobbed on the river before being swept under.

'Is it school?' He sits up slowly, his bunched fists rubbing his eyes.

'No. It's Sunday.' I try to whisper, without making it obvious that I'm being secretive. 'I thought you and I could go for a little walk. Here you go. One hand up.' I pull his right arm out of his pyjama sleeve. 'Then the other, that's right. Clever boy.'

'I'm tired,' he complains, flopping back onto his pillow.

'I know, darling. But we won't go down by the river this time, OK?' I reassure him, sitting down on his bed and leaning close to him.

'Do you think Lucky Ducky is OK?' he asks anxiously.

'I'm sure she is. She has her babies to look after. And, one day, the bad pictures in your head will go away, I promise. We'll make *new* pictures. How about that? In fact, I have an idea. How about we go somewhere nice in the car? Even *further* away from the river.'

'OK.' Billy perks up at the idea, his sleepy frown evaporating. 'Will Daddy drive? He said he'd let me hold the steering wheel next time.'

'Actually, I thought you and I might have a special day.' I reach over to pick up his clothes from the chair next to his bed. 'Just the two of us. Would you like that?' I glance towards the door, before quickly helping Billy pull on his joggers, sweatshirt and socks.

He tips his head to one side, considering. 'Can we have hot chocolate with marshmallows and squirty cream?'

'You bet.' I press a quick kiss to his cheek. 'I just need you to do one thing for me first, before we can go.'

'Brush my teeth? Do I have to?' he groans. 'I haven't even had breakfast yet.'

'No. That's OK. No teeth brushing.' I smile. 'I mean, I want us to play a little game. What do you reckon?' I pause, knowing I've caught his interest now; Billy loves games. 'It's a new one. But I think you'll like it.'

'Is it like hide-and-seek?'

'Ah, I know that's your favourite. And yes. It's kind of like that. What you need to do is get back into bed – yes, that's right, in your clothes – and lie down really, really still. Even if Daddy comes in to check on you, stay quiet and keep your eyes shut. Can you do that?'

'Easy-peasy,' Billy boasts, clambering back into bed.

'Good boy. Lie down, then. Shh. Just like that. *Perfect.*' I pull up his Thomas the Tank Engine duvet, tucking him in tightly. 'And when I'm ready, I'll come back and get you. OK?'

'OK!'

I give him one last kiss, then whisper: 'Then I'll tell you the next part of the game.'

Chapter 61

My heart is beating furiously as I close Billy's door softly behind me. It's a risk getting him dressed and ready, but I need to be prepared. My hands shake on the doorknob when I peep through the crack again, anxious to make sure Billy is still lying quietly in his bed.

'Everything OK?'

I jump as Daniel appears behind me. 'Oh. Yes. Same as usual. He wasn't really awake.'

'Ah. Good. Things must be getting back to normal.' He smiles. 'I was just getting some water.' He lifts his glass, as though raising a toast. 'Heading back to bed. You coming?'

'In a minute. I feel a bit too awake now. Think I'll make myself a mint tea. Might help to soothe me. You go on back to sleep.' I risk giving him a gentle shove. The skin of his chest is unexpectedly cool; I wonder how long he's been out of bed. 'It's still early.'

'Or late. Depending on your point of view.' One eyebrow quirks.

'Sorry? Oh. Yes. That's right. Although I think we're definitely

298

closer to today than yesterday now.' I force a smile.

'Yeah. And it's the weekend. *Family* time.'

He winks, then turns and strolls back to our bedroom. I watch until he's safely inside, groaning in frustration when he leaves the door ajar.

Immediately, I abandon my plan of getting dressed in the bathroom: it's too close to our bedroom. Instead, I slip downstairs to the kitchen, heading for the basket of clean laundry. I dig through it to find underwear, black jeans and sweatshirt, then I bundle them up and head for the corner furthest away from the door.

I'm just zipping up my jeans when I remember that I'm supposedly making mint tea. Quickly flicking on the kettle, I dash back to the kitchen door and peer out. The hallway is empty, the apartment so quiet, I could hear a pin drop. I wonder if Billy is still obediently pretending to be asleep, waiting for the next part of the game, or if he's genuinely nodded off. Despite his smiles, I know he's physically and emotionally exhausted after the last few days.

I also know that what lies ahead is probably going to be even tougher for him. For me as well. But I have to do it. I can't stay here any longer, knowing that Daniel definitely lied about Eve, and Billy – maybe about Jack, too, and quite possibly Bea.

My husband might not be a spy, as I flippantly imagined, but he is keeping secrets from me. Huge ones. Sadness rolls over me in waves as I realise I no longer trust him.

I need time and space to decide what to do about that; I need to stop letting Daniel fix things, and start fixing them for myself.

Chapter 62

I can't believe we've made it out of the apartment, and all the way down to the underground car park, without being discovered. I feel dizzy with tiredness and the exertion of walking down six flights of stairs. My legs are trembling and my back is in agony from carrying Billy.

After waking him with a gentle shake, then pulling on his duffle coat and trainers, and my grey jacket and boots, before creeping out of the apartment, I decided to avoid the lift – in case the sound alerted Daniel. Hooking my handbag over one shoulder, I cradled Billy against the other, carrying him all the way down the service staircase.

He wanted to bring his safari backpack – the one he always takes whenever we go on our little adventures, 'hunting pirates' on the ferry across to Ham House, or 'stalking lions and giraffes' in Richmond Park – but I told him we needed to travel light, so we could move faster. Excited by the game, he grinned and placed a finger to his lips.

'Shh, Mummy. Be *quiet*. We don't want Daddy to hear us.'

My eyes filled with tears as I wished it really was a game, and that Daniel would be joining us and we'd all go for a long walk, ending up at our favourite café, chatting and laughing as we planned which movie to watch later.

More than anything else, from the moment Eve appeared in the school playground four days ago, I've feared the loss of our happy family. I spent so many years yearning for it; I've loved Daniel so much for giving it to me.

But not at any price.

*

'As soon as we get inside, we need to keep our heads down,' I remind Billy now, setting him down before swiping my security pass to open the door to the car park.

'OK!' he whispers, half-crouching, half-walking next to me.

His stealthy, stooping prowl is adorable, and I feel wobbly with guilt about deceiving him. 'Sweetheart, you know I love you more than the sun, moon and stars,' I tell him.

'Shh!' Billy says again, then points to the security cameras.

'You're right,' I whisper, bending down. 'Let's go.'

Taking hold of his hand, I stay one pace ahead of him as we shuffle around the outside edges of the car park, staying low, ducking behind cars. Most are so big, Billy hardly needs to stoop at all, but I can tell he is thoroughly enjoying the spirit of 'the game' and would happily crawl along the concrete floor, if I asked him to.

'There's our car.' I point at Daniel's black BMW. 'Over there.'

Suddenly, I feel overwhelmed. *This is it.*

Once I leave the underground car park, there will be no going back. Daniel is fiercely clever; he's proved that much. He will know for certain that I've guessed his secret; he'll realise I've run away – and taken Billy with me. I'm not even sure he'll come after us.

The possibility that he will makes fear tingle through me. I'm not physically scared of Daniel, although I realise now that Eve probably was. I remember her constant wariness of him, her insistence that I check he wouldn't be angry with her about the police arriving . . .

That fear makes it all the more remarkable that she found the strength to tell her story at all – even if it was only half of it. I have a sixth sense that she didn't tell me about Daniel bribing her with the boat because she didn't want to destroy my marriage.

Eve wanted Billy to have a happier life than she'd had, and she saw for herself that her dream had come true. Billy *was* happy. I was happy. Only it was all based on a lie.

'Is the car door stuck? Won't it open?'

'Sorry? Oh. No, it's fine, sweetheart.' As Billy prods my arm, I drag myself out of my turbulent thoughts and, after one last glance around the car park, reach into my jacket pocket for the key, clicking the remote locking control.

'Too loud!' Billy grabs my hand when the car beeps.

'Come on, *run*,' I tell him, squeezing his hand tight and pulling him along.

We make a dash across the car park, weaving between sports cars and four-by-fours, expensive, luxury vehicles that seem to symbolise everything I'm leaving behind. I look down at Billy, my heart breaking at the trust shining out of his dark eyes. *If he was asked to choose between his parents, would he pick me?*

I feel another stab of guilt as I recognise that I'm not giving him that choice – just as Eve took it away from him, and me, when our sons were born. *I needed to find Sean a mother. I found you, Ruth*, I remember her saying to me.

In one way, she made the most terrible, horrendous mistake. But I know she only wanted the best for Billy, and I vow to myself that I won't let her down, or him. I will fight to give him the security and happiness Eve wanted for him, too.

'You're going to sit up front, next to me, Billy. Like a big boy,

302

OK?' I open the car door and reach into the back for his child-safety seat. Securing it into the front passenger seat, I quickly lift him up and fasten the seatbelt across his chest.

'Look, Mummy! The garage door is opening. I didn't press anything, honest,' he adds, a little furrow appearing between his soft brows.

'It's all right, sweetheart. I know you didn't.'

My heartrate accelerates as I stare at the metal security grille, slowly cranking its way upwards. I haven't pressed anything, either. The garage door opens automatically when a car approaches it from the inside, but from this distance I would need to use a remote control. I haven't pressed one, so either someone else has – or a car is approaching from the outside.

'Maybe it's Arthur,' Billy suggests, referring to the building's caretaker.

'Clever boy. I bet you're right,' I say. I don't tell him that Arthur has been off sick for a week – frustratingly so, or he would have seen Finley trick Billy into going with him on Friday morning. Breathlessly, I keep scouring the dimly lit car park.

'Can I have pancakes for breakfast if we win?'

'Sorry? Oh. Of course, darling.'

'Hooray! Oops. I forgot.' Billy claps a hand over his mouth. 'I'm supposed to be quiet.'

'It's OK, love. I don't think anyone's out there, after all.'

Relaxing a little, I reach out to squeeze his knee, at the same time turning on the ignition. Pressing my foot on the gas pedal, I let the revs build before releasing the handbrake. The car glides forward and I steer it towards the garage door, noticing that the security grille stands wide open now. We're ten feet away when there's a loud bang on the rear window.

In reflex, my foot jerks out to hit the brake, and I fling my left arm across to press against Billy's chest, restraining him as he lurches forward. 'Are you OK?'

'Did we hit something, Mummy?'

'No. I don't think so.' I swivel around but can't see anything. 'Maybe it was a bird. I saw that happen, one time. A pigeon got lost and flew in. Then it panicked, flapping around, bumping into windscreens.'

'Poor birdie.' Billy's chin wobbles. 'It wanted to fly away, and it got *smashed*.'

'I'm sure it managed to escape,' I reassure him. 'Birds are clever, aren't they?'

'They're lucky. I wish I could fly.'

As his head dips, I worry that he's remembering falling from the boat. 'Shut your eyes, darling. Imagine we're soaring up into the sky.'

Obediently, he closes them. 'Over the rainbow.' He's smiling now.

'That's right. We're going to fly over the rainbow. Just you and me.'

I release the handbrake again, fixing my eyes on the exit. There's no sign of blue skies; it's still dark. But through the open garage door, I can see streetlights. Cars. *Freedom*.

My eyes flick to the rear-view mirror, to check it's clear behind. It's not, and I gasp in shock as I see Daniel's face pressed against the glass. His eyes meet mine and he mouths something. I don't even try to work out what he's saying; I stamp my foot on the accelerator.

'Too fast!' Billy shouts, as the car shoots forward.

'Sorry, love, but we don't want to lose the game, do we? Hold on tight. Here we go!'

Chapter 63

My hands are shaking as I jam the gearstick up into first and then down into second, feeling the tyres spin when I hit the slope leading from the underground car park to the street. Billy grips the edges of his seat as we bump over the security hump at the top, and I almost hit a bollard, my attention distracted and my eyes flicking constantly to the rear-view mirror.

There's no sign of Daniel, but the shock of his blue eyes boring into mine is still pulsing through me. My foot quivers on the clutch as I shift gears again and pull across the forecourt, out on to the main road.

Just as the car begins to pick up speed, Billy grabs hold of my hand and calls out: 'There's Arthur!'

'What? Where?' I take my eyes off the road, only for a fraction of a second. Then I hear the sound of splintering glass as the car veers into the bus shelter at the side of the road.

I'm still reeling in shock when a voice from the back seat almost makes me jump out of my skin: 'I told you once before, Ruth. You shouldn't have *run*.'

Daniel's voice sets goose bumps crawling across my skin, but I keep staring straight ahead, frantically trying to come up with a plan. Only my brain and body seem to have frozen.

'You caught us, Daddy!'

'So I did, son.'

'I got to sit in the front seat,' Billy says proudly, even as I bite my lip in frustration that, if he'd been sitting in the *back*, I would have automatically activated the child locks and Daniel wouldn't have been able to open the door and get in.

'You're growing up, Billy. I think Mummy and I sometimes forget how quickly that happens. How fast time passes. How we need to make the most of every single second. It's Sunday. We should be having fun *all together*.'

'Like our game of hide-and-seek?' Billy's soft brows pucker.

'Exactly. That's what it was all for, isn't it?' Daniel says, and I know he's talking to me now. 'All the years of trying to have a family. All those false starts and bumps in the road.'

'Mummy hit the bus stop,' Billy points out, when I still don't reply.

'Oh, don't worry about that. Arthur's back. He was poorly for a few days, but he's back on duty again now. He'll take care of the bus stop. I'll get the car fixed later. That's what daddies are for, isn't it, Billy? *Fixing* things.'

*

I drive without paying attention to where I'm going, doing a circuit of west London, looping back on myself without noticing, or caring. At least the driving doesn't require too much concentration: the roads are getting busier now, but the traffic has yet to hit its peak, and the car glides along, almost as though it has a will of its own.

I lose track of time and place, but when I realise that we're approaching Kew Bridge, I know my unconscious mind is now making all the decisions, drawing me back to the place where my nightmare began.

It feels like I'm retracing my steps, back in time to Thursday morning when I first fled from the school playground, dragging Billy away from an uncertain past – never realising I was hauling him into a far more unsettled future.

As we cross the bridge, I glance over the side, my brain taking a snapshot of the river view I will never be able to look at again without feeling a mixture of horror and sadness.

'Taking us anywhere nice?' Daniel asks from the back seat.

'To hell and back? Oh, but I'm forgetting. That's where we've just been.'

'Do you want to talk about it?' he says, as casually as though we're chatting about a bad day at the office.

'I've heard enough lies to last me a lifetime,' I say bitterly, accelerating over the brow of the bridge, desperate to get away from the river now.

'Then how about we stick to the truth.'

'I reckon you've forgotten what that means.'

'I haven't *forgotten* anything.' His blue eyes stare at me from the mirror again; I refuse to look at them. 'But I admit there are some things I thought you were better off not knowing.'

I don't reply, concentrating on changing lanes, then slowing the car to a standstill at the traffic lights beyond Kew Green. Sitting at the junction, I listen to the powerful BMW engine rumble and try to decide which way to turn. I feel at a crossroads, in every possible way.

The lights turn green; I rev the engine. Making an instant decision, I take the left-hand turning, heading down Mortlake Road. 'If you want to talk, we can do it *here*,' I say a few minutes later, steering the car into a small driveway, pulling up outside a gated entrance.

'Doesn't look much like a café to me.' Daniel leans forward, resting a hand casually on the headrest of my seat, as if we have indeed just popped out on a family excursion and have stopped off to investigate a new theme park.

'It isn't,' I tell him, finally meeting his eyes. Shifting the car into neutral, I pull on the handbrake and switch off the engine.

'Looks a bit grim,' Daniel comments, when he realises I'm serious about us getting out.

'It's actually the most special place on earth,' I whisper.

My eyes fill with tears, blurring my vision, but it doesn't matter: I don't need to look out of the window to see the tall, red-brick pillars spanned by black iron gates guarding a driveway that winds through a garden I know will be slumbering beneath autumnal bleakness.

I've been picturing this place constantly in my mind, ever since Eve first mentioned it. Now I want to see it for myself. I want to see where my son's ashes were scattered.

Chapter 64

Every step hurts. *Someone else* carried my baby boy here; *someone else* cried as his little life was scattered on the breeze. Or maybe they didn't. Mary was probably long gone by then; Eve had already found consolation with Jack. Daniel was busy buying her a boat . . .

'I know you were in my study,' he says quietly at last. 'You went through my papers.'

We've been strolling for a few minutes, silently, aimlessly following a long, winding path bordered by a low privet hedge. I've been trying hard not to think of the rambling walks Daniel and I used to take through Greenwich Park in the early days of our relationship – a lifetime ago, when I used to sneak out of the flat I shared with Bea.

I deliberately kept Daniel away from her, I remember, in case she fancied him and tried to steal him, just like she did my ideas at work – not to mention Finley, seemingly oblivious to the fact that I never wanted him in the first place.

But this is one thing I can't blame Bea for stealing. Eve was the one who took my baby from me. *And my husband helped her.*

'Paper, Daniel. Just the one. There was only one paper of any interest to me.' I stop walking, turning to look at him, the man I would once have trusted with my life.

He stops walking too, shifting Billy higher against his chest into a more comfortable position. 'I promised you the day I married you that I'd always take care of you, Ruth. I meant it. All you ever wanted was a child. *I* wanted that for you. Only, I couldn't give you one.'

'I was devastated, too. But I never asked you to steal someone else's.'

'I didn't steal Billy,' Daniel insists, holding him tighter.

'So you keep saying. The thing is, I'm not sure I believe you anymore.'

'No, you don't *want* to believe. That's different. But there are times, for all of us, when we have to confront things we don't like. I didn't *like* that our baby was born so poorly, he didn't survive. I didn't *like* that there was a sulky teenager in the next bed showing zero interest in her own child. Not while I knew you and I would give him all the love in the world.'

'Eve was a damaged young girl. You knew that. You took advantage of her.'

'No. I didn't.' His face flushes now. 'Oh, I'm not claiming that I had any great altruistic intentions. I simply saw there was a way that two wrongs could, for once, make a right. Her loss was our gain. I realised that. I can't pretend to regret it.'

I glare at him. 'We're not talking about bank accounts, Daniel. You can't switch a baby from the debit to the credit column and think that balances everything out.'

'I didn't *do* it,' he repeats, keeping his voice low, so as not to wake Billy. 'I didn't switch those babies. I never asked Eve to do so.'

I pick up on the hint. 'You didn't ask her to. But you did know that she had. Is *that* your story now?'

'I'm not the one who likes making up stories. I left that to Eve.

She played a blinder, didn't she? Coming up with that magazine interview rubbish. She knew *exactly* where to find us. She just didn't expect anyone to find out what she'd done. But I did,' he finally admits.

I feel like someone has poured ice-cold water over me. 'You did know . . .'

For a few moments, Daniel doesn't reply. Then he sighs. 'Not at first. But by the time I realised, it was all a done deal. The midwife made sure of that.'

'Hang on.' I refuse to let him divert the conversation into an attack on Mary. 'You knew Eve had switched our babies, even in the hospital, and you didn't tell me. Not then. Not for *four years*.' Even though I strongly suspected it, I'm crushed by his admission.

Once again, Daniel falls silent, turning away as though to hide his face. His shoulders, even broader in his thick padded jacket, judder slightly. When he turns back towards me, I realise he was suppressing a sob. His blue eyes are desolate, his flushed cheeks wet with tears.

'I swore on my life that we'd bring home a child, Ruth. I *never* break my word.'

Chapter 65

I spot a bench and head slowly towards it, my legs suddenly feeling weak. Daniel follows and sits down next to me; I'm relieved that he leaves a gap of a couple of feet between us.

As he adjusts Billy's position, I look at my darling boy's face, studying his soft curls and dark brows, his high cheekbones and little pointy chin.

I've kissed and cuddled him a million times, never realising he wasn't my own flesh and blood. My heart shattered when I finally had to accept the truth; now Daniel has ground it into smithereens with his forced confession that he knew all along.

'You're going to have to tell me everything. From the beginning.' I stare straight ahead. I can't bear to look at Daniel, but I'm desperate to hear what he has to say.

'The beginning,' he echoes. 'That's what it *should* have been. Our baby was born. I thought it was the start of our family life. It could so easily have been the end.'

'Mary told me Billy was hypoglycaemic. That's why he was

poorly. He responded to treatment, but our son . . . Do you know what was wrong with him?'

'The same. More or less. Apparently, low glycogen stores are common in slightly premature babies. They were given identical treatment, only . . .'

'Billy got better and our baby didn't.' I grit my teeth to stop myself from crying. '*Why not?*' I ask desperately, knowing it's a question that will torment me for the rest of my life.

Fleetingly, I remember once telling Daniel that I felt I'd been born under a lucky star. I've never felt more cursed; ironically, I have a sense that Eve is the only person who would truly understand that. But she's gone, and I only have Daniel's word for everything now.

'I don't know,' he says simply, as though that's the end to it. 'He looked perfect to me. Yes, he was lethargic after the caesarean. He looked almost grey. He didn't move, or cry. I was terrified to leave him. I went with him to special care. You were still in recovery.'

'I was also sedated,' I point out, groaning inwardly that I'd been oblivious to everything happening around me – powerless to stop it.

'Yes. Which is another reason I insisted on going with him. To watch over him. There were so many babies. Huh, believe it or not, I was paranoid about an accidental mix-up.'

I turn to look at Daniel now, but his eyes are fixed on the tall yew trees that line the perimeter of the memorial garden. The wind rushes through them, but I don't feel the cold. My mind is far from this place – tracking Daniel's, back in the hospital, four years ago.

'You said he was perfect. By that, do you mean . . .' I bite my lip, picturing fragile limbs, tiny fists. I recall my fear and confusion when I looked at first one baby then the other, their crumpled faces a blur as I battled pain and the drugged lethargy of heavy medication.

'He didn't have webbed fingers. He was so small. Clearly

struggling. But he had your pert nose. My blue eyes.'

'The first time I properly saw Billy, his eyes were dark.' I grind my teeth harder, hating having to hear these details from Daniel. I can't stand not knowing for sure whether he's simply playing on my sympathy, yet again trying to twist his way out of trouble.

I've seen for myself how expert Finley is at gaslighting and manipulation; it occurs to me that Daniel has more in common with his former friend than he'd like to admit. Not just the competitiveness they both share, but their capacity to blame others for their own failings.

'Yeah, well. By the time you were well enough to visit special care, Billy was already in our son's crib. The switch was signed, sealed and delivered.'

'Everything changed in those few short hours.' I close my eyes, remembering how long they'd seemed at the time. Now it feels like it all happened in a heartbeat.

'I guess it did. Mary saw to that. I left our baby in her care, that first time. She said she needed to complete her checks. That the doctor was on her way to do her notes. Mary told me it was best if I went to be with you. So I did. And I never left your side, I swear.'

'You didn't need to, did you? You'd already seen him,' I say hoarsely, opening my eyes to stare wretchedly at Daniel. 'You saw our *son*. You picked him up. You held him.'

'Briefly.' A muscle twitches in his clenched jaw. 'Long enough to realise it was a different baby the *next* time I saw him. When I finally got to take you up to special care.'

'You rushed out of there two minutes later, looking like you'd seen a ghost,' I remember, also recalling Mary excusing his behaviour as being the natural stress of a new father. *How bitterly ironic.* She'd known *exactly* what had caused his shock, I realise now.

'I was floored,' Daniel confirms. 'Our little boy's eyes were now black instead of blue. His hair was dark instead of fair. He had webbed fingers on his right hand. I kept staring and staring at

314

him. Checking his notes, over and over. Looking at the little ID bracelet on his wrist. I was . . .' He pauses, pinching the bridge of his nose. 'Floored,' he repeats, his voice cracking.

'Yet you let me go in by myself. To see him alone. All the time knowing it wasn't even our baby.' Tears threaten again, and I dig my nails into my palms to stop them.

'I'm sorry. I'm so sorry, Ruth. I was shattered. *Confused.* I kept doubting myself, thinking I'd got it wrong. I sat in the waiting room, agonising over what to think, what to do.'

'What *did* you do then?'

Daniel groans. 'What did I do? I freaked out. Only in my head, of course. I kept thinking: *there's been a mistake.* Someone will sort it out. Then I went to talk to the doctor.'

'I saw her walk past you,' I recall. 'So you followed her up the corridor. Spoke to her. You *didn't* tell her you'd noticed the mix-up. Why not, Daniel?'

The enormity of that moment hits me: Daniel made a unilateral decision he'd had no right to make, and it changed all our lives, for ever. Eve made a terrible choice, but so did he.

So did I, I acknowledge. Five years ago, when I decided not to mention that night at the hotel. The consequences of that were bad enough; they don't come close to the impact of Daniel's decision. I know I will struggle to live with my guilt; I wonder how he'll handle his.

'I was going to,' he protests. 'Then the second doctor joined us. She said there was a problem with the *other baby*. The one born at the same time. She meant *our boy*, Ruth. She was trying to be discreet. She shook her head. Only a fraction, but I knew exactly what she meant, and I . . . I kept quiet. I knew I should have said something. I couldn't bring myself to.'

'You should at least have told *me*.' I wipe away the tears I can no longer contain. They spill over now, running down my face, their saltiness stinging my cheeks, half frozen by the icy air. I shiver, pulling up the collar of my grey jacket. 'After I fainted,

315

Mary took me back to my bed on the ward . . . and you were there. Why didn't you tell me *then*?'

'Because I knew it would break your heart. I couldn't do that. I wanted you to be happy. It's all I've *ever* wanted.'

I shake my head, struggling to believe him capable of such a monumental deception. 'And has it made *you* happy? How do you live with yourself? How do you *sleep* at night?' Bitterly, I remember envying how well he sleeps – how I put it down to his clean conscience.

His jaw clenches tighter. 'With difficulty. But we have to move forward, don't we? Yes, I've had plenty of long, dark nights. I've had to keep reminding myself: *I wasn't the one who made the switch*. I just didn't draw attention to it.'

'That doesn't let you off the hook. Not legally. Nor morally.'

'It was a moment's crazy impulse, Ruth. I swear. I've relived it a million times, wondering what I should have done differently. Then I look at Billy, and I can't regret it. I know that makes me a bad person. I'm genuinely sorry about that. But I watch you and Billy together. Playing. Laughing. So happy. So *right* together.' He shakes his head. 'In all honesty, I can't help but feel everything has worked out for the best.'

Immediately, I picture Eve's dark, haunted eyes and replay her sad words: in the hospital, on her boat and in our apartment. I remember her intense self-loathing mixed with painful longing for her son – her confusion about how to reconcile the two.

'Best for who, though?' I say quietly.

Daniel swivels around on the bench. 'For Billy. For *us*. I thought of *you*, Ruth. Waiting in your hospital bed, bursting with excitement to hold your son. After all we'd been through.'

'Yes, after all we'd been through, Daniel. *Together*. I thought we were a team?'

'We were. We *are*. We win together. We lose together. Your pain is mine, sweetheart. I looked down at that tiny baby, and all I could see was piles of sleepsuits and teddy bears. All the little

316

things you'd tucked away at the back of your wardrobe. Every hopeful, excited, secret online shopping order each time you believed you were pregnant.' He slants me a sad look. 'Did you think I wouldn't know?'

Ghost babies, I think, and my broken heart aches unbearably. 'I'm sorry. You're right. I didn't think you knew about that. But I couldn't tell you, because—'

'Because you knew it would tear me up. Just as I knew leaving that hospital without our little boy would destroy you. I couldn't bear to watch you go through that agony one more time. I couldn't stand it *myself*. I know you've always dreamed of being a mum. You lost your mother. You never knew your father. But I lost mine, too.' Daniel breaks off, burying his face in Billy's curls. 'I wanted so much to be a dad,' he says at last.

'I know, Dan.' His agony takes me right back to our first failed round of IVF: the first time a doctor broke the bad news to us. 'It's the reason I suggested the name Billy, remember? To honour your dad. To pass his memory on to your son. *Our* son. Only he wasn't ours.'

'But he *is*. In every way that matters. Eve didn't want him. *We did*. That's all I could think about. I listened to those doctors talking about our dying son, and I said nothing. That's my only crime, Ruth. *Silence*. I listened. I kept quiet. I didn't tell the doctor she was talking to me about the wrong baby.'

Chapter 66

The picture Daniel is painting is temptingly plausible. He makes it sound like he was a desperate dad, acting on a moment's impulse, principally out of love and concern for me: innocent of any crime; guilty only of covering it up. It makes my head spin, yet I can almost see how trapped he felt by tragic circumstance.

I sit quietly on the bench, huddling inside my jacket, wanting to believe he's telling the truth, battling with my own conscience. I know Daniel is waiting for me to forgive him, to turn to him for a hug, as usual. I also know that if I do, he'll expect us to go home and carry on as though nothing has happened. Our marriage, our home with Billy, will be as it always was.

And it has been the happiest four years of my life.

I feel myself weakening, lured by the prospect of the family life I've dreamed about ever since I was a little girl crying myself to sleep each night, missing a mum I never knew.

'I make multimillion-pound decisions under huge pressure every day of my life,' Daniel says suddenly. 'I never panic. I panicked in that moment, though. But it was the right thing to do. For everyone. I have to believe that. Like I say, Eve didn't want her baby.'

'How did you even *suspect* her?' I frown, thinking back to those intense days in hospital. 'I can still hardly believe what she did, and she admitted it to my face.'

'Oh, I didn't suspect her. Not at first. I genuinely thought there had been a dreadful mistake. But Eve gave *herself* away. Most people do when they've committed a crime.' Daniel's mouth hardens. 'They make little mistakes. They don't cover their tracks properly.'

Immediately, I think of the paperwork I found in his study. If it hadn't been for that, I would never have known Daniel bought Eve the boat – I would never have run away from him. But I'm too anxious to hear the rest of his story to distract him by pointing out his own slip-up. 'What gave her away?' I say instead.

'Her cockiness. She thought she'd got away with it. She was overconfident. We'd both seen her sobbing into her pillow. Throwing her books around. Wailing like a banshee. Five minutes later, I spotted her smoking outside with Mary, joking around like everything was fine. *Not* like her baby was at death's door,' he says pointedly.

'Really? I never saw that.'

'Her grief was one big act, Ruth.'

I remembered Eve admitting as much to me. 'Perhaps. But, honestly, I don't think Eve truly knew *what* she felt.'

'Well, I do. She was *relieved* she didn't have to take responsibility for a baby. She was terrified when I called her on it, of course. But she was happy for the babies to stay swapped. *So* happy that she promised she'd never tell anyone. I just needed . . . an insurance policy.'

'You offered to pay her off.' Despite his insistence that he panicked, I know how fast Daniel would have acted to secure the 'deal' he wanted.

'Eve said she didn't want money. She wanted to see the world.

I was actually joking when I said: "I'll buy you a boat, then." But she jumped at it.'

'Maybe she didn't feel she had any choice.'

'There's *always* a choice. Eve didn't *have* to accept the boat. She didn't *have* to manipulate that midwife into swapping the babies.'

'You didn't have to keep quiet about it,' I point out.

'Exactly. We're all adults. We make our own choices. We have to accept the consequences. Good *and* bad.'

Actions have consequences. We have to take responsibility for our mistakes. That's what Bea said to me in the playground four days ago, back when I thought all I had to worry about was a vengeful friend and a drunken one-night-stand that cast doubt on whether Daniel was my son's father – not that I'd loved and cared for another woman's child for four years.

'I'm prepared to stand by my mistakes,' Daniel continued. 'Eve wasn't. She fucked up good and proper. Then she thought she could simply erase the past like it never happened.'

'You say we're all adults. But Eve was scarcely more than a child herself when she had Billy. Or Sean, as she called him. She wanted him to have a good life. She thought we could give that to him,' I say, instinctively defending her. 'Jack was the one who messed with her head.'

For all Daniel is portraying Eve as selfish and heartless, I saw the depth of her emotion when she talked about the life she'd had – and the life she wanted for her child. I simply don't believe she was faking it. After all, she gave her own life to make sure it happened.

'And we have. Yes, I made a deal with Eve. No, I'm not proud of it. I wish it hadn't had to happen at all. But I stuck to my side of it. I went home, bought a boat and arranged for it to be moored further up the Thames.'

'You've always wanted a boat,' I mumble, almost to myself, wondering if Daniel had already had one picked out – a boat he'd dreamed of owning himself, but my stupid fear of the water had stopped him getting one.

'Not as much as I wanted our boy.' He groans. 'Look, Eve presented the opportunity. I took it. Simple as that. All she had to do was keep quiet.'

'With a canal boat as added incentive. That's a pretty big insurance policy,' I say ironically, remembering what Daniel called it. 'Not easy for Eve to turn down. Or to arrange, I imagine.' I frown, also recalling that the date of sale was three days after Billy was born.

'Like you said, I've wanted a boat for years. OK, I had one picked out. All it took was a phone call. While Eve was busy earning her Oscar, crying her eyes out, I put an envelope with the details on her bed. Two weeks later, I checked on the boat. It was gone. So was Eve.'

'But she came back.' *On Billy's first day at school.*

'Stupid girl.' Daniel's voice is ragged. 'I thought she was bluffing. Trying to scare me into paying her more hush money. I thought, if I kept denying it, she'd give up and go away. I knew she wouldn't call the police. She had as much to lose as I did.'

'But she *didn't* give up.'

'More fool her. Maybe if she had, she'd still be alive.'

'Or maybe life didn't feel worth living until she knew her son was going to be OK.'

'Sure. Well, I gave her time with him, didn't I?' Daniel says, as though Eve was an ungrateful child. 'She played with Billy the whole time you were at Kew Gardens with Bea.'

'She looked terrified when I came home,' I remember. 'What did you *say* to her?'

'I just pointed out her options. I was perfectly reasonable. Only she refused to drop the act. *Jack* was the one who really had her terrified. That's why I called the police about his licence. I knew if I could get Jack out of the way, I could persuade Eve to leave us alone. For good.' His mouth twists. 'Then Finley showed up and put on a performance of his own.'

'And now he's gone, too. Just like Bea. Just like Jack. And Eve . . .'

I can't bear to look at Daniel's face, and I turn away, my heart pounding as I glare around the cemetery gardens. Desolately, I wonder if there is any kind of plaque or memorial to my son – anything I can touch, to try to conjure up a physical connection with him.

Daniel takes hold of my arm, forcing me to look at me, and his blue eyes are bright with tears, exactly as they were on the day I went into labour, when he first showed me the nursery he'd secretly been filling with specially chosen clothes, toys and gifts for our new son.

All that love. *All those lies.*

'Ruth, sweetheart. What we have is so good. It's all we've both ever wanted. Please, don't throw it away.'

Chapter 67

I sit quietly, staring at the colourless sky, trying to absorb everything Daniel has told me. For all he's painted himself as accidental collateral – an innocent parent who got swept along by a young girl's impulse to profit from an unwanted baby – it all seems too . . . *convenient*.

Everyone who caused him a problem is now gone. They can't present their side of the story – and, as Daniel himself said: *there are always two sides to everything.*

My phone buzzes. I take it out, tensing as I see a text from the school. It's just a bulletin ahead of the new week, but the thought of ever taking Billy back there fills me with horror. Every day would be a reminder of what's happened. But he can't stay at home for ever.

Home. The word makes me want to curl up and hide. Growing up, I never had a real home. Daniel was the one who finally gave me a sense that I belonged somewhere. And Billy was the one who completed that feeling. But like Bea's marriage, our happy family was a sham. Unlike Bea, I didn't know it. *Can I simply pretend none of this ever happened?* Daniel accused Eve of trying to erase the past. I know how she felt; I wish I could do the same.

I tap on the screen of my phone, loading my camera roll, quickly scrolling past photos of the river, the houseboats – random snaps I've taken with the idea of sketching them later. Pictures of Billy spin across the screen: eating cake in the café, feeding Lucky Ducky, playing football with Joseph on what should have been his first day of school . . .

I hold my breath as I suddenly notice Eve in the background of one shot, watching him. I'll never forget that moment, her fierce snarl and angry eyes. Then, as I look closer, I see how *happy* she looks, caught off guard as she gazes at Billy.

Daniel has portrayed Eve as the worst kind of selfish, self-centred person, but I *knew* her. I'm sure of it. When I first met her, she was a lost soul in search of a soul mate. Later, she latched on to Jack. But in the hospital, she latched on to *me*.

Exactly as I did to Bea, I recognise, being brutally honest with myself. Bea wasn't fixated on me; Finley made that up to suit his own wicked purposes. But she did need my friendship, as I needed hers. As, deep down, Eve needed mine.

All three of us had known terrible losses in our lives. We'd each lost our mothers and were struggling to become mums ourselves. I wonder if, had things turned out differently, the three of us might one day have become good friends.

I wonder, too, if Eve's choice to become an artist was inspired by the love of art I shared with her during that intense time in hospital. I think of her reminding me how we 'see the truth in pictures'. Her photo of Billy as a baby in her arms first hinted at the truth about *him*; now, as I stare at the snapshot of Eve in the playground, I see the truth about *her*.

Daniel paid her to stay away, and Jack bullied her into coming back – but I'm convinced Eve made her decision to give Billy up in that very first moment, right there in the playground. I look again at the photo, and I can see it in her eyes: *she'd seen*

Billy . . . Sean . . . was happy, and that was enough for her.

Over the next forty-eight hours, she bounced between Jack and Daniel, both trying to push her in opposite directions. Now Jack is gone, too. It's a clean sweep: no witnesses remain.

'What would you have done – if Eve hadn't drowned?' I ask Daniel, and suddenly my chest feels tight with fear about a possibility I haven't considered until this moment.

He closes his eyes, frowning, and doesn't answer.

The feeling of dread knots tighter. 'Did you even *try* to save her?'

'Of course!' He turns to face me, his eyes full of pain. 'But maybe . . . well, Eve being gone certainly makes the situation a whole lot simpler. Don't pretend there isn't a part of you that feels the same. And that's *OK*. Whatever it takes to keep Billy. Keep us *together*.'

'No, Daniel. I *don't* feel the same.'

'Really? Can you honestly say you would have done anything differently – if you'd been in my shoes?' Daniel sounds impatient now. 'Think about it, Ruth. Two babies. One dying. You have a split-second to make up your mind what to do. Now *you* decide.'

'I could never, ever steal another woman's baby. And if you have to ask me that question, you don't know me at all.'

'But I *do* know you,' Daniel pleads. 'You know me, too. I'm not a criminal. I didn't want *any* of this to happen. It was an accident. But I was in too deep to turn back.'

I remember him saying that when I first invited Eve up to our apartment – when the pain of contemplating that I might lose my son was tearing me apart. *But I'd already lost him*. And Daniel already knew. I'm not sure I can ever forgive him for that.

'You let Eve show me Billy's photo. I touched her baby's clothes.' I can feel my body start to tremble. 'You *lied* to me.'

'Maybe I did the wrong thing. But it was for the right reasons.'

'So the end justifies the means? I would give my life for Billy, but—'

'You wouldn't take someone else's to save him?' Daniel challenges, his question as good as a confession that, however unconsciously, he let Eve drown. 'Look, please, I want us to get on with our life. Be the family we were always meant to be. I know you want that, too.'

'Will you *please* stop telling me what I want, what I would do.'

'We can get over this, Ruth. I know we can. We can be *happy* again. We can be a family. You want that too. I know you do.'

'Yes. I do.' I draw in a deep breath. 'But not at any price.'

*

The wind picks up. I feel like I'm frozen to the bench. I wanted to come here – I felt an overpowering urge to be close to my little, lost boy. But I have no idea even where they scattered his ashes. It feels like he's more lost than ever.

'No more lies, Ruth,' Daniel says quietly. 'I've told you everything. I promise. There's nothing to be frightened of anymore. It's just you, me and Billy.'

'And a mountain of legalities,' I point out.

'I'll take care of it all.'

'And what do we tell Billy? The truth?'

'What's more important: the truth, or our son's happiness?' Daniel prevaricates.

'I'm not sure it's possible to have one without the other. If you've learned nothing else over the last few days, surely you've learned that?'

'I'm not a philosopher. I'm a husband. And a father. At least, if you'll let me be?'

His mouths curls in the warm smile I have loved since the day he appeared in his best friend's place and turned my whole world upside down. I've barely spent a day apart from Daniel since; I can't imagine all the days of my life to come without him by my side.

326

'I love you, Daniel,' I say hoarsely, and I feel like I'm dying inside.

'Me too you. For better, for worse.' He reaches out and takes hold of my hand, kissing the tips of my fingers one by one, as he's always done whenever I have a wobble.

I sigh, leaning against him, and he lifts his arm to rest it around my shoulder. I twist around, looking up at him, studying his face, as I've done more times over the last few days than I have for months. Perhaps years. I *do* love Daniel, but maybe love isn't enough.

'I love you, Dan,' I repeat. 'But I can't live with someone I don't trust. I can't spend each moment of every day wondering if there's something else you're not telling me.'

'No, Ruth. *Please.*'

Daniel's smile vanishes, and for the first time ever, I see genuine fear on his handsome face. I reach across him, but instead of taking his hand, I lift Billy out of his arms. 'Mummy,' he murmurs, but I know he's not really awake.

I kiss his cheek and smooth back his soft dark curls, then I settle him against my shoulder, slotting my thumb into his warm palm, waiting for his fingers to curl around it, exactly as they always have, for the whole of his short life.

'It's time to wake up, Billy,' I whisper against his ear. 'We're going to find that rainbow.'

Epilogue

My darling boy.

I visited the memorial garden again today. There is a little plaque; it has your name on it. It's not your *real* name – Billy has that for safekeeping. Even so, I traced my fingers over the brass plate, closed my eyes, and I thought only of you.

I wondered if you knew I was there five years ago, when I stood next to your cot in the hospital, never realising you were mine. I wondered if your blue eyes opened, just for a moment, and you saw me. Did you cry when I walked straight past you? Did you feel sad when I didn't stop to look at you, or stroke your face, pick you up and cuddle you?

I feel sad. About so many things, but mainly because I never got to hold you – not in your first moments of life, or your last.

But I want you to know you will always be my first boy.

*

It was my dream to have a child. Sometimes, dreams turn into nightmares. Billy still can't go near the water, and we don't live

329

by the river anymore. The penthouse has been sold, and we've moved to a small cottage near Richmond Park. We go there every day. I sketch and paint the deer, while Billy runs through the long grass, pretending he's on safari.

My artwork has really taken off now. I hang my paintings in my own little gallery just off the high street. That was my other dream, and in the end, I worked hard and made it happen, all by myself. The thing about dreams, you see, is that they aren't the same as wishes. Wishes have to be *granted*: you can't buy them, and you can't steal them.

Your daddy tried too hard to make my wishes come true, and all that was left of our marriage was a handful of dust that blew away in the wind. He's moved away now; I don't know where, and I won't ask. I no longer trust he will tell me the truth. One day, maybe, we'll be able to talk again. But not yet.

Billy says he doesn't miss him; I know he just doesn't want me to be sad. I've told him it's OK to cry, and we're busy trying to make lots of new, happy memories. He's at a different school now, close to our new home and not too far from Bea's old house. As I guessed, she never came back from Scotland. We're not in touch very often, but she did send me a framed photo of herself with Ophelia – and Michael. Her son.

At last Bea is happy; I hope Finley will let her stay that way. He's been released on bail, pending further investigation. I was shocked when I found out he's free again – however temporarily – but, somehow, I wasn't surprised. He's always been a slick talker; I can only pray that, eventually, he'll get caught in his own web of lies.

In the meantime, I hope there will come a time when I can stop looking over my shoulder . . . for Finley, and for Jack, too. He may have been bribed to go away, but he could still return. After all, Eve did. No matter how deeply we bury the past, it always finds a way to come back and haunt us.

At night, I see all their faces: Finley, Jack, Daniel, Bea and Eve. I think Billy does, too; sometimes I catch him saying their names during his imaginary play. At least his nightmares seem to have eased. Which reminds me: it's time for his bedtime story now.

His favourite is one I wrote myself, and illustrated with my own artwork. It's called *The Little Boy Who Lives in the Stars*. That's what he calls you, my love.

Every night, before he goes to sleep, Billy looks out of his bedroom window at the sky, and says nighty night to you . . . and Aunty Eve. He says he hopes you're looking after each other, 'up above the moon in heaven'. One day, I hope I'll be there with you both.

Until then, I'll see you in my dreams, my precious boy, and we'll do all the things together that I never got to do with you: I'll watch you run through the park with the sun shining in your beautiful blue eyes. I'll hold you in my arms and count your toes, kiss your fingers. I'll tell you that I love you more than the sun, moon and stars.

Can you hear me? Don't be frightened, darling. Mummy's here.

Acknowledgements

This story has haunted me for some time, and I would like to acknowledge the tremendous editorial expertise of Belinda Toor in helping me transmute the nightmare in my head to the story on the page! Belinda, you are as kind as you are clever. Thank you for all your astute insights, constructive suggestions and genuinely uplifting enthusiasm for this book. It has been an absolute pleasure working on it with you.

Big thanks also to Audrey Linton for loving the book, too, and for your fabulous support and super helpful guidance through every stage of the publishing process. Speaking of which, I'm incredibly grateful to everyone 'behind the scenes' who has worked so hard to turn my words into an actual book and send it off into the world looking its best. My sincere thanks go out to the whole HQ team: copy editor, proofreader, designers, marketing wizards, and all the other energetic and creative people involved in turning an author's dreams into reality.

Being a published author – seeing my stories connect with readers all around the world – continues to be my dream, and I'd like to pay warmest gratitude to Eugenie Furniss and Emily MacDonald at 42MP for helping me keep it alive. The flame that fuels it is without doubt the love and support of my husband

and children – with vocal cheerleading from Jessie, my faithful Cavachon companion, who hasn't a clue what I'm doing when I tap away at the laptop for hours on end, but never leaves my side anyway.

Paul, Hani and Rafi – I can't thank you enough for inspiring, championing and being right by my side throughout all the highs and the lows. Writing is frequently a tough mountain to climb, but the thought of you always spurs me on – and I'm beyond thankful for your encouragement (and coffee/chocolate supplies) whenever I stumble, and for your care and kindness when I fall. No matter where my books go in the world, you are at their heart, and you are the beat of mine.

Keep reading for an excerpt from
The Secret Keeper's Daughter ...

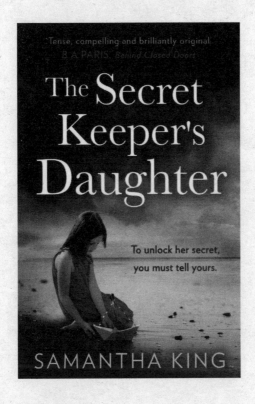

Prologue

The North Sea was my mum's final resting place, but even before then I found a strange sort of comfort living so close to it. Dad always hated it, of course, complaining about its 'bleakness', its 'savage unpredictability'. But that's why I loved it. Dirty, gunmetal grey one moment, then ethereal silver the next, somehow it gave me hope that all my troubles would eventually pass over too, like the changing currents and ever-shifting clouds.

The eager rush of its waves breaking on the shingle beach of our little stretch of the Heritage Coastline was also my favourite noise. As a child, I would lie in bed at Sea View, eyes tightly closed, letting the crashing roar drown out the worries in my head. And when I grew up and had a home of my own, I still relied on the sea to lull me to sleep, even though by then I spent each night safely wrapped in Jordan's arms.

Then we had you, Marley, and I fell in love with a new sound. *Your voice.*

*

337

You were such a noisy baby, and you grew up into the chattiest, most inquisitive child. As we picked our way across tide-sculpted drifts of gritty sand each morning, you would fill your little bucket with stones and your mind with facts: about the incongruously mystical white orb of Sizewell Power Station that seemed to hover, UFO-like, in the distance; about the famous Scallop sculpture facing impassively out to sea, its hinged steel shell spread wide in stoic defiance of the buffeting winds and furiously pounding waves.

You fired endless questions at me, about the hovering gulls that kept plaintive company with us overhead, the fishing boats with their tangled nets strewn out to dry, enticing us with the salty whiff of adventures. Sometimes I conjured up imaginary ones for us, and when you were old enough, you dreamed up even more colourful stories of your own.

Your inventiveness astonished me; you were like a little magpie, collecting new words like pretty shells. Then, one day, a few weeks ago, everything changed. We still walked along the beach before school each day, but you asked no questions; you told no tales. In fact, you began to speak so rarely that when you did, I wanted to scoop up each and every word and hoard them like diamonds in a treasure chest. A worry box, as it turned out.

I can't take my eyes off it – that jewel-spangled box on the kitchen dresser. Here I am, flat on my back on a paramedic's stretcher, half-blinded by pain and a dark curtain of hot, sticky blood, while my chest is rhythmically, urgently pumped – and all I can think about is the words buried inside a glittery old shoe box. No precious gems, in fact, just sharp pebbles of fear. If I close my eyes, I can picture them: five little words; one devastating secret.

I wish you'd told me sooner. No, that sounds as though I blame you. I don't, darling. All I mean to say is that I wish I'd realised what you were worrying about, before it was too late. Before you were snatched away from me; before your baby brother was wrenched so brutally from my arms. I can't stop thinking about that, too. His little pink face all crumpled, blue eyes searching frantically for me. Then the world went black.

That's not your fault, either. I've got a hole in my heart, you see. One of nature's cruel little quirks. *Atrial septal defect*. ASD. That's what the doctors call it. Mostly, it's fine. Medication helps, and when it doesn't . . . well, sometimes, when I'm stressed or frightened, when my heart wants to beat faster and finds it can't, then it simply . . . stops.

This time, I think it might be for good; I can feel that my battered body wants to let go. Only the weaker it becomes, the fiercer my brain rages. *Why has this happened? Why? Why?* That small yet frighteningly enormous word. It's eating away at me, hungry for answers. If it's the last thing I do, I need to find them. Find *you*.

But memory is my only guide, and the only clues I have are the seven notes you left for me. It's been just one terrifying hour since your last one, and seven traumatic days since the first. Since we made that wretched worry box together . . .

Chapter 1

Sunday – Seven Days Before

'Now *this* is perfect. Look, Marley. What do you think?' I smiled, but I could barely breathe as I strolled back into our kitchen and saw you sitting bolt upright at the table, exactly as I'd left you ten minutes earlier. You hadn't moved an inch while I searched the cottage. Or, to be honest, sat on my bed tearing my hair out, wondering what on earth was going on with you.

I didn't tell you that, of course. I told you I was looking for something we could turn into a treasure chest. 'Half-term's over. It's school tomorrow. Last chance for us to get messy and have fun!' I'd coaxed, hoping the idea might excite you. You didn't even look up.

'What do you reckon, love?' I prompted again, holding out the box like I was still a teacher prepping for the afternoon art lesson – only not to a class of lively primary school kids, this time, but to one unnaturally quiet, scared-looking seven-year-old. 'I found it under my bed. No idea how long it's been there. Or what used to be in it.'

That was the first lie I'd ever told you, but my problems could wait; yours couldn't. It wouldn't help you to know what *really* happened to the contents of that glossy white cardboard box, or how it had haunted me for so many years.

Even now, dazzled by the fluorescent glare of hospital lights, I can picture it; even as anaesthetic pumps through my veins, my fingers tingle as I imagine touching its smoothness. Doctors crowd around me, but it's other faces I see – other voices from the past that clamour accusingly in my head. Yours. Your daddy's. My parents'. *Amy's.*

'It looks new.' At last you spoke, your little hand reaching out to hover, butterfly fretful, over the pristine box. 'Isn't it bad to spoil it?'

'No, love, it's fine. It's empty. See?' I shook the box nonchalantly, trying not to remember the last time I'd held it – the angry words and shocked sense of betrayal.

Tentatively, you plunged your hands inside it, and when they emerged, they were filled with frothy almond-white tulle. *My bridal veil.* I genuinely *had* forgotten about that, and I shivered as I watched you crown yourself with the gauzy silk, wishing for the thousandth time that my own mum could have watched me do the same eight years ago.

'Can I keep this?' you lisped.

'Of course, sweetheart.' I took off the veil and tucked it inside the chest pocket of your dungarees, where it couldn't taunt me with reminders. 'As long as I get to keep you.'

'Forever-together-whatever?'

'Till the seas run dry.' I leaned forward to seal what was usually our bedtime promise with a kiss on your forehead.

'Just you and me?'

'Well, we mustn't forget about—'

'Daddy.' Your voice was a squeak. 'And *him.*' Your dangling foot nudged repeatedly against the smart red carry-cot tucked, as usual, under the kitchen table.

'Hmm. We'll have to start calling your baby brother by his name, don't you think?'

'Benjamin.' You chewed it over in your mouth like a sour sweet.

'Don't you like it? Daddy chose it. It's *his* daddy's name. Isn't it, Benji Boy?' I cooed, stooping to pick up your squirming baby brother. He let out a soft, milky burp, and I laughed, turning to smile at you. But your face was blank, your eyes shadowed.

'Can we call him BB instead?' you whispered.

'BB? Oh, I see. Benji Boy.' It hit me that I should have asked you to help choose his name, to make you feel more involved. Maybe that was the simple explanation for your recent mood change: jealousy of all the attention on your new brother; resentment at having to share it with him. I knew how *that* felt. 'Yes, darling. We can call him BB, if you like.'

'Will Daddy be cross?'

'Cross? Why would that make him cross?'

You shrugged. 'For not doing what he says.'

'Well, *we* have a say in things around here too, don't we?' I teased, but you didn't smile. I sighed, frustrated that I had no more clue now about what was bothering you than I'd had for the entire half-term break; all I knew for certain was that you weren't yourself. I tried again to cheer you up. 'Look, I know it's all a bit new, having such a little person around. But it doesn't have to stop us playing *our* games, does it?'

'I don't like games.'

'Really?' I recognised the lie and felt my stomach flip. *What else weren't you telling me?* 'Hmm, I bet I can think of a good one.'

I looked around, determined to find something to entertain you. Only as my gaze trawled our small, bright but messy kitchen, all I could see was boxes of nappies stacked in one corner, a wicker basket near the Aga piled high with freshly washed baby clothes. Bibs and baby toys spilled off the blue-painted rocking chair you used to pretend was a sailing ship, before it became the place where I fed and rocked BB to sleep.

I groaned inwardly, knowing the same scene was repeated in every room of our tiny, two-bedroom fisherman's cottage, wedged in the middle of a pastel terrace fifty metres from the beach. Guiltily, I wondered if the mess, the chaos, was bringing you down.

'OK, how about a silly-rhymes contest?' That *always* got you giggling. I settled BB back in his carry-cot, then leaned on the kitchen table, pretending to think. 'Right, let me see. The pig, who was eating a fig . . . jumped on the sofa to chew Grandma's wig!'

'Did Grandma Olivia have a *wig*?'

'Oh. Well, she . . .' Torn between reluctance to talk about my mum and relief that *something* had finally piqued your interest, I decided to roll with it. 'She had beautiful hair, actually. At least, before she got ill. It was like a river of silk, my dad used to say.'

'A river?' Your eyes widened. 'Like the one where Daddy goes fishing?'

'Sorry?' Jordan always had the daily catch delivered to the restaurant kitchen at the country club where he was head chef; I'd never known him to go fishing himself. He loved sailing and spent half his life on the sea, but . . . 'Has Daddy ever taken *you* fishing, Marley?'

You shook your head, clamming up again.

I couldn't let it go. 'Has he taken you out on his boat at *all*?'

'I wish I had hair like Grandma. I hate my curls.'

I registered the deliberate change of subject, but let it pass. 'I felt the same about mine when I was your age. But I love them now. You will too, one day. My hair's chocolate-brown like Grandma's, but yours is just like your daddy's. Like pockets of sunshine. It's *beautiful*.'

'It's not. It's messy.' You tugged angrily at it. 'Leah called me Mop Head.'

'She called you *what*?' My heart jumped at the nickname, a memory hammering in my head, distracting me from niggles about Jordan. 'Well, that wasn't very kind, was it? Nor is it true.' I reached out, scrunching your soft, golden ponytail between my hands.

You shrugged. 'I don't care.'

'Are you sure, love?' I searched your eyes for the truth. 'I know Leah's your best friend, but . . . has she been teasing you? Is that why you've been a bit quiet lately?'

Another shrug.

'Best friends do fall out sometimes,' I said brightly. 'Look at me and Aunty Amy. I've known her my whole life, and we still have squabbles.' More memories roiled; I pushed them away. 'They blow over, though. That's what friendships are like.' I lowered my voice. 'You can tell me, you know? If you've been worrying about Leah. Or . . .' Breathlessly, I brooded over your question about whether Daddy would be cross. 'Someone *else*?'

This time, you shook your head until your hair spilled out of its ponytail, half covering your face. Selecting a matted strand, you chewed the end.

'OK,' I relented, not wanting to push too hard and scare you off. 'Well, try not to pay any attention to what Leah said. *I* love your curls. And so does your daddy.'

'He doesn't! He said they're a nuisance. My hair got tangled at the beach, and—'

'The beach?' I grabbed your hands, looking you straight in the eye. As far as I was aware, you hadn't left the house all day. 'When was this, darling?'

Your eyes filled with tears. 'I wasn't supposed to say, Mummy! I didn't mean to!'

'You weren't supposed to say *what*, Marley?' I asked, and my faulty heart beat faster.

Chapter 2

By the time I'd bundled BB into his buggy and helped you with your jacket and boots, before slipping into my own, we'd both calmed down. I grabbed some stale, leftover bread for the seagulls, then ushered you out of the back door, bumping the buggy down the step. 'OK, sweetheart? Here, you can push BB for me. You mustn't worry, Marley. Everything's fine.'

I'd managed to cajole out of you that Jordan had taken you to the beach early that morning – 'for a walk'. I hoped a stroll with *me* might help you to relax and say more; we'd always had our best chats wandering along the pebble beach.

'Are you upset, Mummy?'

'Why would I be upset, love?'

'Daddy said it was a secret. I was to be quiet and not say a word.'

I paused, key still in the back door. 'He said that?' I turned to look at you over my shoulder, but you'd already hurried through our small back garden, disappearing into the alley beyond. 'Wait, Marley! Don't run off!' I called out, concerned at how easily you'd managed to unlock the gate; I hadn't even realised you knew the security code.

'I'll push BB, Mummy.' You manoeuvred yourself in front of

me as soon I caught up with you, angling yourself between me and the buggy. 'You *said* I was to push him.'

'So I did. Although the buggy's a bit heavy, and I'd forgotten how bumpy this path is.' I pushed harder to roll the sturdy pushchair along the pebbly path leading straight to the beach, trying not to feel bad about the subtle manipulation: taking you back there to see if it would prompt further confessions about that morning.

Returning to the scene of the crime, I tried not to think, surreptitiously glancing at the spot where Jordan secured his motorbike on days off. You'd refused to say if he'd taken you out on his boat; I wondered if he'd ever secretly given you a ride on his bike . . .

'Can we go home, Mummy? I don't want to go.'

'Come on, nearly there. The fresh air will help BB nod off.' I knew that would please you. 'Oh, Marley, careful!' I exclaimed as you tripped, slipping between me and the buggy.

'I told you! We need to go *home. Now,* Mummy!'

Your face flushed scarlet, and I had a strong feeling that you'd deliberately engineered the fall, to force me to turn back. But *why*? You'd always loved the beach . . . what could possibly have put you off going there? The burst of anger was so completely unlike you that I crouched down, cupping your face in my hands. 'Are you OK? Are you hurt?'

You pulled back, wrapping your arms around yourself, knees hunched.

'Sweetheart, let me see.' I brushed your hands gently aside, gasping when I saw purple, tender-looking bruises. They were recent, but not fresh; they couldn't possibly have been caused by your trip just now. 'Marley, how did you get these?' I asked quietly.

'The ground was really hard,' you mumbled. 'The stones hurt.'

'When? Just now? Or . . . this morning?' I tried to keep my tone even, not to yell in panic, but I couldn't entirely contain my frustration. 'What on earth were you *doing*?'

'Daddy said it was just our little game.'

I don't like games, I heard echo in my head. 'What sort of game?'

'But I got sand all in my hair. I tried to get it out, Mummy. I'm sorry.' You leaned your head on your knees, burying your face.

'Silly bean, you don't have to apologise. That's what half-term is for, isn't it? Getting messy and having fun.' I smiled, even as I continued to puzzle over what 'game' you'd been playing, and why Jordan had taken you out without telling me. He *never* did that. 'So?' I asked casually. '*Did* you have fun?'

Your body hunched even tighter, as though you were trying to disappear into yourself.

I watched you for a few moments, then glanced along the narrow path leading to the beach, racking my brains to think of any possible reason for going there so early, before I was even awake. 'OK, well, let's get you home. I'll speak to Daddy later.' I forced myself to breathe slowly, feeling a fluttery pain in my chest as my heart started to thump.

You looked up at me, eyes wide, pupils narrowing to pinpricks in the bright October sunshine. 'No. Don't tell. Please.'

'But . . .' I didn't want to make a promise I knew I wouldn't keep. 'OK, don't worry. I know, why don't we stop by the café and pick up something nice for lunch, then home for a bath? I'll sort those sandy tangles out in no time.'

*

Not even pizza from The Kitchen café, followed by a browse around The Thorpeness Emporium afterwards, could cheer you up. Usually, you loved exploring the shelves packed with old curiosities and colourful bric-a-brac – it had always been your favourite thing to do with my dad, who loved antiques – but you practically ran out of the shop, refusing to look. I lost my appetite completely, and neither of us spoke as we wandered home.

After bathing BB, I filled the tub for you, kneeling down to shampoo your hair. 'That better?' I soothed, working my fingers slowly through your knotty, sandy curls.

You nodded, scrubbing at your face as tears rolled down your flushed cheeks.

'Marley, love. Please, talk to me.' I stared at your bruised knees, my heart aching. But not even a bubble-blowing competition could coax any joy, and afterwards we skipped our usual hairdryer game of pretending we were caught in a tornado. In silence, I helped you fasten your dungarees, and we made our way down-stairs to the kitchen.

The first thing I saw was the box, still sitting in the middle of the table. I lifted the lid, wishing I could look inside your mind so easily. 'We were going to make a treasure chest, weren't we? Or maybe . . . this would make a great post box, don't you think? Our own special, private one. Shall we decorate it?'

I stood up and took two strides to the kitchen dresser, throwing open the cream-painted pine doors and taking out the big craft box holding all my old classroom supplies: stickers, buttons and gems. Sparkly bits of material. After setting it on the table, I hunted in the dresser drawer, pulling out a pad and pen.

'I hate writing,' you protested, but I saw your eyes fix on the little notebook.

'You don't have to write much,' I encouraged, without pointing out that, usually, you loved writing. 'Anything that's made you smile. Or feel sad. Or angry. Scared, even.' I paused, waiting, hoping you'd say something. *Anything*. 'Or you could draw a picture.' I sat down at the table again, doodling a heart with your name inside it. 'Then fold it up and post it in here. See?' I flapped the lid again, a white flag of surrender.

The idea for the worry box had come to me in the middle of yet another sleepless night. I'd used one many times before – in the classroom. But that had always been anonymous: a chance for any child to get things off their chest without stepping out of the shadows where they felt safe. I had no idea if a sparkly box at home would work the same magic; all I knew was that it felt like my last chance to find out what was troubling you.

If it failed, I was going to find a counsellor. For reasons I couldn't fathom then, Jordan was dead set against the idea, and in truth I wanted you to talk to *me*, just like you used to, chatting on the way home from school, in the bath and at the beach. Your withdrawal frightened me. I knew you were hiding something; I just didn't know what it was.

'Post it how?' Head tilted to one side, you sized up the box.

'Well, let me see.' I reached over to the craft box and took out my scissors, eyeing the blades dubiously. Half-blunt from years hacking away at egg boxes and milk cartons, the paraphernalia of endless school projects, I wasn't sure they'd be sharp enough. 'I might need to use a knife,' I mused. 'Oh! Sweetheart, mind your fingers!'

The scissors were too big for your tiny hands, and blood rushed dizzyingly to my head as you grabbed them, lifting them high before stabbing those half-blunt blades through the cardboard lid, as fiercely as though you were thrusting them deep into someone's heart.

I never guessed whose face you were imagining – who, in your terrified, traumatised mind, you were fighting off. I saw only sparkly red shoes, a stranger's suitcase in the hall at Sea View. I remembered being a child myself, the same age as you are now . . . and I remembered Amy Jackson's smile, the day she accidentally came to live with us.

Writing, for me, is an escape from the knots and tangles of everyday life – but it also helps me to unravel real emotional dilemmas. I was inspired to write *Not My Child* after pondering: *what does it really mean to be a mother, and how far would I go to protect my child?*

After thousands of school drop-offs and pick-ups over the years, the playground felt like the only place to open my story. Gossip is rife at the school gate, but for the most part it's harmless. Yet I've always wondered what I would do if it wasn't . . . if someone approached me with a devastating accusation about my child – one that made me doubt everything and question everyone: my friends, my husband, even myself.

When dreams become obsessions, people are capable of desperate acts, both to make their dream come true, and then to protect it. What looks like a perfect marriage, a perfect family, or even a perfect friendship, can in fact hide a multitude of sins – and a secret web of deception can be unravelled with the tug of one loose thread, one simple question: *whose child is this?*

In contemplating this scenario, I have taken imaginary footsteps down some very dark alleys, and I now have a stronger sense of what matters most to me about being a parent: love or biology. I have also contemplated how I might react if that relationship were questioned or threatened. I hope my story has given you pause for thought, too!

Isn't that the beauty of fiction? To live another life, for a short while, through made-up characters who nevertheless reflect our own frailties. The other beauty is that the writer can conjure up a happy ending. But, in truth, happiness means different things to each of us. Were you rooting for a different ending? Who do you sympathise with most: Ruth, Daniel, Bea or Eve?

I'd love to know, and I wish you happy reading – and happy families.

Samantha King

Dear Reader,

We hope you enjoyed reading this book. If you did, we'd be so appreciative if you left a review. It really helps us and the author to bring more books like this to you.

Here at HQ Digital we are dedicated to publishing fiction that will keep you turning the pages into the early hours. Don't want to miss a thing? To find out more about our books, promotions, discover exclusive content and enter competitions you can keep in touch in the following ways:

JOIN OUR COMMUNITY:

Sign up to our new email newsletter:
http://smarturl.it/SignUpHQ

Read our new blog www.hqstories.co.uk

🐦 https://twitter.com/HQStories

f www.facebook.com/HQStories

BUDDING WRITER?

We're also looking for authors to join the HQ Digital family!
Find out more here:

https://www.hqstories.co.uk/want-to-write-for-us/

Thanks for reading, from the HQ Digital team

If you enjoyed *Not My Child,*
then don't miss these unputdownable
novels from HQ Digital!

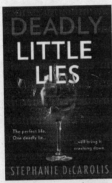

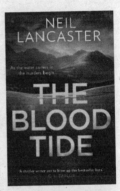

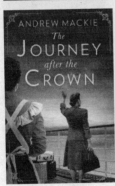